Sus…
lum…
'I…
asked.

'No, I find it exciting,' she said. Then a crescendo of thunder hit a new peak, and she clapped her hands over her ears.

He put an arm around her, his hands brushing against her breast. She turned and lifted her face to him. Their lips met, and their tongues touched teasingly. He undid the sash of her robe and slid his hands inside.

Susan shuddered. 'Do we dare? Somebody may come in at any time. None of the others can possibly be sleeping through this.'

He moved her in the direction of the leather couch. His breath was hot on her face. 'I don't give a damn. I want you now, and I'm going to have you.'

Around them the house trembled and groaned while thunder rolled and lightning flashed, illuminating the erotic tableau on the couch. The tempo of their passion mounted to match the frenzy of the storm.

'Don't let it end,' she begged as he kissed her harder and harder. 'Please don't let it end.'

UNHOLY DESIRES

Stephanie Blake

THE SHERIDAN
BOOK COMPANY

UNHOLY DESIRES

This edition published in 1994 by
The Sheridan Book Company

By arrangement with Random House
Random House, 20 Vauxhall Bridge Road, London SW1V 2SA

Printed and bound in Great Britain by
Cox & Wyman Ltd, Reading, Berkshire

ISBN 1-85501-655-9

PART ONE

1

Jan Danzig's fingers flew across the keys of her electric portable with the dexterity and assurance of a virtuoso. For ten years she had reigned as Hollywood's foremost – and most feared – gossip columnist. She was labelled the 'hatchet woman' by her peers in the media, though only behind her back – far, *far* behind.

She was a handsome, Nordic-looking woman of fortyish with snub-chiselled features and pale-blonde hair clipped in a mannish fashion, perfectly straight with short bangs falling over a high, sloping forehead. Her attire was masculine, too: a tailored herringbone pant-suit worn over a white silk shirt fastened tight at the throat with a black string tie.

Her column began:

DANZIG'S DIARY

Here I am, sitting aboard a luxurious Cessna 421, *Golden Eagle*, playing out the fantasy of every red-blooded screen buff, rubbing shoulders, playing kneesies, and quaffing martinis with two of Hollywood's immortals.

I smile across the table at Richard Lemon, matinee idol, Shakespearean actor, winner of the Academy Award for Best Actor of 1965, and nominated six times for the Oscar . . .

The smile belying the thought: *Over the hill for the past ten years, the strong, craggy features sagging now like a Watts tenement, the organ-reed voice gravelled from a quart of gin and four packs of cigarettes a day, the physique gone the way of all flesh, neglected and abused like a rejected lover, the photographic memory once heralded for its ability to retain an entire script after a single reading now reduced to dependency on cue cards to master a ten-minute scene, and with ten or twenty takes at that!* That would be the obituary for *Sir* Richard Lemon reserved for the roman à clef she was writing. She glanced up at Lemon, a caricature in his white flannel trousers, blue blazer, and absurd red beret.

> And sitting beside Dick, her hand snug in his, the fabulous, gorgeous Laura Devane, movie glamour queen of all time and the former Mrs Richard Lemon. Neither time nor tide has tarnished her ivory-cameo beauty or dulled the glow of the enormous blue eyes that earned her the tribute, among her Japanese fans, 'she of the heavenly eyes.'

Horseshit! You need a bulldozer, not a shovel, Danzig! Laura, you truly rate a Congressional Medal of Honour for valour above and beyond the call of duty in the face of overwhelming odds for your endeavours in the Second Battle of the Bulge. You can't win out over second childhood, baby! Baby fat, that's it – an irreversible return to the womb, as it were. At forty-six, you bear a remarkable resemblance to the photograph of the twelve-year-old Laura Devane displayed in an ancient fan magazine, the renowned classic aquiline nose and high cheekbones slowly submerging into accruing lard. The most expensive beauty salon in Beverly Hills can masquerade the hair and the complexion, but all the chin straps in the world cannot obscure the dewlap!

Jan stared at the movie queen covertly. Like Lemon, Laura was a Kewpie-doll caricature of her former self. The thousand-dollar Halston 'casual dress,' however, worked miracles – a flowing burgundy chevron'd jersey, deeply vee'd into a button-down front, that slenderized the torso and showed off the famed Devane boobs to good advantage.

> This is a historic reunion for Dick and Laura in a double sense, personally and professionally. Not only have they kissed and made up after an estrangement of five years, but they have signed to co-star in Monarch Studio's blockbuster film about the infamous Lincoln County Cattle War, *Blood on the Sun*, to be shot on location in Lincoln County, New Mexico . . .

Jan Danzig stopped typing and looked up as a slender young fellow in green coveralls and matching peaked cap came into the cabin from the cockpit. He flashed a boyish grin: 'We'll be taking off in fifteen minutes, folks, three o'clock.'

'You said two o'clock when we boarded,' Lemon said irritably.

'I know. I'm sorry about that. We're waiting for the other four passengers, who are coming to Denver by shuttle.'

Laura smiled her sultry smile and fixed her bedroom eyes purposefully on the flight attendant's crotch, her famed and antiquated method calculated to overpower males. 'That's all right . . . Larry. It *is* Larry, isn't it?'

His name was plainly embroidered above his breast pocket.

He blushed and backed away, intimidated by the Devane charisma, which, though waning, was still potent. 'Yes, ma'am. Thank you, ma'am.' He touched the peak of his cap and fled back to the cockpit.

Laura chuckled. 'Cute, don't you think, Jan?'

'Divine.'

Jan Danzig met Laura's faintly mocking gaze unflinchingly, her grey eyes impaling the actress like twin daggers. Laura knew damned well, as did everyone else in the film crowd, that Jan was a lesbian and proud of it!

Lemon peered out of the round port beside his seat. 'I say, I do believe our tardy cellmates have arrived.'

The two women followed his gaze. Gunning across the field from the terminal was a Jeep bearing four passengers and their luggage – a black man and woman and a white couple.

'So, we're gonna have spades for company,' Laura said with displeasure, lapsing briefly into her native Bensonhurst, New York, accent and manners. 'Swell.'

Lemon's left eyebrow lifted and his clipped British accent became even more pronounced. 'Equality and fraternity, isn't that what your constitution says? Or is it the French constitution? No matter, it's all bullshit in any case . . . Hmmm, he's a good-looking buck, isn't he? I wonder if it's true what they say about Negro men?' Then, with sly malice: 'Is it, Laura dear?'

Laura's face turned crimson, and her mouth twisted in an ugly snarl. 'You sonofabitch! I ought to—'

Jan observed, with ill-disguised delight, that the muscles in Devane's upper arm tensed and her hand clenched as a prelude to smashing him in the face. Lemon saw it, too, and flinched. To the columnist's disappointment, however, Laura controlled the impulse and snapped at her ex-husband:

'Heavy-handed humour. Can't keep the German in you from surfacing, can you, darling?'

Now *his* face reddened, and he mumbled contritely, 'Sorry about that, sweet. Bad joke. Really sorry.' He stared into his empty martini glass. 'Anybody for another?'

The women declined, and Lemon got up and walked aft to the small but well-stocked service bar in the tail section.

The new arrivals boarded the Cessna while the airport attendant stowed their luggage in the baggage compartment. The black couple were indeed attractive, Laura had to admit. He was not exactly Harry Belafonte – he lacked the West Indian delicacy of feature – but in a long camera shot he could qualify as his stand-in. His white seersucker suit was well-tailored and immaculate.

The girl was a genuine beauty – she could 'pass' in California's beach resorts where tans were a dime a dozen – soft, wavy black hair, enormous, wide-set eyes, and a mouth and chin that could present the camera with either profile. She wore an Oxford-cloth beige dress with a narrow shoulder yoke and short sleeves, and sandals that revealed frosted-blue toenails.

The white pair were classically all-American, he tall, lanky, in Levi slacks, a sport shirt worn outside his belt, and tan loafers. While he was good-looking, his face had a certain simian mien, owing to a too-toothy grin, and his brown hair was as short as that of an army officer, which is what Laura pegged him to be.

The 'little woman' – Laura was certain that is how he referred to her – was a statuesque, leggy girl in her late twenties, with auburn hair that fell softly around her broad shoulders. Her features were as strong as an Amazon's, and her almond-shaped grey eyes were disquietingly penetrating when she introduced herself:

'Hi there, you all. I'm Susan Brandon and this is my

husband, Kevin.' Suddenly her eyes widened, her mouth formed an oval, and she clapped one hand to her left cheek. 'Oh, wow! I don't believe it! Kevin, do you realize who these folks are?'

Kevin stared at Laura and then at Lemon in utter bewilderment. 'Well, sure now. Hell, of course.' His eyes pleaded with Susan: *Get me out of this!*

She obliged. 'Sure you do, honey. They're famous movie stars, Laura Devane and Richard Lemon. This is a real pleasure, Miss Devane and Mr Lemon.'

Flattery will get you everywhere, lady! Jan Danzig looked on with disgust as Dick and Laura responded to Susan Brandon's recognition with gushy smiles and vigorous handshakes.

From behind the Brandons, the black woman spoke up: 'I hope this means that you and Mr Lemon are coming out of retirement, Miss Devane. Do you know, I saw the last picture you two made together six times? *Inglorious Victory* – I'll never forget it.'

In such a windfall of adulation, Laura could handily shelve her racial bias for the duration of a short plane trip. She rose and pushed past the Brandons to welcome the black newcomers. 'Darling, how sweet of you to remember. That was so long ago. Would you believe I'd forgotten the title of that film until you recalled it for me?'

Jan rolled her eyes. *You fucking narcissist, you remember the day, date, and precise time when you shot your first screen test, and that was a hundred years ago!*

'This is my husband, Larry Bostwick. I'm Jennie,' the black girl said, with a distinct note of pride. 'We're going to New Mexico, where Larry is doing research for his new novel.'

Jan's interest perked up. She had a thing for novelists, especially black ones, who were not all that conspicuous, at least in Hollywood. 'Good luck, Mr Bostwick,' she said. 'Have I ever read anything of yours?'

Bostwick ran a finger around the inside of his collar, obviously self-conscious. 'You may have. My last novel was titled *Black Absalom.*'

She reacted genuinely. 'Why, of course! I should have recognized your name. You sold it to the movies, am I right?'

'Well . . . Universal has an option on it.'

Jan couldn't resist putting in a plug for herself so as not to remain partners in anonymity with the Brandons. 'When I get back to Hollywood, I'm going to put an item about you in the L.A. *Times.*'

'Oh? You must be Jan Danzig,' he said. 'I've read your column.' His grin was wry. 'You sure know how to put the needle to a lot of big shots.'

'You'd better believe it, Clyde.' She cast him a conspiratorial wink.

'I used to read you religiously when Kevin taught at UCLA,' Susan Brandon exclaimed. 'You're even better than the *National Enquirer.*'

'Touché!' Dick said, and he and Laura exploded into boisterous laughter.

Jan went pale with anger. She wet her lips as a preamble to delivering one of her notorious Danzig scathing retorts, but the moment was averted for both her and Susan when the pilot poked his head out of the cockpit and announced:

'We're ready to take off. Please sit down and fasten your seat belts. And no smoking, please.'

They scrambled to comply. The cabin of the Cessna was handsomely appointed, with two banks of plush, club-style seats, which could hold eight passengers, and between them, a foldaway table. Lemon, Devane, and Danzig occupied one set; the Bostwicks and the Brandons the other.

'Coincidence that Mr Bostwick is going to New Mexico to research a book,' Susan commented. 'Kevin is researching his doctorate thesis on the religious culture of the southwestern Indians.'

Bostwick responded with interest. 'Say, I'm fascinated by Indian lore and religion myself. After all, the Indians have suffered more injustice in this country than any other minority, bar none.'

His wife winced and laid a cautioning hand on his knee under the table. Jennie shrank from Larry's penchant for engaging even the most casual strangers in discussion about racial prejudice.

'That's the truth,' Kevin agreed with enthusiasm. 'Two years ago I led a protest march at the Tule River Indian Reservation in California.'

'And he spent the night in the pokey, too,' Susan said laconically.

'No kidding!' Larry's face lit up. 'I've been that route myself, man. Montgomery, Little Rock, Atlanta. Put 'er there, my man!' He extended his right hand over the table, palm up.

Without hesitation, Kevin delivered a resounding slap to the upturned palm. 'Right on!' The two of them grinned at each other like kids.

'Tell me about the gig you played at Tule, Kevin.'

Their wives exchanged smiles of empathy and relief. If Kevin Brandon had been a Reagan conservative, the mood of this conversation would have been altogether different, and unpleasant for everyone there.

They could feel the twin wing engines purr to life as the *Golden Eagle* taxied slowly to the head of the assigned runway. There was a Lear jet ahead, revving its engine for takeoff.

Up in the cockpit, the pilot radioed the control tower: 'Tower, this is Cessna four twenty-one, licence number N81129.'

'Roger, Cessna four twenty-one. You're bound for Lincoln City, New Mexico, right?'

'Roger.'

'Wind from the southeast at ten miles an hour,' the tower informed him.

'We read you. What's the latest weather report from that area?'

'They're getting some very freaky weather down there – heavy thunderstorms, lightning, *lots* of lightning – and there are unconfirmed reports that some small twisters are sweeping northwest across the Panhandle.'

'No sweat; we'll steer clear of turbulence. Well, here we go. Over and out.' The pilot swung the Cessna around so that her nose was pointed down the runway into the wind. To his copilot: 'Trim for takeoff.'

'Half flaps.'

'Throttle full; brakes off.'

The engines whined higher and higher to a banshee pitch, and the *Golden Eagle* raced down the strip faster and faster, nosing up sharply and taking to the air as gracefully as her namesake. A few minutes later, the No Smoking

Fasten Seat Belt signs went off back in the cabin.

Dick Lemon was the first one out of his seat, cigarette dangling from his mouth as he headed for the bar. 'Anyone for a libation? Come along, men, and name your poison. I don't mind tending bar, but I will not play steward to you hale and hardy young chaps and your lovely ladies.'

Kevin and Larry unbuckled their belts, slid out of their seats, and ambled after him.

Susan beamed at Jennie. 'I'm so pleased that Kevin and Larry are hitting it off so well.'

'How *about* those two?' Jennie feigned indignation. 'They're already making plans that do *not* include us – camping out in the desert, exploring old Apache burial sites.'

'Between you and me, Jennie, they can have the desert and the snakes and the Gila monsters and the Apaches. I'll opt for sitting around the motel pool, sipping tall, cold drinks and reading my historical novels. I picked up a new one at the terminal newsstand just before we boarded, a real adventure with lots of romance and passion.'

The black girl grinned. 'There's a difference between romance and passion?'

'Of course there is. When we go to bed with our husbands, *that* is romance.' She winked slyly. 'Now, if we happen to latch onto a pair of muscle boys poolside while our hubbies are frying in the desert, what we do with them, well, *that* comes under the category of passion.'

Jennie threw back her head and laughed. 'Oh, Susan, you're outrageous!'

'Who's outrageous?' Kevin said as he and Larry returned to their seats with a tray with four tall glasses. When they were settled, he lifted his glass in a toast: 'To new friends. One day may they become old friends.'

'Right on,' Larry said with pleasure. 'I had a feeling from the start that this trip was going to be something special.'

For no reason at all, a cold chill scampered along Susan's spine.

2

Richard Lemon and Laura Devane, soon after the Cessna was airborne, retired to the bar in the tail section, and there, perched on high bar stools, they studied their scripts for their forthcoming motion picture.

Laura slapped Dick's hand as he reached for the gin bottle. 'For Christ's sake, Dick, haven't you had enough? You've degenerated into a bad study as it is, without fogging your brain with booze.'

He wore the ugly, belligerent sneer of a man who had had one, two, three drinks too many. 'Listen to you, Lady Macbeth. Shit! You can't even recite Shakespeare properly, much less memorize any of it.'

'Fuck you, Limey!' A nasty smile filtered through her sullenness. 'Or would you prefer "Fuck you, *Zitrone*"?'

'Bitch! I'd like to wring your fat neck.'

'Try it, buster!'

She picked up a heavy old-fashioned glass, but quickly set it down as she saw Susan Brandon tripping down the aisle towards them.

'Excuse me for interrupting. I realize you're rehearsing your lines, but could I have another drink?' Susan said.

'Rehearsing our lines . . . ' Laura said, and she and Dick exchanged looks, both choking on suppressed laughter. The absurdity of the woman eased the tension between them.

Lemon cleared his throat. 'Yes, my dear – what is your name again?'

'Susan.'

'Dear Susan, yes, Laura and I were rehearsing our lines.'

'God only knows they shouldn't need any rehearsing,' Laura said tartly. 'Dick and I have repeated them over and over and over.'

The two actors laughed at the inside joke, which only

bewildered Susan. 'Oh?' she said blankly.

Dick removed his horn-rimmed glasses and pushed them and his script aside. 'Never mind, my sweet. Here, let me have your glass. What are you drinking?'

'Gin and tonic, but please, Mr Lemon, I can fix it myself. I wouldn't dream of intruding – '

'Intruding? Laura, did you hear that? Fact is, love, we are delighted and grateful to you for offering us an opportunity to – how do you Yanks say it? – "goof off." Actors, artists, writers, they are all born lazy, slothful, indolent; you name it, we are guilty. It's such a bore to toil for a living.'

'You haven't done much *toiling* of late, dear Richard,' Laura said wilfully.

He ignored her and prepared the drink for Susan, placing it on a coaster on the bar and indicating the stool beside Laura. 'Do sit down and join us.'

She looked anxiously at Laura, but those marvellous blue eyes projected utter affability. She had to say it: 'I hope you'll excuse me for saying it, Miss Devane, but for years everybody has been raving about your beautiful eyes. Has anyone ever told you that the movies really don't do them justice? I mean, it's like your eyes are filled with quicksilver; they keep changing shade from one second to the next.'

Oh, what a delightful child you are! 'You are very generous to say that, Susan. It is gratifying to think that after all the years and all the booze, my old orbs still retain some of the old magic.' She patted the stool beside her. 'You heard Dick. Do sit down and join us, by all means. Where will you and your husband be staying in New Mexico? You said he was doing research of some sort?'

'Yes. I'm not sure where we'll be staying. Kevin hasn't quite made up his mind where he wants to start. Probably we'll start off from Lincoln City.' She rolled the glass Dick had set before her around in her palms. 'My family, my ancestors, all came from Lincoln County. My great-great grandparents owned a cattle ranch back in the eighteen hundreds.'

'You don't say.' Dick Lemon's interest perked up. 'Were they, by any chance, involved in the Lincoln County Cattle War?'

A hard edge intruded into Susan Brandon's voice as she replied, 'Very much involved. My great-great grandfather was a first cousin to Alexander McSween.'

'McSween!' Dick and Laura exclaimed in unison.

Dick pointed a finger at her and said with excitement, 'Would you believe that *I* am to portray Alexander McSween in the movie *Blood on the Sun?* By Jove, what a remarkable coincidence!' He called to Jan Danzig, 'Hey, Jan, did you hear that?'

Jan turned and looked at him vacantly. 'I'm sorry, Dick, I was concentrating on my editing.'

'Stow the bullshit, love,' he said with affection. 'Everybody in Hollywood knows that you can hear the grass grow. Anyway, I think it's bloody supernatural. Here we're aboard a plane with four total strangers, and one of them turns out to be the great-great grand-daughter of Alexander McSween, the chap I'm portraying.'

'McSween wasn't my great-great grandfather, Mr Lemon; he was my great-great grandcousin, I guess you might say.'

'No matter. Let me say how proud I am to know such a lovely great-great grandniece . . . Here, love, let's have a kiss for Cousin Dick.' He leaned across the bar, clasped a hand behind the nape of her neck, pulled her to him, and kissed her lightly on the lips.

'Always was a ham,' Laura quipped, 'like all method actors. He has to believe that he *is* Alexander McSween.'

Jan Danzig got up and joined them at the bar. She lit a cigarette with a heavy gold lighter.

Laura wrinkled up her nose. 'They really should ban smoking on planes and trains, any public place.'

'That would be a violation of our civil rights, my dear,' Dick said as he, too, lit up. 'Smokers deserve the same protection as homosexuals and – ' He bit it off in time, but the nervous glance he aimed at the Bostwicks betrayed him.

'And blacks,' Larry Bostwick finished for him in a bland voice.

Pinned in a corner, Dick Lemon held his ground. 'I suppose they qualify as well. *I* am a firm believer in equality for all without regard to race, colour, religion, or sex.'

Laura fixed him with an expression of contempt: *You*

fucking hypocrite!

'About the movie and the Lincoln County Cattle War,' Jan inquired of Susan Brandon, 'was Alexander McSween truly related to you?'

'Yes, he was,' the girl responded proudly, delighted that these big celebrities were according her a measure of distinction.

'I'm rather vague on what happened during that period of history in New Mexico,' Larry Bostwick said.

Susan deferred to the stars of the film and to Jan Danzig, but they were all looking expectantly at her. Eagerly she began: 'Well, the war had been fermenting for more than a decade. In the eighteen sixties, the New Mexico Territory was divided between two powerful livestock empires, the Chisum and Murphy spreads. Quite literally, they owned the territory, including all the lesser ranches in their districts. The small outfits bought their stock from the feuding giants and traded at the "company stores" operated by them. Of course, they had no other choice. At first there was healthy competition between the two spreads for rich government beef contracts, but the fur began to fly when the advantage gradually swung in favour of the Murphy spread, who won the backing of the Lincoln County sheriff and the territorial governor through bribery and blackmail.

'Now, the Chisum spread was managed by Alexander McSween and a young Englishman named Jack Tunstall – '

'Ron Willard is playing Tunstall,' Lemon interrupted. 'I'm sorry, Susan, I didn't mean to step on your lines.'

'Not at all.' She blushed and continued: 'The Murphy faction was led by two Irish goons named Dolan and Morton. It came to a head when McSween and Tunstall accused Lincoln County Sheriff Brady of taking graft from the Murphy Company and embezzling tax funds. In retaliation, Sheriff Brady issued a warrant for the arrest of Jack Tunstall on trumped-up charges and deputized Morton to form a posse and intercept Tunstall, who was taking a herd of valuable horses across the state line for sale. The posse caught up with Tunstall and his men on the range, and Morton served the warrant. Realizing they were badly outnumbered, Tunstall agreed to accompany the posse back to Lincoln City. But, just as he was reaching for his gun to hand it over to Morton, shots rang out, and Jack Tunstall fell off his horse dead.

'The night Tunstall was murdered, a strange phenomenon occurred. As the sun was setting, its rays reflected on wisps of vapour beyond the horizon, creating the illusion of a crimson spray falling upon the desert – "blood on the sun," the Indian medicine men described it.'

Lemon snapped his fingers. 'So *that's* where they got the title for the film.'

'Call it superstition, whatever, the Indians were right,' Susan said. 'For the next year, the Chisums and the Murphys shed their own and others' blood, robbing, killing, raping helpless women, razing Lincoln County to the ground, all in the name of Chisum and Murphy honour. The horrible irony of it all was, there were scores of innocent victims crucified because they happened to be unwilling constituents of the two cattle dictatorships.'

'And how did your great-great grandparents fit into this conflict?' Jan wanted to know.

'As I said, my great-great grandfather was first cousin to Alexander McSween. McSween was killed in an ambush not long after Tunstall, and my great-great grandfather, Ike Norton, led a party that gunned down McSween's killers. In doing so, he also signed his own death warrant. It was a hot August night and – '

She broke off as, abruptly, the Cessna began to buck and yaw, sending Kevin, the Bostwicks, and Jan Danzig into a heap on the cabin floor. Laura, Susan, and Dick managed to keep from falling by holding on for dear life to the bar.

It was over in five seconds, although the plane continued to shimmy like a scared bird as she plunged ahead through unexpectedly rough air.

The copilot came out of the cockpit. 'Sorry about that, ladies and gentlemen. We've run into some turbulence. Would you please return to your seats and fasten your seat belts?'

'*Turbulence?* That is the understatement of the year, young man. How is it you let it sneak up on us without any warning?' Lemon demanded. 'I mean, what is radar all about? Surely you've been keeping track of the weather reports on the radio, haven't you?' The actor was livid.

'Yes, we have, sir.' The copilot's smile was sickly. 'We've been trying to fly around the turbulence and stay above it, but sometimes Mother Nature hits you with a sneak punch. Quickly, please, go back to your seats.'

There was a mighty clap of thunder and a dazzling flash of lightning that lit up the cabin a brilliant blue-green, and the Cessna's trembling increased. The passengers endeavoured to restrain their rising panic as they proceeded in orderly fashion back to the club seats. Susan and Jennie clung to their husbands with one hand and with the other clenched the arm rests, so tenaciously that even the black woman's knuckles were white. Jan Danzig, straight and stiff in her seat, face frozen like a mannikin's, stared out at the pyrotechnic show raging all about the plane.

Before she had been engulfed by the sudden storm, the *Golden Eagle* had appeared to them as strong and secure as the Rock of Gibraltar, as majestic as the king of the sky from which she derived her name. Now she was reduced to a frail toy, a plaything of the elements, flung in all directions by the buffeting winds, shaken by thunderclaps like a terrified mouse in the jaws of a cat. There was a heart-stopping, deafening explosion as a lightning bolt struck the tail assembly, and eerie blue-green St Elmo's fire danced und crackled all over the fuselage. The Cessna's wings looked like giant sparklers.

Jennie Bostwick screamed and hid her face against Larry's chest. 'We're on fire! We're going to crash!'

'Easy does it, love,' Dick Lemon reassured her. 'Only St Elmo's fire, a luminous electrical discharge. This old girl is built to endure far more punishment than this little blow.'

Laura was scared to death, and she was certain Dick was, too. It was one of his most admirable traits, grace under pressure.

'Gallows humour,' she muttered.

What transpired next was a dream sequence played out in agonizing slow motion. The incessant clapping of thunder had overshadowed the sound of the Cessna engines. It was not until Susan shouted and pointed out a window that they became aware of the shocking truth.

'The motor! Something's wrong with it!'

The engine on the port wing was dead, its propeller rotating this way and that like a weather vane.

'Jesus Christ!' Kevin gasped.

The seven of them sat immobile, like figures in a tableau. Finally Dick broke the menacing silence:

'What do they say? "See Naples and die." May I rephrase that for you, boys and girls?'

'Shut up!' Laura spat at him.

The pilot's voice came over the intercom, barely intelligible through the static: 'Ladies and gentlemen, I have to tell you that one of our engines is malfunctioning.'

'*Malfunctioning?* It's bloody well stopped!' Dick shouted.

The pilot went on: 'Please stay calm. There is no immediate danger. I am going to take the ship down and look for a spot to make an emergency landing. I repeat, there is no danger. The Cessna can remain operational with one engine. But, in view of the foul weather, I believe it advisable to put down someplace until the storm is past. Thank you.'

While the plane descended in a steep but level glide, the copilot rushed back into the cabin and began handing out pillows and blankets from the overhead lockers. 'In case we have a rough landing, better cushion your faces and chests with these.' He went back into the cockpit.

'That, dear people, is a euphemism for all time. "Rough landing" indeed. What the man is saying is, we are about to crash.'

Funereal silence settled over the cabin as the Cessna hurtled downward. From the way the wings dipped from one side to the other, and the fuselage kept bouncing like a rubber ball rolling down a flight of steps, it was clear the pilot was encountering enormous difficulty controlling the ship. The storm had shrouded everything in Stygian blackness, but with each flash of lightning, the landscape below was starkly illuminated – a patch of desert far below; suddenly a mountain peak so terrifyingly close, it seemed to be reaching out for the Cessna; a series of wasteland punctuated by canyons; another mountain range; then, dead ahead, atop a high mountain with nearly vertical sides, an awesome mesa – an enormous flat, rectangular surface more than a mile long and half as wide.

'Here we go, folks,' the pilot informed them. 'Hold tight!'

With only several hundred yards to go, it appeared that the Cessna, bombarded by hurricane-force winds and lashed by sheets of rain, would not survive; she would slam into the rock wall of the mountain. Then a providential updraft lifted her fifty feet into the air like an invisible hand, and the landing gear cleared the rim by no more than a foot. The *Golden Eagle* touched down hard on the rough terrain and careened across rocks and ruts and tall grass.

'Not an ideal landing,' as Dick remarked, 'but a landing nevertheless.'

Mercifully, the passengers were not aware of a potentially fatal hazard that lay ahead. As bountiful as the winds had been moments earlier, they abruptly turned fickle and did a 180-degree reverse, literally 'turned tail.'

In the cockpit, the pilot battled the controls and the brakes. 'Where did that fucking tail wind come from? If it doesn't let up, nothing is going to stop this bird!'

The one functioning engine's prop was in reverse on full power, the brakes were on full, and yet the ship seemed to be gaining momentum instead of decelerating. Straight ahead, and looming up larger and larger, was a grove of slender trees and tangled underbrush. Stoically resigned to the inevitable, pilot and copilot braced themselves against the imminent impact. Amid the din of shattering glass and the screech of rending metal, the Cessna cut a swath through the woods. It was an eternity for the passengers in the cabin, huddled in their wildly whipping seats, flung about in their strained seat belts like dolls, with their faces buried in pillows and blankets.

The once-proud *Golden Eagle* came to rest at last with a final death scream, broken and twisted and dismembered like a great bird demolished by a hunter's shotgun.

No one spoke for a long time. It was as if they were poised on the edge of oblivion, and a single sound would send them all catapulting into the valley of doom. There was only the howl of the wind and the drenching rain assailing the battered plane.

3

It was dark in the cabin except for the dim illumination provided by lightning filtering through the crown of the wood.

Dick Lemon finally spoke: 'Is everyone all right? Laura?'

'I'm alive, Dick, and with no broken bones that I can feel.'

One by one the others affirmed that they were alive and well, though badly shaken up and in mild shock.

Kevin unbuckled his seat belt and stood up. 'When the copilot passed out these pillows, I thought I had a glimpse of some flashlights in the overhead locker.'

He could not budge the sliding doors at first because the metal tracks were twisted out of alignment by the force of the crash.

Larry joined him. 'Here, let me give you a hand.'

Between them, the two men managed to move the door enough so that Kevin could reach inside with one arm and feel around for the flashlights.

'Eureka! Pay dirt!' He produced two heavy-duty electric lanterns of the type campers use. They projected powerful beams that could be adjusted from long-distance spotlight to wide-angle flare. He gave one to Larry and turned his own light on the bedraggled-looking group.

Dick began to chuckle. 'You ladies look as if you had spent a rough night with the Sixth Fleet.'

'Up yours, Lemon,' Laura snarled. 'You don't look as if you just stepped out of a drawing room yourself, old chap. And your rug has slipped, Dickie.'

It precipitated a good deal of laughter, unnecessarily loud and on the verge of hysteria; yet it eased the tension.

'What about the pilots?' Susan inquired.

'What about them, yes.' Kevin walked to the front of the Cessna, leaning against the forward slope of the floor. He pushed open the door and shone the beam inside the cockpit. 'Hey, you guys, are you – '

He stopped with his mouth agape, paralyzed with horror at the grisly scene that assaulted his eyes. The windshield had been pulverised by tree limbs that reached inside the cockpit like skeletal arms and hands. One as thick as a man's wrist had punctured the pilot's forehead between the eyes and passed through his skull and out the back of his head. As for the copilot, a wedge of glass from the windshield had decapitated him as cleanly as a guillotine.

'Oh, my God! Jesus!' Kevin backed out of the cockpit, shut the door, and leaned back against it, his hands trembling so violently that he almost dropped the flashlight.

'What is it, man?' Larry came down the sloping deck to his side.

'They've had it.'

'You certain? Maybe I'd better have a look.'

'*No!* I'm sorry; didn't mean to shout. It's just that . . . man, you don't want to know how they got it. You'd see them in your nightmares for the rest of your life, believe me.'

Stunned silence pervaded the cabin, and Jennie began to cry softly.

Larry went to her and put his arms around her. 'It's all right, baby. We made it OK. Nothing we can say or do will help those poor devils.'

'So what do we do now, chaps,' Lemon said: 'sit back and wait to be rescued?'

'Sit back? You must be kidding,' Kevin answered. 'You saw what kind of a place this is before we landed. Hell! We're perched on top of a huge mountain. It wouldn't surprise me if no human has ever set foot on this mesa. You ever see that ad on TV where they have this car sitting on the flat top of this mile-high spire? That's our situation, only this one is a helluva lot bigger.'

'But surely they'll send search parties to look for the wreckage after the storm clears?' Susan said.

'Spot the wreckage?' Kevin went to a broken port and shone the light upward through the thick foliage. 'My dear girl, we are effectively buried in the middle of these woods. No chance a rescue plane could spot us from the air . . .

No, our only hope is to wait until the rain stops, then build a big brush fire out in the open, saturate it with aviation fuel – God, it's a miracle the tanks didn't blow us to kingdom come – and light it as soon as we hear any trace of a plane engine.'

'I do believe the storm is just about over,' Dick ventured.

He was right: The thunder and rain were abating, and the lightning was growing more sporadic and distant.

'Anybody want a drink?' he asked. He borrowed Larry's light and walked stiffly back to the bar. When he reached it, he recoiled in horror. 'What heresy is this? "Oh Fate! Take away thy heavy hand. Death is the fairest cover for her shame that may be wished for." '

'*Much Ado About Nothing*, act four,' Laura said with sarcasm. 'That's all we need now is Richard Lemon trying to recite Shakespeare.'

'Much ado about *plenty*, my dear,' he said wistfully. 'Our booze rations are demolished, *finito*.'

'The one bright spot in this horror show,' she retorted. 'Ladies and gentlemen, you are going to be privileged to witness one of Richard Lemon's most dramatic performances. It's titled *The Day the Booze Ran Out*. Should be a gem. He hasn't gone an hour without a nip in years.'

Lemon tossed the neck of a broken gin bottle at her feet. 'Shove this up your fat arse, Miss Devane.'

'All right, you two, knock it off,' Kevin moderated. 'We've got our own show to get on the road. It's just about stopped raining, Larry. Want to scout around outside with me?'

'Sure thing.' He handed his lamp to Jennie. 'Here – you guys keep the home fires burning.'

'Not on your life,' she objected. 'I'm coming with you.'

'Oh no you're *not*,' he said firmly. 'We don't have any idea what we'll encounter out there – snakes, wild animals . . . You sit tight. We won't be long.'

He and Kevin went to the door at the tail and released the heavy steel lug fasteners. The door opened out and around. Kevin swung the light about, surveying the crash site. Because of the angle of the Cessna, the ground was ten or more feet below the floor of the plane.

'Looks like a thick bed of soft duff down there,' Kevin surmised. 'I think we'll be OK.' Handing the light to Larry, he sat down with his legs dangling outside, holding fast to the door jamb, and levered himself out of the plane, nimbly landing ankle deep in a ground cover of rotting leaves and branches. 'Just like in the circus,' he called up to Larry. 'Toss down the lantern and join me.'

The black man accomplished the feat with a dexterity equal to Kevin's, and the two of them walked back along the long swath the Cessna had cut through the woods. They emerged from the trees into an open field. The heavy rain had ceased, but there was a thick overcast and a steady drizzle.

'From the look of things, I imagine we'll be stuck here at least overnight,' Kevin said.

Larry gazed around at the dreary desolation. 'You're optimistic, I'd say. Looks to me like we might be stuck up on this plateau forever. I can see it now – the Swiss Family Robinson.'

Kevin nudged him with an elbow. 'So much for your prognostications, buddy. Look!' He pulled Larry around.

'I'll be damned!' exclaimed the black man.

Circling around the right side of the grove of trees were three horsemen – lean, lanky fellows wearing ponchos and sombreros. Kevin and Larry ran towards them.

'Hey! Are we ever glad to see you guys!' Kevin shouted in pure euphoria. 'Where did you materialise from ? It's a miracle, like the genie from out of Aladdin's lamp!'

The lead rider answered him in a voice that was shaded by an indefinable accent. 'Not really a miracle. We saw your plane crash-land from back at the ranch house, no more than a mile from here on the other side of the mesa.'

'Ranch house! Did you hear that, Larry? And we thought we were hundreds of miles from civilization.' Closer scrutiny revealed that the three men were American Indians – gaunt faces, high cheekbones, hawkish noses, and deep-set black eyes.

Their spokesman cracked a restrained smile. 'Well, Skull Mountain is not exactly "civilization." You're a long day's ride from the nearest sizable settlement.'

'Skull Mountain!' Larry looked at Kevin. 'This is getting weirder and weirder.'

'Yes, from the air the mesa bears a resemblance to a death's head and crossbones.'

'We were too preoccupied to notice,' Kevin said. 'What about this ranch? Why would anyone build a ranch on top of this godforsaken mountain?'

'The Ames place was built up here over a hundred years ago by Mr Ames's great-great grandfather. Mr and Mrs Ames retain it as a vacation home. Their permanent home is in Connecticut.'

'Mr Ames is a cattleman?'

The Indian smiled again. 'Hardly. He's a stockbroker. It's more of a token ranch. We have some cattle, and horses and barnyard stock. The three of us, Quannah, Luke, and myself – I am Son of Running Deer, but they call me Chief – manage things for the Ameses year round. The village of our people is two miles down the mountain.'

'I see . . . Look, our friends are still on the plane. We all need food and shelter and fresh clothing.'

'Of course. Mr Ames would have sent the jeep or the pickup truck to fetch you back to the house, but the storm washed out the bridge over the ravine, and the horse path is impassable for motor vehicles. How many of you are there?'

'Seven. The pilot and copilot are dead.'

The Indian made a clucking sound with his tongue. 'It was an evil wind, as Gall said it would be.'

'Who is Gall?'

'The medicine man of the village. He predicted two days ago that the gods would hurl bolts of lightning and thunder down on Skull Mountain, and torrents of rain to wash away the evil and sin that lurks here.'

'Evil and sin?' Kevin and Larry looked at each other in astonishment.

Chief shrugged. 'It is nothing. The people of the village are still very primitive. I am a Christian.' Then, as an afterthought: 'And not superstitious.' Somehow he did not sound very convincing. 'Now, let us go to your people.'

Lemon and the four women were removed from the wreckage. Wrapped in blankets, they were put astride the Indians' horses, Dick and Laura on one horse, Jennie and Susan on the second, and Jan Danzig on the remaining mare. Kevin and Larry agreed to take turns on the open spot on Jan's mount.

They started out at a slow pace, with the guides leading

the horses by the reins. It was a rugged route, over a steep rise behind the woods, then along a narrow rocky ledge that ran parallel to a raging stream with foaming rapids.

Observing that the women's faces were white and taut with fear, Chief reassured them: 'Do not look down. Trust the horses. They are very sure-footed.' To the men, he said, 'Would you believe that not many hours ago this was a dried-up, dusty gulch?'

'I'd believe anything about this place,' Larry said. 'There's an aura about it that reminds me of the Black Forest of Germany. It smacks of invisible gnomes and witches, maybe even a dragon or two.'

The Indian smiled, a distant, secret smile that bore some condescension.

'Do you have many storms as bad as this one?' Kevin wondered.

'Many, many, some even worse. In the past fifty years, twenty-six people have been killed by lightning on Skull Mountain. It is a bad thing to be outdoors during a lightning storm. Years ago, Mr Ames's father put up a series of shelters all over the mesa in the event that any of the family or guests got caught away from the house by a sudden storm. Sometimes they come without any warning at all, like this.' He snapped his fingers. 'The floors of the shelters are covered by rubber mats.'

Kevin let out a long, awed whistle.

'What a ghastly place to live,' Laura said.

'There is great privacy here,' said Chief.

'I shouldn't wonder,' Dick muttered. 'This Ames chap must be a bloody eccentric.'

'He's a bloody saviour, for my money,' Susan declared. 'What do they do at the Indian village when there is an electrical storm?'

'Rubberized tepees,' Jennie offered.

'It is not the same there as being up here on top of the mountain. There are heavy deposits of metal on the mesa,' Chief replied.

'It's one giant lightning rod, is that it?' Kevin theorized.

'Something like that.'

Laura cast a fearful glance at the sky as the overcast became luminous with sheet lightning. 'Jesus! Is it going to act up again?'

'It is possible,' Chief said. 'Anything is possible on Skull Mountain.'

With the exception of the Indians, they all cringed as a brighter flash lit up the dark sky.

'You've got one helluva bedside manner, Chief,' Larry told him. 'How much farther?'

The Indian pointed to the northeast. 'We must go over that hill and down a ravine – high ground; the water has drained away by now – and then we will shortly reach the ranch.'

Kevin had replaced Larry on the horse Jan Danzig rode.

'Can you believe it, Professor?' she said. 'When we started out, I figured this was going to be just another milk run. What a story! First time "Danzig's Diary" is going to make the front page.'

'I'm happy for you,' he said flatly, thinking of the two dead men in the wreckage of the Cessna *Golden Eagle*.

The house appeared as they struggled up a steep incline out of the ravine – a two-tier sprawling affair strung out across a hillside, as natural a part of the rugged, primitive landscape as a huge snake. A bright red barn sat off to one side and below the house. Through its open barn door, two horses could be seen stomping restlessly in their stalls. There was a small corral at the side of the barn. The scene was barren of either grass or flowering shrubs to suggest domesticity, yet the setting was near perfect for this particular dwelling.

'Wonderful-looking place, but where is the livestock?' Susan asked.

'In the meadow beyond the hill,' Chief told her. 'Hardy stock.'

No sooner had the horses halted by the front porch, a flagstone patio with a flat roof, than the heavy front door swung inward, and a tall, muscular man wearing Levi's and a checkered work shirt greeted them: 'Welcome! We've been expecting you.'

His hair was steely grey and wavy, his nose was prominently aquiline, and his craggy features were compatible with the sharp, rugged lineament of the land and the house. Susan judged him to be in his mid-fifties; she liked his wide, toothy smile.

He was soon joined by a woman, tall, erect, with a

handsome, rather than voluptuous, figure. Her brown hair was worn in a casual upsweep, rather untidy, but the effect was calculated and suited her clean good looks; she could have been his sister. Her attire was casual, too: tailored fawn velvet trousers and lemon-yellow turtleneck velour shirt.

'I'm Walter Ames,' he said, 'and this is my wife, Nancy. I won't waste time on amenities. You all must be soaking wet and in need of some food and rest. Do come in. Pedro, our all-around man Friday, is getting your rooms ready and a change of clothes for each of you. There are nine, am I correct?'

'*Were* nine,' Kevin demurred. 'The pilot and copilot were killed.'

The smile was wiped off Ames's face. 'Damned shame! I'm sorry. Lucky thing you *all* weren't killed. I can't tell you how relieved Nan and I were when you came riding up out of the ravine. No broken bones or scrapes? We have a fairly extensive first-aid room here. Out here in the wilderness, cut off from civilization, it pays to be prepared for emergencies.'

They all assured him that they were in excellent physical shape, if a bit weary.

'I could use a bath, a nap, and a thick steak, in that order,' said Laura Devane.

'And you shall have it, my dear lady.'

'First in the order would be a stiff drink,' Dick suggested.

'A good order at that.' Ames laughed. 'Come into the living room. There's a roaring fire awaiting your pleasure. It never gets too warm for a fire up in these parts, especially at night.'

He led them down a short hallway and through an arched doorway into a spacious room richly appointed with a blend of American Colonial, Georgian, and modern provincial furniture – lots of raw pine hand-sanded and polished to a mirror surface. Two wide leather couches faced each other across a kidney-shaped coffee table in front of the largest fireplace any of them had ever seen.

'My great-great grandmother and her girls used to cook chow for twenty-five family and hands in that inferno,' Ames said.

Kevin estimated that the lot of them in the room could

stand erect in the monster and there would still be room for a second team. A pyramid of logs six feet long and a foot in diameter, glistening with embers, burned slowly on a cast-iron grate large enough to contain an ox. Ames invited them to sit down, and took their drink orders.

'I'll attend to it, darling,' his wife said. 'You stay with our guests.'

When they'd settled themselves comfortably around the fire, it suddenly occurred to Kevin: 'Mr Ames, how on earth did you know there were nine of us aboard that plane?'

'Why, it was on the radio just before Chief brought you back here. Your disappearance has created quite a furore.' He removed a pipe and tobacco pouch from his back pocket and tamped the ragged, sweet-smelling weed down into the bowl with his thumb. He appraised Laura and Dick. 'You must be the famous Laura Devane and the equally famous Richard Lemon. I saw you perform on the New York stage back in nineteen sixty-four.'

'*Hamlet*,' Dick confirmed with a smug, satisfied glance at Laura.

'You were marvellous.'

'Thank you, sir,' he said with genuine gratitude.

'And, of course, any accolade I could offer Miss Devane would only be a case of carrying coals to Newcastle.'

'Try me anyway,' Laura said, flirting with her eyes. She licked her lips in speculation: *I'll bet he's a great stud.*

Ames looked at the Bostwicks huddled together in the centre of the one big couch, next to the Brandons. 'And you are Lawrence Bostwick, the eminent novelist. My wife and I thoroughly enjoyed *Black Absalom*.'

'I'm truly flattered, Mr Ames,' Larry said self-consciously. 'Never figured to find a fan way up here.'

'Oh, we have all the creature comforts on Skull Mountain: radio, television, telephone – '

'Telephone!' Laura cried. 'Oh, Richard and I *must* use your phone and let the film crew waiting for us at Lincoln City know that we survived the crash. The producer and director must be tearing out their hair. There are already millions invested in that picture. All of the interiors have been shot, so there is no way they could salvage the project if we were dead.'

The others offered that they, too, had worried relatives and acquaintances to notify.

Ames's expression was pained as he lit up his pipe with a long wood match. 'I'd be only too happy to oblige you, but I'm afraid there's a hitch.'

'The phone line is down,' Susan guessed.

'Afraid so.'

'Well, then,' Laura said, 'couldn't one of your ranch hands drive to the nearest town that does have phone service and put in a call to the studio for us? We'd be more than grateful and prepared to reimburse the messenger handsomely.'

Ames massaged his square jaw. 'That's a dead end, too, for the present. Mud slide wiped out the sole road that goes down the mountain. One of the Apaches rode up earlier to tell us. No, I regret to say – to my delight and to your understandable concern – you are our captive houseguests until the road is opened or telephone service is restored, at which time we can call for a helicopter to fly you off Skull Mountain. I must tell you that there is virtually no hope that they'll get air-rescue search teams into the air before tomorrow, not until this foul weather clears up. Ceiling is no more than a hundred feet at present. Clouds have a way of hanging around this mesa for days, something to do with electrical charges in the clouds and the metal in this mountain.'

'Christ!' Laura moaned, and clasped her head in her hands. 'Dick, the press ghouls are probably writing our obituaries as we sit here.' She cast a dagger look at Jan Danzig. 'Yours too, darling.'

Dick chuckled. 'Yes, Jan, you'll be getting a taste of your own medicine.'

Nancy Ames served the drinks, and Dick proposed a toast: 'To our genial host and hostess. If one must become involved in an air crash and plunged down on top of a mountain, may they have the good fortune to encounter such gracious rescuers.'

'Amen. I'll drink to that,' said Laura, and the others lifted their glasses.

Susan stared across the top of her wine goblet directly into the ice-blue eyes of Walter Ames. Something about those eyes made the fine hairs at the base of her neck tickle.

'Ames . . . ' she said, and everyone looked at her inquisitively.

'Yes?' Walter Ames's eyes narrowed thoughtfully as he regarded her. 'What is it, Mrs Brandon?'

'How long has your family lived in this part of the country?'

'My great-great grandfather was instrumental in settling the New Mexico Territory, came out west in eighteen fifty.'

'And the Ameses had a ranch in Lincoln County,' she said with certainty.

He put down his highball glass and moved closer to her, studying her face, his head cocked to one side. 'Mrs Brandon, why is it you look so familiar to me? Not that we've ever met. It's just there is something haunting about you, rather in the nature of *déjà vu*.'

'I know,' she said evenly. 'I feel it, too – a face out of an ancient tintype.' She inhaled deeply. '*My* great-great grandfather was Ike Norton, and he had a ranch in Lincoln County as well.'

Ames looked incredulous. 'Ike Norton! My God! I can't believe it!'

Kevin put a protective arm around his wife's shoulders. 'Steady, darling.' He looked up at Ames. 'I guess this is a bit traumatic for you, too, Mr Ames.'

Ames shook his head. 'I should say so.'

'I say, what are you all talking about?' Dick demanded. 'I smell a mystery hereabouts.'

'No mystery, Mr Lemon,' Ames said ruefully. 'My great-great grandfather, James Ames, fought on the Murphy side in the infamous Lincoln County Cattle War back in the eighteen seventies.'

'What a remarkable coincidence!' Dick Lemon declared. 'Even more so because Laura and I were on our way to Lincoln City to shoot exteriors for a movie we're starring in about that very war, Mr Ames.'

'More than remarkable coincidence,' Laura said; 'it's positively supernatural.'

'It's a very small world, that's all,' Kevin said with strained joviality. He stood up and pulled Susan with him. 'I say it's time we got out of these wet clothes and into a warm tub.'

'Me, too,' Laura agreed. She regarded Susan and Walter

Ames with open curiosity.

Later, Dick chided her, 'You behaved as if you thought the two of them were aliens from outer space.'

'Not necessarily from outer space,' she mused.

4

When they were alone in their room, Susan Brandon stripped off her wet clothes and sashayed into the bathroom, flaunting her shapely buttocks for Kevin's benefit. Four years of marriage had not dulled her pleasure in arousing him sexually; nor had they desensitized Kevin's ardent response to the charms of her magnificent body. Seeing her naked now, he felt the same magic he had the first time she had undressed for him.

Her breasts were large but so firm that she could go without a bra and evidence no obvious sag; her nipples were pale pink and slightly turned up – 'to match your nose,' he liked to tease her. There was a band of white flesh across her bosom and another across her flat belly, no more than a half-inch above the base of the triangle of thick pubic hair, that contrasted vividly with the bronze tan over the rest of her voluptuous thighs and good calves.

Kevin removed his own clothing and padded into the bathroom after her. Susan was already under the shower. He surveyed the large sunken bathtub, and his loins were afire at the thought that occurred to him. His erection was full, and his testicles ached with desire for her. 'Susan,' he said in a tremulous voice, 'forget the shower and let's take a bath together. Haven't seen a tub like this since that honeymoon lodge we went to.'

She drew aside the shower curtain and peered out at him. Her eyes widened. 'Well, now, will you look at that! Little Willie certainly has grown since last I saw him. This calls for emergency therapy. OK, hop in.'

As he stepped down into the tub, she bent over and flipped the handles that plugged the tub and directed the water from the shower head to the tub spout, and her bare bottom swelled up invitingly.

'Praise the Lord!' he breathed heavily, and grabbed her around the waist.

She pretended to be shocked, and gasped, 'You lecherous sex maniac! Don't you dare! Ohhhhh! You *did* dare!' She straightened up and moved back against him as he slipped his member between her thighs, wet and slippery with soap. 'Oh, sweetheart, love of my life . . . Hurry, sit down; I'm as hot as you are . . . Funny how carnal we can be so soon after what we've come through. I mean, up until this instant, the idea of indulging in sex while those poor pilots are lying alone and dead in that plane would have been repulsive to me, and now . . . '

Kevin sat down with his back against one side of the tub, and Susan straddled his hips. The warm water filling the tub around them had a strong aphrodisiac effect on him. Usually in control of his performance, he felt he must explode the instant he penetrated her. 'I can't hold back much longer,' he moaned.

'You won't have to. Here, stay still and let this little piggy go to market.' She took his hand and directed his index finger to her clitoris. 'There now.' She closed her eyes and rocked back and forth on top of him.

Seconds later he lunged up, grinding his pelvis against her soft, fleshy bottom. His first paroxysm was so powerful, Susan felt that her vagina would split. A delectable fantasy. Moments after, her own orgasm commenced, and Kevin groaned as the warm velvet sheath contracted on him vicelike. Their spasms went on forever, it seemed, until Susan felt that if they persisted much longer, she would faint from sheer ecstasy.

Afterwards, as they lay entwined in the steaming water, she said in a small, breathless voice, 'Would you believe that was the best ever? I mean, they're all wonderful, with rare exceptions, but this . . . ohhhhhh!'

'For me, too. I've read somewhere that living through a disaster that came within a hair of claiming your life has the effect of stimulating and expanding your sexual appetite. Probably something to do with survival and a redoubled appreciation of the body's life force.'

'Whatever you say, Professor.' She giggled. 'I'd better turn off the water before the tub overflows and floods the floor below. Just imagine everybody rushing up here and finding us *flagrante delicto.*'

He slapped her backside. 'The way I feel, I could perform in an X-rated movie without inhibition.'

'Feel like seconds? I do.'

'You're on, lady, but let's get into the sack this time; my butt hurts from pounding the hard porcelain.'

They made love a second time, and afterwards lay in each other's arms in a swoon of lassitude and deep satisfaction.

'Penny?' she said finally.

'I was thinking about Ames.'

'What about him?'

'That's what I want *you* to answer.'

She said nothing.

'Susan, the man is not responsible for what his great-great grandfather did over a hundred years ago.'

Her face clouded over with an obstinate look he'd seen before and did not admire. She was such a sweet, even-tempered girl for the most part, understanding and generous to a fault. Vindictiveness was an alien trait to her nature, one he put down to a 'family characteristic,' which manifested itself in her on rare occasions.

The first time it had surfaced was soon after their marriage. They began double-dating with a couple who lived in the same apartment house, and the girl and Susan had become best friends. Once, on a weekend trip to Malibu, they had offended Susan in a manner so insignificant, Kevin could not even recall the circumstances. After they returned to Los Angeles, Susan refused to speak to her friend, and no amount of reasoning with her on his part could sway her decision. He remembered vividly a final encounter between the girls:

Susan's friend had said in desperation, 'This is insane. I don't even know what I did to you. The least you can do is to tell me what it was.'

And Susan's hard grey eyes had impaled her. 'Precisely. And that proves how insensitive and untrustworthy you are. Good-bye.'

After she had closed the door in the girl's face, she had turned to him: 'My mother and grandmother always told me, "If anyone hurts you, even accidentally, then they don't care as much about you as they pretend, and they don't deserve your love, friendship, or respect." '

Kevin had been stunned by her rigid intolerance. 'For God's sake, Susan! All of us are human; we're not perfect. We do things that later we may regret sincerely.'

She had regarded him with a cryptic smile, arms folded underneath her breasts. 'You're entitled to your opinion, Kevin. One thing, though: Never, but *never,* cheat on me!'

He had been speechless and, for a passing moment, frightened of her.

Now, holding her naked underneath the thin coverlet, he knew instinctively what she was thinking about: the Norton Massacre, as it came to be known in Lincoln County. The bloody outrage of it had been kept alive like a festering wound down through the generations – from Amy, who had witnessed the horror, to her daughter Candice; and from Candice to Peggy, who was Susan's mother. And now it was Susan who was bearing the guidon, lying passively in his arms and silently venting her spleen on Walter Ames and all of the Ameses who had been before him.

'Kevin, you couldn't understand, and I don't expect you to. You're not a Norton. It's a family thing.'

'A vendetta in this day and age, coming from an intelligent, rational woman like you?'

'Intelligence and reason have nothing to do with it. Nothing on earth can ever absolve the Ameses from their eternal guilt. They will wear it like an albatross around their necks until the last of the line perishes.' With that, she kissed him lightly on the lips, smiled lovingly, and closed her eyes.

He dozed soon after, so he did not witness the transformation that stole over her features as she twisted restlessly and whimpered in her nightmare. It was like Dr Jekyll metamorphosing into Mr Hyde, her mind racing fiercely back into time . . .

5

1878 . . . Ike Norton stood on the wide front porch of his home, watching the sun balanced on the mountain peaks to the east. Viewed through the early-morning haze lifting out of the valleys, it was a gigantic, shimmering ball of fiery orange. 'Gonna be a scorcher for sure,' he said.

His son Jack spat a gob of tobacco juice in the direction of a lizard sunning itself in the cracked mud at the foot of the steps. 'What's on the schedule for today, Pop?'

'Paul's taking a crew out to repair the fence on the North Ten. I want you to take the ten horses I sold to Pete Fleming over to his spread. He'll pay the first of September.' He ran a hand over his thinning grey hair, already damp with perspiration.

Norton was a tremendous, raw-boned man, whose work shirt and trousers seemed several sizes too small for him. As the old saw went, his muscles had muscles. His two boys, Paul and Jack, were replicas of their father, only more slender; their guts did not spill over their gun belts the way Ike's did. Jack wore chaps over his pants and sported a ten-gallon Stetson.

The young man was suddenly sombre. 'Ma says you're thinking of taking her and Amy into Lincoln City later this afternoon. You figure that's smart so soon after we raided the Kelly spread? Word's out that Jim Dolan and Billy Morton have upped the price on our heads, payable not "alive or dead," just "dead." '

Ike's face creased in a leathery grin. 'Them rattlesnakes don't scare me none. Besides, I'll take a dozen of the lads along with us just in case.'

His youngest child, a daughter, came running out of the house. 'Papa, Jack, Ma says to come in for breakfast right now.'

Ike bent and swept her up into the air and onto one brawny shoulder. His hands were as big as a bear's paws and just as hairy. 'And how's my sweetie this morning?'

Amy was dwarfed by the two giant men, so that she appeared younger than her twelve years. She was a dark, intense child with small features and long black hair hanging down her back in braids. Her eyes were the colour of jade. 'Just fine, Papa.' She hugged him ferociously and kissed his cheek.

He carried her into the house and down the long hall to the kitchen, the second largest room in the ranch house. It was dominated by a huge banquet table that could seat twenty people, and it was usually occupied by groups of one number or another from six in the morning until dark. Ike Norton had forty hands working for him, and they all ate at different shifts. Molly, his wife, and her two nieces, Flora and Maud, enjoyed few respites from their herculean labours seven days a week, and it was taking its toll on them. All of the ranchers' wives and daughters looked ten years older than their true age from the ravages of hard work.

There were ten hands besides the family at breakfast that morning, devouring stacks of wheat cakes, thick slabs of bacon and ham, platters of scrambled eggs, and home-baked bread and pies. Conversation was animated during the meal.

'Hear Calvin Yates was killed in the Tamale Saloon day before yesterday.'

'Dirty Murphy bastards!'

'Watch your language; the child is here!' Molly shouted sharply.

'Sorry, ma'am.'

'Zeke, you and Les go along with Jack to the Fleming place with the horses.' Ike handed out the daily work assignments. 'Morris, you and Teddy will pick a crew to help Paul out at the North Ten, and Solly, you – '

He was interrupted by the unexpected arrival of a stout man in a striped 'city suit,' with a string tie at the throat of his white shirt and a jaunty derby on his head. Bob Collins came bursting through the back door in a state of great agitation. He was a Chisum attorney and accountant.

'Bob, what in tarnation are you doing out here so early?'

Ike demanded, putting down his fork.

Collins collapsed into a chair and removed his hat to use as a fan. 'Big trouble, Ike. James Ames and Billy Morton are leading a big gang, over a hundred men, into Lincoln, and they're out to get you for the Kelly job.'

James Ames and Ike Norton had been rivals for years, competing for eastern beef contracts and striving to outdo each other in every other ranching endeavour. Ames was the biggest and most influential private ranch owner in the Murphy empire. Norton was his counterpart in the Chisum dynasty.

Ike grunted. 'Good. I been hankering for a showdown for a long time. We'll have the varmints all together in one place and wipe 'em out like a den of rattlers.'

Collins raised his bushy eyebrows. 'That's exactly what Dolan and Morton are saying about you and yours, and they outnumber you two to one.'

'Hell, my boys are worth three of the Murphy gang, man to man.'

'Ike Norton, there'll be no showdown on our property.' Molly had left the stove and was standing over him with her hands braced belligerently on her ample hips. 'The womenfolk of this county are sick and tired of all the murder and rape and pillaging that's been going on here for the past year. And it's all got to be meaningless. Poor Jack Tunstall has been long dead and buried. Nobody even thinks about him anymore. His name is just an excuse to carry on this stinking war. Yes, you enjoy it. All of you, both Murphy men and Chisum men, you behave like irresponsible children, like that Bill Bonney, not even dry behind the ears and already he's murdered God only knows how many men.'

'Billy the Kid, yeah.' A murmur of admiration and approval circulated around the table.

'Billy's one of the best and most loyal and reliable men we've got on our side,' Ike told her.

' "Loyal and reliable"?' she mocked him. 'That's so ridiculous it's sinful. Billy the Kid kills because it gives him a thrill, and that's why he joined up with the Chisums. It gives him a licence to kill and torture. Same with most of the other gunmen, too.'

Ike pushed back his chair and stood up. 'I've got no time

to palaver with you, woman. Lads, we've got to start getting ready for Ames and Morton and their army. We'll give 'em a hot reception when they arrive. We're gonna have to forget the North Ten and Fleming's horses until this nut's been cracked. Jack, you and Paul attend to rounding up all of our boys. We'll assemble out at the barn in one hour.'

'Please, Ike, listen to reason,' his wife pleaded. 'You can call on the law for protection – the army at Fort Stanton.'

'Molly,' he said gently, putting an arm around her plump shoulders, 'you know how much sense that makes. Dolan and Morton have Governor Axtell in their back pockets, and Colonel Dudley as well. No, we Chisum people have to take care of ourselves, and we will . . . Jack, Paul, Morris, Teddy, all of you, let's get cracking!'

The men tramped out of the kitchen, full of excitement, anticipation, and high spirits. Bob Collins was left alone with the women.

Little Amy went over and stood in front of him. 'Are you going to stay here and help us, Mr Collins?' she inquired.

He sighed and mopped his forehead with a red bandanna. 'I think not, missy. Gunfighting is out of my line.'

'I'm glad for you, Bob,' Molly said. 'You'd better get out of here while there's still time.'

'Yep.' He stood up, put on his derby, and patted the top of Amy's head. 'Now, you take care, little lady, and help your ma and your cousins get things ready.'

Get things ready . . . The expression had a special connotation for the residents of Lincoln County in the year 1878; no one – man, woman, or child – needed any instructions. The men would choose defensive positions that would give them an advantage. Outside the most strategic windows, they would erect barricades and barbed wire to repulse a frontal assault by the enemy. The other windows would be boarded up altogether. The women, meanwhile, would lodge mattresses and furniture against the open windows to serve as shields against the attackers' gunfire.

Amy was put to work piling up ammunition and spare pistols and rifles at the defensive sites. Stores of food were carried into the house from the outbuildings and storage cellars. Water was no problem, as there was a well beneath the kitchen, and the sink pump could provide an endless supply.

Ike appraised the situation for his men when they gathered in front of the barn: 'I'd say we're in pretty good shape, boys. We can sit out a siege for two, three weeks. Bob Collins is going to spread the word soon as he gets back to town. Couple days from now, we'll have Chisum reinforcements pouring in from all over Lincoln County, and the Murphy thugs will be caught in the middle.' He rubbed his calloused hands together, pleased with the way things were working out. 'Jack, send out scouts to high ground, where they can give the word when Dolan and the Murphys come into view. The rest of you come with me into the house and we'll set up our positions.'

They tramped after him, kicking up dust with their boots, a straggling army of forty-odd men. 'Boys' was more like it; no more than a handful were over twenty-two years old, though most of them had been in the saddle for ten years as hired hands. And, to a man, they were naïvely prepared to die for Chisum honour and personal glory.

The rest of the morning and all through the long, tense afternoon, the forward scouts lay on their bellies on top of two high ridges on either side of the valley in which the Norton spread was located, watching for the advancing Murphy army. At sunset, Jack Norton rode up to the north ridge on his black gelding:

'No sign of 'em yet?' he asked.

'Nary a one. Maybe it's all a false alarm,' was the reply.

Jack scratched his stubbled chin. 'No, they're probably lying back behind those mountains waiting for dark. All right, boys, let's pull back to the house.'

After supper, the Norton men and their cowhands lounged about on the big front porch or played poker on wood tables Ike had ordered put up in the front yard.

Ike pointed to the northeast. 'Smoke. That's their cook fires. They'll move in after dark.'

'You figure they'll attack tonight, Pa?'

'No, but the dark will give 'em an advantage while they're staking out their positions. We won't be able to pick 'em off so easy even if they get right in close to the house. Time we moved inside and got some shut-eye. Tomorrow is gonna be a long, long day.'

Three men were stationed at each of the barricaded windows on the four sides of the house, twelve windows in all. The remaining four men, along with the three Nortons, would be on roving patrol when the attack came, ready to assist wherever they were needed.

Molly, Maud, Flora, and Amy were quartered in a large, windowless room on the second floor – a store-room, actually, for mattresses, pillows, cots, and other household goods.

'Not likely any bullets will find their way in here,' Ike told them before bidding them good night. 'These here walls are three-inch pine boards. You can leave the door open for ventilation, if you want, until the action starts.' He kissed each of them tenderly, his eyes misting over when he came to Amy. 'You get a good rest, little darling, and I'll see you in the morning.'

When he was gone, Amy put her arms around her mother. 'Don't fret, Ma; we'll all come through this fine. Norton men are worth two of each Murphy man, maybe three.'

Molly sighed. 'Child, you sound just like your father . . . Flora, Maud, you take the big bed; Amy and I will make out with the smaller one.'

Flora and Maud, the daughters of Molly's sister Kate, had been sent by their parents to America to escape the starvation in their native Galway. They were dark, pretty girls with Irish blue eyes and saucy figures. Molly suspected that both of them had rolled in the hay with some of the hands more than once, but she kept her peace. After all, they worked from dawn till dusk seven days a week, and there was little else in the way of recreation in Lincoln County.

Molly lay awake long after the others had fallen asleep, fingering her rosary beads and praying for deliverance. The attack came at dawn, when shapes were fuzzy and without substance in the cold blue light.

'Jesus Christ!' a man at one of the east windows shouted. 'Look what they're doing! They're using our cattle for cover!'

'Sneaky bastards!' Ike ranted. 'Stinking cowards, using innocent animals for shields!'

The Murphy men were driving the frightened beasts directly towards the east side of the ranch house and moving in close behind them in a low crouch. The defenders, manning the three windows on that side, were hard-pressed to sight on a target, and the Murphy men continued to pepper the windows with random shots. Far behind them, other Murphy men, armed with high-powered rifles, poured volley after volley at the house.

'Keep down behind the barricades,' Ike ordered, 'and hold your fire until they try to climb over the outside breastwork!'

It was sound strategy, for when the cattle split off into two waves just before they reached the house, they exposed the men hiding behind them at near eyeball-to-eyeball range from the defenders inside.

'Now!' Ike roared.

Pistols and rifles barked in staccato repetition as the attackers scrambled on top of the barricades. Now the advantage was dramatically reversed in favour of the Nortons. One after another, the Murphy soldiers were either blown back to the ground or became tangled in the barbed wire, where they were quickly and coldly dispatched by the gunmen inside. The survivors threw down their weapons and fled in disorderly retreat.

When the last one was gone, Ike called out, 'Cease fire! We flushed 'em out like a covey of quail.'

'Look there!' a hand shouted. 'Someone's comin' out wavin' a white flag!'

Ike's eyes narrowed suspiciously. 'What's Ames up to now, I wonder. Sure enough they ain't giving up this easy.'

It was Jim Ames himself, a red-faced, beefy man dressed entirely in black – boots, trousers, shirt, and Mexican sombrero – who was swinging the white cloth, fixed to a rifle barrel, back and forth like a pendulum. When he was fifty feet from the house, Ike called to him:

'Stop right there and state your business, Ames!'

'Will you let us send a detail of men to take out our dead and wounded?'

Ike didn't retort immediately. He tugged at his short grey beard and looked from one of his sons to the other. The boys shrugged. Finally Ike made up his mind. 'All right, Ames, but they've got to be unarmed, and don't try any funny business.'

'You've got my word. And' – he hesitated – 'thanks, Norton.' He began to walk away, then stopped and turned. In a voice that was almost conciliatory, he said, 'Ike, I want you to know there ain't nothing personal in what's happening, as far as I'm concerned. You've always been square with me. I'm only following orders. You picked the wrong man to hit on when you killed John Kelly. Kelly, he was Murphy kin.'

'Don't matter, Jim, who he was. Alex McSween was *my* kin. Neither one of us is responsible for what's happening, Jim. It's the code.'

'The code,' Ames repeated, shaking his head. 'Sometimes I wonder . . . ' He left the thought unfinished.

'No you don't, Jim,' Ike Norton said quietly. 'Both of us, we do what's gotta be done.'

He watched the other man walk back to his troops with a heavy heart, but his determination never wavered.

The lull in the fighting continued until four-thirty that afternoon. Periodically, Ike would go to a window on the second storey and watched the Murphy forces through a telescope. The last time, he came downstairs looking very grave:

'Something's up. A band of Apaches just rode into their camp. Be on the alert, boys.'

Shortly thereafter, the Apaches rode around the house, screaming a savage war chant. The defenders took a few potshots at them, but the range was too great.

'Just like they do attacking a wagon train,' Jack murmured. 'What in hell are they up to?'

The answer was not long in coming. At the completion of the ritual ride, the Apaches discarded their rifles and took up powerful war bows.

'Jesus,' Ike exclaimed, 'they're dipping them arrows in pine tar! This could mean real trouble!'

Minutes later the Indians began to lob fire-tipped arrows onto the roof of the house.

'Paul, take a detail of men out the back way and get up on that roof. We've got to beat out them fires before they get a chance to spread!'

Armed with blankets soaked in water, six men slipped out the back door and climbed up to the roof on a ladder, all the while under constant fire from the Murphy men. Ike Norton had his men keep up a steady return fire to cover his exposed men on the roof, but in vain. The fiery arrows kept coming in faster than they could douse the small blazes. Three of the six fire fighters were hit, and the remaining three were unable to control the rapidly spreading conflagration.

'It's hopeless!' Paul shouted. 'Get back down. The old place is a goner.'

The last one down the ladder, Ike Norton's eldest, took a slug clean through the back of his head and died instantly.

Inside the house, there was chaos.

'I ain't gonna die in here, Mr Norton!' one of the hands cried. 'I'm gonna surrender.' And before anyone could stop him, he ran out the front door, down the steps, and across open ground with his hands high in the air, shouting, 'Don't shoot! I wanna give up!'

'Poor damned jackass,' Ike lamented.

There was a fusillade of shots from the Murphy ranks, and the running figure did a crazy dance like a puppet on a string and went tumbling end over end in a shower of dust.

'Jack, go upstairs and get the women down here,' Ike said. He fastened a white shirt to a rifle barrel, as Ames had done earlier, and walked out onto the front porch, waving it. 'Ames,' he shouted, 'I want a truce! You give our women safe passage, we'll surrender and give up our weapons. We're your prisoners!'

'It's a fair offer,' Ames said. Then, to a gunman with an ugly scar running down his right cheek: 'Your gang had no right to shoot that defenceless man, Higgins. No more shooting, and that's an order!'

Jesse Higgins laughed, showing the blackened stubs of his teeth. There were sixteen notches on the butt of his Colt. He and his gang of fifteen were hired killers, who had no more love for the Murphy men than they had for the Nortons. Murder was their trade; they did it for fun and profit.

'Looky here, Murphy's paid us to kill off Nortons, and the job is only part done. Ain't that right, boys?'

He stepped behind Ames and shoved the muzzle of his pistol into the small of his back. Three of his men had the drop on Morton.

'All right, one false move out of any of you Murphy boys and your bosses both get it, understand?' Higgins said. 'Maybe they're gettin' too old and soft for this kind of work, but I reckon you young bucks want to finish the job. Am I right?'

There were half-hearted expressions of agreement from a few, and the others soon followed along like sheep.

Higgins marched forward to meet with Ike Norton. Hands on hips, he leered evilly. 'You got a deal, Norton. Send out your women and then come out yourselves without your weapons. Better be quick about it; your place is going up like tinder.'

The roof of the house was a solid sheet of flame now and on the verge of collapse. Ike ran back to the house. Molly, her nieces, and Amy were huddled together, their faces tear-stained and stark with terror.

'It's all right,' he comforted them. 'You'll be taken to Lincoln City. Get rooms there and wait until you hear from me.'

'When will that be, Ike?' Molly asked in a quavering voice.

'Can't rightly say, Molly. Now, get before this place comes down around our ears.' He kissed them all goodbye and ushered them out onto the porch. 'Don't be scared. Everything's going to be all right. Start walking, and hold your heads up proud.'

Molly smelled trouble the instant she saw who had taken charge of the enemy camp. 'Jim Ames, I thought *you* were in charge of this bunch,' she said.

'As you can see, I have been removed from command, Mrs Norton.' He indicated the gun that Higgins held on him.

'Far as I can see, there are no more than a dozen or so of his kind. You've got over a hundred men.'

'Shut up, you fat cow,' Higgins yelled, 'or I'll throw you to the Injuns!' He smiled grimly. 'All righty, a couple of boys take the women back out by the barn. We'll be with you shortly.'

Before they led the women away, Molly looked at Ames

with scathing contempt. 'You break your word to Ike and the other men and you'll be living with it for the rest of your life. No, for all eternity the Ames name, all of your descendants, will be cursed. I'll see you and yours in hell, Jim Ames!'

'Get that old harpy out of here!' Higgins bellowed. When they were gone, he holstered his pistol and picked up a rifle. 'All right, boys, here they come. Fire at will.'

Ames, his face pale and tense, grabbed Higgins's arm. 'You can't shoot them down in cold blood! We made a truce. They're surrendering in good faith.'

Higgins threw back his head and laughed. ' "Good faith"! What in hell you think this is, Ames, a Sunday-school picnic? This is war, man! Now, get your gun and do your duty, or I'll tell the Murphy brass what a lily-livered sucker they chose to lead this fracas.'

Stretched out in a ragged line, the Norton men came walking across the clearing with their hands in the air, old Ike Norton front and centre. Halfway to the barricades where Murphy men were standing, they heard Higgins give the order: 'Fire!' Coldly and unemotionally, the Murphy army fired volley after volley into the defenceless victims, never ceasing until all of them were lying prostrate on the sun-baked earth.

Higgins put down his rifle and strolled towards the twisted, bloody forms strewn all about. Methodically he kicked a man here, another man there, looking for signs of life. One man groaned, and Higgins drew his pistol and put a shot between his eyes. 'Do as much for a horse,' he said.

Before he was through, he had dispatched three others who were still alive. He stood over Ike Norton, who was conscious and alert, and blew smoke away from the muzzle of his Colt. 'Well, well, well, look what we got here – the *big* man himself. Say your prayers, old man, because you are about to take a long trip into oblivion.'

'You scum bag!' Ike snarled. 'You got a yellow streak down your back from here to Mexico. You talk big with a gun, but I seen you blubber and plea for mercy one night in Laredo. Remember, Higgins?'

'You sonovabitch!' He kicked Ike savagely in the side, and there was the sound of ribs cracking.

The old man groaned and closed his eyes.

Higgins straddled his body and bent over, so that the muzzle of his pistol was no more than six inches from Ike's forehead.

'Hold it, Higgins!' Jim Ames shouted from behind him.

The gunman turned slowly, and a sneer spread over his face as he regarded Ames standing ten feet away with his legs spread and his revolver in his hand.

'Well, well, well, so Mr Ames wants to play games. Put that thing away, fucker, before you get hurt.'

'No, Higgins. You've pushed me around for the last time. You were right when you called me lily-livered. Molly Norton was right, too. I'm going to have to live with the infamy that was perpetrated here today for the rest of my life, maybe through all eternity, but there is one debt I can pay back to society: stomp you out like the rattlesnake you are. All right, Higgins, make your move!'

Higgins swung swiftly to the side, presenting a narrow target to his foe, and the six-gun in his hand cracked twice. Ames took one shot in his left shoulder; the other grazed his right hip. He was slow in returning the fire but more accurate. His two shots hit Higgins squarely in the centre of the chest. An expression of shock and disbelief was stamped on the gunman's face, frozen forever until he would turn to dust, for he was dead before he hit the ground.

Ames stepped over him and staggered to where Ike Norton was lying. He knelt down and lifted the dying man with his good arm, cradling him against his bent knee.

Ike grinned and winked at him. 'Nice piece of shooting, Jim.'

Tears streamed down Ames's cheeks, and his blood dripped from the shattered shoulder and mingled with the blood of his longtime adversary. 'I didn't want this to happen, Ike. I let that slimy bastard push me around.'

Ike's eyes were hard and unforgiving, and his grin mocking. 'No excuses, Jim. You let it happen. You broke the code.'

'Damn the code!' Ames said in helpless frustration. 'If it wasn't for the code, we wouldn't be killing one another; we'd be tending our ranches and beating these guns into ploughshares, like the Good Book says. Damn the Murphys! Damn the Chisums! Damn the Ameses and the Nortons!

One of these days we'll all be together in hell, Ike.' He saw the other man's eyes glazing over, and laid him back gently on the earth. He took his hand and held it until the death rattle slackened to a faint gurgle. 'To think that we might have been good neighbours, friends,' he said dolefully, and collapsed on top of the dead man from loss of blood.

'Let's get him over to the wagon, men!' Morton shouted. 'Put compresses on that shoulder; we've got to stop the bleeding. Then we'll ride him back to Lincoln City and find a doc.'

Inside the barn, the women heard the sound of the distant shooting.

'You stinking cowards,' Molly screamed, 'murdering innocent men!' Tears streamed down her face as she clutched Amy to her bosom.

The four men who were guarding them ignored her, their attention focused instead on Maud and Flora, who were cringing together against a horse stall.

'Tie up the fat old biddy and the kid,' their leader ordered. 'We got important business here before the others come.' He opened the empty stall and leered at the girls. 'All that straw makes it nice and comfy, right, ladies? Bet it ain't the first time you did it on a haystack, eh? You look like hot little wenches. Get inside, and be quick about it!'

Molly and Amy put up a heroic struggle against their tormentors, but they were subdued and tied to a post with horse reins. Then the captors gathered round the door of the stall and watched as Kirk Adams began to undress Maud. Their mouths were contorted with brute lust, and spittle bubbled on their lips.

Adams was a vile brute, a brawny, squat man with arms like an ape's. One hand snaked out and gripped the neck of Maud's summer frock. He tore it off down to the waist. Flora screamed, but her sister was paralyzed with terror. Unable to resist, she stood as still as a mannikin while Adams stripped off her shirtwaist and camisole, exposing her small, firm breasts. He stretched out both arms and covered them with his huge hands.

'Now, don't say you don't like it, little lady. But the best is yet to come.'

When he ripped off her skirt and lace drawers, for the first time she spoke: 'No, no! Please don't hurt me! Don't do this to me!' Whimpering, she covered her breasts with one arm and her crotch with the other and backed off as he advanced upon her until her back was against the wall.

Adam's laughter was hysterical with lust. 'Damn! I ain't had a young piece like this in years!' He unbuttoned his fly and exposed his enormous erection.

'Oh, no! I'll die!' Her eyes rolled back in her head, and mercifully she fainted.

Undeterred, the big man spread her legs and slipped between her flaccid thighs. He ravished her without bothering to remove his trousers.

Flora did not fare as well as her sister. She put up a terrible struggle as the remaining hoodlums tore at her clothing like wild dogs after a frightened doe. Adrenaline surged through her veins, and it took all three of them to contain her.

'Damned little tigress!' one of them panted. 'If you want it the hard way, that's how you'll get it.' He punched her in the face with all his strength, knocking her unconscious to the straw, and they fought over her as if she was a piece of meat and they starving beasts. The biggest man won the right, and the other two turned to Adams.

'Come on, Kirk, you got your rocks off; now give us a turn.'

Grumbling, he got off Maud and spat tobacco juice into a corner. 'Hot damn! Best piece I ever had. Tight as a virgin.' He wiped his mouth with the back of his hand. 'Well, almost.'

One after the other the four raped each of the girls two times. Their revelry and the women's nightmarish ordeal were terminated when Morton entered the barn with a detail of men.

'What the hell is going on here?' he demanded. His eyes widened as he saw the girls lying naked and bloody on the floor. 'Jesus Christ, what kind of filthy bastards are you? Wait till Mr Ames hears about this.'

'Ames?' Adams laughed derisively. 'If your Mr Ames ain't careful, Jesse will turn him over his knee and spank him.'

'Your boss is dead, Adams,' Morton said levelly, 'shot by Jim Ames.' He looked around at his men, and there was unspoken communication among them.

Adams and his cronies had divested themselves of their weapons in order to attack the women, and now, literally, they were caught with their pants down. Casually Adams strolled in the direction of his rifle propped against a beam. He never made it. Morton drilled him three times with a six-gun, and his men mowed down the other three.

'That's that,' Morton said, holstering his gun and ordering his men to untie Molly Norton and her daughter. 'We'll take 'em over to the Carney ranch. They're Chisum people.'

'We'd rather walk, you scum!' Molly shouted as her arms and legs were freed. 'Don't think killing those mad dogs changes anything. You and Ames and the rest of your kind, you stink to the core.' To Amy she said, 'We'll wrap the girls in blankets and hitch up the wagon and take them over to the Carneys.'

'Where's Daddy?' Amy blubbered.

Molly's mouth was a thin grey line. 'Daddy is dead, dear. He's gone to heaven, and so have Jack and Paul.' Then, shaking her fist at Morton and the others, she cried, 'May the lot of you be rotting in hell before the year is out!'

Billy Morton would never forget the hellish wrath in her eyes as long as he lived. He shrugged and turned his gaze away from her accusing glare. 'Come on, boys,' he said in a subdued voice. 'Time to be burying the dead.'

That night, lying with her daughter in the cosy double bed in a spare room at the Carney ranch, Molly repeated her vow of vengeance against the Ames clan. 'You must never forget, child. You must keep the memory of your father and your brothers alive. Never let your hatred of the Ameses become dim with time. One day the Nortons will even the score against them, you wait and see.'

'Are you sure Flora and Maud will be all right?'

'Dr Stevens says they'll be just fine physically; but I'm sure their minds and souls will be scarred forever after what they've been through.'

Amy shivered. 'It must be terrible to be raped.'

'Sheer hell, and that's *another* score to settle with the Ameses.'

Good as her word, Molly wore her hatred against the Ameses like a badge of honour. She and Amy and her nieces spent the winter with Ike's brother Seth in Texas.

Meanwhile, the Norton spread in Lincoln County was cared for by sympathetic neighbours. Rumour had it that James Ames put up the money to rebuild the ranch house and replace the livestock Ike Norton had lost during the savage Lincoln County Cattle War, which ended in a tense but binding truce between the Murphys and the Chisums.

'Will you be going back this summer, Molly?' Seth inquired one night near the end of April.

'It depends on what Bob Collins has to tell me when he gets here tomorrow. In his letter he mentioned some rich Easterner who's made an offer for the spread.' She gazed out the window to where Amy was playing tag with Seth's two daughters. 'Sometimes I think I should take Amy to another part of the country; so many bad memories in Lincoln County.'

'I think you're right, Molly. Ada was saying the same thing to me just last night. Course you're more than welcome to stay with us. We've plenty of room, and you'd be a big help to Ada.'

'Thank you, Seth. I'll sleep on it.'

The following day, Bob Collins arrived in Amarillo on a stagecoach. Seth picked him up in a wagon and took him back to the ranch.

Molly embraced him warmly. 'Still sporting that same old suit and derby,' she chided. 'Fatter'n ever, too.'

He chucked her under the chin. 'Glad to see you didn't lose your sense of humour and – ' He bit his tongue as her eyes flashed like flint against stone.

'Not about some things, Bob. Come in and have some lunch and lemonade.'

Over lunch, he told her about the offer for the Norton spread. 'Big oilman named Tyler, and he's powerful enough not to be partisan to either the Chisums or the Murphys. He might just be the force to put the damper on the old rivalry once and for all. And the price is more than generous.'

'I think so, too. You have my power of attorney to accept.'

'I have a writ for you to sign right here,' he said, withdrawing a document from his inside pocket.

After lunch, Molly signed the power of attorney in Seth's study, and they had a drink of homemade corn whisky to celebrate the sale.

'What'll you be doing now?' Bob asked.

'Seth and Ada invited me to stay on with them, but I've been thinking. I have a sister living in Sacramento, California. I think I'll take Amy and the girls out there and see if we like the country.'

'Hear tell it's wonderful country,' he said, 'and beautiful weather all year round . . . How are Flora and Maud?'

'They're all right – lots more subdued than they used to be.'

'That's understandable,' he said sympathetically, noting the pain in Molly's eyes. 'At any rate, I think it's a good idea to find yourselves a change of scenery. I happen to love this godforsaken part of the world, but it can be grim, 'specially in winter.'

That evening at supper, Molly announced her plans to Amy and her nieces. They all liked the idea of going to California, though Amy had one reservation:

'It won't be forever, will it?' Her eyes were hard obsidian. 'I mean, we have a score to settle with the Ameses, right, Ma?'

Molly leaned over and stroked her hair. 'You bet we do, darling; but there's no hurry. Sometimes vengeance, like plum wine, gets sweeter and richer with age.'

Amy smiled and stared into the future . . .

6

Susan awoke with a start. Someone was knocking at the bedroom door. She sat up and called out in a groggy voice:

'Yes? Who is it?'

'It is Pedro, Señora. Señora Ames asked me to tell you that dinner will be served at eight.'

'Thank you, Pedro. We'll be down shortly.'

It was pitch dark in the room. She fumbled for the switch

at the base of the lamp on the bed table. Her eyes ached in the abrupt assault of bright light. Beside her, Kevin stirred:

'What is it? Who was that at the door?'

'Pedro, the houseboy.' She looked at her watch on the table. 'My God, it's seven-fifteen! I can't believe we've been asleep all this time. Hurry, darling, Mrs Ames is serving at eight.' She threw back the covers and got out of bed.

Kevin sat up and stretched. 'I needed that. A wench like you can really spend a man.'

'Complaining?'

'Not on your life! I'm famished. I could eat a horse.' He swung his feet to the floor.

Susan went to the bureau and took out a pair of blue stretch pants and a striped cardigan. The Ameses had thoughtfully provided them all with loose-fitting slacks and shirts and sweaters so that proper fit was unimportant. Footwear was no problem, either; in the basement, Ames kept many pairs of jogging sneakers and hiking boots in a variety of sizes for the use of visitors who cared to exercise.

'Very chic,' Kevin said when she was dressed. He chose a heavy ski sweater and Levi's.

'My hair is still damp,' she said, and gathered it at the back of her neck with a red bow.

They were the last to arrive in the living room, where the others were chatting over drinks. Richard Lemon looked at them with amusement:

'What kept you two so long, as if we didn't know?' He lifted an insinuating eyebrow.

Susan hated herself for blushing. 'We fell asleep. You should have roused us sooner.'

'Not at all,' Nancy Ames assured her. 'The rib roast won't be done for at least another twenty minutes.'

'And it's a monster,' her husband said. 'Could feed an army.'

'I could outeat an army, I'm so damned hungry,' Dick said.

'Amen,' said Kevin.

'Do you do your own cooking, Mrs Ames?' Susan asked.

'Yes, with a big assist from Pedro. There are no limits to his talents.'

'Anything I can do to help?'

'We've already offered,' Jennie Bostwick told her. 'Nancy says Pedro doesn't allow strangers in his kitchen.'

'That's right, and please call me "Nancy," Susan. This is a very informal occasion. I do apologize for not providing more original attire; but, ladies, my wardrobe is at your disposal if you'd prefer a dress.'

They demurred in a chorus.

'I think we look positively splendid,' Dick declared, noting his companions' rugged attire. In a perfect western dialect, and pretending to strum a guitar, he sang, ' "I'm back in the saddle agin . . . back in the saddle agin . . . " '

Walt brought drinks for Susan and Kevin. 'Please smoke if you wish. There are cigarettes and cigars on the coffee table. I'll stick to my old corncob.'

'Walt was telling us some fascinating lore about the Indians who live in New Mexico, Kevin,' Larry Bostwick said. 'You'd be interested. You know, of course, that drugs play a major role in their religious ceremonies. By coincidence, Walt, Kevin and I were discussing the subject on the plane, just before – ' He stopped abruptly and then went on in a shaky voice: 'Would you believe I've been blocking out that plane crash in my mind for the past hour?'

'As well you should, Larry,' Walt said gently. 'Dwelling on misfortune is futile and unhealthy.'

'Yeah, guess so.' Larry ran a hand through his short, curly hair. 'You were saying, Walt, that the ingestion of drugs is not indigenous to the Indians in the Southwest or to this point in time.'

'True. People all over the world have been taking drugs for various purposes since the beginning of time. Our ancestors discovered weeds and plants that, when eaten or smoked, could induce miraculous changes in feeling and perception – "consciousness-altering drugs," we call them today: fly-agaric mushrooms, hemp, caffeine, tobacco, cocoa leaves, scores of others. Homer wrote about it in the *Odyssey:* Ulysses and his crew entrapped in the land of the Lotus Eaters, where the population was on a permanent high from eating a fruit that induced euphoria and caused the men to forget about their homes and families.'

'And let's not forget about the ancient South American Indians,' Kevin said. 'The Incas gave their messengers cocoa leaves to chew to give them the endurance to run fifty miles over mountainous terrain.'

Walt nodded and pointed the stem of his pipe at Kevin. 'Correct. Cocaine increased their stamina and endurance; in fact, it was the only thing that made life bearable for the impoverished and underfed Indians. Then there are the Vikings. They took an essence of fly-agaric mushrooms before they went into battle. Yes, the ancients were spacing out on psychedelics long before Timothy Leary cooked up LSD in a laboratory.'

'It's been said that Coleridge wrote *Kubla Khan* after an opium trip,' Larry said.

'But I still fail to see the connection between drugs and religion,' Jennie said.

'In the beginning, we had the tribal medicine man, who was both physician and religious leader and whose powers were supposedly God-given. His knowledge of herbs, substances that healed and stopped pain and created euphoria, truly must have seemed supernatural.' Walt placed his pipe in an ashtray. 'In my own opinion, the visions allegedly witnessed by all of our famous religious prophets – Moses, Christ, Mohammed, numerous others – were induced by hallucinogens. Yes, religion and drugs have always been inseparably bound together.'

'I hate to interrupt this fascinating subject,' Nancy said, 'but Pedro just flashed me the high sign. Dinner is ready to be served.'

'If you care to, we can listen to the radio while we're eating, hear if anything has developed since the last bulletins I heard,' Walt offered.

They were unanimous in their consent.

'By all means, old man. I can't wait to hear *Variety's* eulogy of me,' Dick said.

Laura snorted. 'I can't wait to hear *Beefeater gin's* eulogy of you, darling.'

The standing rib roast, served on a huge pewter tray, was a gourmet's delight.

'Done to a turn,' Walt said as he carved.

'My God! My mouth is actually watering,' Dick said. 'I always imagined that phrase was a writer's invention.'

The thick slabs, swimming in the rare meat's juices, were augmented by rich brown gravy, asparagus tips, red cabbage, and glazed, oven-browned potatoes.

Before he sat down, Walt switched on a radio on the sideboard. The static was horrendous, but with patience he managed to find a news station that was intelligible. It was stated that a series of freak rainstorms and tornadoes was sweeping across Texas, Louisiana, New Mexico, and Colorado. Loss of life and property exceeded that of any storm in fifty years. One ship had been sunk in the Gulf of Mexico, and numerous others were in distress. A train had been wrecked in the Panhandle, and three passenger planes were missing, including the Cessna *Golden Eagle*, which:

> . . . carried seven passengers, including famous film stars Richard Lemon and Laura Devane, as well as noted Hollywood columnist Jan Danzig. It is believed that the Cessna charter plane crashed in a violent storm somewhere near the Colorado and New Mexico border. Air-search rescue efforts have been hampered by continuing rain and high winds. The weather bureau predicts there will be little improvement in prevailing conditions until late tomorrow afternoon . . . Now for the local sports news . . .

Walt turned off the radio. 'No sense spoiling a good meal with any more bad news.'

The Ameses were curious to learn more about Laura and Dick's new film.

'*Blood on the Sun* – a good title,' said Walt. 'Doesn't that have local significance?'

Dick replied, 'Yes, it was an Indian superstition that on the afternoon Tunstall was shot, the sunset was red with blood. Must have been some atmospheric phenomenon. At any rate, it persisted throughout the Lincoln County War.'

'And to think that Walt's and Susan's relatives fought each other,' Jennie said. 'Sort of like the North and the South in the Civil War, brother against brother.'

'Not exactly,' Susan denied. 'The Nortons and the Ameses were not related. The only blood between them was bad blood.' Her gaze rested on Walter Ames and didn't waver even when he averted his eyes.

The others, feeling the sudden tension in the air, hurriedly changed the subject.

'I wonder how the weather is now,' Nancy said. 'Walt and I have been invited to a religious ceremony down at the Indian village tonight. It would be quite an experience for you to witness, particularly Larry and Kevin, with their work in the field.'

'I'll have a look out front,' Walt said, rising. He had finished his meal.

'I'm finished, too,' Susan said. 'I'm so stuffed I may burst. Think I'll go out on the porch and have a cigarette. I hate to smoke at a dinner table with non-smokers. Will you excuse me?'

Kevin stared after his wife thoughtfully. Her excuse for following Ames was exceedingly feeble. There was no doubt in his mind that she wanted to be alone with the scion of the man who had been responsible for the Norton Massacre, and her purpose troubled him deeply.

It was windy and raw on the big front porch and pitch black, but the rain had stopped, as had the thunder and lightning. Walt peered into the darkness. He did not recognize who it was until she inhaled deeply on her cigarette and it glowed briefly, illuminating her face.

'Well, hello,' he said with surprise. 'The lovely Mrs Brandon. What are you doing out here? You'll catch cold.'

'My sweater is quite warm, thank you. Well, are we going to the Indian village later on?'

'If the storm doesn't flare up again, we should have no difficulty driving down there in the pickup. I'll ask Chief to reconnoitre the road.'

'Where are the hands?'

'The bunkhouse back of the barn. But you still haven't answered my question: Why did you come out here?'

The cigarette glowed again. 'Why, I came out here to be alone with you, of course.'

His laugh was dry, brittle. 'Of course! You know damned well you hate my guts. I've heard stories about you Norton women, the perpetuation of the grudge you hold against the Ameses past, present and future.'

She laughed lightly. 'Don't be ridiculous, Walt. That's been over for a long, long time.'

He sounded mistrustful: 'Has it, now? I wonder.'

'Stop wondering. I was telling the truth. I find you an extremely attractive man.'

'And old enough to be your father.'

'Hardly that. Anyway, I've always favoured older men.'

'You didn't marry one.'

'A pity.' She sighed. 'At Kevin's age, one's career takes precedence over everything else: home, family' – a pregnant pause – 'and bedroom performance.'

'Jesus!' he said under his breath. 'You *are* a candid female, aren't you.'

'Female I am indeed – a female with a hankering for a strong, virile male.'

She crushed out her cigarette with her toe and moved closer to Walt. Musk and perfume wafted up into his nostrils. Her arms slid slowly onto his shoulders and around his neck – *like snakes,* he thought with a shiver – and her lips pressed, warm and moist, against the pulse on the side of his throat.

'You can't be cold when I'm so hot,' she whispered.

'I don't know what your game is, lady,' he said in a husky voice, 'but I've never been one to back away from a challenge.' He took her in his arms roughly and kissed her, feeling her lips part and her moist tongue slip into his mouth –*the imagery of snakes again!*

Susan tensed as the powerful thrust of his manhood wooed her loins and his hand went underneath her sweater and stroked her bare belly, working its way up to her breast, caressing it gently. She put a hand down between their bodies, unzipped his pants, found his turgid member, and stroked it. 'You're a big one, love. I can't get my fingers all around it.'

'No!' He disengaged her hand from his erection. 'This is not the time or the place. Nancy will be looking for us.'

The words were no sooner spoken than the front door opened and his wife called out, 'Walt! Susan! Are you there?'

They separated quietly, and Walt zipped up his fly. In a remarkably composed voice, he answered, 'Yeah, we're here, hon. I think it's clearing.'

'Good. I do want to go to the village. Come on in and have some coffee and brandy. *Brrr* . . . it's chilly out here.

You must be frozen, Susan.'

'No, you have warm sweaters, Nancy.' She preceded Walt into the dimly lit foyer and followed Nancy to the parlour, where Pedro was dispensing coffee and snifters of brandy.

'Ahh, I see our two defectors have rejoined the flock. What were you doing, necking on the porch swing?' Dick leered.

Walt laughed easily. 'Those days are gone forever. My arthritis will not tolerate cold or acrobatics. Oh, for the good old days. Let me tell you, Dick, when I was twenty-one, I could – as the young folk today phrase it – "make out" on an ice floe or a red-hot beach.'

They all laughed, and Jennie asked Lemon, 'Dick, Larry and I were wondering . . . When you play those torrid love scenes with all those different sexy ladies, does it turn you on?'

Dick laughed. 'You're damned well right it turns me on. I remember one picture I was in with Marilyn Monroe.'

'You're dating yourself, Dickie,' Laura said archly.

'Never mind; Marilyn was timeless.'

'As well as bra-less and pantie-less.'

'Exactly. In any case, we were doing this love scene in a meadow of Swiss edelweiss on the side of a mountain. I was nuzzling her throat and her cleavage when unexpectedly she began to slide. I made a wild grab for her, and my hand slipped under her skirt clear up to her snatch. It was an "elevating" experience, if you know what I mean, gents.'

Laura yawned. 'Richard "elevates" at the drop of a hat.'

'Panties, love,' he corrected her.

'The party is getting ribald,' Nancy observed with a smile.

Susan was keenly aware that Nancy kept casting covert looks at her and at Walt. No doubt she had good reason to be suspicious of her husband. After all, he was an Ames, and not a one could be trusted.

'What time does this shindig begin at the Indian village?' Dick wanted to know.

'Midnight,' said Walt.

Dick winced. 'That's way past my bedtime, old chap.'

'It will be worth it, I promise. Besides, you can sleep late tomorrow. Why don't you catch forty winks now? We won't be leaving for another hour.'

Pedro entered the room. 'Señor Ames, Chief wishes to speak with you.'

'Send him in, Pedro.'

The Indian came in, sombrero in hand. 'I just returned from the village, sir, and the roadway is muddy but passable. No problem for either the jeep or the pickup.'

'That's a mercy . . . Chief, do you think the villagers would object if we brought along our guests to the ceremonial lodge tonight?'

The Indian looked perplexed. 'I will ask Gall. I do not know.'

'It will not be the same as it was with that film crew that came to the lodge two years back,' Walt explained. 'Tell your people that we have the utmost respect for your Holy Spirit and the sacred ground of the ceremonial lodge, just as we respect the sanctity of our own churches and synagogues and holy temples of all faiths. What we see tonight, we will observe with reverence.'

Chief nodded curtly, and the hint of a smile creased his leathery face. 'It is good, then. I do not have to ask Gall. He will respect your respect.'

'Thank you, Chief. Listen, how is the road below the village? When will it be passable, do you think?'

'It is hard to say. The washout was very, very bad, the worst I've seen. The canyon bridge, even it's down.'

'The bridge,' Walt whistled in awe. 'I've never seen it down in forty years.'

Chief was solemn. 'What is even worse, Gall says the storm is not yet over. He says that tomorrow it will renew itself with greater ferocity.'

'Shit!' cursed an exasperated Laura. 'We have got to get word to the studio, to Lincoln City.'

Walt shrugged helplessly. 'My dear Laura, if it were possible, I would carry you down that mountain piggy-back, but – '

'Hell! My guess is, it will be bright and clear by morning,' Dick said. 'I mean, what does this witch doctor know, anyway?'

The Indian fixed him with a laser-beam stare. 'Gall is not a witch doctor. He does not practise voodoo. Gall is a man of God – he is close to God – and he knows that God is angry with Skull Mountain. The evil here offends God.'

'Evil?' Jennie said. 'What kind of evil? I mean, we in this house are the only ones on Skull Mountain.'

'Precisely,' Dick quipped. 'You heard what the man said, sweetie. If the shoe fits, then, I suggest, those of us to whom the charge applies must wear it in good grace.'

Chief turned and walked out of the room.

'Evil?' Laura was visibly disturbed. 'My God! I'm beginning to feel like a character out of *Ten Little Indians*. Remember, their invisible host invited them to a mansion on a desolate island in order to punish them for crimes they had committed in their past?'

An uncomfortable hush settled over the group. Once again the tension in the air was palpable.

Dick Lemon made an effort to dispel the miasma:

'Here we are, as ornery a bunch of sinners as ever got together in one room.'

'Not necessarily just we in this room.' Susan said. She looked straight at Walter Ames. 'You know the old expression, "The gods visit the sins of the fathers upon the children." '

7

The two-mile ride down to the Indian village was an experience in itself. The narrow dirt road was oozing with mud, hubcap deep in places, and even though the pickup truck had four-wheel drive and snow tyres, it bogged down three times, and the men had to get out and push. One half-mile stretch was along a sheer cliff that fell off beyond the iron guardrail into a bottomless abyss.

Lemon, Devane, and Danzig sat up front with Chief, who was driving. The others sat in the van on drop benches on either side.

'If I had known it was going to be like this, I would have

stayed back at the house,' Laura complained.

'Be a good sport, love,' Dick advised her. 'I've got a bottle of gin in my coat pocket, so if things get dull, we can party.'

Walt called to Dick through the open window in the partition that separated the van from the cab, 'Don't break out any booze during the ceremony. That would be sacrilegious. Besides, you'll get the high of your life on mescaline.'

'Are you serious?' Dick said with interest.

Walt grinned. 'Sure; chewing peyote buttons really turns you on. And the ceremony is open to anyone who wants to participate.'

Kevin frowned. 'Count Susan and me out. We're anti-drug people, even over-the-counter drugs like aspirin and Dramamine. The only thing I ingest is food, booze, and nicotine.'

Larry Bostwick shook his head. 'Booze and nicotine – hell, man, they're two of the worst drugs of all. Well, suit yourself, Kevin. For myself, tonight I intend to fly.' He extended his arms to the sides like wings and swooped this way and that.

Susan giggled. 'And let me speak for myself, my darling husband. *I'm* with Larry and Walt.'

'Susan!' He was shocked. 'What's got into you tonight?'

'Nothing, darling.' She nudged Walt's thigh with her knee. 'Not yet.' In the darkness of the van, she and Walt exchanged a conspiratorial glance.

'I think we've arrived,' Dick called back.

The road took an abrupt dip, plunging the truck into a pocket of ground fog.

'Jesus Christ!' Laura exclaimed. 'Talk about London fog, I can't see a foot beyond the headlights.'

Chief was unconcerned and did not even slow down; he knew every twist and turn in the road by heart. The truck emerged from the fog into swirling mist, and the Indian village appeared as they came around a sharp curve.

It consisted of about forty ramshackle shanties and a run-down general store. In what approximated a village square sat the ceremonial lodge, a big dome of mud, animal hides, and tree bark ornamented with colourful designs – animals, flowers, birds, and mythical figures that were half-man, half-animal – painstakingly fashioned from stones held together by clay.

As they disembarked from the truck, Chief introduced them to the elders of the tribe and to the medicine man, Gall. 'Gall is one hundred and five years old,' he said matter-of-factly.

The ancient Indian was truly one of nature's wonders; though his skin showed the ravages of time, giving him the appearance of those great eroded rock faces of the High Sierras, his dark, deep-set eyes were frightening, and his voice was strong and steady: 'Welcome to our humble village. Friends of Mr Ames are friends of our people.'

'Walt practically subsidizes them,' Nancy whispered to Larry and Kevin. 'They adore him.'

There were bonfires blazing all around the lodge, casting grotesque shadows on the low ceiling of fog. It began to drizzle again.

'Come inside and take your places,' Gall invited them. He did not join them immediately.

The interior of the ceremonial lodge was dimly illuminated by torches fastened to the walls. The frame of the structure consisted of young saplings stripped of bark and bent into arched supports. In the centre of the lodge was a stone altar shaped like a quarter-moon, about five feet across at the cusps. It was black and as smooth as if it had been polished by a lapidary. A fire pit had been carved out of the centre, a bowl two feet in diameter. There was about the place the aura of a cathedral, a sense of peace and wellbeing.

'We'll sit back in the spectators' section,' Walt told them. 'Follow me.'

They sat in the last row, cross-legged on the earth floor with their backs against the wall. The air smelled of incense, and it had a pleasantly narcotic effect.

'I'm beginning to feel high already,' Susan whispered to Jennie. 'And sexy.' She looked at Walt and winked.

At exactly midnight, Gall led a procession of worshippers into the lodge, sixteen men and eight women.

'A quorum congregation,' Walt explained to them. 'This ceremony is comparable to the Catholic Sacrament.'

The men wore buckskin tunics that hung midway down the thigh. Narrow leather headbands and knee-high leather stockings completed the simple ensemble. The women were garbed in flowing, voluminous floor-length gowns that looked like white silk. Walt confirmed it:

'The China trade introduced silk to North America, and the sailors made out like thieves, trading it to the Indians. They told them it was angels' hair, and the Indians believed it because they had never seen any fabric as delicate before.'

Gall wore only a loincloth and was barefoot. On his head was a skullcap of feathers that in shape resembled a yarmulka. His torso, amazingly sound for one of his age, was painted red, blue, and green, as were his thin but wiry arms.

'Blue for the sky and water, green for Mother Earth, and red for the life of mankind,' Walt said, looking at Kevin and Larry, who were both scribbling furiously in pocket notebooks. 'Let me know if I'm going too fast for you.'

The sombre marches sat down around the half-moon altar in a circle. The medicine man took up his post between the horns of the crescent, facing the altar. Two fire tenders stood at attention on either side. Sitting opposite the medicine man across the altar were the ceremonial musicians. One cradled an iron water-drum covered with animal hide between his legs; the other held a long whistle.

'Made of eagle bone,' Walt told them. 'Those seven knobs on the side of the drum represent the stars of the Big Dipper.'

The worshippers bowed their heads while the medicine man began to chant: 'The sky is holy, the earth is holy, the water is holy, the birds of the forest are holy . . . '

It was a liturgy that embraced all things large and small in the universe, from the sun and the moon and the planets to the miniscule red ant. His recitation was accompanied by the drummer tapping softly on the taut hide, simple rhythms at first, increasing in complexity and tempo. When joined in by the whistle, it had an exotic, haunting tone reminiscent of the East Indian lute.

The tenders lit the tinder under the logs, stacked together in the form of a tepee, in the fire pit. When the fire began to blaze, they sprinkled herbs and spices on it. Quickly the fragrance filled the lodge; it was like nothing any of them, with the exception of the Ameses, had ever smelled before.

'I feel light-headed,' Susan said.

'You're hyperventilating,' Walt said. 'Try to breathe slower.'

At the conclusion of the prayer, the medicine man placed a dried-up, furry-looking button on the altar. 'Everything that *is* is holy.'

In a chorus, the congregation echoed it back, with the same intonation.

'That's a mescal button he put on the altar,' Walt said, 'cut from the top of a peyote cactus.'

The medicine man pointed to a man seated in the circle. 'Let us hear your prayer.'

The man lifted his face and his arms to heaven and began to chant in a rambling singsong more intriguing for its hypnotic effect than for its profundity; 'Oh, Holy Spirit, grant me long life, good health, and a faithful wife. May my mares and cows foal . . . '

Each man and woman, in turn, recited his or her personal prayer, most of them unimaginatively alike in content but unique in delivery. During the prayers, the medicine man began to roll on the altar herb cigarettes that looked like the black twisted cheroots popular in Mexico. They were handed to the person on the right, to be inhaled deeply and then passed around the circle.

Walt lit two of the cigarettes that Chief had obtained from Gall, took a long drag on one of them, then handed both to Larry and Kevin. 'Go on, Professor. It's not the hard stuff. Go on; it won't bite you.'

On frequent occasions, Kevin and Susan had politely refused to smoke marijuana when pot parties were fashionable on campus among a sizeable percentage of the faculty as well as of the students. There had never been a real temptation to experiment – until tonight. The piquant aroma of the burning herbs, mixed with the scent of the cigarette smoke, wafting up into his nostrils made Kevin light-headed, as giddy as if he had drunk two stiff martinis. He felt good, filled with affection and a sense of camaraderie for the people around him.

Susan expressed it: 'One for all and all for one. C'mon, Kevin, don't be a party pooper. Here, give it to me.'

He withheld it. 'No, I'll give it a try. What the hell! You

only live once.' He put the cigarette to his lips and gingerly puffed, sucking the smoke deep into his lungs. His toes and fingertips began to tingle. It was a highly pleasurable sensation, like that of the initial rush of blood to the genitals at the onset of an erection. Exhilarated, he passed it on to his wife.

'Here we go,' she said gaily. She took a deep draft of the smoke. '*Wheeee!* I needed that! Hey, Walt, old chum, where can I buy a deck of these weeds to take back home?'

He smiled. 'You can't. There are some things money can't buy.' In the dimness of the lodge, he surreptitiously dropped a hand on the inside of her thigh.

From this juncture, time became irrelevant. A second seemed infinite; an hour abbreviated to the wink of an eye. What transpired now was a 'trip' in every sense of the word, a trip through an exotic territory of new dimensional space and colour and excitement and heightened experience – Alice in Wonderland, Gulliver in Lilliput.

To the accompaniment of the eagle whistle and drum, the medicine man sang a stirring song of the great Golden Eagle that had battled fire and ice storms to bring life to the universe. The earth, the moon, the planets, the stars were eggs placed in the sky by the Golden Eagle.

Susan was glassy-eyed; she spoke in a monotone: 'Golden Eagle – that was the name of our plane.'

The worshippers around the altar added their own background to the medicine man's performance, crying, moaning, shouting, swaying back and forth to the drum's beat.

One of the fire tenders held up a buckskin bag as the medicine man announced, 'It is time for partaking of the flesh of the Holy Spirit.' He took the bag from the tender, passed his hand over it, and muttered a prayer. Then he went around the circle, handing each person a small, furry button like the one on the altar.

'Like the wafer and wine of Christian Sacrament,' Larry said to Kevin.

Walt took a similar bag out of his pocket and dispensed buttons to each member of his party.

'A regular pusher,' Susan joked. 'What do we do with them?'

'Chew it very thoroughly,' he said, 'And try to stay as

relaxed as possible and breath normally; otherwise mescaline will make you nauseated.'

Susan placed the button between her back molars and cracked it open. It had the texture of a peanut shell, but the contents were sharp and bitter. Her tongue burned long after she had swallowed it. She belched as acid invaded her oesophagus, and kept swallowing to stop the bile from rising into her throat. She took a deep breath and held it.

Walt passed around mint antacid tablets. 'Stay loose, boys and girls. Here, these will help some. You have to keep mescaline down for at least fifteen minutes for it to be effective.'

The antacid helped.

The Indians were swaying back and forth and praying in counterpoint: 'Everlasting thanks to the Holy Spirit, who is all things to all creatures'; 'Eternal damnation for the forces of evil'; 'Oh, Holy Spirit, we are but weak mortals, and without your strength and supernatural power, we are at the mercy of the evil-doers'; 'Repent, you sinners, and you shall be redeemed.'

'My God,' Laura hissed, 'They sound like Holy Rollers, southern evangelists.'

'Do you get the impression that they are addressing this litany to you, dear Laura?' Dick said.

'Oh, shut up!'

Susan felt like a drowning swimmer going under for the last time, only there was no fear or panic. The voices were a wind in her ears, punctuated by the monotone of the drumbeat. Time had no order, no sequence, in her mind; past, present, and future were concurrent, the three dimensions all brought together on one plane.

As if by magic, she was back in the Cessna as it plunged through the forest and crash-landed, every detail recalled vividly: the shocked expression on Kevin's face when he turned away from the cockpit . . . It was as though she was operating a motion picture projector with the power to resurrect any given episode of her life with the flick of a switch: fast forward and reverse; speed up and slow motion; freeze frame.

She opened her eyes and the mirage was gone. Her perception was becoming astonishingly more keen as the mescaline diffused through her body – sights, sounds, smells. The firelight from the altar was so dazzling, she couldn't bear to stare directly at it. She held out one hand and examined it. She could see the skeleton and tendons under the sheath of flesh and muscle, the solid core of her. *Her*.

Then the onset of terror. She was shrinking like Alice after ingesting the magic potion – smaller, even smaller. She screamed for Kevin to help her, but it was too late; she was a miniscule speck among giants, an ant to be ground under a heel. She whimpered and covered her eyes to blot out the sight of her imminent destruction. When that did not grant her swift mercy, she opened them – and the terror increased. She was no longer a diminishing inanity; now she began to expand until she dwarfed the others inside the lodge, filling up all the available space. Soon she would crush them, and the walls would explode, sending fragments of clay, wood, bark, and hides into the air.

Summoning up all her willpower and self-control, she managed to find her 'sea-legs.' You had to ride with the drug the way a surfer rides the crest of the big wave: relax, stay loose – above all, maintain your balance. After a while she closed her eyes again and took a madcap trip back into time . . .

A hot July day in 1905 . . . Mrs Amy Norton Day and her daughter, Candice, arrived in Lincoln City, New Mexico, for a vacation. However, a holiday was subordinate to Mrs Day's true purpose in returning to her birthplace.

When Molly Norton, Amy's mother, sold out the Norton spread back in 1878, she retained 200 acres of land at one corner of the property, which a geologist friend of her husband's forecast would one day be a rich source of petroleum. After her death in 1890, the deed reverted to Amy, the sole remaining Norton heir, along with other holdings, worth well over $1 million. With the advent of the motor car, the demand for petroleum throughout the world had quadrupled by 1905 and was still increasing by leaps and bounds.

Early that spring, Amy had received a letter from the law firm of Collins, Collins, and Worth, in Lincoln City, advising her that both the Seneca Oil Company and the Standard Oil Company had submitted bids for her 200 acres, which adjoined land holdings owned by Standard Oil. At the time, her husband, Carlton F. Day, a wealthy sugar importer, was in Hawaii on company business. Their family lawyer advised her to postpone any decision on the offers until she and Carlton could travel to New Mexico and negotiate with the participants. But, being a strong-willed woman who knew her own mind, and considered it the equal of any male intellect – including that of her husband, a man of renowned business acumen – Amy decided that she and her daughter would visit Lincoln City in the summer.

'A combination of business and pleasure,' she told Candice. 'I haven't been back to New Mexico since I was just about your age.'

The girl nodded solemnly and compressed her lips. 'Since Grandfather was murdered by the Ameses.'

Amy put her hands on her daughter's shoulders and looked into her eyes, eyes uncannily like her own, of an ambivalent hue; depending on the refraction of light, they would appear grey, pale green, or pale blue. 'We just might run into the Ameses, child,' she said.

Candice Day was anything but a 'child.' At nineteen, she was two inches taller than her mother, and her willowy, well-developed body had a feline sensuality; whatever she did, it was with economy of movement. In appearance she was a Norton through and through. She did not share the dark, intense looks of her mother – Candice's hair was the colour of honey and her complexion fair – but they had the same cameo profile (slightly aquiline nose, strong chin) and the same large, almond-shaped, wide-set eyes. What's more, Amy had passed on to her daughter a common legacy of hatred for the Ames clan. From the time Candice was old enough to understand, she had been indoctrinated, immersed, in the history of the Lincoln County Cattle War and the grisly details of the Norton Massacre.

'Yes, Candice, they will pay for their infamy, the Ameses – pay and pay and pay, over and over and over again.'

Candice frowned. 'But so much time has gone by, Mother, and nothing has happened to them yet.'

Amy smiled sweetly and patted Candice's cheek. 'Well, dear, maybe the time has come.'

When they arrived at their destination on the morning of

July 3, 1905, they went directly to the Carlton Hotel, the most elegant hotel in Lincoln City.

'It's named after Father,' Candice joked.

'It's why I chose it,' Amy said seriously. 'A hunch. Maybe it will bring us good luck.'

Their suite was comprised of a well-appointed sitting-room, two bedrooms, and a bath. They discarded their dusty travelling gowns and took hot baths. Then they chose attire – 'appropriately ladylike for a rustic western city,' as Amy phrased it.

For herself, Amy picked out a three-tiered, ankle-length gown of pima cotton in an Old English flower print, full at the bosom and nipped in at the waist by a cummerbund. 'I think the prairie-plaid flannel would look nice on you, dear.'

Candice wrinkled up her nose. 'It's rather gauche, Mother.'

'My dear, this is not San Fransisco. We are country girls at heart, who have returned to the site of our humble origins.'

Candice gazed at her with comic disbelief. 'Moth–*er!* The ladies at the club should hear how you talk.'

'Never you mind, young lady,' Amy said, affecting a strong midwestern drawl. 'Now, git into that thar dress before I paddle yer bottom. And speaking of bottoms, yours is indecently exposed. Who told you you could wear my Parisian lingerie? That chemise is scandalous. Why, you can see right through it.'

'Isn't that the purpose?' Candice asked slyly. 'I imagine that's why Father brought it back from France for you.'

'You are an impudent daughter and far too precocious,' Amy chided her, but with affection.

'Because I know all about sex?' Candice said innocently. 'After all, it was you who taught me.'

'I explained sex to you, but I did not give you permission to practise it. What's more, you do *not* know *everything* about the subject.'

Candice smiled impishly. 'Then we must resume our lessons, Mother.'

Amy threw her hands in the air. 'That will be enough, young lady. Now, get dressed and fix your hair before the lawyers arrive. They are due at the hotel at noon.'

Candice slipped the gown over her head and surveyed herself in the mirror. 'It's not all that bad at that.' She fluffed the frill top of the blouse with her fingers and buttoned the pearl buttons down the front. Below the waist sash, the skirt was long and billowy.

'You look lovely, dear. I've always liked you in cotton; it clings to you and makes you look very feminine. The colour becomes you, too.'

'I preferred the rose myself.'

'No, it was cheap-looking; the fawn is better. No matter, sit down there at the vanity and I'll do your hair. You should really have it cut, you know; it's almost down to your behind.' She combed out her daughter's long, silky hair and began to braid it across the top of her head, securing it with an embroidered-silk barrette with artificial flowers.

'Do you think the old Mr Collins will come himself?' Candice asked.

'Uncle Bob? Goodness, I doubt it. He must be in his eighties and retired. Probably his oldest son, James – he's the nominal head of the firm now – and one of the law clerks.' She sighed in reminiscence. 'When your grandfather hired Bob Collins, he had a one-room office behind the funeral parlour. Now, I understand, they have an entire floor in a downtown office building. Yes, I must admit, this city is a far cry from Lincoln City as I knew it.'

Candice stared at her mother in the mirror. 'I wonder if the Ameses have changed along with everything else.'

'Some things, some people, the more they change, the more they stay the same.'

8

James Collins bore a strong resemblance to his father, except that he spoke with an accent affected at Harvard Law School and his suit was tailor-made.

When he entered the suite, precisely at noon, he took both of Amy's hands in his and kissed her cheek. 'Amy, I can't tell you how good it is to see you. You look fabulous, beautiful as ever, and, – he looked across her shoulder at Candice – 'not possibly old enough to have a daughter so grown up. Lovely, too. Takes after her mother.'

'Flatterer, but thank you, anyway. Yes, this is my daughter, Candice.'

James shook his head in wonderment. 'I don't know where the time goes, Amy. It seems like only yesterday when I used to ride out to your father's place with my dad. Your brother Jack and I were great pals, remember? He and I – ' He paused self-consciously, aware that all of the light and gaiety had drained out of Amy's beautiful face. 'I . . . I . . . I'm sorry, Amy. I didn't mean to resurrect unpleasant memories.'

'That's all right, Jim. How is your father?'

'Dad, he's chipper as a forty-year-old. Lost a lot of weight and all his hair, but he still comes to the office twice a week. We'll all have dinner with him some evening before you leave.'

'What's happened to the old Norton spread?'

'Well, as you know, your mother sold out to an eastern firm. After the turn of the century, they broke it up into smaller parcels and took bids. Which brings us to our business – '

In the background in the foyer, a slim young man in a pinstripe blue serge suit cleared his throat.

Collins whirled around. 'Oh, I *am* sorry, Benson. In my excitement at seeing Mrs Day, I forgot all about you. Amy, this is one of our law clerks, Fred Benson. Benson, Mrs Day and her daughter, Candice.'

After the amenities were observed, Amy suggested they sit down in the parlour. 'There's a good-sized coffee table there on which to lay out your documents. I'm sorry I can't offer you any refreshments, perhaps we can call down for some coffee or tea.'

'No thank you, Amy. As a matter of fact, when we're through here, I'd like to take you out to lunch.'

'How very thoughtful of you, Jim. We'd be delighted.'

The transaction was concluded in less than half an hour, Fred Benson serving as witness to Amy's signature on the contract Collins had drawn up. A smiling Collins then took a cheque out of his portfolio and presented it to her:

'As was agreed by both parties, here is a cheque for four hundred and fifty thousand dollars. It's quite a windfall, you must admit.'

'To be sure, Jim.' With casual indifference, Amy placed it on the coffee table underneath an ashtray. 'However, money isn't everything in life.'

There was a twinkle in his eye. 'That's easy for you to say. You are a very rich woman – I daresay the most beautiful rich woman in the world.'

'You'll be turning my head with all these compliments, Jim. Now, you said something about lunch. I'm starved.'

'Splendid . . . Here, Benson, take these back to the office like a good fellow and draw up the brief on the Wilson case so I can go over it later today.'

'Yes, sir.' Benson put the contracts in his briefcase, bowed to Amy and Candice, and departed.

'I made reservations for one-thirty at the Cattle King Restaurant. It's one of the finest eating places in the state – in the country, for that matter.'

'I'll reserve judgment until after lunch,' Amy said, smiling.

The restaurant was indeed, as Collins promised, extremely impressive, with four separate dining rooms on two floors and a broad, curving staircase sweeping up to the second storey.

'Italian marble,' Collins said of the steps. 'The crystal chandeliers are imported from Denmark, and Don Carlos Lopez, the Spanish impressionist, did the wall murals.'

The motif of the murals was distinctly southwestern – cactus, natural-stone steeples, snow-capped mountains rimming a blazing desert, cattle and wild horses – but as it might have been conceived by el Greco.

The head waiter, in formal wear, bowed to Collins. 'Your table is ready, Mr Collins.'

'Thank you, Jimmy. I would like to introduce my guests, Mrs Amy Day and her daughter, Candice, from San Fransisco.'

The waiter bowed. 'Madam . . . Miss . . . We are honoured to serve you.' As he led them to a round table at a bay window overlooking the main street, he informed Collins, 'By the way, sir, Mr Ames would like to speak with you before you leave. He's in the bar, I believe.'

Collins chuckled. 'In the bar, eh? Then I have plenty of time.' He ordered whisky and water, while Amy and Candice selected claret lemonades.

'Ames . . . ' Amy said. '*The* Ames family?'

'Stan Ames, son of Carl Ames. Carl was James's eldest son. I'm handling a business transaction for young Stan. Fine lad.' His brow furrowed. 'I don't suppose you and Molly ever learned what happened to Jim Ames, did you?'

'What *did* happen?' Amy asked evenly, and glanced at Candice.

'He was gunned down one night on his way out of the Palace Saloon.'

'Hardly a novelty in Lincoln City,' Amy said, buttering a roll.

'No, this was ten years after the Chisum-Murphy war. Lincoln City, the whole county, had become real civilized.'

'Blood grudges die hard,' she said. 'You should know that, Jim.'

'No, nothing like that. The gunman who shot him had arrived in Lincoln City the very morning of the day Jim was killed. As far as anyone was able to ascertain, he had never been to Lincoln before in his life. And he had a return ticket for Denver the very next day.'

'That *is* odd' – she caught her daughter's eyes – 'isn't it, dear?'

Candice was listening attentively to Collins, but she was looking at her mother – looking at her very intently. 'Yes, it is, Mother.'

'But there was something even stranger,' Collins went on. 'The morning after the shooting, the sheriff received an anonymous telegram notifying him that Jim Ames's killer was registered at the Sentry Hotel, a fleabag on the other side of town, and that he was armed and dangerous. Well, let me tell you, whoever sent that wire knew full well it was a death warrant. The Ameses are a popular and powerful force in this city. Ten deputies went over to the hotel to interrogate the suspect, but he wouldn't admit them to his room and tried to escape out the window and over the porch roof. By the time he reached the ground, he had more holes in him than a piece of imported Swiss cheese.'

'What an intriguing story, Jim. Did they ever learn who sent the telegram or why?'

'Nothing definite. Speculation was that the party who sent the telegram had *hired* the assassin.'

'Difficult to prove without witnesses, I imagine.'

'Impossible. The one witness was a dead man. Well, enough of such depressing talk. Would you like to order now?'

'I think so. I'll have the filet mignon, au gratin potatoes, and pearl onions with baby peas and Belgian carrots. What about you, Candice? Candice! Wake up! Whatever were you thinking about?'

'Oh!' The girl started and gazed at her mother with eyes far wiser than her nineteen years. 'Nothing important, Mother; nothing important at all.'

When they had been served, Amy suddenly said to Collins, 'I was just thinking, Jim, it's a shame to keep that young man – Stan Ames, was it? – waiting in the bar. Why don't you have him join us up here?'

Collins put down his fork and stared at her incredulously. 'Invite an Ames to sit down with *you?* Amy, I can't believe what I'm hearing!'

Amy laughed. 'The old family-feud legend. Jim, don't be silly. What happened twenty-seven years ago is ancient history, water under the bridge. What on earth could I possibly hold against young Stan Ames? Why, he wasn't even born, I'll bet, when all that mess happened.'

'Following year.' His round face brightened. 'I'm so pleased to hear you say that, Amy. Hate can be a very heavy load to carry around year after year.'

'It went to the grave with my mother,' she said.

'Well, all right, if you say so. I'll have Stan paged in the bar and invite him to join us.'

Moments later, Stanley Ames appeared at their table. He was a tall, good-looking young man with rugged features and blonde, curly hair. His blue eyes were mischievous when Collins introduced him to mother and daughter. 'You could be sisters. There's no way you can be this young lady's mother, Mrs Day.'

'You are a charming liar, Mr Ames,' Amy said, smiling. 'Won't you sit down?'

'If you will excuse my appearance. I didn't expect to be in the dining room.' He was wearing a tweed sporting outfit, with low riding boots and a white silk ascot knotted loosely at his throat.

'You look very presentable.'

He sat between Amy and Candice. 'If you will give Jim and me a few minutes of business conversation, then we'll get on to more interesting topics – namely, about you two lovely ladies and why you are here in Lincoln City.'

'As a matter of fact, we have just concluded some business of our own,' Amy said. 'I sold a parcel of land to Standard Oil.'

He whirled in her direction, mouth agape, and his blue eyes widened. 'The Norton land you were telling me about, Jim? Why, then you – '

'Yes, my maiden name was Norton.' The smile remained pasted on her face. 'Don't look so shocked, Mr Ames.'

His face was flushed, and his discomfiture was patent. 'Amy Norton . . . I had no idea. Are you sure you wouldn't prefer me to leave? If you do, I will understand perfectly.'

'Don't be so stuffy, Mr Ames. I requested that you join us.'

He was still self-conscious. 'I must say, that's very magnanimous of you, considering – '

'Let's not consider what is past and done. Now, why don't you and Jim discuss your business while Candice and I visit the ladies' lounge and freshen up.'

She rose, and Candice followed her into the lounge. As they reapplied their makeup at the vanity, Amy said casually:

'What do you think of Stan, dear?'

'He's very attractive.'

'He's got his eye on you.'

'Do you think so?' Candice said coldly.

'He'll ask you for a date before the afternoon is over.'

The girl shrugged. 'What shall I tell him?'

'That you accept with pleasure, naturally.'

'He's an Ames.'

'Yes, he's an Ames.'

She turned, and mother and daughter looked deeply into each other's eyes, eyes cold and hard and flinty.

When the women returned to the table, they all had coffee and dessert, and Jim and Stan brandy.

'You chose a fortuitous time to visit Lincoln City,' the young man advised them. 'Our Fourth of July picnic is one of the biggest and best in the territory. I would consider it a privilege, Mrs Day, to escort you and Candice to the festivities.'

'That's very gallant of you, Mr Ames, and we accept with gratitude' – she looked at her daughter – 'don't we, dear?'

'I can hardly wait. I dearly love fireworks and picnics.'

Jim took a gold watch out of his vest pocket. 'I say, I'm going to be for my next appointment. Stan, will you do me the favour of seeing Amy and Candice back to their hotel?'

'I'd be delighted.'

Back at the hotel, Stan walked with them to the elevator. Amy offered him her hand, and he held it briefly.

'I consider it my very good fortune to have been present in the Cattle King today and to have made your acquaintance,' he said.

'*We're* the fortunate ones, Mr Ames.'

'Thank you for saying so, but please, call me "Stan." ' His eyes avoided her steady gaze. 'And once again, thank you for not holding me in contempt for being an Ames.'

'Let's not dwell on that subject any further. Good day, Stan, and we'll be looking forward to the picnic with great expectations.'

He took both of Candice's hands in his and looked into her eyes. 'What marvellous eyes you have, the two of you. I can't make up my mind what colour they are – blue, grey, or green.'

'It depends on what mood we're in,' Candice told him.

'There, now! It's uncanny. Just a moment ago I saw them as green, and now they're slate grey. Remarkable!'

'Thank you, Stan. Goodbye until tomorrow.'

The two women stepped into the elevator, and the doors slid closed. They looked at each other with conspiratorial smiles.

'I didn't know you were so fond of fireworks and picnics,' Amy remarked.

'I positively loathe them – all that horrible noise and

insects in the food.'

'You must think positively, dear. I'm sure the day won't be completely wasted.'

9

On the morning of 4 July, 1905, Amy and Candice were rudely awakened by a string of Chinese firecrackers exploding in rapid succession in the street beneath their bedroom windows. It was 7:00 A.M.

Candice sat up in bed and stretched her long, slender arms over her head, yawning. Then she arched her back, her rose-tipped breasts thrusting up and out. Candice preferred to sleep in the buff unless she was sharing a room with a friend. She scratched her flat stomach with both hands, relishing the feel of her smooth, velvety skin, then ran them up her torso and cupped her breasts. She shivered with pleasure. Candice enjoyed being a woman, a woman, however, who was long overdue in employing her womanhood as God intended – possessing a mate and enjoying his hard male body, his manhood. She shivered again, but, with great willpower, overcame the warm, pleasurable lassitude that was pervading her flesh and leaped out of bed. *What you require, my girl, is a cold bath.*

Amy was just climbing out of the tub when Candice walked in.

'I see the fireworks got you up early, too, Mother.'

'Yes, and that's the way it's going to sound all day. Tell you what – I'm going to call down and order us breakfast. Let's have it in the room.'

When Candice had had her bath, they sat down to a hearty meal of sausage, eggs, and home fries. Over their second cup of coffee, they smoked long, thin French cigarettes.

'If your father could see us now,' Amy said.

Candice chuckled. 'I've been tempted to tell him of late. I really hate this duplicity, Mother.'

'He would have apoplexy.' Amy laughed. 'The American male is not yet prepared to acknowledge the equality of women.'

'That is *their* problem, and the sooner they face it and cope with it, the better it will be for them. Women's suffrage is right around the corner, and that will pave the way for female parity in every walk of life.'

'Bravo!' Amy clapped. 'Men are such naïve creatures. They think of us as being frail, fragile, helpless little things with tender sensibilities that quail in the face of life's sordid realities. Little do they realize that there is, within the feminine heart and brain, a durability and relentless determination and tenacity that makes a woman capable of performing deeds many a man would blanch at the mere contemplation of.'

Candice smiled. 'Yes, Lady Macbeth.'

Amy leaned over the table and patted the girl's hand. 'It's time we got dressed. We wouldn't want to keep Stanley waiting.'

They chose simple summer frocks – Amy an Oxford-cloth striped dress with a narrow shoulder yoke, shirring, pearl buttons on the front placket, and a self-tie belt; Candice a beguiling sundress in a green cotton floral print, with an elastic-smocked bodice that whittled in her waist.

Amy ran a hand over her daughter's bare shoulders and looked with misgiving at the upper mounds of her breasts brazenly peeping over the top of the square neckline. 'Don't you think it's a mite too daring for a Fourth of July picnic, dear?'

Candice's eyes changed from light blue to steel grey. 'I'm in a daring mood today, Mother.'

'Good. I like to see that. You remind me of myself when I was your age.'

Both put on wide-brimmed, floppy straw hats against the torrid New Mexican heat.

At 10:00 A.M. Stan Ames arrived to pick them up in his own carriage. He was wearing tan riding breeches, brown boots, and a white silk shirt. A small peaked cap sat at a rakish angle on his blonde head. 'You both look ravishing,' he raved.

'And you look very handsome,' Amy said, returning the compliment.

The fairgrounds on the edge of town was the site of the picnic, and by the time they arrived, it appeared that the entire population of Lincoln City was congregated there. When Candice suggested it, Stan laughed:

'You're not far wrong. There's almost a one-hundred-per cent turnout out for the Fourth of July shindig.'

The event was pure bedlam, a cacophony of fireworks of every size and variety, and human voices, everyone expressing himself or herself at the top of the lungs.

Candice ducked as a Roman-candle ball lofted a few feet over their heads. 'This could be hazardous to one's health,' she quipped.

'Soon as we're out of this area, things will calm down,' Stan said. 'This is reserved for the pyrotechnic people. We're on our way to the picnic grounds. Say, did you ever participate in a sack race?'

Candice winced. 'I'm afraid I'm not the athletic type, Stan.'

'I can't believe that. You look in fine shape.' He blushed. 'I'm sorry, that just slipped out. That is to say, your shape . . . er, your figure, it is absolutely – ' He broke off in confusion.

Amy and Candice laughed at his embarrassment.

'You had better stop while you're ahead, my boy,' Amy teased.

Candice looked at him coquettishly. 'Please don't. I am not in the least bit offended by men admiring my figure.' She hooked her arm in his. 'Come on, now, Stan, don't be a prig.'

Stan stopped abruptly in mid-stride and cleared his throat. 'This is a bit awkward for me, but it has to be said. The two of you were very generous and forgiving in your acceptance of me yesterday, but does your amnesty apply to the rest of the Ameses? My older brother, Robert, is here, along with his family and my sister, Louise. If you'd be more comfortable with some other party, that can be arranged.'

Amy touched his arm and smiled. 'Stanley, I told you yesterday, what happened between the Ameses and the Nortons in the past is ancient history. Candice and I will be delighted to join your family group.'

Relief flooded his face. 'That's wonderful. I can't get over what beautiful people you are, Mrs Day – on the inside as well as the outside.' He glanced meaningfully at Candice.

'One thing, Stan,' Amy added: 'Although Candice and I harbour no ill feeling towards the Ameses, it might be discreet if you withheld the fact that we are Nortons. It just might spoil *their* day. You know, guilt feelings; it could be awkward. Why don't you introduce us as your friends "the Days" and let it go at that?'

He thought about it and nodded. 'You know, I do believe you're right, Mrs Day. All right, you two beauties, let's be on our way.'

With Amy and Candice on either side of him, holding snugly to his arms, Stan led them to a large wooden table, set in a grove of pine trees, where the Ames clan was gathered. Amy was outgoing and voluble, and she and the Ames women were shortly chattering away like old friends.

Stan whispered to Candice, 'They seem to be hitting it off very well indeed. Would you like to go for a stroll with me, Candy?'

She arched her eyebrows. ' "Candy"? No one has ever called me that before.'

'I can't believe that. It's so obvious: You look sweet enough to eat.'

'Do I, now?' She cocked her head to one side and regarded him with a penetrating look.

He flushed but was not intimidated. 'Yes, you do, my girl, and I may devour you before this day is over.'

Candice placed a hand on her left breast and feigned trepidation. 'Dear me, do I dare wander off alone with a beast like you?'

'Live dangerously.' He tucked one of her hands in the crook of his elbow and they were off.

He took a circuitous route through the trees, across a footbridge over a babbling brook, and up a hill, the top of which afforded them a panoramic view of a green meadow that stretched away to the foothills of a majestic mountain range.

'Why, it's beautiful! I was beginning to think that New Mexico was all sand and Gila monsters,' Candice exclaimed. She stooped to remove her sandals. 'I have a wild desire to walk barefoot through that green grass.'

'Bully for you. I'll join you.' He took off his riding boots and socks. 'We can leave them here until we return.'

Holding hands and swinging their arms exuberantly, they marched through the knee-high grass at a brisk pace. Within a half-hour they arrived at the base of a steep hill that, at its summit, was 1,000 feet above the valley floor.

'Game to try it?' he inquired.

Candice collapsed in the grass. 'I'm game for anything, but first let's take a breather.'

He lay down beside her with his head braced on his hand, leaning on an elbow.

Candice picked a long shard of grass and put it between her teeth. 'It's sweet,' she said.

He leaned over her; their eyes were so close, their vision was blurred. 'Not as sweet as Candy. God, you're a lovely creature!'

' "Creature"?' She frowned. 'I'm not sure I care for that appellation.'

'It's a compliment. The animal kingdom boasts far more beauty than mankind. You remind me of a lovely tawny cat.'

'*Meowwww* . . . ' She raked his face gently with her nails.

'Did you really mean what you said before, that you're game for anything?'

In reply, she reached up and around his neck and insistently drew his face down until their lips met. An innocent, tender kiss at first; then, as their ardour waxed, it grew more intense. He lifted her to a standing position and cradled her in his arms. She pressed her body hard against him and opened her mouth to receive his tongue.

'Jesus!' he uttered as her hand crawled down his body and found his hard, straining penis.

She disengaged herself from him briefly to pull down the bodice of her dress. The sight of her bare breasts inflamed him uncontrollably, and he caressed them reverently.

' "Little pillows for the gods" – that's what the Greeks called them,' he said. 'Succulent fruits.' He buried his mouth and nose between them in her perfumed cleavage. 'I told you you were sweet enough to eat, and that is what I intend to do.' He lavished kisses on her bosom, took her red, taut nipples between his lips.

Candice moaned and writhed in passion, and her eager hands undid his belt and pants buttons. His erection sprang free, and she cherished it with loving fingers.

'I want you, Stan. I think I shall die if you don't make love to me.'

With trembling hands they divested themselves of their clothing and faced each other, kneeling, devouring each other with unabashed desire.

'For the first time in my life I'm in love,' Stan said breathlessly. 'Do you think you could ever love me?'

'What a silly goose you are, Stanley Ames. Here I am, naked before you and begging you to make love to me, and you make idle chatter. Come and take me before I go up in flames.'

She lay down on her back and opened her arms and legs to him. He came down upon her gently until their bodies were joined, breast to breast, belly to belly, loin to loin, thigh to thigh. With assurance she grasped his tumescent member and guided it to her vagina.

'I hope you're not disappointed that I'm not a virgin,' she said casually.

For an instant he was rendered immobile, and his erection began to subside. *Damned bitch to say such a thing at a time like this! And I thought I was madly in love with her. What a damned fool!*

'What's wrong, darling?' she asked.

He shook his head to clear it. 'Nothing . . . nothing at all.'

'But why are you going soft? Oh, please, my darling, don't stop now.'

'I . . . I'm sorry. Must be a case of belated conscience. I shouldn't have compromised you like this.'

'*Compromised* me?' Her tone was faintly contemptuous. 'Don't be silly. It was I who asked you to make love to me. What is it, Stan? Does it bother you so to know that I've been with other men?'

'Men?' His pain was compounded. There had been more than one. How many, for God's sake? *Two, four, six, eight; Candy's the gal they appreciate!* He got up slowly and began to dress.

Candice followed his example, turning her back so that he could not see the gleaming satisfaction in her face, the bright, hard glee in her eyes. 'You promised to take me up to the top of the hill.'

'Yes,' he said dully, 'to Lovers' Leap. Say that's ironic.' His laughter was like the rustle of dry straw on a neglected grave.

'Tell me, why is it called Lovers' Leap?'

'Apache folklore. A princess and a lowly brave fell in love. Her father banished him from the tribe. They met here one last time, climbed to the top, and, hand in hand, leaped off the precipice together.'

She clasped her hands as she adjusted the bodice of her dress. 'How romantic! Maybe when we're up there, you might be inspired to try to make love to me again.'

'Don't make fun of me, Candice . . . Come along!' he said sharply, and started up the grade with long strides.

The view from the mountaintop was glorious. The stark, craggy New Mexican terrain stretched away in all directions, a veritable lunar landscape, broken here and there by patches of greenery and the sinuous blue strip of a river. To the south, the fairgrounds were laid out like a miniature scene beneath a Christmas tree, men, women, animals the size of ants scurrying about.

Candice reached the top at least five minutes after Stan, out of breath and perspiring. He was standing with his back to her, almost at the edge of the sheer precipice that plunged down to the valley floor, staring off into space with his arms folded across his chest. She stopped a few yards short of the drop.

He looked back across his shoulder with a surly smile. 'What's the matter, honey, scared of heights?'

'Height makes me dizzy, and don't call me "honey." '

'What do others call you?'

'Others?'

'The men you've slept with.'

'You're a rude, crude man, Stanley Ames. I imagine it goes with the heritage.'

'When did they find the princess and her lover?' she asked.

'I don't know; maybe never. It's a long way down, and those rocks must have done a brutal job on their bodies –

chopped them up, food for the wild animals.'

'How horrible.'

He laughed harshly. 'They never felt it. Actually, it's not a bad way to go. Better than lingering with a gunshot wound.'

'Like my grandfather and my uncles?'

'What's *that* supposed to mean?' His attention was suddenly caught by a large eagle hurtling down into the valley in a vertical dive, wings folded back smoothly against its body, bent on some prey the human eye could not detect. 'Look at that, will you!' he exclaimed. 'What a beauty!'

'In reply to your question, Mr Ames . . . ' She stretched out her hands in front of her and advanced towards him.

Back at the picnic grounds, Amy was playing a game of hearts with Louise Harkness, Stan's sister, and Robert Ames's wife, Laura. The men were playing horseshoes nearby and drinking beer out of icy mugs. To one side a lavish 'groaning board' was laden with platters of shrimp, oysters, and clams flown in from the West Coast; roast corn; a side of barbecued beef; a suckling pig with an apple in its mouth; and a variety of home-made breads, rolls, and pies.

Laura and Louise howled with glee as Amy was euchred into winning a trick containing the dreaded queen of spades.

'The Black Maria,' Laura chortled. 'Thirteen points against you.'

'Not to mention the four hearts she picked up last trick,' said Louise.

'Unlucky at cards,' Amy said gaily.

'Lucky in love,' Louise teased.

Amy laughed. 'I barely get to see my love these days. He's off to Hawaii this trip.'

'Wouldn't marry a travelling man myself,' Laura declared.

'Well, Carl is not exactly a travelling man. That is, he's not in sales. The trouble is – ' The rest of it choked in her throat as a bloodcurdling scream rent the air.

The men dropped the horseshoes and ran towards the source of the scream, which was repeated in an even higher pitch. Amy clapped her hands over her ears as she and the other women followed the men at a slower pace.

A huddle of baseball players were congregated around first base, all talking loudly and excitedly:

'She came out of thin air.'

'From the direction of the river.'

'What happened to her?'

'Dunno. Barefoot like that, she couldn't have come from too far.'

'Must have fallen in the water. She's soaked to the skin.'

'Who is she, anyway?'

Robert Ames pushed his way through them and gaped with disbelief when he saw the pale, unconscious girl lying on the ground. 'Jesus Christ!' he said. 'It's the girl Stan invited to the picnic. Name's Candice Day. She and her ma are visiting from California. What's wrong with her?'

'No telling. She came staggering across the field, all out of breath and babbling crazylike. Then she started screaming and passed out.'

'Let me through!' a woman cried from the outer fringe of the gathering crowd. 'That's my daughter they're talking about!'

A path was cleared, and she came forward and knelt down beside the girl and cradled her in her arms. 'Candice, baby, what happened to you?'

Robert flung his arms out. 'Clear back and give her air. Somebody get Doc Peterson. He's around here someplace. And fresh water!'

Two men carried Candice to an empty picnic table and laid her down. Not long after, Dr Petersen arrived, carrying his black physician's satchel. The sleeves of his striped shirt were held up by red elastic arm garters; his long, drooping moustache was speckled with beer foam.

'Lift her head up, please,' he said, and Amy complied. He took a bottle of smelling salts out of his bag and removed the stopper.

Candice moved and whimpered as the pungent fumes wafted up into her nostrils.

'She'll come around presently,' he assured Amy.

Candice opened her eyes; they were glazed with horror.

'Like a petrified animal,' someone muttered.

'Can you tell us what happened?' Amy asked gently.

'Yes, please try,' Robert begged, in a voice fraught with anxiety. 'Where's my brother? Were you attacked by Indians? outlaws? wild animals?'

'Easy, easy,' the doctor cautioned. 'Not too many questions at once. She's still in shock.'

It was another ten minutes before the stricken girl found her voice. She could speak barely above a whisper, but she was rational and intelligible. She told her story falteringly:

'Stan . . . took me to this place called Lovers' Leap. It . . . it's high on top of a mountain. The view was beautiful . . . Then he began to tease me about being afraid of heights. He . . . he stood right at the edge of this steep precipice and pretended he was going to jump, and then . . . and then it happened. He must have slipped on a rock or something, and he lost his footing, and then . . . Oh, God! I can't bear to think or talk about it anymore. It was horrible!' She buried her face in her hands and began to sob hysterically.

Amy took her daughter in her arms; tears were streaming down her face as well. 'My poor darling! What a terrible thing. How awful that you had to see such a thing.' She cast a covert glance at Robert Ames.

Ames's face was stamped with grief and incredulity; hell was mirrored in his eyes. 'I've got to get out there right away,' he said. 'Got to find my baby brother.'

Sam Harkness, his brother-in-law, put an arm around his broad shoulders and said in a quiet voice, 'We'll go with you, Bob, but there ain't no hurry. If Stan fell off Lovers' Leap, ain't no way he's alive.'

The big man began to cry like a baby and collapsed onto the grass.

Off to one side, Robert Collins stood by the side of his son, James. Age had shrivelled his once rotund form; as with a piece of ripe fruit, time had sucked out his juices and reduced him to a shrunken hull. His mental faculties, however, were as sharp as ever they had been. To his son, he commented, 'Well . . . it seems the Norton curse has struck again.'

The following day, Amy and Candice Day checked out of their hotel and took a carriage to the rail depot. Jim Collins was there to bid them farewell.

'Candice wanted to remain for Stan's funeral,' Amy confided to the attorney, 'but I don't think it would be advisable.'

'I agree. She's been through enough.'

Candice stood to the side, immobile and expressionless, like a zombie. When it came time to board, Jim kissed Amy's cheek and took Candice's hands in his:

'Goodbye, my dear. This, too, will pass away, as all tragic memories do.' He watched them climb the steps, and stood there until the train pulled out of the station.

Amy waved to him from the window of their compartment. Then she removed her bonnet and put it on an overhead rack.

There was a knock on the door, and a white-jacketed black porter poked his head into the small cubby. 'Lunch will be served from eleven-thirty on,' he informed them.

'Good,' Candice said after he closed the door. 'I am simply famished.'

'Me, too,' Amy agreed. 'How are you feeling?'

The girl grinned. 'Positively fabulous!'

Amy leaned over and patted her knee. 'Good girl.' Then, after a pause: 'Grandpa Norton would have been proud of you.'

10

Richard Lemon was as fascinated by the ever-changing patterns of his hallucinations as he was by a magician sawing a woman in half on a stage. He *knew* it was an illusion, but a part of him wanted to accept it as reality. The laces of his sneakers were snakes, wriggling out of the metal eyelets and crawling away towards the fire. Oblivious of what was happening inside the lodge, at breathtaking speed he went spiralling down the sides of a long tunnel of such brilliant and beautiful colours that his eyes filled with tears.

It was like a ride he had taken as a child at an amusement park, only more thrilling.

Now he was back in the lodge, and his spirit was detached from his body. He was watching himself standing naked on the altar, while the audience laughed and jeered at him. Why were they laughing? With abject mortification, he looked at himself, at his huge, purple erection. One after another, the women came to him and rubbed it. He shut his eyes and savoured the paroxysms of an orgasm that pulsated all over his body: loins, belly, arms, legs, even his head . . .

'Richard! Wake up this instant!'

A powerful hand was shaking his shoulder. It took him a long time to awaken; he was still holding fast to the euphoric aftermath of his sexual pleasure.

'Richard!' The hand slapped him hard across the face, and he sat upright, gasping and holding his smarting cheek. Fear flooded through him as he saw his father standing over the bed, every inch the soldier even in his black silk dressing gown – a handsome man, but in a cruel, hard way, like an eagle, his steel-grey hair clipped to a length of one-half inch. Old to have a fourteen-year-old son, but he had married his English wife late in life. He had little patience with his frail, sensitive son.

'You're making a mama's boy out of him!' he would berate the woman. 'A sissy! No wonder his classmates make fun of him!'

During World War II, General Zitrone was appointed the commandant of a highly specialized and little-publicized prison camp in the Black Forest. The 'enemies of the state' incarcerated there were all females ranging in age from thirteen to forty-five. The function of this camp, *Der Schadel und Totenkopf* – Skull and Crossbones – was to supply inmates for the network of government-operated houses of prostitution the Third Reich maintained for the 'heroes' of the Wehrmacht, the Luftwaffe, and the dreaded SS in reward for overrunning all of Europe and most of Russia. The general had repeatedly urged Richard to accompany him on his rounds inside the compound, but the boy was reluctant, and his mother was adamant in her support of his stand.

Privately, she ranted at her husband, 'Don't you think Richard and I know what's going on inside that hellhole? We can hear the crying, the screaming, the wailing like a chorus of the dead.'

The Zitrones lived in a Bavarian chalet on a grassy hill overlooking the camp.

And so the son continued to be a source of shame, disappointment, and frustration for the man who had been awarded the Iron Cross in World War I by Field Marshal Hindenburg personally. Richard had been dishonourably discharged from the Hitler Youth Corps for wetting the bed, and for that infamy his father would never forgive him until the day he died.

As the boy came fully awake, sitting there in bed, he realized that his father had pulled off his bedcovers. And then he saw, with horror and panic, what had happened.

He had dreamt that Frieda Schultz, the daughter of one of the general's staff officers, a precocious thirteen-year-old with a plump woman's body, invited him to go up into the hayloft with her, an invitation that half the boys in his class claimed to have accepted. There he watched her taking off her clothing, his lust so great he was unable to breathe. A habitual masturbater, Richard unbuttoned his pants with trembling fingers, but Frieda called out, 'No, let me do it,' and undulated over to him, wearing nothing but a lascivious smile, her enormous breasts swinging from side to side. Then, miracle of miracles, she reached into his open fly and pulled forth his stiff, hot penis. Weak with ecstasy, he let his eyes roll back in his head as she stroked his member gently back and forth. And then . . .

His irate father was standing over him, contemplating the untidy evidence of his nocturnal emission.

'You *schweinhund!* Do you know that you woke up your mother and me with your moaning and groaning and thrashing about? You pig!'

'I couldn't help it, Papa I swear!' Shaking like a leaf, he began to cry.

The general administered another swat on the side of his head, which sent him tumbling out of bed to the floor. 'Now, stop your blubbering before I take a cat-o'-nine-tails to your behind. And clean up that mess at once! I'll decide what to do about you in the morning.'

His wife looked at him aghast when he stomped back into their room, his face red with fury. 'Ludwig, what happened? What did you do to Richard?'

'Less than he deserved. Are you aware, madam, that your beloved son is a sex pervert?'

'Ludwig!' Her voice rose two octaves, and she clutched at her throat with a hand; she thought she might swoon.

Isabelle Clayton Zitrone had been brought up in a generation of English girls who were indoctrinated with the belief that a female was obliged to participate in sex with her husband, albeit reluctantly and only in the pitch dark, but under no circumstances was she ever to speak, or even think, about sex with her husband or anyone else.

'Yes, your little precious masturbates all day and dreams about it at night. He just had a wet dream now. Would you like to help him clean it up?'

'Oh, Ludwig!' She fell back on her pillow and closed her eyes.

'I'm warning you, Isabelle: From now on, *I* am taking charge of that pantywaist, and I will not tolerate any interference. Is that understood?'

'Yes, Ludwig.' She was utterly defeated at the notion that her dear, sweet little Dickie could be so gross and depraved as to – Her mind refused to accept what her husband had told her.

At five-thirty the following morning, Richard was awakened rudely by the clap of a leather riding crop on his backside.

'Up, and be quick about it!' the general barked. 'Roll call is at six o'clock in the compound.'

'In the compound?' the bewildered boy said.

'Yes, the compound; that is where you will be working every day from now on.' His anger was fanned as Richard's chin began to quiver and tears welled up in his soulful blue eyes. 'If you don't stop this nonsense, I will thrash you in front of the guards and the prisoners in the centre of the courtyard. Now, *mach schnell!*'

Richard leaped out of bed and put on his clothes hastily, the uniform of so many lads his age in that era: shirt, heavy sweater, *lederhosen*, and knee-high wool socks. Then, following two steps respectfully behind the general, who was resplendent in his black and gold SS uniform and officer's cap, with its heavy gold swastika on the front, Richard Zitrone marched to the prison camp with the resignation of a doomed soul going to the scaffold.

Der Schadel und Totenkopf inspired terror in Richard even from the outside, with its high stockade fence topped with barbed wire and its ominous watchtowers bristling with machine guns. At night it was even more menacing in the glare of powerful spotlights constantly sweeping the interior of the camp and the courtyard outside.

As they approached the main gate, his heart accelerated so fast he could not count the individual beats, and his knees threatened to give way. *Dear God, don't let me wet my pants. He would kill me for sure!*

The guards at the gate snapped to attention and raised their rifles to port arms: '*Guten morgen,* Herr General.'

'*Guten morgen.*' Zitrone returned their greeting with a perfectly executed salute.

After the general and his son had passed through, one guard turned to the other in astonishment: 'This is the first time little Dickie boy has come within fifty feet of the compound. Wonder what's up.'

The majority of the guards working inside the camp were matrons – big, brawny women with heavy, sullen faces – supervised by a team of SS officers. When the general and Richard arrived, they were busy getting the inmates into formation for morning roll call.

As General Zitrone inspected the ranks, Richard, tagging at his heels, kept his eyes on the ground, afraid of what he would see in the women's faces if he looked up. He was amazed at how young and pretty many of them were, some no older than he. Unlike the inmates of most other Nazi camps, these females were well fed and well scrubbed. Their short-skirted drab uniforms were clean and neat. But their eyes were haunted by the ordeals and indignities to which they were subjected day after day, with only worse damnation awaiting them in the future.

After inspection, the prisoners were herded off in small groups by the matrons to commence their daily chores. General Zitrone went to his office and sat down behind his enormous mahogany desk.

'Sit down, Richard!' He indicated a chair at the front of the desk. He picked up the phone and ordered his male secretary: 'Send Corporal Muller in to see me as soon as possible.' Then, ignoring his son, he went to work on a stack of documents piled high on his desk blotter.

Richard squirmed and fidgeted as time dragged on endlessly, speculating on his fate. He bolted upright in the chair at the sound of a sharp knock on the general's door.

'*Komme!*' snapped the commandant.

The door opened, and a tall, mannish-looking woman marched up to the desk and saluted. 'Corporal Muller reporting, Herr General.'

'At ease, Corporal.' He leaned back in his big leather swivel chair and tapped a pencil against his front teeth. 'You know my son, of course?'

'Yes, sir.' She cast a contemptuous glance in his direction. The personnel of the camp took a secret, perverse satisfaction in the knowledge that the much-decorated and much-feared war hero was ashamed of his effeminate son.

'Corporal Muller, I wish you to take Richard to section nine and give him a Cook's tour. Have him express his preference and confine the two of them in Ward A. Do I make myself clear?'

'Perfectly clear, Herr General.' Corporal Muller had to exert all of her willpower to restrain her laughter, for inwardly she churned with hilarity. She looked at Richard, who was cringing in his chair and quaking with alarm. *So, our little bed-wetting mama's boy is going to lose his cherry. This will be something to witness. Oh, I have just the little tart for his kind – number 23.*

General Zitrone snapped his fingers at Richard. 'Now, be off with Corporal Muller! Today we are going to make a man out of you whether you like it or not. Dismissed!'

Richard was almost as intimidated by Corporal Muller as he was by his father. She had powerful forearms and a thick neck, and there was a huge strawberry birthmark on her left cheek that lent her a particularly threatening aspect. He followed her dutifully out of the administration building and across the compound to where the prisoners were policing up to a small yellow building behind the main barracks.

'The prisoners in section nine are being processed for shipment to their destinations,' she explained matter-of-factly. 'A fine crop of beauties; you'll see.'

As they approached the building, Richard had a wild impulse to make a break for the main gate, but his legs felt too weak. They entered the processing office, where a half-dozen guards were cutting shipping orders.

'Sergeant Gutenberg around?' the corporal inquired.

'She's in the back.'

'Come.' Corporal Muller strode to a metal door with a small observation window and led Richard into the confinement area, down a long hall with doors on each side of it. 'You look around while I make arrangements with Sergeant Gutenberg.' She left him by himself and walked to the end of the corridor, then turned into another corridor out of his sight.

Richard stopped in front of one of the doors and peered through the observation window. He was shocked to see a number of females lounging around on army cots in their underclothes – not the heavy underwear worn by the other prisoners, but filmy, lacy silks and satins, the tools of their trade, so to speak. One voluptuous young girl, who reminded him of Frieda Schultz, was bare-breasted. In his fantasizing, the mere image of a naked woman was sufficient to give him an instant erection; but, when confronted by women in the flesh, he was less than bold. His member was a withdrawn, shrivelled worm!

Richard moved from one door to another until he reached the end of the corridor. In each room there were women in various stages of undress; yet he felt no arousal, only anxiety.

'Herr Zitrone!'

He recoiled from the harsh sound of Corporal Muller's voice.

She came around the corner and stood in front of him with her arms folded across her chest. Her smile was reptilian. 'Well, young man, have you appraised the merchandise?'

He was speechless.

'No matter,' she said. 'I will select a girl for you myself' – the smile widened – 'a rare delicacy, guaranteed to please a gentleman of your special needs. Come with me.'

He followed her around the bend into a short hallway that terminated at a door painted bright crimson. She opened the door and motioned him to enter. Richard obeyed, and she patted him on the back.

'You can get undressed,' she said. 'Your friend will be here shortly.' She closed the door, leaving him alone.

It was a rather pleasant room, with a window high on the back wall, through which sunlight spilled a radiant trapezoid on the floor beside the bed – a real bed, with a coverlet and a snow-white pillow. The only other appointments were a washstand and two straight-backed chairs. Corporal Muller's voice rang in his ears: *You can get undressed* . . . He began to tremble, and his teeth were chattering.

He shrank back against the windowed wall as the door opened and Muller shoved a young girl into the room. No more than fifteen years old, she was quite pretty, with brown eyes and long black hair that fell down to her buttocks. Her only garment was a diaphanous slip, which provocatively displayed her firm, plum-sized breasts and the dark triangle of her pubic hair.

'Enjoy yourself, Herr Zitrone,' the corporal said tauntingly, and closed the door.

The girl, seeing the shock on Richard's face, smiled reassuringly. 'You look like a scared rabbit. Is it the first time you've been with a girl?'

He nodded dumbly.

'That's all right. There has to be a first time for all of us. I'll never forget my first time. I was just thirteen, two years ago this June. My father was a college professor. We lived on the outskirts of Berlin. The Gestapo came to our home in the middle of the night. They had a warrant for my father's arrest. They claimed he preached Communist doctrine in his classes. They raped my mother, myself, and my ten-year-old sister, nine of them in all. Then they took us away to a holding camp. A week later we were separated. I don't know what happened to either of them or my father. Dead, no doubt.'

Richard was appalled. 'How can you speak of such vile atrocities so matter-of-factly, almost as if they had happened to some other family?'

Her smile conveyed no warmth or humour. 'One learns the cardinal rule of life: The will to survive is far stronger than the worst degradation these pigs can inflict on me . . . I cannot keep count of how many men have enjoyed my body. It is of no consequence. They can possess the flesh, but they cannot possess me.' She tapped a finger over her heart. All right, let's get on with it. What is your name? You must be someone special to rate such privileges.'

'I am Richard Zitrone. My father is the commandant of the camp.'

Her eyebrows arched. 'Well, now, that *is* an honour indeed – Herr Zitrone's son.' She giggled. 'Isn't it ironic? Men are always bragging about seducing a virgin. Now it's my turn. Do you know, Richard, you will be *my* first virgin?'

She pulled the slip over her head and tossed it on a chair. She was small-boned and a half-head shorter than Richard, but her body was exquisitely mature. Her skin was the texture of fawn velvet.

'Relax, lover.'

She placed a hand behind his neck and kissed him on the lips. Her other hand undid his belt and fly buttons. His pants cascaded about his ankles, and his undershorts shortly followed. She plied his penis and his testicles with both hands, to no avail.

'What's wrong with you?' she demanded with some irritation. 'Don't you find me desirable?'

He shook his head. 'It's not you.'

'Then what?' She pressed her soft belly against his loins and undulated her hips.

Richard remained flaccid and without sensation.

'You must be a faggot, is that it? Perhaps you'd prefer one of the male guards?'

In despair Richard flung himself face down on the bed and began to sob.

The girl clapped a hand to her forehead. '*Sheiss dreck!* Stop it, you fop! Do you know what will happen to me if I don't cop your cherry? Muller warned me that your father will be most displeased if his little boy doesn't achieve manhood today.' Her eye caught sight of a broom handle propped up in one corner. She went and got it and came back to the bed. Brandishing it in both hands, with all her might she whacked it down hard on his pale buttocks.

Richard let out a howl and reared up on his knees.

The girl struck again.

'Oh, Jesus!' He grabbed his buttocks and leaped off the bed. The pain was so intense, he couldn't stand still. He ran around the small room like a rat on a treadmill, all the while massaging his smarting flesh with both hands.

She kept after him like a tigress, swinging the broom handle – a clout on his shoulder, another on an arm, a fierce shot across the genitals that drove him near insane with pain. It served as a trigger. Abruptly the pain was obliterated by anger and outrage. He had never experienced such intense emotion in his life. Growling like a mad animal, he attacked her, tore the broom handle out of her grasp and commenced beating her with it. Screaming, she ran to the bed, trying to escape from his wrath. She crouched against the wall with her knees drawn up, covering her face and shoulders with a pillow. It was futile. He pounded her until her body was crisscrossed with welts and her pretty face was a bloody mask. He ceased only when his arms became too weary to wield the weapon. He let it fall to the floor and stood over her, gasping for air and swaying from side to side.

He looked down, and , to his amazement, his penis was hard and erect, and he felt agonizing desire such as he had never known before, not even in his dreams of Frieda Schultz. Consumed with bestial lust, he flung himself down on the unconscious girl and ravished her. Three times he achieved orgasm before he rolled off her and lay immobile from exhaustion.

How long he remained beside her with eyes closed, savouring the sweet hiatus, he could not recall. His reverie was interrupted when the door opened and Corporal Muller walked into the room. Her smile was demonic:

'You seem to have thoroughly enjoyed yourself, Master Zitrone. Your father will be proud of you. In spite of what everyone believed, you are his son after all.'

And that was only the beginning.

For the next year, Richard never missed a day at the *Schadel und Totenkopf* camp. In the room behind the crimson door in ward A, he indulged in orgies he had never dreamed of in his most erotic fantasies. He knew that Corporal Muller and other guards watched him from concealed observation posts, but it did not inhibit him. In fact, the knowledge that he had an audience titillated him and inspired him to even grosser and greater excesses. It was during this period that Richard Zitrone came to the conclusion that he was born to be an actor.

All good things must come to an end; he was fatalist enough to realize it. And so, on the day the general came into his bedroom early in the morning to inform him that he would no longer be permitted to visit the stockade, he just shrugged philosophically.

'The thing is, Richard, we have been receiving complaints that our merchandise has declined in quality. You really have been exceedingly rough on the girls in section nine. I hope you understand?'

'Of course, Papa.'

The general embraced him. 'You are a man at last, my son. When the war is over and the Third Reich is victorious, I will see to it that you and I have a private audience with the Führer himself. We are old comrades.'

Two years later the war *was* over, but with a result other than the one General Zitrone had envisioned. Two weeks before Germany's capitulation, Richard and his mother fled across the border to Switzerland. And in January of 1946 they returned to his maternal grandfather's estate in Sussex, England, at which time they changed their surname to 'Lemon.'

11

Richard Lemon opened his eyes, and he was back in the Apache ceremonial lodge, distastefully aware of the warm, wet discharge in his undershorts. Exerting all of his willpower, he battled the inclination to drift off to yet another experience. The people around him were reacting to the peyote in a variety of ways, some laughing hysterically, others raving and ranting like madmen, writhing in agony and ecstasy on the earth floor.

Lawrence Bostwick was sitting cross-legged, immobile as a buddha, eyes closed in deep meditation, employing the drug to plumb still greater depths of the controlled trance state of mind. At the peak of his high, he was miraculously endowed with absolute omniscience by the Holy Spirit. All knowledge was his. There was nothing in the universe he did not possess an explanation for. The true nature of life and death, all existence was revealed to him as if God had unveiled his painting of the universe for Bostwick's eyes alone.

Even time was in his power. With the snap of a finger he could transform himself back to any age and aeon: be there when Columbus set foot on the shore of the New World; weep with the mourners at Calvary as the Roman soldiers nailed Christ to the cross; marvel at the spectacle of Satan being cast out of Heaven, falling like a pinwheel into the Dark Pit. He saw the devil's face as clearly as if he were right beside him. And Lucifer's face was the face of Lawrence Bostwick! But his own fall from grace had not been so dramatic . . .

Lawrence Bostwick had been a college sophomore in 1963 when 200,000 blacks and whites demonstrated in Washington, DC, in support of Negro demands for equal rights. Tears had streamed down his cheeks when Martin Luther King, Jr, gave his most memorable speech: '*I have a dream that this nation will rise up and live out the true meaning of its creed: "We hold these truths self-evident, that all men are created equal . . ."* '

All the demonstrations that followed, all the freedom marches, all the Vietnam War protests – and the growing discontent, disillusionment, and bitterness he suffered as the gains were made with such maddening slowness. The assassinations of President John F. Kennedy, his brother Robert, and Martin Luther King, Jr, and a tour of duty in the Green Berets in Vietnam, drove him to the outer limits of humanity and civilization. He became a zealous black militant and enlisted members for an underground force called the Black Watch.

The Black Watch preached subversion to break down discipline, harassment of white officers, and, in special cases, even murder, as well as a variety of other terrorist acts. 'Fragging' of white officers was commonplace in the Mekong Delta sector.

In later years, reflecting back on this phase of life, Bostwick was incredulous. It was an era of insanity, a *war* of insanity, and the men who were caught up in the maelstrom of blood and horror, they were madmen. That young zealot who resembled him, he was not Lawrence Bostwick, author, scholar, man of letters. He was not the gentle, reserved man of affluence who belonged to a posh country club where he played golf and bridge with white judges, financiers, lawyers, and physicians, and who thought nothing of Jennie's dancing with them while he danced with their wives.

He wanted to believe the theory that the body's cells completely replace themselves every seven years; only then could he rationalize the acts of the *other* Lawrence Bostwick that fateful night in Nam:

Sergeant Bostwick's platoon had ambushed a force of Vietcong and sent them scattering in confusion, leaving behind many dead and wounded. The wounded were taken back to camp for interrogation, and after they'd been questioned, the company commander summoned Bostwick to his tent:

'Sergeant, good work. You have dropped a very rich plum into our lap.'

'Captain?'

'One of the prisoners is a colonel in a top-security special-service branch of the VC. When Nam G-2 get their hands on him back in Saigon, the bastard will wish he had gotten it out here in the jungle. Anyway, pick him up at our G-2 tent and put him under special guard.'

'Right on, Captain.' Bostwick rolled off a casual, almost impudent salute and left to perform the mission.

The prisoner was tall for a Vietnamese, and wore the distinctive black pyjamas of the VC. His head was swathed in bandages, but he was otherwise in good condition. He spoke English fluently. Bostwick put him in a tent with a cot and a small table, befitting his military status, and stationed three guards outside.

'Need anything before I go?' he asked the officer.

'I would appreciate a cigarette.'

Bostwick took one himself and tossed the pack to the man. 'Keep 'em. There's a half-dozen left.' He lit his own with a Zippo lighter and gave the VC a pack of paper matches.

'Thank you, Sergeant. My name is Lum. What's yours?'

'Bostwick.'

'Where is your home?'

'It *was* in Mississippi.'

'Mississippi? Ah . . . well . . . ' There was a shrewd calculating look in his eyes. 'I do not envy you growing up in a racist place such as Mississippi.' And with a hint of condescension: 'Then again, I suppose there is racism *wherever* one goes in the United States. One must contend with racism if one has a coloured skin. I myself, when I attended Stanford, was the victim of white prejudice, so I can sympathize with you.'

Bostwick ignored the ploy. 'I've got to be going.'

'Sergeant, one last thing.' He stepped close to Bostwick and placed a hand lightly on his arm.

Bostwick stared at him coldly. 'You should know better, Colonel Lum, than to touch an enemy soldier. Man could get shot that way.'

Lum removed his hand. 'I am sorry, Sergeant, and inasmuch as you introduced the possibility, I would like to request a favour of you . . . Shoot me. Execute me here and now.'

Bostwick regarded him with suspicion. 'What the hell are you talking about, man? I'd end up in the stockade myself for abusing the Geneva Convention – not that you guys give a damn about any conventions.'

'You don't understand, Sergeant. Do you know what the government interrogators will do to me back at Saigon? They will draw and quarter me. They will gouge out my eyeballs. They will dismember me an inch at a time: a finger, a toe, my penis . . . '

Bostwick shuddered, recalling how gleeful the captain had been at the very possibility: *'The bastard will wish he had gotten it out here in the jungle.'*

'Brother – all men of colour are brothers – we have both been fighting oppression from the day we came into this white world. I implore you to show me the mercy I would show you if our positions were reversed. Help me to die with mercy and dignity . . . Sergeant, if you won't do it yourself, let me have your pistol.'

'My pistol? Not on your life.' He hesitated, his mind racing: *I feel sorry for you, you poor bastard. I've seen some of the atrocities the glorious Vietnam brass have committed under the guise of interrogation. I've killed so many of you, what does one more matter?* 'Sit down and finish your cigarette. I'll be right back.'

'You have earned my eternal gratitude, Sergeant. You are a good and just man.'

Bostwick went back to his quarters and rummaged in his duffel bag until he found the Chinese-made automatic pistol he had lifted from one of the dead Cong as a souvenir to be sold to some greenhorn fresh from the States on his next leave in Saigon. 'What the hell!' he muttered. 'There's plenty more where this came from.' He removed the clip and extracted all but one of the shells, then tucked it inside his shirt underneath his waistband and walked back to the tent.

Of the three guards, two were white PFCs and one a black corporal, also a secret member of the Black Watch. He laughed when Bostwick returned:

'Hey, man, you must be sweet on that Commie officer. Whatcha do, bring him some goodies?'

Bostwick removed a fresh pack of cigarettes from his fatigue-jacket pocket. 'Just some smokes.'

Corporal Cook hooted. 'Come on, man – that mother was trying to kill us tonight!'

'Sure he was; that's his job.' Bostwick stared down the other black man. 'You got any idea what's going to happen to him when the Nam G-2 get him? Worse than anything happened to your great grandpappy back in Georgia. You dig, *man?*'

Cook shrugged and turned away sullenly while Bostwick entered the tent.

'Sergeant, what have you for me?' In the lamplight Lum's eyes were bright with fever.

'Keep your voice down,' Bostwick cautioned. He took the pistol from inside his jacket and offered it to him. 'You had better make the first slug good, because that's all you're going to get.'

A crafty expression flitted across the man's face; it

triggered some gut instinct in Bostwick that almost caused him to change his mind and retrieve the weapon.

Lum saw the indecision in Bostwick's face and reminded him softly, 'You promised you would help me die.'

'Like hell! I said I'd think about it.'

'And you did, and you made a moral commitment. Please, Sergeant, don't let me down.'

'Oh, shit!' He shoved the pistol roughly at him.

The colonel took it and smiled. 'I thank you, Sergeant. May God be with you.'

'I don't believe in God.'

'Neither do I.' The smile was mocking. 'Well . . . I suppose we should say good-bye.' He held out his right hand.

Bostwick only nodded and left the tent. He lit a cigarette as he walked slowly across the encampment to his quarters. Not bothering to light the lamp, he flung himself down on the bed and waited, staring at the coal of his cigarette. When the shot finally rang out, he looked at the luminous dial of his watch. Only three minutes had passed. The report of the pistol ignited commotion throughout the compound. It was followed by a fusillade.

Playing out his role, Bostwick ran out of his tent and joined the crowd milling around in front of the tent where the colonel had been confined.

'What the hell is going on here?' Bostwick yelled. 'Cook! Where the hell are you, Corporal? You're supposed to be in charge here!' He pushed his way through to the front rank.

The faces of the two white guards were pasty and fraught with shock in the glare of the spotlight. 'Sarge . . . ' one of them croaked.

'Come on, spit it out!' he barked. 'What happened?' Bostwick's eyes were drawn to a shapeless, dark mass off to one side outside the circle of the spotlight. 'What the hell!'

'Sarge' – the PFC found his voice – 'it's Cook. That slimy Red must have had a gun stashed on him someplace. While Cohen and me was circling to check the back of the tent, he jumped Cook out here and shot him in the chest. He . . . he's dead. So is the prisoner. We blew the fuck to pieces.'

Bostwick stood there numb, speechless. A statement by a

soldier in the crowd fell harshly on his ears:

'Can you imagine that stupid bastard thinking he could get away with a stunt like this? And only one shot in the damned pistol at that!'

Bostwick shook his head and spoke quietly: 'No, it wasn't that way at all. He didn't believe for one minute that he could escape. You see, the thing is, he wanted to get just one more of us before he died.' He swallowed with difficulty. 'That is what is known as fanatic dedication to a cause. Winning this war means that much to them – to a man, they will die to accomplish it – and that, my good buddies, is why, in the end, it's gonna be the Cong who win all the marbles here in Vietnam. We might as well pack it in now.'

There was an abbreviated hearing into the incident. No decision was reached on how Colonel Lum had obtained a weapon. A G-2 lieutenant took the heat off Bostwick and onto his own shoulders:

'Only way it could have happened is that we figured he had been thoroughly searched when he was brought in, so we didn't bother. He must have had the gun in his boot.'

'You had no right to make that assumption, Lieutenant!' the captain said.

'I know, sir, but me and my men haven't had any sleep in twenty-four hours. We're ready for the funny farm.'

The captain debated convening a court-martial board to try the lieutenant for negligence of duty, but thought better of it. He couldn't afford to lose such a good man. He couldn't afford to lose *any* more men, good or bad. He rubbed his eyes and waved a hand at the group of officers and noncoms in his quarters. 'All right, case closed. Dismissed.'

Bostwick would never dismiss it for the rest of his life. He had murdered a brother, the same as if he had pulled the trigger himself. One thing the episode accomplished: From that time on, Lawrence Bostwick renounced violence and bloodshed as a means to achieve an end, no matter how worthy.

Jennie, his wife, had always known him as a pacifist, espousing the doctrines set forth by Dr Martin Luther King, Jr. She would have been shocked if she ever found out that gentle Larry had once been a zealous militant.

12

Walter Ames was shaking him by the shoulder. 'Wake up, Larry. The water is being brought around.'

A tender was passing among them with a pail of water and a common dipper. Ordinarily fastidious about drinking out of glasses or cups that others had put their mouths to, Larry Bostwick could scarcely wait to lave his parched throat. When the dipper was passed to him, he gulped it down greedily. Cold as ice crystals, sweet as nectar of the gods . . . Nothing would ever taste as good to him again.

Each time the dipper was refilled, the tender would recite: 'Pray to the Holy Spirit to bless this water that the universe may be preserved.'

The water, and whatever else had been put into it, seemed to act as a partial antidote to the hallucinatory stage of the experience for Bostwick – for the time being, at least. He felt – or thought he felt – quite normal now, although his powers of perception were still super acute. He heard the Indians around the altar all speaking at once, reliving the history of past hunts and famous battles joined in by their ancestors. Group ego-tripping, he thought at first; but then it hit him that they were speaking not to one another but to themselves.

Susan Brandon was way, way out in space. She watched dispassionately as Laura Devane rose from her place and walked in a trance to the altar. Kneeling before the medicine man, she recited:

'Forgive me, for I have sinned, Holy Spirit.'

'That is why you have been summoned here tonight,' Gall said, 'because all of you have sinned. The Holy Spirit says that wherever you walk, you desecrate his earth.' He waved the sceptre over her head and cried, 'Hail to the Holy Spirit! Hail to the Earth Mother!'

He handed the sceptre to Laura, and now Susan saw that the sceptre was also a pipe stuffed with herb tobacco. Laura put it to her lips and inhaled deeply. When she exhaled, the cant went all around the altar:

'The smoke the Earth Mother breathes is the life she brings to us . . . Oh, Holy Spirit, can these damned souls be redeemed? Let us have a sign, Holy Spirit.'

For Susan, reality and unreality gradually were merging like the twin images in a stereoscope. She gasped as Laura suddenly disappeared in a puff of smoke, and in her place, there materialized a huge lion with a jet-black mane. It snarled and shook its head from side to side, the tufted tip of its tail twitching menacingly.

Susan blinked, and when she opened her eyes again, the lion had been transformed into a giant golden eagle. It spread its wings – wings that almost spanned the walls of the lodge – and sprang into the air. Susan leaped high and seized the bird's talons as it soared to dizzying heights. They were suspended in a maelstrom of colour as the eagle flew in a spiral arc, up and up, and around and around, the sides of the conical tunnel, higher and higher in ever-increasing arcs until they burst through the ceiling of the universe into the kaleidoscopic palette where God mixed his hues. And the chanting rang in her ears:

'Earthmaker, Earthmaker, hear out the Earth Mother. This is your Sacrament, and let me hereafter perform your miracles.'

Now Susan passed into oblivion, her brain drained of dreams by the mescaline. She settled into empty blackness gratefully. A voice, far distant, wafted to her on solar winds: 'Suuuu– sannnn . . . *Susan!*' She opened her eyes. Kevin was shaking her by the shoulder: 'Sue, are you all right? Wake up.'

She felt as though she had been on a drinking binge. She groaned and cradled her head in her hands. 'Ohhhhh . . . I feel *terrible*.'

'Join the club,' Jennie Bostwick said.

Larry was on his hands and knees, shaking his head from side to side. 'I feel like I just went ten rounds with Muhammad Ali.'

Walter Ames was on his feet, shaking his head over the sad state of his guests. 'Best get up and work out the kinks,' he advised them.

Richard Lemon yawned and stretched. He looked around the empty room. 'Where did the Indians go?'

'The prayer meeting broke up about an hour ago. It's daybreak. Time to go, boys and girls. Chief is waiting in the pickup. Better hurry. The weather doesn't look too good.'

His remark was emphasized by the rumble of thunder in the distance. They scrambled to their feet and walked, weary and leaden-legged, to the truck.

'Shit!' Laura complained. 'It's starting to rain again. We'll never get out of this horror show.'

'Horror is right,' Richard agreed as they piled into the truck.

'Amen,' said Larry Bostwick.

Susan smiled in reminiscence. 'I enjoyed it thoroughly.'

'I don't remember a damned thing,' Kevin said.

'The best part,' Susan said, 'was when Laura turned into a lion.'

'A lion?' Laura said with disbelief.

'A lion.' Susan laughed. 'That was the work of the Holy Spirit. The medicine man said you were a sinner, and the Holy Spirit punished you by turning you into a lion.'

'He said we *all* were sinners,' Walt told her.

'I saw it, too,' Jan Danzig said. Her eyes were still glassy. 'The lion and the bird – the golden eagle.'

'That's incredible!' Susan said. 'If we were hallucinating, how is it possible that we both saw the same thing?'

'Apache magic,' Walt said. 'Mass hypnosis. Did anyone else see what Jan and Susan saw?'

'I did,' Jennie affirmed. 'A lot of other weird things, too. Larry, I dreamed you were back in Vietnam.'

'I don't want to hear about it,' he told her sharply. 'I just want to go to bed.'

'So all of us *are* secret sinners,' Jan said with malicious satisfaction. 'After we recover from this session, we should sit down and have a group-therapy session. Confession is good for the soul, so they say. Anybody for confession, lads and lassies?'

Silence was her answer. The truck seemed to leap off the road as a bolt of lightning struck nearby and the thunder that followed it deafened them.

'Jesus Christ!' Kevin said. 'Maybe the Holy Spirit is after

us at that!'

They reached the house without further incident and disembarked. No sooner had they gathered on the porch than rain descended like a waterfall, and it was black as night again.

'In the nick of time,' Walt said as he opened the front door. 'Anybody care for a nightcap before we hit the sack?'

'Just let us die in peace,' Richard groaned.

'A day of miracles,' Laura exclaimed. 'Ladies and gentlemen, in all the years I have known this blighter, I have never heard him turn down a drink before.'

' "And the truth shall set ye free," ' Lemon intoned, and with bent head and sagging shoulders, he started up the long staircase.

'One thing I should caution you about,' Walt said before they all parted at the head of the stairs. 'Like many hallucinogens, mescaline has a sneaky way of coming back to haunt you. Periodically you may experience still more hallucinations like the ones you had last night – milder ones, to be sure; but don't panic. Then again, you may not. Well, I guess it's time to pack it in. I can't tell you how pleased Nancy and I are that you were able to accompany us to the ceremony. I'm sure it's been a rich experience that you will remember for the rest of your lives.'

'Just fabulous,' Susan agreed.

Larry was laconic. 'Yeah, a real ball.'

Later, lying in bed, Nancy Ames said to her husband, 'Hold me tight, Walt; I'm so cold.' She lay with her back to him and fitted her body against his, spoonlike.

'You're trembling like a leaf.'

'What do you think about what Gall said, that we're all sinners?'

His laughter did not ring true. 'Oh, come on now, Nancy; you've seen Gall go through his act before. Like all good showmen, he's got to have versatility in his performance. Tonight the theme was Sin on Skull Mountain.'

'I wonder.'

'You're still under the spell of the mescaline.'

'I don't need mescaline to conjure up my special visions. Hardly a night passes that I don't – '

He clamped a hand across her mouth and admonished her, 'Stop it, Nan! Not another word! I'm getting tired of this guilt trip you're on. Five years have passed. It's time you forgot it.'

She tensed against him. 'Tired of my guilt trip, or plain tired of me? I saw you and that Brandon girl flirting. And I know damned well what was going on out on the porch when I surprised you two.'

He shoved her away roughly. 'You're becoming more paranoid every day. Susan Brandon is a callow child. I treat her with the same courtesy I extend to all my guests, nothing more.'

Her voice was drained, full of resignation. 'You are tired of me, I sense it, just as you became tired of – ' it stuck in her throat like a bone – of *her*.'

'Damn it! I've had enough of this drivel. I'm going down and have that drink after all!' He flung off the covers, grabbed his bathrobe from a chair, and stormed out of the bedroom, slamming the door behind him.

Nancy lay there curled up in a foetal position, sobbing silently into her pillow. She'd have the recurring nightmare tonight; of that she was convinced . . .

Shortly after World War I, the Ameses sold out their billion-dollar cattle empire, and the surviving sons and daughters took their shares and went their separate ways. Walter Ames's father, Glenn, who had been investing in the New York Stock Market for years, moved his family to that city and bought a partnership in one of the most prestigious brokerage houses on Wall Street. He also bought a lavish mansion in Connecticut.

The Ames estate, Manorhaven, was a showpiece in that wealthy community referred to in the high-society columns of both Hartford and New York newspapers as the 'Connecticut Gold Coast' – five acres fenced in on three sides by wrought iron and, on the fourth, by a steep bluff rising from the white beach. The Tudor mansion sat on the high point of the property like a gem on green velvet. Its opulent rooms – twenty in all – and manicured lawns and terraced gardens had graced the covers and slick pages of *House Beautiful* and *Better Homes and Gardens* so many times, even Sam Brown, the chief gardener had lost count.

Nancy Carlson Ames would never forget her first sight of Manorhaven. A nurse at Mt Vernon Hospital in Westchester County, she had been approached with an unusual job offer in 1974 by Dr Lewis Lanz, a prominent neurological surgeon who was frequently called into the hospital as a consultant. Nancy's relationship with Dr Lanz became close after she served as his scrub nurse on a particularly difficult operation.

One day he summoned her to his office and asked, 'What would you say to giving all this up and becoming nurse and companion to a rich woman who lives in Connecticut?'

'Nothing, Doctor. I love my work. I don't want to sit around on my butt playing lady-in-waiting for some wealthy dowager.'

'It's not what you think. Kate Ames is an extremely attractive and intelligent woman in her mid-thirties, and she's not a hypochondriac. In fact, I've never had a patient with more guts. Never complains, always a bright smile, no matter how bad her pain is. A real classy broad.'

'What happened to her?'

'She was injured in an automobile accident, her husband's sports car. He was drunk and doing over a hundred miles an hour.'

'Him I couldn't work for. Sounds like a prize stinker – spoiled, shallow.'

'Hold it. Couple of years back, I would have agreed with you. He was a real hellion, but the accident changed him. He's come about a full hundred and eighty degrees – no more drinking and carousing, nose to the grindstone from dawn to dusk. His father left him a brokerage firm in New York. Walt let his partners run it for him until the past few years. Now he's hell on wheels, a gung-ho broker.

'Look, I know you and Kate would hit it off great. You'll get to love her like the rest of us do. Besides, she needs a top pro like you to care for her. She's a very sick lady. Come on, at least consider it . . . One more thing: You'll earn five thou a year more than you do at the hospital.'

That was the decisive factor. The year before, Nancy's father had a coronary and was forced into semi retirement. As a consequence, her mother had to return to work as a sales lady, and it was a constant struggle to make ends meet. If she accepted the position in Connecticut, she could contribute to the household, and her mother could stay home.

'It's a deal,' she told Dr Lanz.

On her next day off, the doctor drove her to Manorhaven for an interview with Kate Ames. The apprehension she had experienced since awakening that morning was aggravated by her first glimpse of the imposing Ames estate.

'I think this is going to be too rich for my blood,' she said wryly. 'How many servants does it take to care for this place?'

'Oh, I'm not sure: five or six, counting the maid and cook and gardeners. You'll like Kate, Nancy. She's not the stereotyped rich bitch portrayed in the movies. As a matter of fact, her background isn't a lot different from your own. She wasn't born into money. Her father was a shoemaker in Brockton, Massachusetts. She worked her way through college, same as you did, and then she met Walter Ames.'

'Just like in the movies after all – Cinderella and Prince Charming.'

They were admitted by Hattie the maid, a small, sparrowlike woman with quick, nervous movements. 'Good morning, Dr Lanz. Mrs Ames is waiting for you on the patio.'

Nancy checked her appearance covertly in the full-length mirror on one of the large foyer walls. She had chosen to wear a rather prim, though form-fitting, lamb's-wool sweater dress of dove grey. *You look very professional, my girl.*

Kate Ames was seated at a white wrought-iron table on the flagstone patio beneath a gaily coloured yard umbrella. She was dressed casually in black velvet slacks and a white satin blouse. But for the wheelchair, she was the personification of the handsome, well-kept matron who belonged to the smart set on the Gold Coast.

She held Nancy's hand longer than a conventional handclasp. 'Oh, Nancy, I've been dying to meet you! Lew has told me so much about you. I've already dubbed you "Saint Nancy." '

Nancy sensed that her smile and exuberance were genuine. 'Hardly a saint,' she said, returning Kate's smile.

'And you're every bit as lovely as he described you, too. Won't you both be seated?'

'Thank you.'

Nancy's reservations were fast melting away, and over

tea and cakes, the issue was sealed when Kate rattled her cup against her saucer and confessed:

'I've been so nervous you wouldn't like us, Nancy. You *have* decided to accept the position, haven't you? Oh, please say you'll come stay with me and be my friend.'

In a common impulse the two women reached across the table and clasped hands.

'I'll be honoured to be in your employ, Mrs Ames.'

Kate leaned back, her face radiant with joy and relief. 'Oh, this is marvellous, Lew! I'll be forever in your debt.'

Dr Lanz reached over and squeezed her hand. 'It looks like you've found yourself a nurse, Kate.'

A little later Walter Ames joined them, and he proved to be every bit as attractive and personable as his wife. When he bent to kiss Kate, Nancy observed how tightly she clung to him, the pain in her eyes, and a lump formed in her throat. To be shut off from someone you love was a cruel thing. Kate Ames was incapable of physical love, Dr Lanz had implied.

It had to be a torture for Walter Ames as well. Nancy appraised his lean, athletic body, his handsome, tanned face, his thick, wavy hair bleached from the sun. She could appreciate how deeply Kate loved him. He would be an easy man to love. A breeze gusted over the patio, raising goosebumps on her arms. A shudder wracked her body.

'*Somebody's walking across your grave,*' her grandmother used to say.

13

From the beginning, Nancy Carlson fit into the Ames household like one of the family. Dr Lanz was right about the two women having a good deal in common. With Walter and his friends and family, Kate never talked about her childhood, but with Nancy she delighted in nostalgic reminiscence:

'I'll bet you had an old brown mutt who used to sleep all day on the front porch.'

'How'd you know? His name was Brownie.'

'Now, *that's* original.'

'So, what did you call yours?'

' "Spot." '

'Tres grand!'

The two of them erupted into a giggling bout that left them exhausted.

'My father used to run the growler down to the neighbourhood bar every night, twice on Saturdays. Bet you don't know what a growler is.'

'You've got to be kidding! My old man's can held five quarts, and the bartender would fill it for a buck.'

Unexpectedly they were sober.

Kate sighed. 'You know something, Nancy? All my life, when I was growing up, I used to dream about getting away from the dullness of a middle-class existence. Now, looking back, I think they were pretty good times.'

'Yes . . . I remember my kid brother used to bug me to death. I could have killed him cheerfully. Then there was a night he almost died from pneumonia, and I sat up all night holding his hand and blubbering.'

'Hey, what is this?' Kate forced a smile. 'If we keep it up, *I'm* going to start blubbering. Say, how about you whipping us up a couple of very, very dry martinis and our breaking out the deck? Gin rummy, a penny a point.'

One night after dinner, when Kate, Walt, and Nancy were sitting in the den watching television, Kate, to Nancy's astonishment, said, 'I don't know about you two, but I've had all this drivel I can stand. I'm going to bed . . . Walt, after Nancy tucks me in, why don't you take a drive into Hartford and see a good movie? I read in the paper that *Papillon* is playing somewhere around.'

Nancy, badly flustered, looked at Walt.

He grinned. 'Damned good idea. I've been wanting to see that; it's attracted so much controversy. What about it, Nancy?'

Nancy seesawed her eyes back and forth between Kate and Walt, then waved her hands feebly and looked down at her rumpled slacks and sloppy sweater. 'I . . . I'm not dressed.'

'You look fine,' Walt assured her. 'Nobody dresses to go out anymore. Look at me.' He was wearing a polo shirt and Levi's.

'Well . . . ' She faltered.

'Any more objections?'

Before she could reply, Kate said, 'Good, then it's settled. Now, help me up to bed, will you, Nancy?'

Traffic was light on the highway to Hartford. It was a beautiful night, the sky resplendent with stars, a quarter-moon reflected in the mirror-still water of the Sound, the air fragrant with the aroma of spring greenery.

'Do you know you've been with us almost a year?' Walt said.

'It's hard to believe. It seems like only yesterday that Dr Lanz drove me up here to meet Kate.'

'Kate . . . yes. She's been a new woman since you arrived.'

'She needed companionship more than she needed an RN, Mr Ames.'

'Damn it, Nancy,' he said in annoyance, 'will you stop calling me "Mr Ames"? You've been calling her "Kate" for months now. I demand equal rights.'

She laughed. 'Hard to break old habits. When I was growing up, before women's lib, little girls were brought up to revere the "great-father" image, and "mister" and "father" were synonymous.'

'Well, I am nobody's father, and' – he was abruptly bitter – 'I am not likely ever to become one.'

Nancy looked away from him and stared out the window on her side. She tensed as his hand came down gently on her knee; but he withdrew it immediately. Accidental? or merely an affectionate impulse? she wondered. There was an interval of silence, as though neither of them wanted to dispel the fragility of the brief, intimate moment when his hand had touched her.

Without warning, he turned off the highway onto a narrow side road that led up into the hills.

'What are you doing?' she asked.

'The hell with the movie! Who wants to sit in a dark, dingy theatre on a night like this? There's this little inn on a lake, used to be a favourite of ours before Kate – '

Neither of them spoke again until they arrived at the inn. 'The Thatched Cottage,' an ancient rustic sign read. It did indeed have a thatched roof.

'It's a picture postcard,' Nancy said. 'I feel like we're in the English countryside.'

The inn was situated on a bluff that fell away to a white beach, silver in the moonlight. 'Tell you what,' Walt said. 'Before we go inside, let's go down to the beach. Feel like wading?'

'No, I'm cold. If I had known we were coming here, I'd have brought an extra sweater.'

They walked down a long flight of wooden steps that led down to the lake.

'Look at all the birds. Are they ducks?' she asked.

'Mostly sea gulls'.

'Are they sleeping? They could almost be decoys, they're so still.'

'Yes. You can always tell when a storm is brewing out to sea, because then the lake is crowded with gulls, all of them seeking a safe harbour until it blows over. Occasionally a swan will honour the humble pond with his exalted presence, and there's always a flock of wild ducks passing through on their way to wherever wild ducks go.'

On the far side of the lake, the rolling hills were shucking off a drab mantle of winter. Nancy pointed out the bright wild forsythia growing along the rim of the beach: 'Look how everything is bursting with life. "Gold dust," my grandmother used to call forsythia. Everything is so beautiful this time of year.'

He studied her profile. 'Yes . . . *everything* is so beautiful.'

She pretended not to know he was watching her. 'The seasons fly by so fast. As we were saying before, it's been almost a year since I've been with Kate.'

'It seems longer than that from another viewpoint.'

She was puzzled. 'What other viewpoint?'

'My special viewpoint. You fit in so well, I get the feeling sometimes that you've always been at Manorhaven, as if things had never been any different.'

'I know what you mean. I myself feel as though I've been living with you and Kate all my life.'

'You're family, Nancy.' He squeezed her hand. 'On the

other hand, it must be monotonous for you, a pretty young woman shut off from life in that isolated house.'

'Not at all. I'm quite happy and content at Manorhaven.'

'You don't know how much that means to me to hear you say it. I don't know what I would have done without you, Nan.'

His intensity made her uneasy. He took both of her hands now and swung her around to face him. For the first time, she realized just how intimate this occasion was becoming.

Better stop it while you can, my girl! She shivered.

'You're cold.'

'Yes.' She grasped it as an excuse to make him let go of her hands so that she could fasten the top button of her sweater. She laughed nervously. 'Strange weather – one minute you're hot and the next you're cold.'

'Yes . . . and you're tired but can't sleep, hungry but can't eat. I know the symptoms well. Diagnosis: spring fever.'

Despite his bantering tone, she knew what he was thinking. A man who looked at a woman the way Walt was looking at her . . . She pushed the idea out of her mind and tried to keep the mood light and frivolous.

'And I know the remedy,' she said: 'sulphur and molasses.'

She was paralyzed – too stunned to resist or protest, or so she wanted to believe – when he put his hands on her shoulders and drew her gently to him. His mouth covered hers in a passionate kiss, and she found herself eagerly responding, her arms slipping around his neck, and her fingers caressing the fine curly hairs at his nape. The urgent thrust of his manhood against her loins broke the spell.

'Walt, please, don't!' she gasped, trying to push him away.

'Why not? Don't try to pretend that you don't like it or that you don't need love.'

'Walt! My needs are of no concern to you,' she said in anguish. 'I should never have let it happen. I want to forget it happened.'

'You say it, Nan, but everything else about you, your eyes, says it's a lie.'

She pulled away from him and walked back to the steps.

He caught her from behind and wrapped his arms around her. She felt his erection pressing into the valley between her buttocks. Her body went slack. There was a bittersweet quality in her voice that was both a sign of yielding and a plea of defencelessness:

'Mr Ames . . . you know lots of women. Why pick on me?'

His hands slid up her body and closed over her breasts. He nuzzled the hair behind one ear, and the heat of his breath melted her. 'Nan . . . Nan . . . is that all you think it is? Sex? Yes, I want you desperately, really want you, damn it, in all ways. How can you be so blind? I'm in love with you, have been for months.'

Nancy closed her eyes and moaned as he fondled her. All the will to resist drained out of her. She was an empty shell needing passionately to be replenished. In total surrender, she squirmed around to face him and put her arms around his neck. They kissed wantonly.

'I want you,' he gasped when they came up for air. 'Here; now.'

She put her fingertips to his lips. 'Yes, my darling. I want you, too, so badly. So long I've wanted you' – her voice cracked – 'God help me.'

'God help us both!'

He led her beneath the steps, where it was dark and the grass was a soft, thick bed. He helped her struggle out of her slacks and panties, then removed his trousers and Jockey shorts. 'Keep your sweater and blouse on so you won't catch cold,' he said.

She giggled. 'One minute you're cold and the next you're hot.'

'You've got it backwards.'

'No, I haven't. Before, I was shivering from cold, but now I'm burning up with fever.' Her fingers encircled his hard, rigid penis and stroked it lovingly.

His hands caressed her belly, her thighs, her mound of love. Gently he lowered her to the ground and kneeled between her open, eager thighs.

With trembling fingers, she guided him to her orifice. 'Made for each other,' she murmured, and cradled his hard testicles in one hand. She matched her rhythm to his stroke. It was all as natural and familiar as if they had been making love all of their lives. 'Oh, my wonderful, darling love!' she cried out softly as her orgasm commenced.

His own began, and they played out the rapturous interlude, striving to prolong the sweet spasms as long as they were able. Then, drained and satiated, they fell back and lay side by side, holding hands, with the innocence of two children.

It was after midnight when they drove through the front gate of the Ames estate. Nancy had been pensively silent on the trip home.

'Penny?' he teased.

'Haven't you heard of inflation?'

She was torn by conflicting emotions: anticipating what lay ahead for her and Walt with contained excitement; dreading it, too. One thing was certain: Life would never be the same for Nancy Carlson again.

They did not look at each other or speak until they reached Nancy's bedroom door. Nancy's mouth was as dry as talc, and the wild beating of her heart seemed to thunder through the deathly quiet house like a kettledrum roll.

Standing sideways to him, she put a hand on the doorknob. 'Good night, Walt.' she said tensely. 'Thank you for a wonderful evening.' *Good God, girl! You sound like Nancy Carlson coming home from her first date at the frosh hop!*

'Nancy . . . ' He put a hand beneath her chin and tilted her face up to his. 'You are very beautiful.'

She shut her eyes, trying to squeeze back the tears, to no avail. He kissed one eye and then the other; kissed her nose, her lips.

She whimpered and pushed him off. 'Walt, not here in her house.'

'It's my house, too. Besides, Kate is sedated and has long been asleep.'

The Ameses occupied separate bedrooms.

She wanted to resist, wanted to stop him. All the while he was kissing her, she was picturing Kate's face, so pale against her pillowcase – her lovely, waxen martyr's face so wracked with suffering. 'No, Walt,' she pleaded. 'Please . . . not in her house.'

'Damn it, Nancy, will you stop wailing like a harpie! I've told you, this is *my* house. Kate never had a pot to piss in before I married her!'

Later, in retrospect, Nancy told herself that this arrogant, insensitive remark was a pivotal point in everything that came to pass for her and Walter, and she should not have disregarded it; but then his mouth had smothered her protests, undermined her good judgment and sense of fair play, and his tongue, probing the inner membranes of her mouth, had so intoxicated her, everything but the yearning of her flesh was obliterated.

She did make a last feeble effort. 'It isn't fair to Kate.'

His flint-hard eyes bored into hers. 'Fairness has nothing to do with it. Kate might as well be dead, for all the wife she can ever be to me; you know that.'

'Yes, I know, but . . . '

'Yes, you know,' he said in a soft, patient voice, like a tutor instructing a student in a foreign tongue. 'Yes, yes, yes.'

'Yes,' she said like a robot, almost swooning as his hand slipped down under the waistband of her slacks and panties and manipulated her clitoris.

'I love you, Nancy, *only* you. And you love me.'

'Yes, yes, yes . . . I love you with all my heart.'

'Then there is nothing else to say or to regret. Come along with me. I need you so desperately.'

He opened the bedroom door and put an arm about her waist. Together they walked into Nancy's room and closed the door silently.

14

Nancy did not wake up until nine o'clock the following morning. Hurriedly she slipped into a dressing gown and rushed to Kate's room. She found her sitting up in bed, eating her breakfast from a tray.

'Kate, I'm so sorry I overslept. I'm not accustomed to

going out at night gallivanting.'

'Not to worry, dear,' Kate said cheerfully. 'Hattie took care of everything: fluffed my pillows, opened the drapes, and served me breakfast.'

'Your medicine – it's an hour overdue.'

'Hattie did that, too. Sit down and join me in a cup of coffee.' There were two cups on the tray. 'And tell me how the movie was.'

Nancy was terrified. Without a doubt Walt had visited Kate before he left for New York. Had he lied and let her believe that they had seen the movie? Or had he told her the truth – a partial truth, at least – that they had gone to the countryside inn instead?

She chose her words carefully. 'Didn't Walt tell you?'

'I hardly had time to say a word to him. He was in such a rush, and I was on the phone when he left for the office.'

She tried not to reveal her enormous relief. Casually she said, 'Walt decided he didn't want to sit in a stuffy theatre. He was feeling a bit nostalgic.'

'Oh?'

'Yes, he took me to a cute little inn he said was a favourite place of yours.'

'The Thatched Cottage?' Kate was beaming. 'I can hardly believe it. He hasn't been back there since my accident. Did he tell you that we were on our way home from there when it happened?'

'No.' Nancy was genuinely surprised.

'Well, I couldn't be more delighted . . . Dear, your coffee.'

'In a little while.' The fact was, her hands were so unsteady she didn't risk pouring coffee.

'So, what did you think of The Thatched Cottage?'

'It's charming.'

'Did you dance? Walt and I used to dance by the hour there.'

'They didn't have music last night.'

'That's right; I forgot. They have a band only on Fridays and Saturdays.'

'Walt and I had two drinks and then we came home.'

Kate lit a cigarette with a gold lighter. 'Do you know what I think, Nan? You and Walt should do it more often.'

Do it? Dear God!

'What's that?'

'Get out and have fun. It isn't healthy for an active man like Walt to be cooped up in this house night after night, any more than it is for you.'

'I never was one for partying. I like to lounge around at night – soak in a hot bath, read a book, and early to bed.'

Kate was very persistent. 'Nancy, would you do me a special favour?'

'Of course.'

She held out a beseeching hand, and Nancy had no other recourse than to grasp it. 'Nancy . . . I don't know what I'd do without you. You are my arms and legs, my eyes and ears. I depend on you for everything.'

It pained Nancy to smile. The muscles at the back of her neck and between her shoulder blades were as taut as steel cables.

'It's my job, Kate.'

'It's not a job; it's a labour of love. You're my best friend, Nan.'

'Of course I'm your friend.'

She was squeezing Nancy's hand like a vice. 'I could ask what I'm about to ask only from my best and truest friend.'

A Klaxon sounded in Nancy's mind. 'Kate, I – '

'It's about Walt. Please, hear me out before you say another word. I don't want Walt to spend the rest of his life in the shadow of this room. He has got to have some recreation.'

'I don't know what you mean, Kate. It seems to me that Walt leads a very active life. I mean, he puts in ten hours a day at his office alone.'

'His work. Since the accident, his whole life has been occupied with the business and what goes on in this house. All work and no play – you know what they say.'

'So, if Walt is pushing tò be a dull boy, what does it have to do with me?'

'If we could only get him to take an interest in his hobbies again, you and I. Summer is almost here. Oh, there are so many things the two of you can do together – golf, riding, swimming – all the things I can't do with him anymore.'

'Kate, I can't do that; you *know* I can't.'

Kate refused to listen. 'It will be good for you, too, Nancy. So good for both of you. I just know that Walt will love the idea.'

'Kate! The answer is *no!*'

The expression of eager anticipation on Kate's face was somehow obscene. There was no doubt whatsoever in Nancy's mind that Kate Ames was intimating that she should sleep with her husband.

'Dear Nan, if you're worried that our friends will talk about you and Walt going out together, forget it. I couldn't care less what those old farts think about it.' Her face mirrored happiness and contentment. 'I feel so good about us, Nan, the three of us – you, Walt and me.'

That night, after Kate was put to bed, Walt and Nancy left the house by the back door and walked across the broad lawn to a path that wended its way through a grove of pine trees to the high bluff overlooking the Sound. A flight of stairs, precariously steep, descended to the beach. At the bottom, Nancy removed her shoes.

'I like to wriggle my toes in the sand.'

'I'm with you,' he said, removing his loafers.

Hand in hand they walked down to the water, lapping lazily at the sand. A wide swath of moonlight stretched away across its still surface like a silvery highway.

'It's never altogether still, water,' he observed. 'The sea is a living thing. Right now it's breathing quietly in sleep.'

She clutched his arm, pressing herself tightly against him.

He hugged her. 'Want to go skinny-dipping?'

'Too cold.'

'We could go streaking and give old Mrs English apoplexy.' He looked in the direction of a large Cape Cod-style villa far down the beach.

Nancy giggled. 'If I take off my clothes, it's going to be back in the bushes, and I won't be running.'

'You vixen, you.' He laughed and kissed the side of her head above her ear.

'Incidentally,' she said with studied casualness, 'Kate suggested this morning that you and I should sleep together.'

'What the hell!' He stopped and faced her. 'You have a perverse sense of humour.'

'No, your wife does.' She related the conversation she'd had with Kate over breakfast.

'I'll be damned.' He rubbed the side of his jaw. His face was very grave. 'It certainly sounds like she was suggesting just that.'

'Not a mere suggestion; it was more like a direct order.'

Frown lines bunched up between his thick eyebrows. 'Well, Confucius say, When rape is inevitable, lie back and enjoy it. One thing: Kate's tolerant view of the situation is going to make it a lot easier for you and me to be together.'

They resumed walking along the beach, each absorbed in his own private meditations. Nancy's calves were aching, and with each step she seemed to sink deeper and deeper into the sand.

It was a Friday night, and by eleven o'clock the dining room at The Thatched Cottage was nearly empty, most of the diners having moved into the adjoining bar, where a band had just set up. Walt and Nancy were dawdling over their coffee and brandy and smoking cigarettes.

Three months had passed since Kate Ames gave her blessing to the relationship between her husband and her nurse. Two or three days a week, through the summer, Walt and Nancy played golf or tennis at the country club, followed by a swim in the pool. Every two weeks they travelled into New York, ate at Sardi's, and saw a Broadway show. And there were nights like this one, when they dined at the Thatched Cottage. It was very much like a courtship, and, as in most courtships, the man and the woman were falling deeper and more intensely in love.

Ben Reardon, the restaurant's owner and an old friend of Walt's, came over to the table and winked at Nancy. 'He can't keep his attention off the band, can he, Nan?'

Walt gritted his teeth. 'I can barely keep my *hands* off them. Jesus Christ! That isn't music; it's pure cacophony!'

'Pure crap,' Ben said. 'I couldn't agree with you more, but that's what the patrons go for, so I stuff my ears with cotton and grin and bear it.'

Walt took out his wallet and removed a five-dollar bill. 'Ben, old buddy, do you think you could induce those cats to play a golden oldie, something Nan and I can dance to?'

Ben laughed. 'I think it might be arranged. Got any preferences?'

'Ask 'em if they know "My Silent Love." '

'You got it? He looked at their empty glasses. 'I'll send over a refill, on the house.'

'I don't want to dance,' Nancy said.

'Sure you do.' Walt put his hand over hers. 'What's wrong with you tonight?'

'The same thing that's wrong with me every night. All we've got to look forward to is sex. There's a hell of a lot more in life than that, Walt.'

He took her hand and pulled her to her feet as the band began to play his request. To his surprise, the guitarist, who modelled himself after Elvis sartorially as well as in his vocal style, knew the words:

'I reach for you like I reach for a star,
Worshipping you from afar,
Dreaming in my silent love . . . '

'You sure know how to pick 'em, Walt – "My Silent Love" indeed.'

'Nothing silent about *our* love, darling.'

'Dead is silent, and you and I are on a dead-end street.'

'I didn't realize it was as bad as all that for you,' he said glumly.

She gave him a scathing look. 'You hypocrite! You know perfectly well that the longer we go on, the more broken up I get inside. You're content to let things stay the way they are *ad infinitum.* You've got the best of both worlds.'

'That's a rotten thing to say. I'm going through sheer hell, same as you are.'

'Then *do* something about it, Walt. I can't go on this way any longer, loving you so but having you only in bed. You know what I am: your surrogate wife. But your real wife is Kate, and she always will be. Walt, I want out. Find another nurse for Kate. I'm serving you two weeks' notice.'

They stopped dancing and stood there facing each other in the middle of the floor.

'No, Nan, you can't mean it. We love each other. I'll never let you go.'

'You can't make me a prisoner.'

'Jesus! Be reasonable! Do you want me to divorce her?'

'I can't tell you what to do. You don't owe anything to me. Kate is your wife.'

'I know, I know, I know. What makes it so hard is, she's a cripple because of me.'

Empathizing with his guilt, torment, and frustration, she melted a little. 'It was an accident, Walt. Nobody blames you, not even Kate.'

He took her in his arms, and they resumed dancing. 'I blame me,' he said miserably. 'I was drunk. It was criminal of me to get behind the wheel . . . What makes it doubly hard, Nan, is that if I left Kate, she'd have nothing. All she has now is her obsessive love for me, so much love that she condones my sleeping with another woman. If I divorce her, it will be the same as if I murdered her with a gun; only it would be more merciful with a gun.'

He lapsed into introspective silence. She could feel his body tense.

'Walt, what's the matter?' she asked, stepping back and searching his eyes.

'No way out . . . until Kate dies,' he mused.

A strange quality in his voice troubled Nancy.

'Until she dies,' he repeated.

The quality was menace now. Nancy shivered, although it was warm and humid in the inn.

'If Kate were dead, Nan – '

'Stop talking crazy, Walt.'

He raised one of her hands to his mouth and kissed the palm. The glow in his eyes was sinister. She could sense his rising excitement as he contemplated the mad idea.

'Why not, Nancy? If I left Kate, it would destroy her, and I don't think either of us could live with that. If I gave you up, I would be destroying you and myself. But if Kate were dead, then all three of us would be free. It's the fairest way for all of us, don't you see? For Kate, the most merciful way.'

'Stop talking about it, Walt. I don't want to hear any more.'

Nancy was filled with revulsion; yet, at the same time, she experienced a perverse sense of fascination, the same kind she'd felt as a child on a school trip to a reptile farm, when she was tempted to reach out and stroke the deadly cobra. 'The most merciful way,' she said involuntarily. It was not her voice speaking. She was possessed, like the demonic monster-child in *The Exorcist*.

'It's going to be so simple,' he said, and his voice mesmerized her, entwined her in its spell the way a spider immobilizes a victim in its web.

'When did you arrive at the Ames residence on September fifth, nineteen seventy-five, Dr Lanz?'

'At five-thirty in the afternoon with my wife. It was Walter Ames's birthday, and along with another couple we had been invited for the weekend.'

'You were Mrs Ames's personal physician?'

'I was, and over the course of our professional relationship, we became close personal friends.'

'Prior to her death, when was the last time you conducted a physical examination on Mrs Ames?'

'One week before the . . . the accident.'

'You don't know that, Doctor. That is our purpose in convening here today: to establish the cause of her death . . . Now, what was your diagnosis of her physical condition after the last examination?'

'She was in excellent physical condition, considering her disability. That is, there is a slow attrition of the muscles, naturally, when the body is deprived of exercise, but other than that – '

'Then you gave her a clean bill of health after the last examination?'

'I did, and Kate was extremely pleased.'

' "Extremely pleased." Are we to assume that she accepted her infirmity philosophically, then?'

'Indeed she did. Except for the first few months after her accident, I can say that I never detected any morbidity whatsoever in Mrs Ames's attitude towards her misfortune and life in general.'

'In your professional opinion, Dr Lanz – and the coroner's jury should keep in mind that it is a subjective judgment – is it conceivable that Mrs Ames may have committed suicide?'

'Absolutely not. As I told you, Kate Ames was a happy woman with an optimistic outlook on life. She loved her husband, she loved her home, she loved her friends. She loved life.'

'Dr Lanz, I am going to query you now about the events of the morning of Saturday, September sixth.'

'Everything happened just as Mr Ames testified before.'

'Nevertheless, for the record, this panel must have your sworn testimony. What time did you arise on the morning in question?'

'Oh, it was shortly after seven o'clock. Walter Ames and I were going to have breakfast on the patio and then play tennis. It was exactly seven-thirty when I joined him on the patio; I heard the clock in the parlour chime the half-hour.'

'And then you ate breakfast?'

'No, we never got around to breakfast. You see, the Ameses had given the servants the weekend off. Kate said she didn't want them to intrude on the intimacy of the occasion. It wasn't as if there was going to be a big dinner party. We wanted to rough it for a few days.'

'Was Mrs Ames present on the patio when you were down there?'

'No, sir. She was making a tour of the gardens in her motorized wheelchair. She did that every morning before breakfast. It was the closest thing to physical activity she could enjoy.'

'Did you see her in the gardens?'

'Yes, I did. At one point she called to us and waved. We waved back. And Walt yelled to her that breakfast would be ready in fifteen or twenty minutes. She said she'd be along presently.'

'Then what did she do?'

'She started off along the path that leads to the bluff where it happened. The last we saw of her was when she entered the pine grove.'

'What did you and Mr Ames do then?'

'We went into the kitchen and started cooking up a batch of hot cakes and sausage and eggs. We put everything in the warming oven and waited for Kate to return.'

'What time was that?'

'Ten after eight. When she didn't make an appearance, Walt began to get worried. I was concerned, too. We decided to go out and look for her. I . . . I . . . Excuse me, this is very difficult. When we reached the bluff, there was no sign of her, and we almost turned back.'

'You almost turned back?'

'Yes. We knew Kate was incapable of descending the long flight of stairs to the beach, so we assumed she had gone back

to the gardens. It was strange. I had this sudden premonition, and I walked to the top of the stairs and looked down . . . One of the most traumatic experiences of my life. There she was, lying crumpled up alongside the twisted wreckage of the wheelchair.'

'What happened then?'

'I sent Walter Ames back to the house to get my bag, and I went down to the beach to see if there was anything I could do for her.'

'Was she alive when you examined her?'

'No, it was quite clear that death had been instantaneous. As a result of her previous accident, Kate Ames's spinal column was very fragile indeed. The impact of this fall virtually pulverized six vertebrae and severed the spinal cord, in addition to breaking her neck.'

'Did you yourself perform an autopsy on Kate Ames's body?'

'I did, and the results were as I just described.'

'Dr Lanz, you were very emphatic in your judgment that Kate Ames did not commit suicide.'

'I am convinced she did not.'

'Then – and once again this is a personal, subjective opinion on your part – how do you account for the fact that she did plunge to her death down those steps? You heard the testimony of Detective-Sergeant Mooney, one of the first police officers to arrive at the scene. Sergeant Mooney stated that the terrain leading to the top of the steps ascends at a grade of ten per cent. The conclusion to be drawn from this is that it would have been impossible for her wheelchair to roll up that incline accidentally.'

'That's true, but remember, her wheelchair was propelled by a motor. Now, if that motor somehow malfunctioned, a jammed valve, the throttle . . . I don't know very much about engines, but on more than one occasion in my medical career, I have witnessed just such a thing occur.'

'I see. All right, thank you, Dr Lanz. You may step down now.'

Hartford *Herald*, September 12, 1975:

SOCIALITE VICTIM OF
FREAK ACCIDENT

Yesterday a coroner's jury ruled that the death of Mrs Walter Ames on September 6 was the result of accidental causes. It is the judgment of the coroner's office that Mrs Ames's motorized wheelchair went out of control on a high bluff overlooking Long Island Sound on the Ameses' Gold Coast estate, carrying Mrs Ames over the bluff to the rocky beach below, where she died instantly. Mrs Ames had been paralyzed in a tragic automobile accident . . .

Walter Ames put down the paper and went over to Nancy, who was standing at the edge of the patio, looking off in the direction of the bluff where Kate Ames had perished. 'A penny?'

'I told you once before, we're in the midst of an inflation.' She turned her head and looked at him. 'You look like hell.'

'So do you.'

'I *feel* like hell. Walt . . . why? Why did we do it?'

Grimly he told her, 'Because there was no other way for us to be together. The whole scenario was written on the winds of time before either of us was born.'

PART TWO

1

Skull Mountain was besieged by thunder and lightning. Fire bolts, ten feet in diameter, assailed the mesa in continuous bombardment. Walter Ames stood by the bay window in his study, a tumbler of scotch in one hand and a cigarette in the other. The raging scene outside reminded him of an artillery barrage he had witnessed at Anzio in World War II, great balls of fire exploding in every direction as far as the eye could see. The house was grounded by ten steel lightning rods thirty feet high, positioned at strategic vulnerable points, so that the likelihood of its receiving a fatal strike was minimal. But then, in all the years Walt had been coming to Skull Mountain, he had never observed a storm so savage.

In their bedroom at the other end of the house, the Brandons stared out the window, awestruck.

'Jesus Christ!' Kevin exclaimed. 'It's like the end of the world!'

There was no need to put on a light. The room was vividly illuminated by never-ending flashes of lightning that appeared brighter than sunlight as they streaked across the sky like so many wriggling electrically charges snakes.

'Armageddon is upon us,' Kevin muttered.

'As the Holy Spirit predicted,' Susan said. 'I'm going downstairs and get that drink Walt offered me. Join me?'

'No, I'm going back to bed. I'm bushed, and my head is splitting from that damned mescaline.'

'Take some aspirin and one of my tranquillizers. They're in my tote bag.' She put on the robe Nancy had hung in the closet and belted it snugly about her naked body. 'I won't be long, hon.'

The house was an enormous echo chamber, reverberating deafeningly with the ceaseless pounding of thunderbolts. Susan was serene as she walked down the long hall towards the study; in fact, she rather enjoyed the magnificent spectacle of Nature displaying her prowess. Overhead, the heavy oak ceiling beams creaked and shuddered, the sound eerily akin to human voices crying out in protest against the attack of the elements. She found Walt standing at the window, his broad-shouldered silhouette sharply defined against the luminous rectangle. Stealing up behind him silently, she put a hand against his back. He was not startled; in fact, it was almost as if he had been expecting her.

'Hello there, Susan,' he said casually. 'Come down to watch the fireworks?'

'I need a drink.'

'Allow me.' He walked to a cabinet in one corner and picked up a bottle. 'Scotch OK?'

'Fine; just a touch of water.'

He mixed her drink and another one for himself.

'Thanks, Walt.' She took a long swallow. 'That's good medicine.'

Although the storm was raging as savagely as ever, its effect on the human senses was diminishing.

'The brain manufactures its own natural opiate,' Walt exlained. 'Same as being under fire in war. It benumbs the mind and the flesh.'

She nodded, hypnotized by a ball of fire that kept skittering about the plateau beyond the house in a dazzling erratic fashion. 'It's as if it were looking for someplace to alight,' she said. She clapped her hands over her ears as the crescendo of thunder hit a new peak.

'Does the storm frighten you?' he asked.

She looked up at him. 'No, I find it exciting.' Her eyes were luminous in the lightning's glow.

'And I find *you* exciting.' He put an arm around her, his hand resting against her breast.

She turned to him and lifted her face for his kiss, moulding her body to his, relishing the demanding jab of his manhood. Their tongues played a teasing game. He undid the sash of her robe and slid his hands inside, stroking her hips and then her buttocks.

Susan shuddered and put her hands inside his pyjama pants. 'God! You are one big man,' she gasped.

He pushed her in the direction of the big leather couch against one wall. 'Shall we dance?' he joked.

'Do we dare? Somebody may come in here at any time. None of the others can possibly be sleeping through this.'

His breath was hot on her face and smelled of whisky and tobacco. 'I don't give a damn! I want you now, and I'm going to have you.'

'I'll keep on the robe just in case.' She lay back on the couch, with the robe fanning out across the cushions, and opened her thighs to him.

Walt did not bother to remove his pyjamas. 'They say Mussolini liked to do it with his pants and boots on.' He laughed. 'There *is* something titillating about it. When I was in Europe in the war, we used to do it standing up in hallways when we took a girl home. Stolen sweets always taste the best, you know.'

She arched her hips to receive his powerful thrust, moaning softly. 'That hurt. I almost felt like a virgin. You could hire yourself out as a stud, Walt.'

'I'm sorry.'

'Don't be. I love it.'

The tempo of their lovemaking matched the frenzy of the storm. Around them the house trembled and groaned, while lightning framed the erotic tableau on the couch. They peaked simultaneously, loins, bellies, chest and breast pounding away at each other, in rapturous ecstasy.

'Don't let it end, Walt!' she begged. 'Don't go soft on me. I want it again. Once more!'

'What a wench you are. It will never be the same as this with any other woman again.'

'Even your wife?' she goaded him.

'Any woman. Fate works in mysterious ways. I feel it in my gut that your being here on Skull Mountain was an inevitable act of destiny. You and I were meant for each other.'

'I think you're right,' Susan said. She had felt that the instant she learned that his name was Walter Ames.

In silence they went on performing like two craftsmen engaged in skilled labour. The second orgasm, for both, was more satisfying than the first in that it was protracted, and sensation was not expended in a brief blaze of passion.

Outside the study in the dark hall, a shadowy figure

stood pressed against the wall, had been there from the onset of the love play between Walt and Susan. When the deed was done, it moved down the hall to the staircase, fading into the shadows.

Walt and Susan made themselves presentable, and he turned on a dim desk lamp.

'Another drink?' he said.

'I'd love it. Got a cigarette?'

'The box on the desk.'

He mixed two more drinks, and they sat down on the couch. There was a lull in the storm, and it was possible to speak again without shouting.

'How long have you and Nancy been married?' she inquired casually.

'Five years and three months, give or take a few days.'

'What a dutiful husband you are. I'll bet you never forget anniversaries.'

He shrugged. 'You know, Nancy is my second wife. My first wife, Kate, died in an accident.'

'Oh, I'm sorry.'

Walt thought he saw a crafty gleam in her eyes, and it discomfited him. Suddenly he felt exhausted. 'After this drink I'm going to bed. I'm getting old for this sort of hanky-panky.'

She laughed and reached over to pat his cheek. 'You old? Never. I wish I could go up and climb into bed with you and Nancy.'

'You do?' He was mildly shocked. 'You're positively depraved . . . Come to think of it, though, it might be fun.'

'Sure. Don't knock it until you try it. We could ask Kevin to join us, too.'

'That does it,' he said with a grin. 'I've had it for one night.' He kissed her tenderly and patted her bottom. 'Now, off to bed with you like a good little girl.'

When he returned to his bedroom, Nancy was lying inert on her right side and her eyes were closed. He climbed in beside her and lay on his back with his hands folded behind his head. He thought of Susan. What a hot little bitch she was. He wondered how many times before this she had cuckolded her husband. What was it Churchill had said about Russia? 'A riddle wrapped in a mystery inside an enigma.' Susan struck him that way, for some unfathomable reason – a multi-faceted creature, the dangerous kind.

Also, for some equally puzzling reason, he thought of his father. Glenn Ames was still on his mind when sleep came, and, perhaps nourished by the mescaline, his father materialized in his dream, one of the most vivid Walt had ever experienced . . .

It was in 1946, the year after the war, that Peggy Dewhurst applied for a secretarial job at the brokerage firm of Ames, Leonard, and Lowe. The director of personnel was so impressed with her scholastic records – straight A's in business administration from Cornell, Phi Beta Kappa, and number one on the dean's list – that he arranged an interview for her with the senior partner, Glenn Ames.

Glenn was even more impressed with her. He believed her to be the most beautiful woman he had ever met. There was about her the quality of a Nordic goddess: tall, statuesque, flaxen-haired, with a classic profile and large grey-green eyes that gave truth to the cliché 'limpid pools.' She had a secretive Mona Lisa smile and an air of aloofness, verging on arrogance, about her. Her body was superb: firm, high breasts that asserted themselves saucily within her tight sweater, and long, shapely legs that she displayed without self-consciousness when she sat down across from Glenn Ames and crossed them. It was the only time in his mature life that he experienced an instant erection merely from the sight of a sensual woman.

'Where are you from, Miss Dewhurst?' he asked. 'I mean, your home.'

'New York City.'

'You were born in New York?' he asked sceptically.

'You're puzzled by my accent – or, rather, lack of it. Well, my family travelled a lot. My father is an army officer.'

'I see . . . My son Walter was recently discharged from the service . . . Miss Dewhurst, may I inquire why you are applying for a secretarial position? I mean, a girl with your qualifications must have higher aspirations.'

She looked him directly in the eye. 'I have extremely high aspirations, believe me, Mr Ames. In his commencement address to the graduating class, the dean of the School of Business Administration advised us that if one is confident in one's abilities, one should not hesitate to accept a job with a successful corporation at the lowest level, because the cream rises quickly to the top.'

Glenn chuckled. 'I like your assurance and candour, Miss Dewhurst. But I fear I have to recast your game plan somewhat. Here at Ames, Leonard, and Lowe we have a surfeit of excellent secretaries. What we are looking for at the moment is a junior administrative assistant to the president, which I happen to be. Do you think you'd be interested?'

'I accept with pleasure, Mr Ames.' She rose, approached his desk, and extended her hand.

'Welcome to the firm, Miss Dewhurst.'

'Thank you, sir. And please call me Peggy.'

'Peggy, yes. I noticed you call yourself Peggy on both your resumé and your application. I assume your Christian name is Margaret?'

'Yes, but I changed it legally to Peggy.'

'Oh, I see.'

It was another suggestion of an elusive quality that, for lack of a better definition, he labelled 'eccentricity.' He rang for his secretary:

'Jennifer, please take Miss Dewhurst to Jim Ransdall's office for briefing.' He nodded to Peggy. 'Randall is my chief assistant. Well, Miss Dewhurst – '

' "Peggy," ' she said with a flirtatious twinkle in her eyes.

She made him self-conscious. 'Yes, to be sure. Well, Peggy, it's been a pleasure to meet you, and I have a feeling that Peggy Dewhurst and Ames, Leonard, and Lowe are going to get along very well indeed.'

After she was gone, he went to a mirror and examined his face. He was flushed and a little giddy. *Damned old fool! You're old enough to be her father!* Yet, he could not shake the conviction that she had been mildly flirtatious. Anyway, it wasn't as if he looked his age. He had most of his hair, his features were lean and the skin tone good, and he kept physically fit at the gym, working out three times a week and playing handball and tennis on weekends. With a rueful smile, he decided to transfer young Walter to the Chicago office. No sense taking chances that his handsome son might turn her head in his own direction.

Glenn Ames's prophecy that Peggy Dewhurst and Ames, Leonard, and Lowe would 'get along very well indeed' was borne out in the next six months. And, when Jim Randall resigned the following June, Peggy was promoted to chief administrative assistant, against the opinion of his two partners.

'You've got to concede that her work here has been brilliant. What she accomplished with the Chapman account alone merits the promotion,' he challenged their objections.

'Granted,' said Lowe. 'A healthy raise is certainly in order, but to promote her over the heads of qualified people who have seniority and are men, well, it's not cricket, Glenn. After all, she *is* a woman.'

Glenn regarded him with a contemptuous smile. 'I don't buy your male chauvinism, Gene. Yes, she is a woman and a damned handsome one at that, but she is also the most gifted member of her department. It's settled, gentlemen. Peggy Dewhurst has the job.'

Carl Leonard could not resist a parting innuendo. 'Are you sure your judgment isn't being prejudiced because she is, as you say, a "damned handsome" woman?'

'Not in the least,' Glenn retorted defiantly.

But, after they were gone, the suggestion nagged at him. It was a typical Ames characteristic to quell self-doubt or uncertainty by meeting any threatening affair head-on. He picked up his phone and dialed Peggy's extension:

'Peggy, would you please come into my office at your earliest convenience.'

She arrived within ten minutes, and without fanfare he broke the news to her:

'As of Monday morning you will be my new chief administrative assistant.'

She stood there like a statue, saying nothing, her eyes wide with disbelief and her mouth open.

Glenn came around the desk and confronted her with his hands on his hips. 'Well, don't just stand there. Say something. Do something.'

Her obedience was swift and extreme. She threw her arms around his neck and kissed him forcefully on the mouth. 'Oh, Mr Ames, you're the most wonderful and generous man I've ever met! Thank you so very much. I'm eternally grateful.'

He felt himself blushing. 'That's not it at all. My decision is strictly objective. You've earned the job by your exemplary record since you came to work for the firm.'

'That may be, but I love you in any case.'

It was a strong statement, even spoken in the euphoric state she was in.

Impulsively, Glenn Ames made a decision. While he was addressing her, he could not believe what he was saying. 'How would you like to celebrate by having dinner with me tonight?'

'I would be delighted to sup with you, sir,' she said coquettishly.

'Splendid . . . Suppose I pick you up at your apartment at eight o'clock?'

'I'll be ready, Mr Ames.'

'Oh, and Peggy, I think it's about time that you call me Glenn.'

She smiled and lowered her eyes demurely. 'I'll see you later on . . . Glenn.'

Glenn Ames arrived at Peggy Dewhurst's apartment on East Sixty-ninth Street at five minutes to eight. As he was getting out of the cab, she came skipping down the steps.

'Perfect timing,' she said gaily.

'My word, you are a remarkable woman: not only not late, but early and waiting.'

He took her to Sardi's. Dinner was a huge success, punctuated by animated conversation and heightened by a magnum of Dom Perignon champagne. A heated debate about the suicide of Hitler and the disappearance of his aide Martin Bormann, had Glenn on the defensive thoughout. He shook his head and held up his hands in resignation:

'All right, let's call it a truce. And let me repeat, you are a *most* remarkable woman, Peggy Dewhurst.'

She smiled, placed her elbows on the table, and cocked her chin in her hands. 'You're pretty terrific yourself Glenn Ames.'

His whole being was suffused with warmth and longing he had not felt since his first love affair as a college freshman. He reached across the table and took her hands in both of his. 'Peggy . . . er, that is, I . . . '

She comprehended his embarrassment and his inability to express what was, patently, a clash of conflicting emotions – very powerful emotions – and deftly she circumvented the issue. 'Glenn, I can't believe it's almost one o'clock. We've been together for five hours, yet it seems such a short time.'

'I feel that way, too.' He pressed her hand. 'Time always flies when you're with someone you . . . ' He faltered again.

'Someone you care for and with whom you have many things in common.' She saved him again. 'I really must be getting home – with deep regret.' She winked mischievously. 'I'm a working girl, you know, and my boss is a martinet.'

The two of them burst into hearty laughter, thereby earning some disapproving glances from diners at nearby tables.

'They must think we're either crazy or drunk,' Peggy observed as they walked to the cloakroom.

'Bunch of snobs,' Glenn dismissed them. 'God! I haven't felt this young in years.'

She tucked her hand into the crook of his elbow and looked up into his face. 'I'm glad, because you *are* young, Glenn. I find you one of the most interesting and attractive men I've ever been out with.'

'Thank you, Peggy; thank you very much indeed. And I find you *the* most attractive woman I've ever met.'

During the cab ride to her apartment, there was a faint undercurrent of tension between them, the kind of strain that arises in a male-female relationship passing from the platonic stage to the corporeal.

He walked her to the door and removed his hat. 'My dear, this has been one of the memorable nights of my life. Thank you so much.'

'It's been wonderful for me as well, Glenn,' she said in a small voice, avoiding his gaze. 'I . . . I'd ask you up, but my place is such a shabby little dump.'

'Don't say that, Peggy; I'll see you at the office tomorrow.'

She started to enter the lobby, then turned suddenly and,

standing on tiptoe, kissed him lightly on the cheek. 'Good night, Glenn.'

The door closed behind her, and Glenn stood there staring at the bare portal, still seeing Peggy, so beautiful, so wholesome, so vibrant, so young. He started as the cabby yelled at him:

'Hey, mac, the meter's running, you know! Something wrong with you?'

Glenn came down the steps slowly and got into the cab.

'You sick or something, mister? You look funny.'

'No, no, I'm not sick; I'm – '

Like the old song from *Call Me Madam: 'You're not sick, you're just in love . . . '*

2

The following Friday, Glenn Ames invited Peggy to the theatre and a late-night supper, and to dinner the Wednesday after that. And for the next two weeks, it was the same: dinner on Wednesday, the theatre on Friday.

'They're getting to be an "item" around town,' Leonard observed dryly to Lowe.

The junior partner shook his head. 'I can't understand Glenn anymore. He and Clarissa have always been so devoted. He's an attractive guy, and plenty of women have dangled their hooks in front of him, but he never took the bait.'

'Not until now,' Leonard said gloomily. 'Our Peggy has him completely under her spell.'

'What the hell!' Lowe tried to find a bright note. 'So he's got the hots for her. Middle-age crisis – it's as common as the cold. He'll bang her until the novelty wears off; then he'll take Clarissa away on a cruise to assuage his conscience, and that will be that.'

'I hope you're right, but I'm not so sure. I have a hunch

he's never laid a hand on her.'

'Come on!'

'No, I mean it. It goes deeper than sex. I think the poor bastard is in love with her.'

On Friday night on the way back to her apartment, Peggy surprised Glenn. 'I'd like you to come in for a drink tonight. I've finally gotten the place spick-and-span, and I bought a bottle of Metaxa brandy for the occasion. I know how much you like it.'

'Miracle of miracles! I was beginning to think you were using the apartment as an excuse because you didn't want to be alone with me.'

'Oh, Glenn, how can you say a thing like that? You know how much I want to be with you.'

'Do you, really?'

Without a word, Peggy put a hand at the back of his neck and kissed him on the lips. 'More than anything else in the world, I want to be near you,' she said.

When they'd reached their destination, and were standing just outside her apartment door, she hesitated before turning the key in the lock.

'It's still pretty shabby, even if it is clean and tidy,' she said.

'I don't care if it's a barn, so long as you grace it.'

She preceded him into the flat and switched on the table lamp. 'As little illumination as possible,' she joked. 'It doesn't look so bad in poor light.'

'It's very nice,' he said mechanically, striving to conceal his disappointment. The living room was small and square, with a dingy white ceiling and drab grey walls. The furnishings were sparse and shabby. Off to one side was an alcove that housed a small gas stove and a counter-top refrigerator.

She hung their coats in the closet and went into the makeshift kitchen to pour them drinks. 'I even bought aperitif glasses,' she called to him.

'Very nice,' he said absently, his displeasure growing with each passing moment. Certainly, he thought, she could afford better digs than this hovel. Ames, Leonard, and Lowe paid her a more than respectable salary. He could not in good conscience let the matter pass.

She brought in the glasses of Metaxa, placed them on the

small, chipped coffee table, then sat on the couch, half facing him, with one leg drawn up underneath her. Her short skirt was drawn up over her knees, affording him a view of her thighs above her stocking tops. It pleased him that she was wearing nylons held up by a garter belt; so much more feminine and provocative than panty hose.

She lifted her glass in a toast: 'To the two of us and a glorious evening. I thoroughly enjoyed myself. Of course, I always do with you, Glenn.'

'To infinitely more evenings like it.'

They touched glasses and sipped the strong, sweet Greek brandy.

Glenn put his glass down and took a deep breath. 'Peggy, I hope you won't be offended by what I'm about to say, but I feel obliged to do it . . . My dear, this apartment is not nearly good enough for you. You deserve much, much better. I mean, I can't tolerate the idea of you sitting alone in a place so depressing night after night. The fact is . . . ' He paused and mopped his brow with a handkerchief. 'God, I am botching this for sure.'

All the while he was talking, Peggy watched him curiously, head tilted to one side, her ruby-red lips a pouting oval, her green eyes intent. She brushed back a lock of golden hair from her forehead before she answered him. 'I don't want you to misunderstand me, Glenn. The salary you pay me is more than fair. However, the truth is, I cannot afford the kind of apartment you are envisioning for me.'

'Oh, come now, Peggy, I can run through *The Times* right now and locate a dozen apartments for rent that are far more presentable than this and at a price you can afford.'

She placed a hand on his arm. 'I'm afraid you're wrong, Glenn. See, what you don't know is that a large portion of my salary goes back home to help support my parents.'

'But I thought your father was an army officer. It may not be the highest-paid profession in the world, but one can live quite comfortably, I should think.'

She hung her head. 'You must have misunderstood me, Glenn. I said he *was* an officer. The truth is, Dad is in a mental institution – the strain of the war and everything. My mother is hard put to get along on his meagre pension.'

He shook his head uncomprehendingly. 'And I always imagined that the government took care of its fighting men and their families. What a shame.'

'Please, Glenn, let's drop the subject. And stop feeling sorry for me. This apartment is quite adequate for my needs.'

'Damn it, no!' He was indignant. 'I will not have you trapped in a chicken coop like this one week longer. Tomorrow I am going to find you living quarters suitable to a woman of your class.'

'I told you I can't afford it.'

'But I can,' he said quietly, and took both of her hands in his.

'But I couldn't accept that.'

'Darling Peggy, you must have guessed it by now, that I am madly and hopelessly in love with you. I'm old enough to be your father, and I don't expect you to reciprocate my feelings, but that's all right. I – '

'Stop it, Glenn.' She silenced his declaration with a hand across his mouth. 'You silly goose. I keep telling you, you are *not* old – not to me, anyway – but you are blind, my darling, not to have sensed that I, too, am in love with you.'

He was incredulous. 'You love me? I can't believe it. It's a cruel hoax.'

'Let me prove it,' she said, tilting her head back, waiting for his kiss.

He took her in his arms and embraced her passionately. The blood was pounding in his loins as it had not done in years. With his wife, he was impotent half the time they made love, or attempted to. Clarissa and he accepted it with resignation. After all, the well runs dry sooner in some men than in others. Now, however, his body throbbed with lust; no, more than lust – youthful, healthy desire. In his most erotic fantasies he could never have visualized this reality.

Peggy slipped her dress over her head and folded it neatly on the table. 'Dry-cleaning prices being what they are, it pays to be neat,' she quipped. She lay back in his arms as he lavished kisses on her face, her neck, the upper mounds of her breasts. 'Let me take off my bra. Here, help me.'

With trembling fingers he unfastened the catch and stripped the bra off her. Her breasts were firm and high, just as he had known they would be, her rigid nipples pink and perkily upturned. His mouth adored them hungrily while his hands explored the satin softness of her thighs.

She lifted her hips off the cushion. 'Take off my panties.'

No woman had ever said that to him; it inflamed him to the edge of delirium. He slipped the filmy bikini panties down over her knees and feet and dropped them beside the couch. Her half-slip was next, and then she was naked.

She flashed a wanton smile. 'Well, come on, slow-poke; it isn't polite to keep a lady waiting.'

Glenn fairly flung off his clothing. To his surprise, he was not the least bit self-conscious about disrobing in front of this young, voluptuous creature, who was watching him brazenly. He was proud of his physique, harder and leaner than that of most men his age; proud too, of the firmness of his erection. When she took it in her hand, he was worried that he might ejaculate prematurely. Shades of adolescence! Talk about a Renaissance man! Glenn Ames was born again!

The joy was almost too exquisite to bear when he entered her: Adam in the Garden of Eden, the first man in the world – the *only* man in the world – and Peggy the only woman. All of the others did not exist. Nothing existed at this pristine moment in time but the two of them.

After it was over, they lay side by side, sipping Metaxa and gazing into each other's eyes.

'When I move to my new apartment, I'm going to take this couch with me. After tonight, I'll treasure it as long as I live,' she said.

'And I'll treasure *you* as long as I live.'

Peggy smiled.

Peggy Dewhurst's new apartment was on East Sixty-fourth Street, overlooking Central Park. It consisted of a large sunken living room with a picture window, a kitchen-dinette, two bedrooms, and two baths. She decorated it herself with American Colonial appointments, except for her bedroom, which was in the style of French Empire, very chic and feminine.

'The best thing about it is the bed,' Glenn joked the first time he visited her. It was a spacious four-poster with a pink ruffled canopy.

She went to him and put her arms around his neck. 'I was hoping you'd think the best thing about the room is me.'

'God! I adore you, my sweet. Do you know, sometimes when I'm with you, I wake up in the middle of the night and think it must all be a dream? I can't believe that you're in love with me.'

She smiled. 'That's the name of a song,' she said, and gently rubbed the front of his trousers. 'Would you like me to prove just how much I love you?'

'Now?'

'Yes; we'll christen the bed.'

When they'd undressed and climbed onto the bed, she pushed him back on the pillows and straddled his hips. 'Tonight mama's in the saddle.' She grasped his full erection and slid her body forward, impaling herself on it, rolling and writhing against him until she felt his spasms commence.

Afterwards he asked her, 'When you're on top, doesn't it have an adverse effect on your orgasm?'

She made fun of him. ' "An adverse effect on your orgasm?" – I say, aren't we a bit clinical tonight? Well, now, let me tell you something, Mr Ames: *Nothing* has ever had an adverse effect on my orgasm!'

His expression was suddenly serious. 'You are the most passionate woman I have ever met.'

'I come from a long line of passionate women. Love and hate, both extremes of the emotional spectrum – no room for middle ground with gals like me.' Her green eyes shone with a strange feline gleam.

'I realize, of course, there have been others before me, but I am curious because I love you so much . . . and I'm so damned jealous. Were there very many?'

She laughed softly and patted his cheek. ' "Daisies don't tell," my mother used to say.'

'I'm sorry, it was a boorish thing to ask. Let's forget I said it.'

'Forgotten.'

'My sweet.' He kissed the palm of her hand.

She lit a cigarette and sat propped up against the pillows. 'Glenn . . . do you think your wife suspects about us?'

'I'm sure it's crossed her mind – not you, just that I might be seeing another woman – but only fleetingly. I'm convinced she doesn't really believe it.'

'No, it's a human foible. No one likes to face up to something that will cause them pain or grief. She'll find a score of reasons why you stay in town so much.'

'There's the badminton tournament this week. They'll cover for me at the club if she phones.'

'What kind of a woman is your wife, Glenn?'

'A fine woman, very pretty when she was young. She's put on too much weight but still makes a very smart appearance.'

'Good in bed?'

'We had a good sex life for years, but for some time now it hasn't worked. My fault, really; I was semi-impotent until I met you.' He leaned over and kissed her ear. 'You've given me new life, darling. Like the phoenix, I have risen out of my own ashes.'

She saw that he was ready to make love again, and put out her cigarette. 'OK, tiger, shall we have another go at it?'

Glenn Ames's idyllic relationship with Peggy Dewhurst lasted six months.

On a bright spring morning in May, Peggy phoned him at the office. 'Glenn, I hate to do this to you at such short notice, but an emergency has come up. My father's taken a turn for the worse. I'm going to fly out there on the noon plane to be with my mother. I'll need a few days off.'

'By all means, take as much time as you need. Peggy, I'm terribly sorry about your father. If there's anything I can do to help, don't hesitate to let me know – money, anything, you name it.'

'You're an angel, Glenn. I'll keep in touch. Be a good boy while I'm gone.'

'I love you.'

She hesitated. 'Goodbye, darling.'

She kept her hand on the phone after it was cradled, staring at it. She could not lie to him that last time, could not tell him that she loved him. She felt genuine compassion for him at that instant. He was a decent man, a kind man, a loving man – and none of it counted because he was an Ames!

Peggy showered and dressed at a leisurely pace: black

lace lingerie, garter belt of black satin – black seemed appropriate for the occasion – a delicate lavender chiffon dress with a tulip front, a flutter-sleeved print, and a light spring jacket; there was a nip in the air. Then she went to the bedroom closet and removed the large leather carrying case from behind her wardrobe. It was heavy, and she listed to one side when she walked, but she didn't have far to carry it – just to her Datsun, parked in the garage in the basement.

She drove down East Sixty-fourth Street to the East River Drive, where she headed for the Triboro Bridge. From the Triboro she would drive to the Throgs Neck Bridge and cross to the Connecticut turnpike.

She arrived at the Ames residence, Manorhaven, at half-past noon, parking at the top of the big circular drive before the front entrance. A liveried butler answered the door and inquired in an austere, nasal voice, 'Can I be of service, madam?'

'I have an appointment to see Mrs Ames, please. My name is Sally Winters and I'm a representative for the Willoughby Camera Corporation in Manhattan.'

He invited her into the large foyer. 'Would you please wait here and I'll tell Mrs Ames that you have arrived.'

Minutes later a woman of fifty-odd years came down the hall, her expression one of total bafflement. She was a nice-looking woman with soft brown hair – a good dye job – and a round, cherubic face. The expensive grey jersey dress minimized the thickness of her waist and hips.

'Miss Winters?'

'Yes, I'm pleased to meet you, Mrs Ames.' Peggy extended her hand.

The woman recoiled. 'No, no, there must be some mistake. I've never heard of you, Miss Winters, or of your camera company.' She eyed the black case on the floor cautiously.

Peggy frowned and took an appointment book out of her purse, riffling through the pages until she found the entry she was seeking. 'Here we are: "Mrs Glenn Ames, Thursday, May eighth, twelve-thirty" Didn't your husband tell you I was coming?'

'No, he did not, and I am at a loss – '

'He must have forgotten,' Peggy cut in. 'Mr Ames came

into Willoughby's last week to buy a motion-camera and projector. He said it was to be a gift for your niece who's expecting a baby.'

The puzzled look left Clarissa Ames's face and she smiled. 'Yes . . . of course. Oh, he's been so absent-minded lately.'

'In any case, Mr Ames wanted your approval of the equipment before he finalized the sale. He said you were an excellent photographer.'

The woman looked pleased. 'Oh, that was *years* ago.'

'Do you have a place where I can demonstrate our product for you? It's the finest amateur equipment that money can buy.'

'To be sure. We can do it in the study. Follow me, Miss Winters.'

Peggy picked up the carrying case and went down the hall after the lady of the house. When they were inside the study, she shut the door, turned, and leaned back against it. She wore a predatory smile – the cat grinning as it is about to devour the canary. 'We won't be disturbed, will we?'

'Not so long as that door remains closed.'

'Fine . . . Well, then, we can begin.'

Glenn Ames received the phone call at 2:10 P.M.:

'Mr Ames, this is Captain Walsh, of the Hartford Police Department. We're at your home, Manorhaven. I'd like you to get here as soon as possible. There will be a police limousine in front of your office at two-thirty.'

'What's the trouble, Captain?'

'It's your wife, sir. She's . . . she's dead.'

'*My God!* How did it happen? A stroke?' Clarissa was being treated for high blood pressure.

'No, not a stroke, Mr Ames, but I'd prefer to say no more until you get here. Goodbye, sir.'

The police limousine was chauffeured by a plainclothesman. Citizens of the stature of Glenn Ames received preferential treatment in delicate matters such as this. The driver was tight-lipped, replying to Glenn's queries in succinct equivocations: 'Yes, sir'; 'No, sir'; 'I can't say, sir.'

When the limo turned in the drive at Manorhaven, Glenn was stunned at the spectacle of an armada of police cars and ambulances and two fire-department emergency vehicles arrayed at the head of the drive, as well as on the front lawn. The front door was open. He bounded out of the car and up the steps. In the foyer, he was met by a stocky man wearing a black top-coat and a crumpled fedora. His complexion was ruddy, and he had a blotchy bulb on the end of his nose.

'Mr Ames?'

'Yes, of course I'm Glenn Ames,' he answered impatiently. 'Now, what's this all about?'

During the trip from New York, an overpowering sense of guilt had been building within Glenn Ames. Clarissa was dead, and the awful truth was that he felt no grief, only some remorse for his dispassionate treatment of his wife for the past five years – the minimal conscience of a righteous man – but overriding that, a sensation of relief. It was as if a nagging burden had been lifted from his shoulders. Now he and Peggy were free – free to love, free to live together, free to legitimize their relationship: *Mr and Mrs Glenn Ames; Mrs Peggy Ames.*

'How did my wife die?'

'Mr Ames, I'm Captain Walsh. Come with me, please.'

Glenn followed Captain Walsh down the long hall, past a battery of detectives and uniformed police officers. When he entered the study, he was stupefied. His wife was sitting in his swivel chair, slumped over the desk, her head resting in a pool of blood, and in her right hand was his revolver.

'Suicide?' he whispered.

'We're pretty certain.'

'But why? Did she leave a note? phone anyone? What about the servants?'

'She didn't say anything to anyone, at least not to our knowledge at this time. The last person who saw her alive was a Miss Sally Winters, who claimed to be a representative for the Willoughby Camera Corporation in New York City, only she didn't check out. The Willoughby people never heard of her, and they have no record that you set up an appointment for her to visit Mrs Ames.'

Glenn's head was spinning. 'Sally Winters? Willoughby Camera? I set up an appointment? What the hell are you talking about, Captain? This is absurd!'

Captain Walsh nodded at a man standing beside the desk. 'Run the film, Baxter.'

In his state of shock and extreme perturbation, Glenn Ames had been oblivious of the motion-picture projector on the table at the far end of the room, and of the easel screen opposite it.

An officer drew the blinds, and the room was in semi-darkness.

'Come over here, Mr Ames,' Walsh said.

Glenn's toes and fingers were numb; so were his lips. *Am I dying?* He felt strange. Everything was unreal. It was not happening, not to him. *The Trial . . . The Castle . . .* Yes, that was it! It was happening to a character out of a bizarre story by Kafka.

Action flared on the screen, dazzling Kodacolour, a man and woman making love on a bed. What raging insanity! The police were actually showing him a stag movie! A close-up of their genitals meshing in frantic rhythm, now a close-up of the woman's face, contorted by lust . . . Glenn's knees caved in; it was as if he had been struck on the head with a sledgehammer. *The woman was Peggy!*

Captain Walsh and another detective supported him on either side.

'It can't be,' he said. 'It's some sort of obscene, sadistic joke.'

'There's more, Mr Ames.'

Now the couple on the screen switched positions and the man was on the bottom. Horrified, Ames recognized his own face, in the agony and ecstasy of climax. On and on it went, and every frame of the film would be etched on Glenn Ames's mind, as enduring as a Greco-Roman frieze: his head buried between Peggy's thighs; his engorged penis encompassed by her sweet lips.

Glenn Ames fainted . . .

Peggy parked the Datsun in the parking lot across from the American Airlines terminal. She did not bother to wipe clean the interior surfaces or the door handles. There was no record of her fingerprints in any official file.

Once inside the terminal, she went straight to the ladies' room, where she locked herself into a stall and took off the red wig. She undid the pins from the tightly rolled buns at the back of her head, and her natural blonde hair tumbled loose. Next she removed the tinted contact lenses that had transformed her green eyes to dark brown. To accentuate her eyes, she had worn glasses with thick magnifying lenses. She flushed the contact lenses down the toilet and put the glasses in her purse, then buried the wig in a trash can and left the ladies' room. With long, exuberant strides, she walked to the boarding gate. In less than ten hours, Margaret Lee Dawson would be back home in San Fransisco after 'an extended holiday in Europe,' as all of her friends believed.

Margaret Lee Dawson, who would one day become the mother of Susan Brandon.

3

Laura Devane stood at a window in her room, smoking a cigarette. An oversized flannel robe was belted snugly around her thickening waist. Dispassionately she observed the savage storm with its earthquaking thunder and pyrotechnic lightning. 'Cool-hand Laura,' she was not so affectionately referred to within the film industry.

No doubt about it, it required more than a pretty face and a good figure to propel a minor talent named Rosie MacFarland from Bensonhurst, New York, to the rarefied heights of universal fame, popularity, and financial reward she had enjoyed in her halcyon days.

Growing up in a household with three older brothers and a father, all of whom were inveterate combatants in the old Irish tradition, Rosie was something of a street fighter herself, and she never outgrew her native instincts.

The first time she stepped onto a stage after being coerced by a good-looking young drama teacher into joining the high-school drama club, Rosie was hooked. 'I never knew the true meaning of life until I was out there on centre stage playing to an audience,' she reminisced in later years.

'It's so wonderful to be idolized by so many people and to get paid an exorbitant salary into the bargain.'

What she lacked in acting ability she made up for in perseverance and stamina. She worked hard at improving her craft throughout high school and after graduation by joining local little-theatre groups.

With guidance from Jim Devane, the drama teacher, she made steady progress, and with the help of a friend of his who was a part-time professional actor off Broadway, she got an audition for a small role, that of a chorine in a musical-variety show. Up until then, her sexual favours had been bestowed on the captain of the varsity football team in high school, on Jim Devane, and on the actor who secured the audition for her. Now she went right to the top and began sleeping on a regular basis with the show's producer. She moved out of the cold-water flat in Bensonhurst and into Sol Margolis's duplex apartment on East Forty-first Street.

Margolis was the pampered son of a rich Jewish widow whose husband had willed her his prosperous garment business. His goal was to direct and produce a smash Broadway show, and Rosie's was to star in that show. Neither ambition materialized, but Margolis's uncle, who was vice-president in charge of media for the J. Walter Thompson advertising agency, made him an offer to produce and direct television commercials, which he accepted, in turn hiring his 'shiksa,' as his mother vitriolically described Rosie, to be the featured performer in a toothpaste commercial and, later, a razor commercial. Her flawless complexion, her clear eyes, her cameo profile came across stunningly on the tube.

'That girl was born for the camera,' the sponsor crowed.

Overnight, Rosie was swamped with offers to appear in a variety of television commercials, but Jim Devane, whose advice and counsel she still sought, although she had stopped sleeping with him, convinced her to proceed with caution.

'First thing you must do is get the best agent in the business,' he said. 'Second, you should think about expanding your horizons. You don't want to sell toothpaste or toilet paper for the rest of your career. You've become a pretty damned good actress over the years. My advice is to head west, young girl: Hollywood. Movies, television – you're a natural.'

She took both pieces of advice, and the agent she hired flew out to the West Coast with a suitcase full of film clips of the commercials she'd made. The response from the studio moguls was unanimous: She was showered with contract offers. All that remained for her to do was to choose the fattest deal, and Rosie MacFarland was on her way.

The first order of the day, when she signed with Universal Pictures, was to select a more appropriate name for the studio's 'rising new star.'

A strong streak of Irish superstition ran through Rosie. 'My favourite movie of all time was *Laura,*' she told Jim Devane. 'Yes, that's it. I'm going to be Laura.'

Devane grinned and gripped her by the arms. 'You figure it will bring you good luck.'

'I feel it in my gut.'

'OK, then try this on for size. From the day you met me back in high school, you've been on a run of good luck. What do you say you and I get hitched? Then the lucky bond will be cemented. "Laura Devane" – I can see it in lights on the marquees of theatres all over the country.'

She thought about it with intense concentration, not seeing him, just staring off into space at those distant marquees. Finally she said, 'I like it. "Laura Devane" – it sounds lucky. All right, Jimmy, I'll marry you.'

The marriage lasted only two years, but the luck endured for more than a decade. Two marriages later, she met Richard Lemon when she played the female lead in his first American film.

From the very first take, it became apparent to everyone on the set that this team had a unique force flowing between them, a mercurial chemistry that caused the atmosphere around them to crackle with electricity. It was not that their personalities complemented each other; on the contrary, they were antagonists, and it was the tension between them, whether the mood of the scene was love, hate, apprehension, or grief, that reached out of the screen to seize the audience in an inexorable vice.

From that first day, their professional and personal lives would be forever entwined. It was an inevitability that the two would marry, just as it was an inevitability that they would be divorced. Despite their incompatibility, however, both Laura and Richard would admit without reservation that the chaotic years they had lived together as man and wife had been 'one helluva good show,' never a dull moment – 'the world's longest party,' Jan Danzig had once defined the union.

'Ruthless ambition' – the term was coined for Laura Devane. The axiom that one must be very careful how one treats people on one's way up because one is bound to meet the same people on one's way down is a respected one in Hollywood – respected by all but Laura Devane. Her battle plan for 'waging' life – war was a metaphor for life, in her lexicon – was to show no quarter to anyone on the way up in the film industry. She believed in wreaking total destruction on her competition: 'That way there's no one with enough power to pull you down.' It was a philosophy that worked for Laura Devane. Her first victim had been Jim Devane.

From the time they arrived in Hollywood, Jim acted as Laura's business manager, an arrangement that worked out satisfactorily until she began to command the big bucks. Her first picture, A *Rage in Heaven*, was an immediate success at the box office, and her name became a household word overnight. Her performance won her a nomination for the Academy Award for Best Actress, but she was beaten out by a more seasoned performer, whose name Laura added to her enemy list (she actually kept such a list).

Although Laura had signed a three-year contract with Universal at a generous salary, her agent, Sidney Carlton, a corporation attorney turned on to show business, demanded that the studio renegotiate. Well aware that Paramount, Warner Brothers, and Twentieth Century-Fox were waiting in the wings like vultures, all praying that the negotiations would fall through, Universal acceded to Carlton's extravagant demands, and Devane tripled her salary per picture.

Jim Devane voiced his disapproval: 'For Christ's sake, Rosie, how could you agree to something so unethical? I mean, Universal gave you your first break. It's more than just a contractual obligation; it's a moral obligation as well.'

'Fuck moral obligations! Fuck obligation, period. And don't give me any more shit about what Universal or anyone else, *including you*, did for me! The only reason anyone in this stinking world does anything for anyone else is if there's a fat payoff for them in doing it. Look out for number one, that's the name of the game. And *stop* calling me Rosie!'

It was about that time that Jim Devane began to drink heavily, and her agent warned her, 'You've got to get that Mick lush off your back, Laura, and get yourself a competent business manager. You're in the big time, and your husband is way out of his depth. Frankly, if you'll take my advice, you'll cut him out of your life as well as out of your business affairs. Listen to your Uncle Sidney.'

'I'll give it careful consideration, Sid.'

It was the same week she began work on a new picture, costarring with a popular singer who had turned his talents to acting with extraordinary success. Cam Douglas had a reputation for being a notorious 'swordsman,' in film parlance, and as his PR sheet at Universal attested, he had cut a swath through a gaggle of females in his lifetime, ranging from teeny boppers to Blue Book socialites.

The first time Laura and Cam met, witnesses swore that sparks flew back and forth between them. That same night they drove out to Cam's beach hideaway at Malibu and raced from the car to the house – 'like two horny teenagers with the hots,' Laura shamelessly described the episode later to intimate friends. Rushing into the bedroom, they got jammed together in the doorway.

'Where's your manners?' she snapped. 'Ladies first.'

'Fuck the ladies.'

'Which is what you do very well, so I hear; so I *hope*. Well, let's get with it, Cam baby.'

In the frenzy they literally tore off their clothing, blouse, shirt, skirt, trousers, brassiere, T-shirt, panties, jockey shorts flying through the air into different corners of the room.

Laura hurled herself upon the bed and opened her arms and legs to him. 'Come on! Hurry!'

He boasted the largest erection Laura had ever set eyes on, deep purple and as smooth as a rhino's horn. It excited her to the point of madness. As he mounted her and descended, she clutched at it with greedy fingers:

'Come to Mama.'

'Hey, take it easy . . . Oh, shit!'

'What the hell is it with you?'

'I just shot my wad. Sorry about that.'

She let out a long, anguished wail. 'You did *what?* You lousy sonovabitch! Now, what about me? If I don't come, I'm going to explode.'

'Not to worry, Laura sweetie. There's more than one way to skin a cat. Hey! I made a funny! Cat, pussy, – get it?'

'Henny Youngman I don't need at a time like this.'

'Relax.' He reversed his position on the bed, threw one leg over her body, and straddled her with his elbows braced on either side of her quivering hips. His hands slid under her thighs and parted them as his head came down on her *mons veneris*.

Laura moaned and writhed feverishly under his expert ministrations – and let the good times roll.

Two weeks later, Jim Devane returned home to their Holmby Hills mansion one night after attending a stag party. He was quite drunk; but soon he would be quite sober.

He parked the car in the garage and let himself into the darkened house by the side door. From the end of the hall, he saw that a dim light was on in the living room. He walked down the hall and stood in the archway, gaping in shock at the spectacle being enacted before his eyes. In a corner of the room stood a white baby-grand piano, and in front of the keyboard, a matching white swivel stool. And there, to his utter disbelief, appeared his beloved bride, Laura Devane, perched licentiously on the lap of Cam Douglas. Naturally, they were both naked; and since Cam's member was not visible, Jim had to conclude that it was snugly ensconced within Laura.

He staggered into the room, numb from the neck down. His expression was one of stupefaction. 'What the hell do you think you two are doing?' he rasped.

The couple did a pirouette on the swivel seat, so that Laura was facing Devane.

What does it look like we're doing, Jimsy?' she replied gaily. 'Help yourself to a drink. We'll be finished shortly.'

As Devane testified at the divorce hearing a month later, 'They never even missed a stroke!'

After the divorce was in the works, Devane went back to New York. A year later, Laura received a letter from his sister informing her that he had died in Bellevue Hospital in the alcoholic ward. Part of the letter still troubled Laura on bad nights in her dreams:

> They say it was the booze that got to him, but you and I know the real truth. It was you who got my brother. You got him as sure as if you had put a hit out on him. Yes, you murdered him, Rosie MacFarland – murdered his heart and his spirit at first and then his mind and his body, you fucking bitch!

Other victims followed in dramatic succession. There was a young ingenue named Beth Courtnay, who played a supporting role in a movie titled *Jennifer's Choice*. Even as she watched the first day's rushes, Laura Devane knew Beth meant trouble. Innocent-looking, doe-eyed, obsequiously deferential to everyone on the set; but beneath the beatific façade, there beat the heart of a jungle predator. So unobtrusively that no one but Laura was aware of it, she would steal a scene, step on other actors' lines, upstage the leading man, all accomplished masterfully. In short, she was a Xerox copy of Laura Devane who had descended on Hollywood five years earlier. Laura resolved that there was not room for the two of them at the studio.

There was an underground impresario by the name of Johnny Wheeler who operated out of Burbank. A tall, good-looking black with skin like polished ebony and a slight Jamaican accent, he had once been a bit player, but decided early in his career that he could profit more by becoming a 'boss player.' His business was sex and drugs – pot, hash, cocaine, peyote, opium, morphine – the life of any good swinging Hollywood party. And as there was no lack of aspiring starlets, every shape, colour, and variety, who would eagerly take a vow of promiscuity if it meant furthering their careers, Johnny's stable abounded with pretty girls, whom he booked for stag affairs, private parties, and intimate hotel rendezvous with visiting VIPs.

Laura and Johnny were good friends. One Sunday she drove out to his posh Santa Monica villa, overlooking the sea, in her chauffeured limousine. Johnny was on his outdoor patio playing gin with two white girls in bikinis.

He was surprised to see Laura but pleased. 'This must be your day for slumming, baby. What are you drinking?'

'Gin and – '

'Tony!'

From around a corner of the house, there appeared a massive man, nearly seven feet tall, broad as an ox and with a face that resembled a beat-up catcher's mitt. Tony Vasile, onetime wrestling champion of the world, second-rate pug, and ex-Mafia enforcer, was Johnny Wheeler's man Friday and bodyguard.

'Gin and tonic for Miss Devane, and bring it into the den.' He winked at Laura. 'You wouldn't be here if you didn't have some private business on your mind.'

She patted his cheek. 'You're so clever, Johnny.'

Ignoring the girls, he took her elbow and escorted her into the den. 'So, sit already.'

She took a cigarette from a slim gold case, and he lit it for her. Then he sat hipshot on one corner of his desk. 'Let's have it, sweetie.'

She waited until Tony had served their drinks and departed. 'I want to ruin someone's reputation.'

He grinned. 'So what else is new? Who is she and what do you have in mind? It *is* a she, isn't it?'

'You're positively clairvoyant. Her name is Beth Courtnay.'

His head bent forward and he began to laugh softly, chin almost resting on his breastbone. 'Hey, what about that! Oh, man, you are really something, Laura. Courtnay, she's the chick who's in that picture you're making. I've heard a lot of scuttlebutt about that wench.' Then, with a sly wink: 'Hear tell she's going to be the successor to Laura Devane in time to come.'

'Her time has already come.'

'What's the strategy?'

'We put her in a compromising situation – a very compromising situation – discredit her Rebecca-of-Sunnybrook-Farm credibility. She doesn't have enough clout at the studio yet to survive a tacky scandal. You dig me, man?'

'I dig. You set it up; I'll arrange the rest.'

'I've invited her to spend the weekend of August sixth at my place on the pretence of going over some key scenes in the script.'

He went behind his desk and made notes on his calendar in small, neat script. 'I'll get to work on it and let you know what's happening.'

'Thanks, Johnny . . . and name your own fee.'

'We'll discuss that when the mission has been successfully accomplished. You want another drink?'

'No thanks. Besides, you have guests. It was thoughtless of me to barge in.'

He chuckled. 'Fuck 'em.'

She groped him in the crotch. 'I suspect that's what you have in mind. Thanks, anyway, and keep in touch.'

As Wheeler watched her get into her limo, he turned and smiled at Tony. 'You ever hear of Lady Macbeth?'

'Naw, I never worked for no Limeys.'

Johnny laughed and slapped Tony's hard-muscled belly with the back of his hand. '*That* lady was a pussy-cat compared to this lady.'

On a Friday afternoon, Laura Devane's limousine picked up Beth Courtnay at her apartment and drove her out to Laura's palatial estate in Holmby Hills. The young actress feasted her eyes on the many enchantments of the property: the majestic iron gate that opened onto a winding private road lined by cedar trees on each side; at the top of the hill, a gravelled parking area that could easily accommodate a hundred cars; and the grand Georgian mansion itself, a sprawling brick structure with classic courses and cornices of white stone and trimmings of white-painted woodwork. 'Feasted her eyes' was a literal phrase. Beth was possessed by a ravenous longing and hunger that was physical as well as mental.

Later, sitting poolside beneath an enormous umbrella and sipping frozen daiquiris with Laura, she was filled with envy. 'Someday I'm going to have a layout just like this, Laura,' she said.

Laura smiled benignly. 'Of course you will, my dear. After all, I didn't get where I am overnight.' *Little twerp! You can't even sit on the same john seat as Laura Devane, much less on her throne!*

Beth's eyes shone with malice and spite. 'Well, you were a model first of all and an actress second. You had to learn your craft. I have a classical background on the stage.'

It required all of Laura's acting ability and discipline to weather that blast and to restrain the urge to hurl the pitcher of daiquiris into the little slut's face. The smile was pasted on her lips.

'All of us must find different paths to the top.'

'I'm glad we can get together about the script, Laura. There are several scenes I have some innovative ideas about. I've already been over them with Jack Sanderson, and he was very impressed. I'd like to bounce them off you.'

And I'd like to bounce you into the pool, you little bitch! The audacity of you to make suggestions to the director! Laura gritted her teeth and listened.

'Take the scene where Clark and I are out on the balcony, embracing, and you come out of the French doors from the ballroom. The way it is in the script, the camera has a medium two-shot of us when you emerge from the background and enter. Now, I think the scene would be far more effective if the camera were to be behind you and dolly along as you walk out onto the balcony.'

Sure you do, you fucking barracuda! You and Clark get the two-shot in any case, and I give the camera the back of my head and my ass! Hold that tiger, Devane! After tonight, the whole thing will be academic, anyway.

'Why don't we talk about it after dinner, dear? We'll lock ourselves in the projection room and thrash it all out.'

For the rest of the afternoon and through dinner, Beth Courtnay talked about little else but herself. That was customarily Laura's role, but, on this occasion, she deferred modestly to her houseguest. She tuned out most of what the younger woman was saying.

'Yes, I'm sure it was at Stratford, *The Crucible*. Miller wrote the part for me, everyone said.' She giggled. 'May I have some more of this bubbly water?'

'Of course. Henderson, some more Moêt for Miss Courtnay.'

The bitch has a hollow leg, and that's all to the good. She's tipsy right now.

After dinner, Laura took Beth to the projection room, a small, unattractive building remote from the main house, camouflaged by trees and shrubbery so as not to present an eyesore to visitors.

Beth was agog. 'Imagine having your own movie theatre! Even the seats are special.'

'And each one an easy chair,' said Laura archly. 'We can seat fifty people.'

Off to one side of the general sitting area was a cosy little room with chairs and sofas arranged in a semicircle in front of a fireplace, and a fully stocked bar in a corner.

'How about a grasshopper?' Laura said. 'It's a great after-dinner drink and goes well with coffee.'

'I'll give it a try.'

When the butler arrived with a silver coffee service, Laura asked him to make a grasshopper for Beth and a brandy for her, then dismissed him. As she poured Beth's coffee, she let a small gelatin capsule in her left hand drop into the steaming brew. It would melt instantly. She then produced two scripts of *Jennifer's Choice*. 'Let's start reading from scene one twenty, the first time Marion suspects that Clark and Gwen are having a clandestine affair.'

'Can we do it standing? I work better when I can move about.'

'The only way to work. All right, Gwen, take it from the top.'

It was a well-written scene: good crackling dialogue that rolled off the tongue trippingly, as the bard might have put it. Laura had to admit grudgingly that Beth was a damned good actress. She truly lived her role, and her voice was crisp in spite of all she had had to drink. Johnny had said that the drug would take effect in about a half-hour. Laura glanced at her wristwatch. Soon.

They were halfway through the next scene when Beth abruptly staggered and bumped into the couch. She put a hand to her head. 'Hey, those grasshoppers pack a wallop.'

'Are you all right?'

'I think so; but I'd better sit down for a few minutes.' She eased herself down gingerly onto a chair. 'Whew! Oh, God! The damned room is spinning.' She placed her hands over her eyes and rocked to and fro.

A smiling Laura stood over her, arms folded, the script

rolled up in one hand. 'Perhaps you'd like to use the john? Cold water might help.'

'Good idea.' Beth's voice was thick now, like a phonograph record playing at the wrong speed. 'I . . . I . . . ' She rose from the chair, took two steps forward, and collapsed on the rug.

Laura kneeled down beside her. 'Beth! Beth, can you hear me?' A sense of triumph filled her. The bitch was out cold – like a stone.

Behind the movie screen, there was a small bedroom. For special parties, Laura would hire a professional projectionist, and movies would run continually for hours for those who cared to watch them. The bedroom was for his use if he wanted to sleep over. She walked back to the room and knocked on the closed door:

'Johnny, the pigeon has pooped out. You can come out now.'

The door opened, and Johnny Wheeler appeared, a roguish smile on his handsome face. 'We're ready, babes. Let's go, you guys.'

Two men came up behind him, one white, one black – sleezy-looking types. They looked vaguely familiar to her.

'Best professional studs money can buy,' Johnny joked.

Then it came to her: They were featured players in porno movies. She must have seen them a dozen times.

'You're in classy company, gentlemen,' Johnny cautioned, 'so watch your manners. This is *the* Laura Devane. Miss Devane, Paul and Ike.'

'A pleasure, Miss Devane,' said Ike, the black man. 'I've seen all of your pictures.'

Laura smiled. 'Can't say I can say the same for your pictures, Ike, but I've seen a *few* in my time.'

The men laughed, and Johnny turned serious. 'No more of this idle chatter. Let's get to work. Where is she?'

Laura took them to where Beth was crumpled up on the floor. Paul, the biggest of the three, stooped and lifted her up in his arms. He carried her into the bedroom and laid her down gently on the bed. Johnny bent over her and patted her on both cheeks. She stirred briefly, but did not respond otherwise.

'She's out good,' he said with satisfaction. 'All right, let's get her clothes off.'

Laura felt a pang of self-recrimination as she watched the men remove Beth's dress, slip, bra, and panties. They folded the articles neatly on a chair and then began to remove their own clothing, totally oblivious of Laura's presence.

Johnny looked at her, frowning. 'Would you prefer not to watch this performance, Laura?'

'Wouldn't miss it for the world,' she said in a hard voice.

He shrugged. 'I'm sure the boys have no objection.'

Ike grinned. 'Not at all. It's always a thrill to have one's peers in the audience.'

'Never get tired of your work, eh, boys?' she asked.

'Do you?' asked Paul.

'No, but your work is so physically demanding.'

'When you got it, you got it; right, man?' Ike poked Paul in the ribs.

Laura's heartbeat accelerated, and a hot flash swept through her body like wildfire. The two of them were better endowed in the masculinity department than any other men she had ever seen, including Cam Douglas. And the sight of Beth's ripe body lying naked and defenceless on the bed induced instantaneous arousal.

'I can hardly wait to get to work,' Ike enthused.

Johnny took from the dresser his Nikon 35-mm single-lens reflex camera with built-in flash and exposure meter. 'Can't beat this baby for jobs like this . . . OK, Ike, you're on first.'

'You want me to go all the way?'

'Yeah.'

'Is she a virgin?'

Laura snorted. 'Like Fanny Hill.'

Johnny was still not satisfied. 'She's limp as a rag doll. It ain't gonna look natural. Tell you what, Paul, take that robe sash over there on the chair, and we'll tie her ankles behind Ike's back.'

Laura's excitement was rising to fever pitch as she watched Johnny and Paul wrap Beth's pliable legs around Ike's waist and bind her ankles together so that her heels rested in the small of the man's back.

'Beautiful!' Johnny said, and picked up the camera again. 'Lights, camera, action!'

Ike had no trouble penetrating her, and when he did, she

let out a faint moan.

'Right on!' Johnny crowed, snapping away furiously, hopping around the bed to shoot from a variety of angles. 'I swear to God, when she opened her mouth, she looked like she was coming!'

'*I* sure am!' Ike said in an ecstatic tone.

Talk about hot pants! I wouldn't mind being in her place right now, Laura mused, savouring the vicarious pleasure the enactment fired up in her loins.

Satisfied with the shots he had so far, Johnny told Paul to replace Ike on the bed. And, with certain novel variations, the performance was repeated.

'Roll her over on her belly and we'll do some takes doggy fashion,' he directed. That accomplished: 'OK, now we go to fellatio. You on the bed, Ike. Paul, you'll have to support her weight; you won't appear in the frame. I'll get in close so that we'll see her only from the waist up . . . No, I've got to get higher to delete Paul . . . Yeah, man, perfect.'

'You said a mouthful,' Laura remarked, bending over for a more advantageous look.

After about an hour, Johnny put down the Nikon and lit a cigarette. 'Let's wrap it up, guys and gals. I've got more than enough to suit your purposes, Laura.'

'I think so. All right, boys, why don't you mosey out to the bar and mix yourselves some drinks? I want to tidy up, and then you can help me dress her. How long will that sedative work?'

'Four hours. Plenty of time. OK, grab your duds, boys, and we'll retire to the lounge.'

Later on, as the three men and Laura sat around the bar in the projection room, Johnny inquired, 'What are you going to tell her happened? You know damned well that little lady is going to know she's been fragged.'

'Leave her to me,' Laura said confidently.

'You're the boss lady.' He looked at his watch and yawned. 'Let's get out of here. I'm bushed.'

'How do you think *we* feel?' Ike jived.

Laura bid them good night and went back to the room to check on Beth. She was fully clothed and sleeping peacefully underneath a quilt.

Laura beamed down at her and recited softly:

' "And by a sleep to say we end
The heartache and the thousand natural shocks
That flesh is heir to, 'tis a consummation
Devoutly to be wish'd. To die, to sleep;
To sleep: perchance to dream: ay, there's the rub." '

She stooped over the bed and patted Beth's cheek. 'Best performance you ever gave, honey. Pleasant dreams.'

The following morning, Laura was eating a hearty breakfast of bacon, eggs, and kippers in the sun-bathed dining room when Beth appeared in the doorway, looking pale and wan, and deeply troubled.

'Well, good morning,' Laura said cheerily; 'or I should say "Good afternoon." The two of us really tied one on last night, didn't we?'

Beth swayed and held onto the doorway jamb. 'I . . . I . . . I'm terribly vague on everything.'

'That makes two of us. You look even worse than I do. I'll have Henderson mix you a bloody mary.'

'No, no thanks, I couldn't get it down. Just black coffee.' She staggered over to the table and sat down with her head cradled in her hands. 'God! I've never blacked out before in my life. Last thing I remember is you and I reading the script in the projection room, and then – ' She broke off helplessly.

'You don't remember Bill and Don stopping by?'

'Bill and Don? You mean, there *were* men with us?'

'Why, of course. I must say that you and Don were getting on very, very well indeed when Bill and I left you.'

'You left me alone, with this . . . this Don?'

'Bill and I went back to the house, put on the stereo, and danced. You and Don were still making out over in the projection room when Bill left.' She smiled and winked. 'I didn't think it would be discreet to interrupt whatever you were up to.'

In a dull voice, Beth muttered, 'I guess that explains it.'

'Explains what, dear?'

'Nothing . . . It isn't important.'

Laura looked at her over the rim of her coffee cup. Her eyes were dancing with glee. *So long, sucker!*

Five days later, four brown paper envelopes were delivered, one each to the chief of Universal Studios, to Jack Valenti, the commissioner of the Motion Picture Review Board, to Beth Courtnay's agent, and to the Los Angeles *Times*. After studying the flagrantly candid photographs contained within the envelopes, the first three recipients agreed that Beth Courtnay's film career was *kaput*. And a headline in the entertainment section of the *Times* ran: 'Universal Ingenue Revealed as Porno Queen.'

Nine months later, living with a run-down musician in a cheap flat in West Hollywood, Beth Courtnay killed herself with an overdose of heroin. The autopsy confirmed that she was pregnant.

4

Laura Devane was still standing at the window when dawn crept across the mesa from the eastern horizon. The ashtray on the windowsill was mounded with cigarette butts. With the onset of daylight the storm slackened off markedly, the thunder retreating across the western mountain ranges, and the lightning flaring only intermittently above the thick, low cloud-cover.

'Like a damned shroud,' she muttered. She put out the last butt, stripped off her robe and nightgown, and went into the bathroom to take a shower. She avoided looking at her naked reflection in the mirror on the bathroom door. The ravages of age and a lifetime of intemperance were too painful to confront this early in the morning.

Back in the bedroom, she struggled into the jeans the Ameses had provided. She could not fasten the top waist-button, but the sloppy-Joe sweater hid the button and the embarrassing roll of fat that bulged over the waistband.

Richard Lemon sat naked on the edge of his bed, smoking a cigarette and contemplating his flaccid penis. He carried on a dialogue with himself:

'Dick, old chap, when was the last time that worm was hard?'

'Too long ago to remember.'

'Do you think, perhaps, that any of the quim here could get a rise out of it? That Brandon wench is leggy, big-titted, and has an arse that's asking to be sodomized. Or what about the black bitch? I'll wager she's insatiable. Nancy Ames – now, she's the mellow, experienced type. Scratch the Danzig dyke. Which leaves us with dear old Laura, probably the best bet for an aging satyr like you; comfortable as an old shoe, too.'

'Listen, you horny bastard, all that's on my mind now is getting off this accursed mountain. By God, it's got to be today! I can't spend another night here. In all my life, I've never had a more vivid, realistic dream than the one last night.' Ames was right: The mescaline had come back to haunt him.

When Susan Brandon awoke, she saw Kevin sitting cross-legged at the foot of the bed, fully clothed and staring at her intently. 'What are you doing?' she inquired drowsily, yawning and stretching like a cat.

'Waiting for you to wake up.'

'It's not polite to ogle someone who is asleep. It's the same as being a Peeping Tom. The Gypsies believe that if you watch a person while he or she is fast asleep, you can steal the soul from the body.'

'But you're not a Gypsy.'

'All of the Nortons have been nomads, Gypsies, ever since they were dispossessed by the Ameses in the Cattle War.'

'You do have that quality at that. Say, what time did you come to bed last night?'

'Not too late. I had a drink with Walter Ames downstairs, and that quieted down my nerves. You were asleep when I came up.'

'You had a drink with Walter Ames, did you?' His gaze was probing. 'It would appear that, at long last, the Nortons and the Ameses have finally buried the hatchet.'

Her smile was enigmatic. 'Then again, things are not always what they appear to be.'

Jennie Bostwick's awakening was a sensual experience. She dreamed that a man was kissing her breasts; only, when she opened her eyes, she discovered it was no dream. Larry had one arm across her body, and his lips were teasing her nipples.

'Hey, man, that's not nice at all!'

'You don't like it?'

'I love it. What I meant was, it is uncivil to make love to a woman when she's asleep. Like getting a gal drunk and laying her.'

His hand stroked her belly and worked its way down between her thighs. 'My apologies. But now that you *are* awake, would you be interested in knocking off a little piece?'

'A very large piece.' She put her arms around his neck and drew his mouth down on hers.

Across the hall, Jan Danzig sat in front of the vanity brushing her short, coarse hair. It had the texture of a man's hair. She smiled at the comparison. Why shouldn't her hair be like a man's hair? She thought like a man. All of her emotions were of a masculine nature.

For example, she had contracted a bad case of the hots for their hostess the moment she set eyes on her. All night she had tossed and turned restlessly, tortured by lurid fantasies of her and Nancy locked in lascivious embrace, engaged in the most erotic acts imaginable. Nancy's rigid nipples thrusting against the palms of her hands; Nancy's round buttocks quivering in her ardent grasp; Nancy's thighs parting to her adoring gaze, revealing to Jan the gateway to the Garden of Eden, wherein she would sip the heady nectar from the tree of life . . . *Steady, old girl, steady!*

She pulled on a sweater and blue corduroy slacks, then walked to the bedroom door and opened it a crack. She peered up and down the hall, noting with satisfaction that the Ameses' door was still closed. As a cub reporter, she'd been told that patience was the biggest virtue a professional newshound could have. She folded her arms and leaned against the wall, waiting. Patiently.

Walter Ames came out of the shower with a towel wrapped

around his waist. He eyed Nancy's attire – dungarees, heavy flannel shirt, and hiking boots – cynically. 'You are an optimist, my dear. Nobody is going to get off the mesa today. Have you seen the cloud cover?'

'At least the storm is over. I think the overcast is beginning to lift.'

He snorted. 'I'll put my money on the Indians. Gall said last night the worst is yet to come.'

Nancy shrugged. 'I thought I'd drive down to the canyon bridge and see just how badly it's damaged.'

'It's down; you heard Chief.'

'What about the old footbridge along the bridle path? It was sturdy enough to ride a horse across.'

'If the main bridge couldn't bear up under the onslaught of the storm, odds are that the footbridge is demolished.'

'Just the same, I'm going to look. Besides, I want to get out of the house and walk.'

'Restless, eh?'

She didn't reply, but her eyes were riveted on him as he dropped the towel and stepped into his Jockey shorts. Walt's naked body never failed to excite her: his flat, rippling belly, narrow hips, muscled thighs and buttocks, most of all his ponderous male sexuality. She forced her eyes away, loathing herself for her vulnerability, for her wild jealousy over his flirtation with Susan Brandon – *hot-pants little bitch!*

Cursorily she asked him, 'What time did you come to bed?'

'Don't know. About four, I think.'

'What were you doing?'

'Drinking. Thinking.'

'I did a lot of thinking myself last night, about home . . . Walt, let's go back to Connecticut.'

'You know damned well I can't go back until I settle things with Galloway down in El Paso. I thought you liked it up here on Skull Mountain.'

'I do. I just wish we could get rid of our damned guests!'

'Tch, tch. Now, is that a convivial attitude? After all, they didn't crash their plane here on purpose?'

'I know,' she said doggedly. 'Just the same, I want them out of here at the first possible opportunity.' *I want that bitch Susan out of here before it goes any further, this thing between you and her.*

'Rest assured they feel the same way, but all of it is wishful thinking. We're socked in from the air, and they sure as hell won't have that canyon bridge operable for days, maybe weeks. However, as soon as the rain ceases permanently, the water level in the canyon will fall fast, and we can drive out across the Frisby conduit.'

Nancy stood up and walked to the door. 'I'll see you downstairs.'

Halfway down the hall, Nancy heard someone call to her and turned.

'Nancy, can I speak with you a moment?'

It was Jan Danzig, standing in the doorway of her bedroom.

'Of course. What can I do for you, Jan?'

Nancy was somewhat intimidated in the journalist's presence. There was something vaguely sinister about her; at the same time, something fascinating. The analogy of the bird and the snake came to her; the bird could easily fly off and escape, yet it could not resist the lure of the reptile. It almost seemed that its fate had been predestined from birth by some avian legacy. Nancy felt like the bird at this moment.

'Come inside, will you?' Jan stepped aside so that the other woman could enter; then she closed the door firmly and, to Nancy's astonishment, turned the key in the lock.

Nancy attempted to make a joke of it: 'We are being melodramatic, aren't we, Jan? What's this all about?'

'It's important enough so that I don't want anyone to disturb us.' She toyed with a cigarette before lighting it.

'Can we make this fast? I have to help Pedro with breakfast.'

Jan studied her through eyelids narrowed against the smoke curling along one cheek. 'Maybe it's better to mind one's own business, let sleeping dogs lie and all that, but my business is to snoop and tell. I've been called hard, ruthless, predatory, brutal, and without conscience. It's how the bloody hypocrites of this world – and that comprises about ninety-five per cent of the population – rationalize their own petty deceits, duplicities, dishonours, and cowardice. Jan Danzig tells it like it is, and anyone who doesn't like it can go screw!'

Nancy was confused and wary. 'What on earth are you leading up to? I don't see what this has to do with – '

'Hear me out.' Jan came close to Nancy and put a hand on her shoulder. 'I like you, Nancy. I sense that you are a woman of deep integrity.'

'Thank you.'

Jesus! You should know the depth of my integrity. It could be measured with the dipstick in the crankcase of your car!

'I won't procrastinate any further. There is something you deserve to know, because even the best of them, men, are bastard chauvinist pigs. They've been exploiting women since the beginning of time, and they're still working at it, even the ones who pay lip service to ERA and let their female associates pick up lunch cheques.'

Nancy felt herself being engulfed by an intangible turbulence as intense as those tangible forces of nature that had downed the *Golden Eagle* Cessna. And suddenly she thought of the terrifying golden eagle that had materialized on the altar inside the Apache ceremonial lodge.

'I don't think I want to hear anymore.' She backed away in the direction of the door.

Jan's glare impaled her. 'Yes, you do want to hear. You do want to hear about Susan Brandon and your husband.'

'That does it!' She turned and ran to the door, fumbling with the key.

Jan sprang up behind her and grabbed her roughly by the shoulders, turning her around and pinning her against the door with her hands braced against the portal.

'Do you know where Walt was last night after we got back from the village?'

'Why, of course,' she lied. 'He went straight to bed with me.'

Jan's smile was condescending. 'If you truly believe that, you're pathetic. The fact is, at four o'clock this morning, your husband was screwing Susan Brandon on the couch in his study.'

Overcome by anger and indignation, Nancy lashed out at the other woman: 'You're lying! You delight in burying people in lies and slander. Oh, I've read all about you, Jan Danzig! You're like a sadistic child pulling the wings off flies and butterflies!'

Nancy's face suddenly dissolved in a wash of tears as the terrible pain tore through her heart like a dagger. *You know she's telling the truth. You knew it instinctively when you woke up this morning.* She was gentle and consoling now.

'Don't let it rip you to pieces, Nancy. He isn't worth it. No man is. Honestly, if I hadn't told you what I saw, I couldn't live with myself. It was disgusting!' *Another twist of the dagger.*

'What . . . what did you see?' Nancy, powerless to stop herself, playing the bird to Danzig's snake . . . She did not resist when Jan put an arm around her shoulders and led her over to the bed.

'You had better sit down, dear.'

Nancy obeyed, and Jan sat down beside her, the arm still about Nancy's sagging shoulders.

'I couldn't sleep, so I went downstairs to find a book in Walt's library, only I didn't go in, because Walt and Susan were in there making love on the couch. The lightning lit up the room like daylight.'

Nancy closed her eyes tight and shook her head from side to side. 'No, no . . . Walt, how could you do this to me?'

'There's more. They did it a second time.' And exercising poetic licence: 'They engaged in all kinds of erotic foreplay, fellatio, cunnilingus, and some other acts that shocked even me, and I've been around a long time.'

Nancy collapsed into Jan's arms, her face buried against her shoulder. Jan stroked her back, her hair, and kissed the side of her head:

'Poor baby. That's it; let it all out.'

Gradually Nancy's sobbing slackened, and her body went still and limp in Jan's embrace. A warm, dreamy lassitude pervaded her. It was pleasurable to be patted and comforted, a reversion to childhood. Jan Danzig's hands were skilled in the art of healing wounds, both physical and emotional. Under Nancy's sweater now, gently stroking her abdomen, one working downwards, the other upwards, teasing fingers slipping inside the elastic of her panties, fondling her breasts, tweaking her nipples . . .

Nancy went rigid as she comprehended what was happening. 'Jan! Stop it! What do you think you're doing?'

'I know what I'm doing, and so do you.' She kissed the

nape of Nancy's neck.

Nancy struggled to free herself, but her strength was no match for the other woman's. Jan Danzig was an athlete; she could beat most men at tennis, golf, swimming, and arm wrestling.

'Don't fight it, darling,' she cooed to Nancy. 'Let yourself go. Once you get used to the idea, you'll realize how wonderful sex can be with another woman, much better than with a man. Men, they're all infantile and selfish, concerned with their own adolescent self-gratification.'

'Let me go this instant or I'll scream for help.'

Nancy renewed her efforts to escape from Jan, but the columnist pushed her back on the bed and pinned her down with one arm and one leg across her body. Her free hand pulled Nancy's dungarees and panties over her hips and thighs and down to her knees.

'Scream all you want, sweetie. Can you imagine what your dear husband would think if he could see us like this?'

'Please, I'm not a lesbian. *Please* let me go . . . Oh, dear God, help me!'

Nancy thrashed about in desperation as Jan lavished kisses on her quivering belly. This couldn't be happening, not to her. She was, quite literally, being raped by another woman! No, it was just a recurring hallucination invoked by the mescaline she had consumed the night before. But Jan Danzig's artful lips were all too real. Nancy gasped and bucked as Jan's tongue found her naval.

'No! No! You must stop. It's . . . it's not right.'

It was the first break in her defences, and Jan, with her worldly wisdom, knew it. Nancy was no longer protesting that she did not want to participate in this act of inverted love, but rather that what they were doing was not right, not acceptable to society.

'But it *is* right,' she assured Nancy. 'All the world has come to realize that, darling. Homosexuality is as healthy and normal as heterosexuality. Whatever feels good has to be right. And this does feel good; don't deny it.'

Nancy moaned, and her eyes rolled up and back in their sockets, and she surrendered to the domination of her partner. She fancied she was lying on a beach with the sun hot and energy-sapping on her nude body. Tepid waves lapped soothingly over her feet and ankles, grew stronger as they reached her thighs and moved higher, even higher, on her body – warm, wet, so, so soothing – until at last a fierce, crashing breaker swept over her, and she was totally submerged in a breathtaking, tumultuous sea of pleasure.

I only wish you would walk in here and see me like this, you dirty bastard! Nancy couldn't wait to confront Walt with the truth:

I made love with another woman, darling, and it was better than it ever was with you!

5

Conversation was curtailed during breakfast. Everyone's attention was fixed on the radio:

> 'The worst storm to strike the tri-state area of Colorado, New Mexico, and Texas in this century is still wreaking havoc over thousands of square miles throughout the Midwest. Torrential rains, accompanied by hurricane winds, thunder, and lightning, have so far taken a toll of human life and property unsurpassed by that of any other natural disaster recorded in the annals of the United States Weather Bureau. Among the casualties are nine commercial aircraft, five of which are listed as missing and presumed downed in remote sections of the mountains. Air-search rescue attempts are being hampered by air turbulence and heavy cloud cover in southern Colorado and northern New Mexico. Among the missing aircraft is a charter Cessna whose passenger list includes famous film stars Richard Lemon and Laura Devane, who were flying from Denver to Lincoln City, New Mexico, where their latest movie, *Blood on the Sun,* is being shot . . . '

'It's the same drivel they've been repeating for the past

twenty-four hours,' Walt said. 'Pedro, turn the damned thing off.'

'Not exactly the same drivel,' Dick Lemon taunted. 'This time they did not refer to Jan. Her newsworthiness has been exhausted . . . Hey, where is she, by the way?'

'Sleeping late, I imagine,' Laura said. 'God knows, none of us got much sleep last night, with all that thunder and lightning.'

Walt Ames put down his fork and frowned on his plate.

Pedro, a small, wizened Mexican, wearing a white jacket, came up behind him and asked, 'Hey, boss, you no like my eggs Benedict today?'

Walt smiled up at him. 'No, Pedro, they're superb, as usual. I was just wondering where Mrs Ames is. She came down before me, didn't she?'

Pedro shrugged. 'I no see her. You want me to go upstairs and look for her?'

'Yes, you do that. Maybe – ' He stopped abruptly as Nancy and Jan came into the dining room.

'Good morning, you all,' Jan said cheerfully.

'Where have you two been?' he demanded.

'I met Jan on my way downstairs, and we decided to go for a walk,' Nancy explained. 'It's positively eerie out there: trees and boulders split in half by the lightning, mist swirling about . . . It's like the beginning of time. I half expected to see a Neanderthal man come lumbering out of a cave.'

'Or a dinosaur,' Jan said. 'I'm famished. Oh, good, eggs Benedict – my favourite.'

Walt summoned Pedro. 'Serve the ladies, and more coffee all around.'

Pedro brought in two more plates from the kitchen, and while he was pouring the coffee, Chief came in the back door. He stood in the kitchen doorway, waiting for Pedro to finish serving.

Walt saw him first. 'Chief, come in. Sit down. Have you had your breakfast?'

'Yes. I just came back from the north meadow. I think maybe we can put the cattle out to pasture this morning.'

'Do you think the storm is over?'

'For the time being. Gall says it is but a temporary lull, but we can take advantage of it.'

'Use your judgment, then. Any casualties among the livestock?'
'No, but the animals all are suffering from a bad case of nerves.'
'Why should they be an exception?' Laura said. 'I'm off the wall myself.'
Dick went to the sideboard and poured a generous shot of gin into his orange juice. 'What are the chances of getting out of here today, Chief?'
'Not good, Mr Lemon. The village sent out two messengers at dawn to Fort Stanton. The army engineers should be here sometime this afternoon to start work on the canyon bridge.'
Laura's fork clattered on her plate. 'You mean to say there's a way out of this never-never land?'
'There's a footbridge. It suffered bad damage, but it's still standing.'
'That's unbelievable!' Walt said. 'The big bridge was knocked down, and that flimsy catwalk weathered the storm.'
'It is a great deal more flexible than the big bridge,' Chief explained. 'How is it said in boxing? "Roll with the punch." '
'God damn it!' Laura said. 'Why didn't you tell us about the messengers? They could have notified the studio that we're alive.'
'It is already done, madam,' Chief said. 'They will tell the authorities that you survived the plane crash.'
'You told them our names? Laura Devane and Richard Lemon?'
'Names do not matter. There will be a rescue party here as soon as it is possible.'
'Devane and Lemon, just two names out of the phone directory in these parts, dear,' Jan reminded her. 'The army boys at Fort Stanton were toddlers in diapers when you and Dick were front-page items.'
'Up yours, Danzig!' Laura growled. 'Dick, pour me a shot of bourbon, will you?'
Dick was not paying attention. He walked over to the Indian. 'Chief, you say these messengers got out across the footbridge. If they can do it, why can't we?'
'Very dangerous crossing, and there is no transportation.

Many miles to walk across rugged terrain to reach the nearest community.'

'You'd never make it, Dick,' Walt confirmed. 'You'd poop out in the wilderness with blistered feet and a dragging ass.'

'Don't be so certain of that,' Dick said. 'I've got a lot of staying power when the going is rough.'

'Staying power?' Laura jeered. 'Just ask any of his ex-wives!'

'Oh, shut your hole, Devane!' he snapped. 'Listen, Walt, you have saddle horses. We could ride out.'

'Out of the question, old man. It's risky enough for a man to cross that bridge. To take a horse over it would be suicidal.'

'I wonder.' Dick rubbed his stubbled chin and took a long swallow of his gin and orange juice.

Walt folded his napkin at the side of his plate and stood up. 'I think I'll have a look outside. Anyone care to join me?'

The 'ayes' were unanimous.

'Can we go back to the plane?' Susan inquired. 'It would be nice to get some of our luggage. After all, Nancy's wardrobe is not inexhaustible. And there are traveller's cheques and valuables in our bags.'

'That depends on whether or not the water in the ravine is down to a passable level. If it is, Chief will take the truck back to the plane and retrieve all of your possessions.' He smiled. 'I don't think you have to be concerned about looters making off with your luggage. The incidence of crime on Skull Mountain is negligible.'

'Very amusing,' Laura said. 'That entire Injun village could live in luxury for the rest of their collective lives for what they could fence my emerald necklace for.'

Chief regarded her with disdain. 'Possibly they could buy back Manhattan Island?'

'I didn't know those Indians were Apaches,' she said guilelessly.

'Oh, Christ!' Dick moaned. 'Why don't you shut up, Laura?'

'Better get some warm clothing,' Walt advised. 'It's cold outside.'

Somewhat later they met in the foyer, bundled up in

sweaters, machinaws, and all wearing hiking boots. Walt led the way.

Dick hugged himself as they emerged into the damp, cold air. 'Reminds me of the English moors, with all that swirling mist. I keep expecting to see the Hound of the Baskervilles come bounding over a ridge.'

The landscape was, indeed, raw and bleak. They clambered over the debris that had been strewn over the flatland beyond the house by high winds. Felled trees were juxtaposed like jackstraws on all sides. One huge boulder had been split cleanly down the middle, and the exposed surfaces looked as if they had been polished by a lapidary.

'White-hot lightning,' Walt said. 'I wouldn't have wanted to be here when it happened.'

They reached the ravine that divided the mesa, running from east to west. The freshet created by the heavy rain was lower and less turbulent than it had been the day before, when they were travelling from the crash site to the Ames place, but it was still too fierce to navigate by jeep or truck.

'What do you think, Chief?' Walt asked.

'If there is no more rain, it will be passable in another hour or so. I'll keep checking.'

'Good . . . Well, we may as well return to the house.'

On the way back, the group disbanded into a straggling column. Walt set a rapid pace, and only Susan kept up with him.

'I hope we don't get out today,' she said in a low voice. 'I'd like one more night like last night.'

'So would I, but I don't think it would be a good idea.'

'Oh?'

'We were both hyped up from mescaline and booze. Now, in the cold light of day, I realize how dangerous it was. Christ! Anyone might have walked in on us – Nancy, Kevin.'

'You know what they say about stolen sweets: The risks enhance the enjoyment.'

'Yeah. Well, it was fun, but I'm getting too old to play chicken with you sexual hot-rodders. Besides, I don't believe you want to break up your marriage any more than I want to break up mine.'

What he didn't say: *I can't afford to break up with Nancy. The bond is far stronger than a wedding licence. We're inseparably bound by blood – Kate's blood!*

Of late, Nancy had been showing signs of mental instability, no doubt from the attrition of a guilty conscience. She was growing possessive and inordinately jealous of him. No predicting what she'd do if she found out he had screwed the Brandon wench. She might even go to the police and confess that the two of them had murdered Kate. No, he'd better mend his fences with his wife and, in the future, exhibit more restraint when confronted by a willing piece of ass.

'I suppose you're right, Walt. I do love Kevin, in my own special way.' She looked at him fixedly. 'Besides, we've both accomplished what we wanted, isn't that true?'

His laughter was uncertain. 'What a curious way to express it.'

She was a strange girl, he thought. From the instant he met her, he had felt that she was not the person she seemed to be: a not-too-bright, attractive young housewife devoted to her husband and their future life together. No, there was something mysterious about Susan Brandon. No matter; in a short while she would be gone from Skull Mountain, along with her fellow refugees, and their paths would never cross again.

At the end of the column were Richard Lemon and Laura Devane. 'You heard what that Indian said about the footbridge? It's a way out of here,' Dick said.

Laura snorted. 'I also heard what Walt said. We're miles from nowhere, and hoofing it ain't my style, Dickie.'

'We can borrow two horses from Ames.'

'Are you crazy? He said it would be suicidal to cross that bridge with horses.'

'Yes, *he* said; but I don't believe him. He wants to keep us here, God only knows why – maybe because we provide company and entertainment for his wife. In any case, from the looks of the weather, we won't get off this bloody mountain today unless we take matters into our own hands. Come on, old girl, you never backed off from a challenge. I daresay you haven't entirely forgotten your riding skills.'

'Are you kidding? I still ride at least once a week.'

'Then, what are you waiting for?'

Laura pondered over his idea. At last she said, 'Let's wait until early afternoon. It may clear. Something positive may develop. As of now, we'll put it on hold.'

Nancy and Jan Danzig were walking together. 'I'd like to get together with you, dear, before we leave here,' Jan said.

Nancy was flushed, torn by all sorts of contrary feelings. Her mind was in chaos. 'I'm not really that way. What happened this morning was an accident. All of us have a bad case of the "morning-after" blues.'

Jan chuckled. 'You weren't acting very blue in my room, dear. *Au contraire!* And it was no accident. I planned it very carefully.'

Nancy could not meet her gaze. 'Well, it *was* for me. I didn't want to. You forced me.'

'I didn't force you to enjoy it. That came from within you.'

Nancy could not deny it. She felt helpless, alone, betrayed – betrayed by her own perverse emotions. And Walt was compounding her perturbation. The way he looked at Susan Brandon, it was obvious he was aching to climb into her pants again. As for Susan, she looked as though she'd be only too pleased to comply. Then again, maybe Jan had lied about Walt and Susan. Nancy wanted desperately to believe that she had, but her intuition told her otherwise.

'If we're stuck here for another night, you can come to my room.' Jan laid a tender hand on Nancy's arm.

'No! And don't touch me!' She pulled away angrily.

'All right. But you *will* come.' It was a declaration, not a question.

Nancy shook her head vigorously. She dared not speak, for in her secret heart she knew that Jan was right. She *would* keep the tryst. The thing of it was, this Machiavellian woman had tapped a stratum of latent sexuality within her that she had never realized existed – a monster in her that Jan had breathed life into, just as Frankenstein had resurrected *his* monster. A vivid image of the scene on the bed in Jan's room flashed across her mind, and hot, prickly heat spread across her belly and buttocks and down her thighs.

With a bitter sense of justice and retribution, she recalled a banality, a platitude, by Friedrich von Logau, translated from the German by Longfellow: '*Though the mills of God grind slowly, yet they grind exceeding small.*'

6

Back at the house, Nancy excused herself and went up to her bedroom. There she sat down at a small writing desk and stared out the window. The sky was darkening again, and a fine drizzle was falling. She saw Dick Lemon and Laura Devane walking in the direction of the barn. It puzzled her that they would be strolling in the rain, particularly since the weather bureau's last report mentioned a new storm that had formed over central Colorado and was sweeping south, accompanied by tornadoes and heavy rain.

She dismissed them and put her pen to paper. She wanted this to be accurate in every detail . . .

September 5, 1975 . . . Walter Ames plotted the murder of his wife Kate in the same way he would draw up a game plan for an athletic event – golf, tennis, handball, or an auto race. As in sports, timing was everything. Precision meant the difference between winning and losing, and this was one game he could not afford to lose.

Each night Kate received an injection to relax her muscles and help her sleep. The highly volatile drug – one of its components was curare – was administered by Nancy with extreme caution. An overdose could send the patient into shock, with fatal results.

Walt's intention was, after the dinner party on Friday night, to sedate his houseguests by drugging their nightcaps. It was a ritual, on such occasions at the Ames home, to drink a final toast before retiring.

The 'right' guest list was essential to the success of Walt's scheme: Dr Lewis Lanz and his wife, Rose; Margie and Jock van Nostrand, Cissy and Paul Marchand. It was the wives who provided the key; all of them, with the notable exception of Kate, were brunettes.

Dinner was a huge success. Endless champagne toasts generated a warm, festive mood. Everyone was giddy and voluble, and the most wretched joke was guaranteed to evoke gales of laughter. It was quarter-past midnight when Walt served a final round of drinks. Dr Lanz claimed the privilege of making the toast:

'To our charming and beloved hosts, Walt and Kate: May all of us meet here for the next hundred years to honour this joyous occasion . . . Walt, happy returns and many, many more on this, your fiftieth birthday.'

'We'll drink to that,' echoed Paul Marchand.

'You'd drink to anything,' said his wife. 'He even drank a toast to Nixon one night. Can you believe that?'

The banter was growing stale, and yawning became ludicrously contagious.

'If I don't hit the sack this instant, someone will have to put me to bed,' Margie van Nostrand said.

'I volunteer!' Paul thrust his hand into the air.

'You wouldn't be in any danger, believe me,' Cissy scoffed. 'Five drinks and he's totally impotent.'

'Wanna lay a bet?' he said indignantly.

'I couldn't even lay a *bet,*' Jock van Nostrand admitted. 'I have never been so tired in my entire life. What did you put in these drinks, Walt?'

Nancy almost spilled her drink, and she dared not look at Walt. He managed a stiff smile:

'One hundred-proof grain spirits, but there's no flavour, so you think you're drinking plain fruit juice.'

Lewis Lanz frowned but said nothing. It was not like Walter Ames to pull a cheap stunt like that, spiking his guests' drinks. However, Walt had been drinking heavily, and alcohol was notorious for lowering the boundaries of good taste.

'Come on, Rosie,' the doctor said. 'Help me make it upstairs.'

Walt walked with the Lanzes to the foot of the staircase. 'Lew, are we still on for tennis tomorrow morning?'

'Definitely. What time?'

'About seven-thirty.'

'You wake me.'

The Marchands and van Nostrands came out of the parlour.

'You bums game to join Lew and me for tennis in the morning?' Walt inquired.

Jock and Paul clamoured in unison, 'You've got to be kidding!'

Walt smiled. 'No sporting blood, eh, Lew? Well, then, I guess it's just you and me.'

Good nights were exchanged, and the three couples went up to bed. Walt went back into the parlour, where Nancy and Kate were chatting.

'Well, are we ready for beddy-by, my bride?'

'I was ready an hour ago.' Kate stifled a yawn with the back of her hand.

'I'll carry you upstairs.'

'No, I'll use the elevator. Besides, in your condition, you might drop me.'

'Yes, that would be a risk.'

He attempted to attract Nancy's eye – she was standing in back of Kate's wheelchair – but she averted her face.

'So, get going, you two. I'll tidy up a bit and then I'll be up to say good night.'

'Yes, it certainly needs tidying up,' Kate said. 'Walt, I will never understand why you chose this weekend to give the servants a holiday.'

He looked offended. 'You can't? I did it for your sake, dear. You're always saying that having servants hovering over you gives you the jitters. I thought this way you'd really stay loose on this auspicious occasion. I can't believe it – fifty years; half a century.'

'Well, you certainly don't look fifty, my darling, does he, Nan?'

'No, he doesn't,' Nancy agreed in a subdued voice.

'And I must say that you two ladies were the belles of the ball this evening. You both look absolutely lovely.'

Kate was wearing an evening gown of pale pink, layered chiffon. Nancy was ravishing in a form-fitting trapunto-stitched evening gown tied at one shoulder – emerald-green satin lined with magenta.

Walt stood in the middle of the living room, smoking a cigarette, watching Nancy push the wheelchair down the hall and out of sight on her way to the private elevator that had been installed after Kate's accident. He waited fifteen minutes, then went upstairs. Outside Kate's bedroom door, he took a deep breath before turning the knob.

Kate was lying on top of the coverlet, clad in a robe and blue satin pyjamas. The week before, Nancy had driven into Hartford and purchased matching pairs of pyjamas and quilted robes with a distinctive floral print.

'Is she out?' he asked quietly.

Nancy nodded. 'According to Merck's manual, she should be in shock within thirty minutes.'

'OK. Now, change into jeans and we'll get to work.'

Nancy did not reply. Her face was a mask of fear and distress as she stared down at Kate lying so still, her expression serene, a half-smile on her lips.

Walt walked over and shook her. 'Snap out of it! We have crossed the Rubicon and there is no turning back.'

She turned away from the bed and walked out of the room in a trance.

Walt looked after her anxiously. *Jesus, baby, don't break down on me now.* He sat down on the bed and felt for Kate's pulse. He timed it at forty-five beats per minute. By the time Nancy returned, dressed in a sweater and jeans, it had declined to thirty-five.

'She's going into shock,' she told him.

'So much the better for her, but we don't want her to die from the drug. If her heart stops, there won't be any blood.'

Quickly he picked Kate up in his arms.

They took the elevator down to the basement level, went through the laundry room, and exited the house by the service entrance. There was only a sliver of a moon, and the sky was so overcast, they were surrounded by near-total darkness.

'Fate's on our side,' he muttered.

Even if one of the guests had been standing at a bedroom window, he couldn't possibly have seen Nancy and Walt – Kate in his arms – disappear into the pine grove and climb the grassy incline to the head of the stairs that descended to the beach.

'Goodbye, Kate,' Walt whispered.

Nancy turned her back with a small moan of anguish. She put her hands over her ears to shut out the awful sound of rending flesh and bone hurtling down the long, steep flight of steps. She blacked out momentarily, regaining her equilibrium when Walt grabbed her roughly and said:

'It's over. Now, pull yourself together. We've got to go down there and see if she's dead.'

'I can't do it!'

'God damn it, you *will* do it! You don't have any choice. It's our own necks that are on the line now!' He took her hand and started down the steps.

It was so dark on the rocky turf below, shrouded by the shadow of the bluff, that the steps, the rocks, the shrubs, the mangled body of Kate Ames appeared only as a grotesque mass.

'All right, you're the nurse; is she dead?'

Battling nausea and revulsion, she kneeled down and fumbled for Kate's hand, pressed her fingers against the wrist. There was no pulse. More than that, she knew the feel of death from serving for years in the operating room at Mt Vernon.

'She's gone,' she said.

'Good.' He pulled out a large canvas tarpaulin he had stashed behind the stairs, and spread it out flat on the ground. 'Now help me get her onto it.' That accomplished, he bundled the body snugly inside it. 'Nancy, you take one end and I'll take the other.'

Together they carried the body to a boathouse a ways down the beach. Inside the boathouse was a walk-in refrigerator, where an earlier generation of Ameses used to hang sides of prime beef, suckling pigs, and a variety of top-quality game to be served at the extravagant parties that were the rage among the social set of that era. Now it contained only some cases of beer, wine, and soda and two Smithfield hams. Walt placed Kate in it, on the floor, and stood up.

'All right, let's get back to the house,' he said.

On the way back, he went over the plan with Nancy for still another time. 'If they perform an autopsy, keeping her in that deep cold will throw off the coroner as to her precise time of death; but, most likely, they won't. I'll protest on the grounds that Kate made me promise never to let anyone violate her body after death. With my connections in Connecticut judicial circles, I don't believe they'll overrule me.'

'What time do you intend to bring her out on the beach?'

'Just before I wake Lew for our tennis game.'

'Suppose someone sees you from a fishing boat?'

'No chance. I own all the property on either side of this cove, and the cove is off limits to strange craft. Listen, there's always an element of risk in any undertaking. Nothing is sure except death and taxes.'

She shivered and folded her arms around her body. 'Death.'

'All right, what's your game plan for tomorrow morning?'

' "Game plan"! Walt, please stop acting as if this were an entertainment.'

'I'm sorry . . . Well?'

'As soon as I get upstairs, I change into the pyjamas and robe that match the ones she's wearing.'

'If you feel bushed, take a nap. I'll wake you up on time.'

'Sleep – after what we've done? God, I don't think I'll ever be able to sleep again! I might dream.'

'Easy does it.' He put an arm around her. 'Bear up. It won't be long before it's all over.'

'Will it ever be over, Walt?'

'Of course it will. Then what do you do?'

'When you go down to the beach, I ride the wheelchair down to the garden and post myself by the fountain.'

'Yes, and for God's sake, don't forget the wig. That's the key to the success of the whole plan. Lanz is our star witness. He sees you from the patio, the only blonde female in residence. It has to be Kate; he'll swear to it.'

'I wave and wheel myself along the path that leads through the trees to the cliff.'

'And we're home free. You push the chair down the steps, where the body will be lying, scoot back to the house through the service entrance, while I distract Lanz in the kitchen, go to your own room, change into fresh night-clothes, and get into bed – neat and foolproof.'

And so it turned out to be: neat and foolproof. She would never forget the moment when Walt and Dr Lanz came to her room that morning.

'We've got some bad news for you, Nan,' Walt said. 'Kate – ' He broke off and covered his face with his hands. Heartrending sobs wracked his body. 'You tell her, Lew.'

There were tears in Lanz's eyes, too. 'Nancy . . . this is going to be a terrible shock to you, just as it was to us.

Nancy . . . Kate is dead. She was out by the cliff in her wheelchair, and . . . and somehow she went over the edge and down the steps. She must have died instantly, from the looks of her corpse.'

Nancy sat up slowly and drew up her knees. 'Kate . . . dead?' She buried her face in the blanket against her up-drawn knees and burst into tears. Her tears were real. Her grief was real.

Against Walter Ames's objections, the district attorney's office insisted on an autopsy, but it was arranged that Kate Ames's personal physician would conduct it. Lewis Lanz, out of deference to Kate's alleged aversion to having her body dissected after death, performed a superficial examination of the corpse, just enough to determine that the injuries to her head and spinal cord were lethal.

'No one could have survived such physical punishment,' he declared unequivocally to the coroner's jury . . .

Nancy Ames looked up from her writing chore and gazed out the window. The rain was coming down harder again. She gathered up the eight sheets of paper she had filled with her small, classical script, folded them, and put them into a large brown manila envelope, on which she wrote Jan Danzig's name. Then she left the room and walked to the head of the stairs, where she stood listening to the murmur of voices in the living room. When at last she identified Jan's unique nasal twang, she went to Jan's bedroom. It took only a moment to prop the envelope against a vanity case on the dresser.

Back in her own room, Nancy sat down at the desk and opened the drawer in which Walt kept a .38-calibre revolver. With complete dispassion, she placed the muzzle against her right temple and blew out her brains.

7

An Indian was cleaning out the horse stalls when Dick and Laura arrived at the barn.

'Would you please saddle up two of the horses for Miss Devane and myself?' The bass-organ voice radiated authority.

Still the Indian hesitated. 'It's very dangerous to ride now. Gall says the storm will return soon.'

'The United States Weather Bureau says otherwise. Now, be quick about it, my good man.'

'Mr Ames gave his approval?'

Dick fixed him with a withering stare, one eyebrow raised haughtily. '*What* did you say?'

The Indian cringed. 'Of course; you would not be here if Mr Ames did not say so. Do you have special horses in mind, you and the lady?'

Laura spoke up with equestrian expertise: 'We'll take the bay and the pinto. I noticed how sure-footed they were when we were coming here from the crash site.'

They were small, compact mountain horses with short, powerful legs and broad backs.

While the Indian readied the horses, Dick talked to him patronizingly. 'Actually, we're off to the Cessna. Miss Devane left a good many valuables behind in her luggage. We want to retrieve them before a rescue team gets here to fly us out.'

The Indian grunted noncommittally.

Dick paced back and forth nervously and kept looking out the barn door towards the house. 'Just our luck to have Ames come out here.'

'Relax.' Laura dropped her cigarette butt and put it out with the toe of her boot.

'Horses ready,' the Indian called to them at last.

'Thank God.' Dick took a ten-dollar bill out of his pocket

and handed it to the Indian. 'For your trouble, my good man.'

The Indian looked at him impassively, saying nothing, his hands at his sides.

'Well, take it,' Dick said impatiently, flipping it in the Indian's direction.

The bill fluttered to the barn floor untouched. It was still lying there when they mounted the horses and rode out into the misty drizzle.

Dick kept glancing back over his shoulder in apprehension until they passed out of sight of the house. 'Whew! I kept expecting to take a slug in the back any second,' he said.

Laura laughed harshly. 'You see too many movies, Dickie!'

Within a mile, they came upon a duff-covered trail leading up into the woods off the right side of the road and wide enough for two horsemen to ride abreast.

'Must be the bridle path they were talking about. Here we go, ducks!' Dick sang out. He was filled with enthusiasm and confidence. 'By George, it will be good to get out of this hellish place!'

'Will it ever! Skull Mountain gives me the creeps. In fact, all of our partners in disaster have something creepy about them.'

He gave her a searching look. 'Except thee and me, eh, my dear? Don't you remember what Gall suggested, that we all share a common guilt? Partners in "sin," not "disaster," I should think would be more appropriate.'

'Knock it off, Lemon. You seem to take a masochistic satisfaction in assuming a burden of guilt. Well, if you get a kick out of doing penance for some hidden vice or crime, by all means go to it. But, for myself, sackcloth and ashes was never my bag.' She put up the collar of her jacket. 'Shit! That fucking old Indian may have been right. It's raining harder. Maybe the storm *is* coming back.'

Dick was in a swashbuckling mood. 'Damn the torpedoes! Full speed ahead! Even if the storm does return, we'll be down the mountain and safe . . . There, up ahead; that must be it!' He urged his horse forward at a canter.

They emerged into a little clearing and came upon the

bridge. It spanned a canyon 200 feet across and nearly 500 feet deep. At the bottom of the gorge, swift-moving white water crashed and tumbled over a bed of huge boulders and jagged rocks.

'Where on earth does all that water come from?' he said. 'It hasn't rained hard since early morning. Every stream on the mountain must ultimately drain into here. Let's have a look at the bridge.'

It appeared remarkably durable, for a footbridge. The construction was basic: four steel cables embedded in concrete abutments on either side of the ravine, the lower pair supporting a heavy steel-mesh platform, the upper two forming the top railings, and steel side posts reinforcing them at ten-foot intervals. The structure swayed slightly in the wind, but not enough to pose any real hazard – or so it appeared to Richard Lemon and Laura Devane.

'Piece of cake,' Laura exulted. 'Come on, Dickie, follow the leader.' She tightened the reins and guided her mount to the bridge.

The gelding pinto was reluctant to heed her wishes. It whinnied, shook its head from side to side, and balked at setting hoof on the span.

'Come on, sissy, you can do it.'

Laura slapped its rump and dug her heels into its sides. She had a way with horses, and at last the pinto moved onto the bridge.

'There! Now, was that so bad?'

Dick's bay followed the leader, as it had been trained to do, and at a leisurely pace the two animals traversed the bridge. They were midway across when the wind and the rain increased.

'Jesus Christ!' Dick yelled. 'Speed it up a bit, will you? This lad of mine is trembling like a leaf.'

Fear seized him as he looked down into the canyon. With the heavier rain, the water level was rising so fast, one could discern it with the naked eye. As the gorge filled, the rocks were submerged, and the teeming torrent reached out for the bridge and its hapless occupants with long, ghostly tendrils of white water kicked up by the wind. A gust swept through the ravine, creating a whining sound. The centre of the strand swayed back and forth in a six-foot arc, throwing the horses against the side rails.

'Oh, my God!' Dick cried out. 'Fuck the horses, Laura! Let's make a run for it ourselves!'

'Dick, don't!'

But he was already dismounted and trying to push past her horse on the narrow bridge. The pinto, frightened by the unexpected presence of Dick at its side, reared up on its hind legs, almost unseating Laura.

'You damned fool!' she shouted as he pushed by and ran for the far side of the canyon, stumbling and clutching at the rails for support.

He was within thirty yards of his goal when it happened. The concrete abutment that held the supporting cables had weathered years of punishment from the savage elements on Skull Mountain. This final onslaught of torrential rain and hurricane winds delivered the *coup de grace.* Dick stared in horror as the two cables supporting the platform tore loose from their moorings, and, as in the slow-motion movie sequences that had always fascinated him as a boy, the steel-mesh strip fell away from the abutment, twisting and undulating like a huge snake as it swung down and away.

As the deck, literally, was pulled out from under him, Dick grabbed one of the railing cables and held on for dear life. Terrified, he saw Laura and the horse dropping off into the churning maelstrom below, their bodies turning over and over until they plunged into certain death. He attempted to haul himself hand over hand to safety, but the wind was determined not to let him go. Or was it the Holy Spirit of Skull Mountain?

'Please, God, no!' he pleaded.

His last thought was that the prayer had served only to incense the Holy Spirit, for it felt to him as though two invisible hands had seized him and wrenched him loose from the cable. The world spun around him crazily as he dropped to his doom. The last sight revealed to his glazed eyes was a wall of boiling water closing over him.

It was Chief who brought the tragic tidings to the Ames house. He told Pedro in the kitchen: 'There was a party gathering firewood downstream from the bridge when it collapsed. There was no way to save them.'

Pedro crossed himself and said a brief prayer in Spanish.

'Your medicine man was right. I heard them speak of the ritual last night. This mountain is cursed.'

'I had better tell Mr Ames.'

The cook blanched. 'Of course – you don't know about Mrs Ames!'

Chief's leathery face creased. 'What about Mrs Ames?'

'She is dead. She shot herself not an hour ago.'

The Indian rocked back and forth, took a step backwards, and sat down heavily in a kitchen chair. He shook his head and touched his fingers to his closed eyelids. 'I must speak with Gall as quickly as possible. Perhaps there is still some way to save the others. I will tell him to implore the Holy Spirit to be merciful and spare them.' He stood up and walked heavy-legged to the kitchen door and out into the driving rain.

Walter Ames, a water tumbler half full of 100-proof bourbon in his hand, was standing at a window with his back to the others when Pedro entered the living room.

The Brandons and the Bostwicks sat around the coffee table in abject silence, each lost in his own thoughts. Jan Danzig chain-smoked as she paced up and down in front of the hearth, her mind racing in high gear. The immediate impact of Nancy's death on her had been devastating – the tears she'd shed, genuine – but she'd soon regained her composure. Jan Danzig was the consummate survivor; thus, overwhelming guilt had given way to regret, then to bitterness, and finally to anger and resentment against Nancy: *You damned silly broad, killing yourself over that turd of a husband! What a waste. How good it was between us; it could have been perfect if only you had been a rational person. You and I might have found true love.*

The last vestige of remorse had vanished when Jan, retiring to her room after the fatal incident, found Nancy's letter. Except for the personal loss to her of Nancy's magnificently sensual body, it was hard to feel pity or sympathy for either Nancy or Walter Ames. They had murdered his first wife in cold blood! And, as Jan refolded the letter and tucked it inside her pantie girdle (she would not trust such a treasure to be away from her person for longer than it took to change her clothes), she made a vow to herself: *I'll see that bastard Ames drawn and quartered by the press and by the courts! The gas chamber is too good for the likes of a swine like him. I want them to throw him in solitary confinement and toss away the key!*

She stopped pacing as Pedro entered and addressed Walt:

'Mr Ames, there is more bad news . . . much bad news. The words stick in my throat.'

Walt turned and looked at him absently. 'What is it, Pedro?'

'Mr Lemon and Miss Devane . . . they take horses and try to get across the footbridge.'

'Damned fools.' Walt said without emotion.

'They in the middle of the bridge, and bridge she break. They fall into the water. They die.'

'Oh, dear God, no!' Jennie Bostwick cried.

Larry took her in his arms. 'It's a terrible thing, honey, but there's nothing we can do for them. They never should have – ' He shook his head helplessly.

'The prophecy of the medicine man,' Susan Brandon said. 'First Nancy, then Dick and Laura. I wonder which one of us is next.'

'That isn't funny, Susan,' Kevin snapped. He went over to Walt. 'Those Indian messengers, do you think they got through to civilization?'

Walt looked to Pedro. 'Did Chief say anything about it?'

'No, he only talk about Mr Lemon and Miss Devane.'

'Not that it makes any difference. We're still socked in. And now that the footbridge is down, I'm afraid there is nothing we can do but sit it out.' He went into the dining room and refilled his glass.

'This is a nightmare,' Kevin said. 'The two pilots, Nancy, Dick, and Laura . . . We're trapped on this mesa with five dead bodies.' He lowered his voice. 'If help doesn't come soon, they're going to decompose.'

'Don't say things like that!' Jennie stood up and went over to a window. 'I won't listen.'

'He's right, though,' Larry said. 'That big freezer in the basement – we could stow them in there.'

'Good idea. Let's talk to Walt about it,' Kevin said.

'You're a couple of ghouls,' Jennie said.

Susan joined her at the window. 'Don't be so uptight, Jennie. Would you like a drink to calm you down?'

'Yeah, bring me the whole bottle.'

Kevin approached Walt and asked him about putting the dead into the meat freezer. 'I realize it must sound grisly to you, what with Nancy and all. You wouldn't participate, naturally. Larry and I – '

'No, no,' Walt interrupted. 'It's the only reasonable thing to do, and I *will* participate. If the rain lets up again, I'll have Chief and some of the hands ride up to the crash site and bring in the dead pilots.'

A jagged fork of lightning shot down out of the overcast and struck an ancient tree no more than 100 yards from the house, splitting it asunder as neatly as an axe cleaves a log in two. It was followed immediately by a thunderbolt so loud that everyone in the house was struck momentarily deaf. The house groaned and creaked like a living thing in pain. Dishes and bottles on the sideboard rattled. The floor trembled as though an earthquake had struck the mesa.

Jennie threw her arm across her eyes. 'I've never seen anything like it!'

'Look, the tree is on fire!' Susan exclaimed.

The others ran to the window and looked out into the storm, raging ferociously once again. The ravaged tree was indeed ablaze.

'It looks like a burning cross,' Susan said.

Larry grunted. 'Sure does. Walt, you got the KKK up here on Skull Mountain?'

'Very funny,' Jennie said angrily.

'How can it burn with all that rain?' Jan wanted to know.

'Lightning generates extreme heat,' Walt told her, 'but it won't be long before it fizzles out.'

Lightning and thunder were besieging the mesa from all directions.

'Like Walt said, this mountain is a giant lightning rod,' Kevin mused.

'Reminds me of an artillery barrage I got caught in in Nam,' Larry said. 'Great balls of fire! Look at *that* monster!'

A perfect globe of fire came hurtling directly at the house.

'Down on the floor!' Walt shouted.

They hurled themselves prone and held their breath. Suddenly the window became a rectangle of blinding fire, and then it was gone.

'What happened?' Kevin asked.

'Bounced right over the house,' Walt explained. 'The lightning rods deflected it.'

'How long can we stay lucky?' Larry said.

'Hard to say,' Walt replied. 'This old place has lasted almost a hundred years. My guess is, it will last another hundred.'

'You're not a gambling man, Walt,' Larry said cynically. 'If you were, you'd figure that after a hundred years, the odds are bound to be against you. I'd say this old house's number is about up.'

'You're such an optimist,' Kevin said.

They stood up and gazed out the window again.

'Look at all those fireballs,' Larry said. 'Looks like the Holy Spirit is playing tenpins. And we, boys and gals, we are the pins!'

8

Jan Danzig walked into the dining room, where Susan Brandon was mixing herself a drink. They were alone.

'What is it, Jan?' Susan inquired. 'You look worried. Then again, we're all worried. Skull Mountain could become the final resting place for all of us "sinners." '

'That's what I've been thinking ever since Nancy – '

'Yes, poor Nancy. I wonder why she did it.'

Jan glanced furtively over her shoulder. The others were still in the living room, out of earshot. She lowered her voice to a whisper: 'I know why she did it – because of you and Walt.'

Susan's composure remained unruffled. 'Whatever are you talking about?'

'You and her husband last night, screwing on the couch in the den. I saw you.'

That would have disconcerted the most imperturbable woman. Susan's high cheekbones were red blotches:

'You sneaky bitch! Don't you have any scruples at all?'

'No more than you. Look, I wasn't snooping last night. I came down to the den to get a book.'

Abruptly it struck Susan like a lightning bolt. 'My God! Yes, you told Nancy!'

'I did.' Jan's eyes held Susan's steadily.

'I can't believe it. You . . . you *monster!'* She placed her hands flat on the sides of her head, as if to keep it from flying apart. 'And she killed herself because of *that?'*

'Partially, but don't run off and join a nunnery to atone for your sin. There's more to it than that. Look, it's too risky to tell you the rest here. I'll go upstairs. Wait a few minutes and come up to my room.'

'I don't want to hear about it.'

'I think you'll change your mind when you hear what I have to say about your Mr Ames.' Her smile was wicked.

'All right, I'll be up shortly.'

While the columnist made her edgy, Susan wasn't about to pass up any opportunity to learn something incriminating about an Ames. When Jan had departed, she carried her drink back into the living room.

'You're really putting it away,' Kevin said with disapproval as she swigged from her glass.

'Eat, drink, and be merry, for tomorrow we may die,' she quipped.

'Correction,' Jennie said. '*Today* we may die.'

A monstrous explosion rocked the house.

'That's it! We're hit!' Larry shouted.

'I don't think so,' Walt said. 'That was outside.'

Pedro came running into the room to confirm it. 'The generator shack was struck by lightning.'

'Impossible!' Walt said. 'The generator is insulated by six inches of rubber.'

'You come see,' Pedro insisted. 'It's on fire.' As he spoke the words, all of the lights dimmed, then went out.

Walt ran into the kitchen, the others on his heels, and looked out the window. Fifty feet behind the house, the small brick building that housed the generator was enveloped in flames. As they watched, the fire was doused by the rain.

'I better go out there and see how much damage has been done,' he said. 'Pedro, you're handy with engines. You come with me.'

Pedro backed off. 'Not now, boss. Pedro does not want to get a lightning bolt up his ass.'

'Pedro has a good point,' Walt admitted. 'We'll wait until there's a lull.'

Susan faked a yawn. 'Well, I think I'll grab a little shut-eye. Coming, Kevin?' When he shook his head, she left the room.

Susan stopped before Jan's bedroom and glanced down the hall to make certain that no one had followed her upstairs. Satisfied, she knocked lightly.

Jan opened the door. 'Come on in.'

Although it was only one o'clock in the afternoon, it was nearly as dark as night. The only illumination in the room was provided by the incessant lightning.

'Now, what is this important item you want to tell me?' Susan asked.

Jan paced back and forth, chain-smoking. After what seemed an eternity to Susan, she blurted, 'Walter Ames and Nancy murdered his first wife, Kate. Nancy was her nurse, and she and Walt had an affair and decided to do away with her. She was a cripple.'

Susan stared at her in utter disbelief. 'You can't be serious!'

'Perfectly serious. Nancy told me herself; that is, she left a written confession on my dresser before she shot herself – every detail, from the inception of the murder plan through its execution.'

'Where is it?'

Jan patted her tummy. 'Right here, and that's where it's staying until we're off this fucking mountain. The reason I'm telling you is that, if anything happens to me, you make sure it gets into the hands of the law. Will you do it?'

'Will I do it? Oh, that will give me the greatest pleasure! Walter Ames a murderer – what about that! But are you sure it will hold up in court? I mean, Walt may claim that Nancy was insane. After all, she did kill herself.'

'That's another thing. I'm going to say that Nancy made a full oral confession before she wrote this letter. A death-bed confession has a lot of weight in court.'

Susan felt so exhilarated, she could have done cart-wheels. What a stroke of luck, a miracle! Walter Ames had been delivered into her vengeful hands by Divine Providence! If there was a heaven, oh, how proud Amy, Candice, and Peggy would be!

'We can do better than that,' she said. 'I'll swear that I was present when Nancy confessed to the crime!'

Jan looked dubious. 'Why would you do a thing like that to a man you cared enough about to bed down with?'

'The only reason I let Walter Ames make love to me was to give me certain leverage over him. It can be of no importance to you, my purpose; that's merely academic now. Nancy's letter changes everything. Oh, I can't wait to get on that witness stand!'

Jan shrugged. In her years as a reporter and Hollywood gossip columnist, she had seen and heard it all: infant molesters, dirty old men and women, grandmother rapers, deviants straight out of psychiatry texts. If crucifying Walter Ames would give Susan Brandon her kicks, so be it. 'All right, if that's how you want to play it, I'm game. But remember, if I don't make it out of here, the confession is pinned inside my girdle.'

'I'll remember . . . Now, I had better go to my room in case Kevin comes looking for me.'

Kevin Brandon stood on the front porch observing the storm. The rain was coming down so hard, the three open sides of the porch appeared to be contained within solid walls of water. He had the odd sensation that he was inside a diving bell, looking out into the unfriendly ocean.

It had been raining almost as hard as this the day he and Burns and Goldman went ashore on leave in Honolulu; but it let up by noon, and they began bar-hopping. Kevin lost count of how many bars they were in. He was drunk as a skunk and smelled like one, too, though he had no great liking for liquor, particularly the rotgut served in the cheap Hawaiian cafés.

Well after midnight, they ended up in a whorehouse in the slums, where the tables in the parlour were covered with dirty tablecloths, and the drinks were served in glasses that had been jelly jars.

There were three girls, one a dyed blonde. Two of them were clad in bras and panties that were so sheer, dark triangles of their pubic hair were visible. The third wore a shorty nightgown, and when she bent over to pour drinks, the cheeks of her buttocks below the hem of the gown could be seen. To Kevin, in his drunken stupor, all three looked desirable. His hand trembled when he picked up his drink, and he spilled it down the front of his trousers.

The girl in the gown knelt in front of him and wiped his lap with a napkin. Her fingers closed over his erection and she giggled. 'You got one big hard-on, sailor. You come upstairs with Lea and I fix you up good. Best fuck ever.'

Kevin thought he must be dreaming. He was in the middle of a carousel, and everything in the room was revolving around him. None of it was real. He struggled to focus his eyes, and caught sight of the blonde straddling Burns's lap while he buried his face between her naked breasts. Her hands were clasped on either side of his head, and her long neck was arched back, swanlike, with her face upturned to the grimy ceiling. She was laughing lewdly. Goldman and the third girl were on their way upstairs, their arms wrapped around each other's waist. The stairs seemed to tilt at a grotesque angle, and Kevin slid off the chair onto the floor with the limp sinuousness of a snake.

Lea stood over him laughing wildly, hands on her hips, her legs spread far apart. He looked up her nightgown at her genitalia and was possessed by lust so fierce and urgent, he almost ejaculated in his pants. She held out her hands to him and helped him get to his feet.

Kevin let her lead him by the hand to the stairs. He floated after her like a balloon, bobbing effortlessly up the stairs and along a dim, narrow hall with closed doors on both sides. When they finally reached a room with an open door, she pulled him in behind her. A single pale-yellow bulb was suspended from the ceiling over an army cot with a bare mattress.

Lea removed her nightgown and sat down on the edge of the cot. Kevin swayed from side to side as she unbuttoned his trousers and let them fall around his ankles. She pulled down his Jockey shorts and giggled as his gorged member sprang up like a jack-in-the-box. His agony was exquisite.

'Hurry!' he said. 'I can't hold back much longer.'

She lay back on the mattress and spread her arms and thighs for him. He kneeled down on the foot of the cot and crawled up between her legs. He was on the verge of penetrating her when the sound of a commotion downstairs echoed up the stairs and through the hall, raucous voices calling for the girls.

'God damn it!' Kevin cursed.

Lea pushed him off. 'Lea go see what matter is. Maybe more sailors want to have girls. I go see.'

'Let someone else see what they want. You can't leave me like *this*.'

She put on the nightgown. 'I go tell them to wait, else they come up here to look for girls. I come back right away.'

Kevin sat down on the bed. 'All right, but make it quick.'

Ten minutes passed and she did not return. He paced the room in a murderous rage, and when he found a half-full bottle of cognac on the closet shelf, he uncorked it and drank straight from the bottle until the raw liquor choked him and brought tears to his eyes. His sexual frustration fanned his anger.

Naked but for his socks and shoes, he went out into the hall to the head of the stairs. Bawdy laughter and loud voices came from the ground floor: Lea horsing around with other American sailors.

'The hell with you, slut!' Kevin muttered. He stalked back down the hall, bouncing off the walls in his drunken haste, mumbling to himself, 'Fucking whore! Listen, kiddo, you ain't the only fishie in the ocean – I mean *pussy*.' His vision blurred, and the hallway shimmered as if he was looking at it through water. 'Atta boy, Kevin, you tell 'em! Kevin Brandon wants to get laid, and li'l Kevin is *gonna* get laid!'

He opened a door and stared dumbly at the two copulating bodies on the bed. They were too occupied to notice his intrusion. He tried two more doors, with the same results. 'God damn! Everybody's screwing but me!'

He grasped the knob of the last door, at the end of the hall, and pushed. The room was silent and in darkness. He felt along the wall inside the doorway and found a switch. Soft orange light glowed from a table lamp next to a large double bed against the far wall. And asleep on the bed was a girl. Her arms and legs were spread-eagled, and her nightgown was tangled up around her hips. One small, plump breast was hanging out of the bodice.

Now, this is more like it.

She was prettier than Lea or the other two girls, and the lust that filled him, as he looked at her, was a form of madness. She was so young – no more than twenty, he guessed – so innocent in her slumber, her red lips parted cherubically and her long hair fanned out across the pillow.

He sat down on the side of the bed, picked up one of her limp hands, and closed the fingers around his erection. *Oh, Jesus*! It was sheer heaven. He slid his hand up between her thighs and said in a voice hoarse with passion, 'Wake up, baby. No more sleeping on the job. The joint is jumping with customers.' He squeezed her thigh hard.

She woke up, gasping in pain. Her dark, round eyes blinked at him, unfocussed still with sleep. On interminable nights thereafter, Kevin would, in macabre recollection, attempt to re-create the swift sequence of events when, with fear and shock, the girl realized that a naked stranger was sitting on her bed:

A blurry face contorted in animal terror; a brown knee drawn up protectively against a white breast . . . Sharp pain exploding inside his brain as her fingernails clawed at his face; he seething with savage anger and inflamed with lust . . .

Her red mouth shaped in a scream that couldn't escape, her breath choked off by his throttling hands on her throat, pressing her back on the bed; pale breasts heaving; knees clenched tightly together, inexorably split apart by his knee; her body convulsing in pain as he went dryly into her . . .

His pain, too. Had there been *any* joy for him? He couldn't remember . . .

Then bedlam exploding in the room; men shouting; women screaming; hands pulling at him, shoving him roughly to the floor; sheer cacophony . . .

Kevin closed his eyes and passed out.

He woke up in another room on another bed. Standing around the bed were Goldman, Burns, and two sailors he had never seen before.

'You drunken pig!' Burns swore at him.

Kevin sat up and put his hands to his aching head. He was wracked by pain and nausea. Worst of all was the formless fear – shadowy dream memories. 'What's happening?'

'You really fucked up bad,' Goldman said.

'What . . . what did I do?'

'You raped that girl, buster,' one of the strangers declared.

Kevin was electrified, instantly sober, all his senses in sharp focus. 'What the hell are you talking about? Rape a whore? That's ridiculous! Knock it off.'

'She was no whore,' Burns said. 'She and her husband just rent a room here. He works the night shift at the navy yard.'

It was insane, absurd! 'They rent a room in a cat-house?' he said with disbelief.

'She's a cousin to Lea. They let the couple stay here until they can find a place of their own. They're poor as church mice. Came over from Maui.'

'All right, guys, let's put our act together,' said Goldman, 'before the husband comes home. The kid is hysterical, wants to go to the police. She's two months pregnant.'

'Pregnant? Oh, Jesus!' Kevin was awed by the enormity of his own self-contempt.

'We'll talk to her,' Burns said, 'make a deal.'

'A deal?' Kevin said dully.

'Sure, there's a price on everything,' Burns said with cheerful cynicism. 'It's not as though we're dealing with an American suburban *hausfrau* with a full belly, a fat bank account, and a husband on the board of Ma Bell. The only thing this kid has in her belly is a kid. And her husband is bringing home only fifteen bucks a week from the navy. Let's see how much cash we can dig up among us.'

'Count us out, buddy,' said one of the strange sailors. 'No business of ours.'

'Aw, come on, you guys. The navy sticks together, takes care of its own.'

'He's right, Jim,' the other sailor admitted. 'Count me in for twenty bucks.'

'OK, I'll go for twenty, too,' said his mate.

Burns collected a kitty of $190 altogether. 'Come on, Goldman, let's go talk to her.'

Kevin sank back on the bed and rolled over on his face. The pillow stank of sweat and sex and he savoured it. He wanted to wallow in a cesspool; he belonged there. Five minutes later, Burns and Goldman returned.

'Mission accomplished,' Burns said triumphantly. 'She's agreed to forget about the whole mess.'

Goldman smiled. 'When you come to think about it, she got more for a piece of ass than a high-class call girl back home.'

'Now, get your clothes on, Brandon, and let's haul our asses out of here,' Burns said.

The night before their carrier sailed out of Honolulu Harbour, Burns, returning from shore leave, went to Kevin's bunk. 'I bumped into our friend Lea on the street. Guess what. That girl you raped? She had a miscarriage . . . '

Kevin shivered uncontrollably as he was jerked back to the present by a monstrous thunderclap directly above the porch. *Must be the end of the world,* he thought.

9

The gigantic thunderbolt was followed by a succession of blasts of even greater magnitude, accompanied by forked lightning and enormous fireballs that seemed to be directed by a malevolent intelligence, unseen but very palpable.

'If ever a situation qualified for the term "All hell broke loose," this is it,' Walt said with awe. 'I've been coming up to Skull Mountain since I was knee high, and there were some whopping bad storms over the years, but *never* anything like this.'

Walt, Kevin, Larry, Jennie, Jan – all of them were pale and drawn, showing the strain and anxiety of the past two days. Only Susan Brandon seemed unperturbed. Her face was flushed, and her eyes glowed with feverish excitement.

Kevin observed, 'You're not high again from eating that mescaline last night, are you?'

'Of course not. I just find this all so very exciting. It's

something we'll be able to tell our grandchildren about time after time, without their getting tired of hearing it.'

'Grandchildren!' Jennie said. 'What an optimist!'

'For my part, if I'm lucky enough to get off this mountain alive, I will *never* talk about the experience or even think about it,' Kevin declared.

'Amen,' echoed Larry.

Jan said nothing, just rubbed her tummy, feeling for Nancy's letter.

'Stomachache, Jan?' Walt inquired.

Her smile was stiff. 'No, I'm just a little hungry.' *When I turn this letter over to the authorities, you are going to have yourself the bellyache of your lifetime, you sonovabitch!*

It was Pedro who gave the alarm. He came running into the living room, which was dark but for two oil lamps burning on top of the mantle, and shouted, 'Smoke is coming down through the rafters into my room!'

'Jesus! Come on!' Walt cried.

Dread engulfed them as soon as they were in the front hall. The smoke was wafting down the stairwell in thin, wispy tendrils. The smell was acrid and ominous.

'Fire!' Kevin said in a whisper. 'Oh, my God!'

They followed Walt up the steps two at a time. The smoke was thicker in the upper hall, and Jennie began to cough.

'Pedro, I think you had better take the ladies back downstairs. This may get hairy. And bring up the two fire extinguishers from the basement,' Walt ordered.

'*Si* señor. And what about the two in the attic?'

Walt looked grim. 'There's a distinct possibility that we may not be able to reach them.'

Jennie, Susan, and Jan went back downstairs with Pedro. Larry and Kevin walked behind Walt to the door leading up to the attic at the end of the corridor. They walked softly, gingerly, and with bated breath, almost as if they were afraid of offending some higher alien force. Walt's worst fears were confirmed as soon as he opened the door. They were enveloped in a ballooning cloud of thick black smoke.

'Get back!' he screamed.

Choking, coughing, gagging, they retreated outside the perimeter of the burgeoning cloud, no longer so dark and impenetrable, as the fire racing down the stairs behind it infused it with a rosy glow.

'No hope anymore,' Walt said in anguish. 'Look, you go back downstairs and alert the others. We're going to have to get out of here.'

'But the heavy rain!' Larry protested. 'Won't it extinguish the flames?'

'No chance. It'll keep the roof wet enough, maybe, but this blaze will gut the entire interior and leave the empty shell of the house standing. Get moving! I'm going to take Nancy's body down to the freezer; it's fireproof. We'll all meet in the front hall.'

The women were waiting at the foot of the stairs. 'How bad is it?' Susan asked.

'The worst,' Kevin replied. 'The house is on fire, and we've got to evacuate.'

'Evacuate?' Jennie and Jan cried out together. 'To where?'

'I haven't the remotest idea – the barn, maybe.'

Pedro came running up with the two fire extinguishers.

'Forget it,' Larry told him. 'It's too late for that. The house has had it.'

Pedro dropped them, clasped his hands together, and commenced praying in Spanish, eyes turned upwards in supplication.

'I hope He can hear you with all this thunder,' Jan commented acerbically.

'Here comes Walt,' Larry said.

The women averted their eyes as Walt carried his wife's body, swathed in a blanket, down the stairs to the cellar. Minutes later he returned.

'What now?' Kevin demanded. 'Do we go to the barn?'

'Too late,' was Walt's funereal answer. 'It's on fire too. The Indians are out there now clearing out the stock. Ranch house gone up in flames, everything.' He threw up his hands in despair.

'The final act,' Susan said in a strange, detached voice. ' "Vengeance is mine," said the Holy Spirit. And he's set to collect right now.'

'God damn you, Susan, will you stop it with that insane drivel!' Kevin snarled. To Walt: 'Where *can* we go?'

'To one of the insulated shelters. There's a sizable one near the ravine to the south, about a quarter of a mile.'

'A quarter of a mile?' Larry said. 'Isn't that going to be terribly dangerous with all this lightning?'

'I afraid so, but we don't have any alternative. Look up there.'

The head of the staircase in the upper hall was a sheet of flame, and it was already licking down the stair carpeting.

'Come on, all of you! In another ten minutes the second storey is going to collapse on this one.'

They trooped after him out onto the porch and gazed dismally at the downpour.

'It's let up a little,' Walt offered. 'At least, there is some visibility.'

He was right. After the fearful barrage of thunder and lightning that had mortally wounded the house, the storm seemed to have peaked and was now withdrawing from Skull Mountain. The lightning was still a grave threat to anyone moving across the field in front of the house; but they would all have to brave it.

Walt buttoned up the collar of his slicker and tugged his rain cap down tightly over his ears. 'Let's go!' He sprang down the front steps and headed south across the open ground at a quick jog.

Strung out behind him, the others kept up with his pace, all but Jan. Pedro fell behind deliberately and held out his hand to her. She was puffing and wheezing, and her gait was unsteady.

'Come, Miss Danzig, take hold. I will carry you if I have to.'

She clutched at his hand like a drowning woman clutching at a straw.

Lightning was still cleaving down trees in the woods to their left. Up ahead, a coruscating ball of fire danced on a rock pile.

'Skirt around that hazard!' Walt yelled back. 'Keep clear of any protuberance that is higher than you are. Our biggest chance lies in the fact that there are so many more attractive targets out here than we present.'

And so they stumbled along, possessed by fear and the sick conviction that if they all got away from Skull Mountain alive, it would be a miracle of no small distinction.

'There it is up ahead!' Walt shouted.

The shelter, resting on a cement platform a foot above ground level, was constructed to hold six people, but could accommodate two more in an emergency.

They were within 100 yards of it when a lightning bolt exploded at the rear of the column. Susan glanced back in time to witness a spectacle like nothing she had ever seen in her life or would be likely to see again in the future: Pedro and Jan Danzig, standing motionless like figures in a tableau, their faces frozen in pain and terror as their bodies limned with dancing fire. They looked like apparitions out of a sci-fi horror film.

No one considered stopping to lend assistance; it was obvious that there was no hope for the two unfortunates. The others reached the hut safely and squeezed inside.

'No room to sit down,' Walt said, 'but the lightning can't get us. We're standing on six inches of rubber insulation.'

Time after time, lightning struck the long steel rod atop the roof, which was grounded to another steel rod, buried in the earth a dozen feet from the shack. Then, unceremoniously, it was all over. The storm swept past Skull Mountain and advanced on a mountain range to the east. Body-sore and weary, drained of emotion, they limped outside.

'It's going to clear,' Walt declared.

The overcast was thinning out, and the ceiling was higher. Directly overhead, there was a soft golden glow filtering through the clouds.

'The sun!' Kevin exclaimed. 'Thank God! I was beginning to think I'd never see it again.' He gave Larry a resounding clap on the back. 'How about that, old buddy?' To his astonishment, the black man staggered and almost fell. 'I'm sorry, Larry. I didn't think I hit you that hard. Are you OK?'

'Sure, sure, I'm fine; just a little rocky. Got to get my sea legs.'

Jennie frowned at him. 'Honey, you look funny. Are you sure you're feeling all right?'

He smiled weakly. 'Now, don't go telling me that I'm pale.'

'Oh, you!' She took his arm and pressed close to him.

Walt and Susan ran back to where Pedro and Jan were lying on the ground, bodies twisted grotesquely. It was apparent they were dead, even before Walt felt for a pulse beat.

'They look smaller,' Susan said, 'withered, as if all of their juices had somehow been sucked out.'

'You're right – the lightning,' Walt said. 'The same as if they'd been electrocuted in the electric chair. We'll come back and get them later in the jeep.'

They walked back to the house slowly, heavy-footed.

'First Nancy, then Dick and Laura, and now Pedro and Jan . . . When will it end?' Susan said.

'It's ended,' Walt assured her. 'We should be seeing blue sky within the hour.'

What really gave them a shot of adrenaline was the sound of a helicopter flying overhead. They couldn't see it, but its very presence was comforting.

'We'll be out of here before nightfall,' Walt told them.

Their morale was definitely on the rise. Even the sight of the burning house could not dampen their spirits. The barn was already a smouldering shell, but the Indians had rescued all of the livestock.

Chief was stoic and philosophical: 'It was not the first storm on Skull Mountain, and it will not be the last.' Even the news of his friend's death did not unduly perturb him. 'Pedro was a good man. He is at peace, as all of us will be one day.'

'Yes, he *was* a good man,' Kevin said thoughtfully, 'not one of us so-called sinners – the evil Gall said is a blight on Skull Mountain. Why, then, didn't the Holy Spirit spare Pedro, Chief?'

'Evil is contagious. He was with that woman, and her evil infected him.'

'That will be enough talk of evil,' Walt snapped. 'None of those who died were evil. Their numbers were up, that's all.' He thought fleetingly of Kate, Nancy . . . 'What's done is done,' he said, more forcefully than he realized.

'Where did you take shelter, Chief?' Susan asked.

'In the generator house. You know the white man's saying: Lightning never strikes twice.'

'I do believe that old saw was positively refuted today,' Walt told him. 'We must have taken at least twenty strikes on the shelter by the ravine . . . Chief, I realize it isn't a pleasant task, but the bodies of Miss Danzig and Pedro have to be brought in.'

'We'll go there in the jeep as soon as we finish checking on the livestock.'

Susan volunteered, 'Let Chief finish his chores. Kevin and I will do it.'

'I can't ask you to do such an unpleasant task. It can wait for the Indians.'

'No, I insist.'

'All right,' he agreed at last. 'Jeep's out back by the barn, what's left of it.'

Kevin drove with Susan sitting beside him, very erect and tense. 'What is this act of yours, darling?' he inquired. 'Why so eager to be a pallbearer?'

She told him bluntly, 'Jan Danzig has something I want.'

'Robbing the dead? I don't believe this!'

'It's something she wanted me to have in case anything happened to her – a letter.'

'What letter?'

'The one Nancy wrote to Jan before she killed herself – a confession. A little over five years ago, Walt and Nancy murdered his first wife, Kate.'

Kevin brought the jeep to a dead stop and faced her. 'What the hell are you saying? You must still be on a trip from the mescaline.'

'You'll see it for yourself. Come on, get this heap moving.'

When they reached the site, Susan leaped out of the jeep even before it stopped rolling, and went to kneel beside Jan's corpse.

Kevin came up behind her. 'What the hell – '

Susan undid the dead woman's belt and the fly of her pants. As he watched with mounting revulsion, she slid a hand down inside Jan's girdle. He turned around so as not to see what happened after that.

Susan stood up, brandishing the letter.

'*Voilà*! We've done it.'

'*What* have we done?'

'Here, read it.' She thrust it at him.

All the while he was reading it, he shook his head incredulously. 'It's the most bizarre thing I've ever heard of. It's obscene! The old medicine man was right: This damned mountain *is* cursed.'

Her eyes gleamed. 'Let he – or she – who is without guilt cast the first stone.'

He glanced at her uneasily. 'What's that supposed to mean?'

'I'm a true believer, Kevin: curses, spells, black magic, voodoo, the Holy Spirit. Come on, we'd better get back to the house. Look, the sun is coming out.'

As if on cue, dazzling bright sunshine inundated the mesa. A strong, fresh, aromatic wind swept away the last halo of clouds from the summit of Skull Mountain. Susan and Kevin loaded the bodies into the jeep and headed back towards the house. On the way, a helicopter, bearing the insignia of the US Army, swooped low over their heads.

Susan waved and shouted, 'Here comes the cavalry!'

Kevin was in a dour mood. 'Listen, what do you propose to do with that letter?'

'Present it to the authorities, of course. I want to see that murdering bastard hang or go to the chair or the gas chamber. I'm not particular how he dies. Just like all of the Ameses who came before him, he's rotten to the core.'

Involuntarily, he drew away from her. She was his wife, but suddenly she had become a stranger. Oh, not a total stranger. He had always recognized a dark, inscrutable side to Susan's personality, but nothing as extreme as what she revealed now.

'So that's been it all along, ever since we arrived here. You've been out to get Walter Ames. That schoolgirl flirtation with him – it was just a device to put him off his guard.'

She laughed and said cryptically, 'Oh, there's more to it than that, Kevin. I mean, Fate brought us here to Skull Mountain. It was preordained, everything that has happened the past two days. But once Walter and I were face to face, I did my share to contribute to his downfall.'

'I think you're insane.' He meant it.

'Crazy like a fox.' She felt for the letter inside her work shirt. Susan was joyful – ecstatic, in fact.

When they got back to the house, or what had once been the house, two helicopters were landing on the turf nearby.

A captain jumped out, followed by two army medics. 'You folks all right?'

'What's left of us,' Walt said.

'I'm Captain Haines.' He shook hands with Walt. 'Are you Mr Ames?'

'That's right.'

'Two Apaches from the village came into Fort Stanton this morning and told us you had a Mayday situation up here. But until the storm cleared out, there wasn't anything we could do. They said a plane crashed here on Skull Mountain yesterday.'

'Yesterday?' Jennie shook her head. 'It seems as if we've been here for years.'

'In a sense we have,' Susan said, with a thin smile.

Walt introduced the survivors. 'Mr Lemon and Miss Devane drowned while attempting to cross the footbridge. Miss Danzig was struck by lightning. The Cessna pilots were killed in the crash.'

The captain surveyed the ruins of the house and digested the account of the related tragedies that had befallen the group. 'It's a bitch!' he said solemnly. 'What you people have been through, it's incredible.'

'A night on Skull Mountain,' Susan said. 'Yes, *quite* a night on Skull Mountain.'

'Well, folks, how about we board the choppers and fly you out to civilization?'

When they were aboard, he instructed the pilot: 'Get on the radio and tell 'em to send a rescue team to the site of the crashed Cessna, take out the pilots and luggage and whatever else these people left in that plane, then stop back here and pick up the bodies of Miss Danzig, the Mexican, and' – he looked at Walter Ames with sympathy – 'Mrs Ames. She's down in a cellar freezer.'

Susan was sitting behind Walt, and her gaze on the back of his neck was venomous. *It won't be long before you join dear Nancy, Walt – not very long indeed!*

10

Susan and Kevin drove Larry and Jennie to the airport at Lincoln City in a rental car. They spent the half-hour before boarding time at the bar.

'Sorry we didn't get an opportunity to research together,' Kevin said.

Larry grinned. 'Oh, but we did. I learned more about Apache folklore from the villagers on Skull Mountain than I could have found out in a dozen textbooks.'

'Real grass roots, all right.'

'How long will you have to stay in Lincoln City?' Jennie asked Susan.

'I have to testify at a preliminary hearing on Wednesday morning. After that, we'll have to wait and see.'

'If they *do* indict Walt, it will have to be in Connecticut, where the alleged crime was committed,' Kevin said. 'There's going to be all kinds of red tape, not to mention that Walter Ames is a very rich and influential man. Quite frankly, I think Sue is baying at the moon. I don't think there's a chance in hell that he'll be convicted.'

Larry sipped his gin and tonic. 'I have to agree with Kevin. The only witness, Nancy, is dead, and that letter constitutes flimsy evidence, to say the least.'

'It's a death-bed confession in essence,' Susan said adamantly. 'You see, *I* heard the verbal confession before she shot herself – Jan Danzig and I.'

Larry and Jennie made no comment to this latest of Susan's revelations, but it was clear they were sceptical.

'They might say Nancy was insane.' Kevin lit a cigarette. 'Normal people don't shoot themselves for no reason.'

'But she *did* have a reason,' Susan maintained. 'She could no longer bear up under the pressure of her enormous guilt for helping Walt murder Kate.'

'There could be another reason,' Jennie said casually, but her eyes darted furtively to Susan and then back to Larry. 'Nancy was terribly jealous of Walt. And, in my opinion, she had good cause to be jealous. Don't you agree, Susan?'

Susan fielded the leading question flawlessly. 'Oh, I don't know. Walt is an attractive man and he knows it. What's the harm in a little innocent flirting? Haven't you ever flirted with a man other than your handsome husband, Jennie?'

'You'd better believe it,' Larry acknowledged. 'When we were going together, this wench nearly drove me out of my mind with her flirting.'

His wife sniffed. 'Campaign strategy, lover. I wanted to make you so jealous that you'd have no recourse but to marry me.'

They all laughed, and the awkward moment was over.

There was an announcement over the loudspeaker system: 'Western Airlines flight forty-six to Los Angeles leaving from gate seventeen. Passengers may begin boarding . . .'

'That's us, hon.' Larry downed his drink and stood up. 'Kevin and Susan, it's been a pleasure meeting you. In the few days we've known one another, I feel like we're old friends.'

'Amen, old buddy.' Kevin shook his hand warmly.

'When you've been through the kind of ordeal we have together, there's a close bond,' Jennie said.

She and Susan embraced, and the men kissed each other's wives on the cheek.

'You take care,' Kevin said, 'and be sure and write and tell me how your research is coming.'

'We're not that far away,' Susan said. 'Come and visit.'

'You, too.' Jennie waved as they walked off arm in arm.

Kevin swished the martini around in his glass. 'Nice guys.'

'The best. Do you know, she's worried about Larry?'

'Oh?'

'You remember when we came out of the shelter and Larry acted sort of vague and dizzy?'

'Come to think of it, yes.'

'Jennie told me earlier that he's had spells of some sort

before. In fact, he had one last night: cold sweats, shortness of breath, nausea.'

Kevin frowned. 'Why doesn't she make him see a doctor?'

'She is, as soon as they're back home.'

Kevin looked at his watch. 'Well, we may as well go back to the hotel and see if there are any messages. The district attorney's office promised to phone us before the day is out. You know, Sue, we've got to get this thing resolved. I can't sit here in Lincoln City indefinitely. I've got research to do.'

'Then don't. I'll sit it out, and you go and do your thing.' She had a certain glint in her eyes that he did not favour. 'What I'm doing is *my* thing.'

'Yes, it would appear that you, your whole family, have made "hating Ameses" a lifetime vocation.'

'Occupation!' she declared.

'Come on, let's go,' he said in annoyance.

They spoke very little on the way back to town. Near the end of the drive, Kevin felt compelled to comment:

'Well, the old medicine man was wrong. The Holy Spirit wasn't out to get us after all. You and I, Larry and Jennie, Walt – we've all come off Skull Mountain intact.'

She smiled. 'Don't count your chickens, Kevin. The Holy Spirit isn't through with Walter Ames; you'll see.'

They had been inside their room only ten minutes when the phone rang. Susan was in the shower, and Kevin answered it.

'Mr Brandon?'

'Speaking.'

'This is Harmon Gunderson at the district attorney's office.'

'Yes, Mr Gunderson, we've been expecting to hear from you. What's up?'

'We've been in touch with the authorities in Connecticut, as well as with Walter Ames's attorneys. To be frank, they are less than enthusiastic about reopening the case.'

'I can imagine. Ames packs a lot of clout in the state of Connecticut.'

'Yes, he does, but it's more than that. I mean, to charge a man with murder on the strength of a letter written by a distraught and desperate woman who killed herself immediately after writing it . . . well, you've got to admit that's pretty flimsy evidence.'

'My wife and Jan Danzig heard Nancy Ames's oral confession as well.'

There was a long silence before Gunderson drawled, 'Mr Brandon, Jan Danzig is dead, and your wife . . . well, let me tell you, the savage Ames-Norton feud is historic legend in Lincoln County.'

'Are you accusing my wife of lying?'

Another long pause. 'Mr Brandon, let me put it this way: Would your wife be willing to take a lie-detector test?'

Silence on Kevin's end, then: 'That's academic, isn't it? The results of polygraph tests are not admissible as evidence in court.'

'I realize that, but they can be extremely influential in affecting opinions both in the DA's office and the police department. It would lend credibility to her testimony if Mrs Brandon would agree to the polygraph test.'

'Well, I see your point, Mr Gunderson, but I can't speak for my wife. Right now she's in the bath. Can I phone you back?'

'That will be fine. You have the number. I'll expect to hear from you. Thank you very much, Mr Brandon.'

Kevin stared at the phone after he put it back on its cradle. He was still deep in thought when Susan came out of the bathroom, wrapped in a bath towel.

'Was that the phone?' she asked.

He told her about Gunderson's call. 'Well? Will you do it?'

She sat down on the bed and crossed her legs. 'No, of course I won't do it. It's an affront to one's dignity, an invasion of privacy. And, as everyone knows, the results are thoroughly unreliable.'

'Not altogether. You'd score points with the police and the DA's office. Believe me, you're going to need all the points you can rack up if you take on Walter Ames in his home state. It's only your word against that letter, and, candidly, Sue, it's one of the wildest things I've ever read.'

'I can convince a judge and a jury,' she said stubbornly. 'Walter Ames murdered his wife. He knows it, I know it, and – '

'You're the only one who knows it, aside from Walter Ames, and he sure as hell isn't going to admit it.'

'Why don't they give *him* a lie-detector test?'

'Maybe they will. All right, the assistant DA is waiting for your decision. I'll phone him and tell him no.'

Gunderson's reply, when Kevin told him Susan's answer, was civil, but the innuendo was clear: 'I didn't think she would . . . Oh, by the way, one new development: Walter Ames has expressed his willingness to appear before a grand jury in Connecticut. In fact, he insists upon it. Claims that even if they decide not to reopen the case, he will demand a hearing in order to clear himself of the absurd accusations your wife is making against him?'

'Absurd? Is that your personal view, Mr Gunderson?' Kevin was becoming nettled with the assistant DA.

Gunderson replied coldly, 'I have no official opinion, Mr Brandon. I am only repeating what Mr Ames told the district attorney and what he told me moments ago.'

'All right, so what happens now?'

'When a grand jury is convened to hear the case, you will be notified to appear in Connecticut on the assigned date. As far as we here in Lincoln County are concerned, you are free to leave any time you please . . . Thank you for *your* cooperation, Mr Brandon.'

Kevin's anger triggered a thought. 'And thank *you*, Mr Gunderson . . . Oh, my wife just said I should tell you that if Walter Ames agrees to take a polygraph test, then she will, too.'

It had the desired effect: Gunderson was caught off guard. 'Oh?' He cleared his throat. 'Well, it's out of our hands, at any rate. Good luck and goodbye.'

Kevin hung up and grinned at Susan.

She was indignant. 'What on earth did you tell him that for, that I'll take a test if Walter Ames does?'

'Psychology, my love. I think I may have scored a point for you with a wild card. If we accept what Nancy said in her letter as the truth, then we have to conclude that Walter Ames is lying, in which case he would never agree to take a lie-detector test.'

Susan looked pleased. 'I never thought of that. Yes, a brilliant bluff. He would never consent.'

Kevin studied her closely. 'On the other hand . . . '

'No, you're right, Kevin. The man *is* a cold-blooded murderer and – '

'That's what worries me.'

'Why so?'

He put his hands on her bare shoulders and looked into her large, slate-grey eyes. 'He might not care for the idea that you, my dear, share his critical secret. He might decide it would be a risky thing to have you testify before a grand jury.'

'You mean – oh, you can't mean – '

'I *do* mean. He may decide to see to it that Susan Brandon will be missing when the grand jury convenes.'

It was a sobering thought, and Susan was shaken. 'He's ruthless enough to try it.'

'And rich and powerful enough to hire the best hands in the business . . . You know, I think we ought to cut this trip short and head back home. I'll feel a lot safer on our own turf. We're far too vulnerable gallivanting around the country.'

'What about your thesis?'

'It will keep; everything does. Besides, with this hassle to cope with, I couldn't keep my concentration. Jesus! How did we ever get into this mess?'

'Kismet, darling.' She stood up and discarded the towel; throwing her arms around his neck, she rubbed her pelvis against his. 'Do you know what we need? Some relaxation. Take off your clothes and we'll hop into bed. Any interest?'

He let out his breath in a long, low sigh, almost a whistle. 'I am your slave, madam.'

11

The Brandons returned to their home in Palo Alto, California, and spent a lazy, uneventful summer. Kevin worked on his thesis for two hours every morning while

Susan puttered in her garden. Afternoons they spent at the beach; evenings at home, just to play it safe. Walter Ames was still very much on their minds.

In early August they were notified to appear on September 16 in Hartford, Connecticut, to testify before a special-grand-jury hearing into the death of Kate Ames.

'At long last!' Susan declared. 'Let's drive into Frisco tonight and celebrate.'

And for the first time since they'd returned from New Mexico, they were not nervous about venturing away from the house. They even took to leaving their windows open at night again.

On August 20 they received a phone call from Jennie Bostwick.

'Jennie! What a pleasant surprise!' Susan said, and called to Kevin in his study. 'Guess who I'm talking to, hon – Jennie Bostwick!'

He strolled into the kitchen and leaned against the sink, smoking his pipe and listening.

'How is Larry?'

'That's why I'm calling,' Jennie said in a strained voice. 'Remember those spells he was getting? Well, I finally got him to have a physical.' She hesitated. 'And . . . and the results are inconclusive. They think it may be his heart, but like I said, they're not sure. His doctor wants him to go to Stanford to see this specialist, Dr Wilson Busch.'

'Stanford's number one for heart men,' Susan consoled her. 'I'm sure it's going to work out fine. My cousin had the same thing; they even had him in intensive care at one time, and it turned out to be nothing. When are you coming?'

'Next Monday; that's why I called. Can you recommend a place to stay while he's at Stanford?'

'Why, *here,* of course.'

'Thanks, but that would be an imposition.'

'We'll be highly insulted if you turn us down, won't we, Kevin?'

He nodded. 'Tell her I'll never read another one of Larry's books.'

Jennie didn't need much persuading, and on the following Monday afternoon, the Bostwicks arrived in their Lincoln Continental convertible.

'Pretty classy,' Kevin said admiringly. 'Obviously it pays

to be a novelist.'

'Only lately,' Jennie said dryly. 'For years we lived on a shoestring, namely my salary as a receptionist.'

Kevin threw an arm about Larry's shoulders. 'Well, come on inside and have a drink, old buddy, and you can tell us what this is all about. Personally, I think you're a gold brick. You look like you could whup Ali in his prime.'

Larry grinned. 'Get off my case, Brandon. It's all *her* doing. I feel fine.'

Jennie bristled. 'Well, you *ain't* fine. The doctor says he's got this arrhythmia – an irregular heartbeat caused by some disturbance in the discharge of cardiac impulses. Maybe they can pin it down here at Stanford.'

They spent the rest of the afternoon drinking gin and tonic on the patio and talking – mostly about their ordeal on Skull Mountain.

'You know, it all seems so unreal now,' Jennie said, 'something that happened to somebody else, not us.'

'I wish it *had* happened to somebody else,' Kevin said.

'Amen,' Larry agreed.

Susan shocked them all by dissenting. 'I'm not sorry it happened.' Conscious of their censuring looks, she amended it. 'I mean, if it hadn't happened, the four of us would never have become friends.'

'I'm all for friendship,' Larry said, 'and I value ours very highly, but think of the price, Sue: seven people dead.'

'What about Walt?' Jennie asked.

'We go east in September to testify before the grand jury.'

Although the sunshine was hot, Jennie shivered. 'Better you than us. Aren't you scared that he might try to stop you from testifying?'

'We were a little squeamish at first,' Kevin admitted. 'But when you examine it rationally, he'd be a fool to do anything to us. It would just put the finger on him, but good. As it stands now, it's his word against Susan's.'

'And there's the letter Nancy wrote,' Larry reminded them. 'I think he's on the hook. So what has he got to lose by eliminating you guys?'

'Thanks a lot, pal,' Kevin said. 'Oh, hell! Let's talk about something pleasant. How's the new book coming?'

'Slow, I hate to say. I've got this crap on my mind when I sit at the typewriter.'

'Sure you have. It'll pass once this Dr Busch gives you a clean bill of health.'

'Sure,' Larry said, but not too convincingly.

They went to bed early that evening. Larry's appointment at Stanford was for eight o'clock Tuesday morning. He and Jennie skipped breakfast but had coffee and juice with the Brandons before they left.

'You have a great location here,' Larry said, admiring the scenery from the patio. 'Right on top of the mountain.'

'It's gorgeous,' Jennie agreed, 'except for that terrible winding road coming up here. It's practically hanging on the side of a rock wall.'

Kevin chuckled. 'Don't look down.'

'I used to feel the same way when we first moved up here,' Susan said, 'but now it doesn't phase me a bit. Just like driving on the freeway.'

Larry glanced at his watch. 'Time to go, love. I don't know what time we'll see you guys. They might even keep me over.'

'If they do, give us a ring.'

Kevin and Susan walked the Bostwicks to their car.

'Good luck, Larry.' Susan kissed him on the cheek.

'See you around.' Kevin punched him playfully on the bicep.

They stood in the drive and watched the long, sleek Lincoln glide down the road and disappear around the first bend behind a wall of trees, then went back to the patio and finished breakfast.

A short while later, Susan was planting geraniums in the garden, and Kevin was reading in the chaise longue on the patio, when two police cars pulled up in front of the house. The drivers got out and walked up the driveway – lean, muscular, sombre-looking men with half-moons of perspiration darkening their uniforms around the armpits.

Kevin sat up and removed his sunglasses. 'What can I do for you, officers?' he asked.

The taller of the two replied, 'Do you know a Mr and Mrs Lawrence Bostwick?'

'Yes, I do. They're our houseguests. Is anything wrong?'

The cop pushed back his cap. 'I'm afraid so. There's been

an accident.'

'How could that be? They left here less than an hour ago.'

'They didn't get very far, sad to say. Their vehicle, a nineteen seventy-nine Lincoln Continental, crashed through a guard rail down the road and plunged into the canyon. They were killed instantly.'

Susan sprang up and ran over to the chaise kneeling behind Kevin and clutching his shoulders. 'Oh, my God!' she gasped. 'I can't believe it!'

'It's true, ma'am. They must have ploughed through that rail at better than eighty miles an hour.'

Kevin kept shaking his head and moving his lips, but nothing came out. Finally he found his voice. 'It isn't possible. Larry isn't – wasn't – the reckless kind. Something must have gone wrong with the car.'

'We'll be checking that out, sir.' The officer stood with his hands on his waist, staring out across the valley below. 'Well, I guess there's nothing else for now. Will you be around later today? We may want you to give a statement.'

'We'll be here all day,' Susan assured him. 'What's going to happen to their bodies?'

'They'll be shipped to the next of kin. Mr Bostwick carried a lot of identification.' He touched the bill of his cap. 'We'll be leaving now. Thank you for your help.'

In silence, Kevin and Susan watched them walk back to the patrol cars and drive off.

'What a bummer,' Kevin said in a hollow voice. He turned around and looked at his wife. 'Do you feel all right? You're the colour of death.'

She looked right through him. 'That's because I've been living so close to death for so long. Ever since we boarded that damned Cessna at Denver, death has never been more than an arm's length away from us, Kevin.'

The sweat trickling down his spine was icy cold. 'Mustn't talk like that, Sue; mustn't even think like that.'

'But it's the truth, Kevin; you know it is.' Her mirthless laughter had the timbre of earth rattling down on a coffin lid. 'Even a thousand miles away from Skull Mountain, the Holy Spirit reaches out to us.'

'Stop talking nonsense!'

'Kevin, don't you realize that we are the only remaining

survivors, you and I?'

'There's Walter Ames.'

'And all the others – the two pilots, Nancy, Dick and Laura, Jan, and now Larry and Jennie – died horrible deaths.'

He grabbed her arms and shook her. 'For God's sake, get a hold of yourself! I'm heartsick over Larry and Jennie, but we mustn't go to pieces over it. Life is terribly unfair.'

'And death is the great equalizer; it plays no favourites.'

'Let me tell you, my dear wife, it is not the Holy Spirit that worries me. Oh, no, my fears are of something far more tangible.'

'What do you mean?'

'Never mind for now. Let's wait and see whether or not the police can determine how the accident occurred.'

At three o'clock that afternoon a plainclothesman in a seersucker suit appeared on their doorstep. Flashing his ID, he introduced himself:

'Captain Jennings, of the Santa Clara County Homicide Division. May I come in?'

'Certainly.'

Kevin escorted him into the parlour, where Susan was sitting on the couch with her legs drawn up underneath her, drinking a martini – her fourth. Her eyes were glazed.

'My wife,' he said, with a note of apology, 'has been under a great strain. She – both of us – still haven't recovered from the shock. The Bostwicks meant a great deal to us.'

'I understand,' the captain said.

'So, Cap, whassa verdict?' Susan said thickly. 'How did it happen?'

'Well, we can't be positive, because the car was a junk pile; it fell two hundred feet straight down onto the jagged rock floor. However, there is the distinct possibility that the Lincoln's dual brake systems had been tampered with. In fact, I'm almost certain the lines were cut. The nodes are too even.'

'I was afraid of that,' Kevin said grimly.

'How well did you know the Bostwicks?'

'Not very, really.'

'Well enough to know if they had any enemies?'

'I'm afraid not. He was a novelist and scriptwriter, and I

suppose all prominent people, those in the public eye, have enemies who bear them grudges. But we're not talking about grudges here; we're talking about *murder.*'

'Mr Brandon, you'd be surprised how many men and women commit murder over trivialities. Perhaps there was something in their past, his or hers . . .'

Kevin walked to the bar and poured himself a drink. 'Captain?'

'No thanks, I'm on duty.'

Kevin drained the glass and then refilled it. 'I think you're barking up the wrong tree, Captain. If the Lincoln's brakes were sabotaged, I'm convinced that whoever did it was not out to get the Bostwicks but my wife and me.'

Jenning's eyebrows lifted in surprise. 'Who would want to kill you and your wife? And why?'

'I'll tell you, Captain, but please sit down. This is going to take time.'

'Shoot.' Jennings sat down on a leather easy chair and lit a cigar.

When Kevin had concluded his story, the captain's cigar was a stub with an inch of white ash hanging precariously from it.

'That's an incredible story, Mr Brandon, but hardly substantial enough to warrant an official accusation against Walter Ames. I read all about the case in the papers right after that monster storm clobbered the Midwest; but let's not digress. You think the Bostwicks' car was mistaken for your car by whoever cut the brake lines. It doesn't hold together. If you were marked for murder, you'd be checked out for weeks – at the very least, days. I mean, these people are professionals. They wouldn't mistake a Lincoln convertible for a Datsun sedan.'

'But here's the key, Captain. Until last Wednesday, Susan's Uncle Fred stayed with us for ten days on his way to Mexico, and he was driving a Lincoln convertible. It was parked in the drive all the time he stayed here. To be sure, it was a different colour, but at night – like they say, all cats are grey in the dark.'

Captain Jennings tugged at his lower lip pensively. 'When are you due to travel to Connecticut to appear before the grand jury?' he inquired.

'September sixteenth.'

'Hmmm . . . a little over two weeks.' He stood up and began to pace back and forth. 'Do you know what I think? I think it would be a wise precaution to keep you under police surveillance until you leave for Connecticut. We'll see you to the airport and notify the Connecticut authorities to have a police escort meet you at their end.'

'Thanks, Captain.' Susan downed her martini and handed the glass to Kevin for a refill. 'I sure would hate to die before Walter Ames does.'

The captain grunted something noncommittal. 'Mr and Mrs Brandon, I'll be leaving now. We'll have a man over here within the hour. He'll do his best to be inconspicuous, so don't do anything to blow his cover. Don't even talk to him.'

Kevin went to the front door with him and watched him walk down the path to his unmarked car.

Susan came up behind him and put her arms around his waist. 'I must be perverted,' she said. 'Whenever I'm in a dangerous situation, I get horny.' She slipped one hand down inside his trousers and shorts and clasped his penis. 'It would appear that we are housebound for the next two weeks, which means we'll be putting in a lot of sack time. Sex, anyone?'

He was slow to respond, but her skilled and persistent fondling eventually produced an erection. 'It's funny,' he said. 'Sex is the last thing on my mind, with all this menace hanging over us yet, as they say, the flesh is weak. I'll go along with you, but my heart won't be in it.'

'Try it; you'll like it.' Pulling up the skirt of her sundress, she slipped her panties down to her ankles and stepped out of them. 'I feel positively wanton. Let's do it right here on the hall rug.' She lay down on her back and held out her arms to him. 'Come to Mama, honey.'

Kevin shook his head in disbelief. 'This is sheer insanity. I feel as if we're back in that ceremonial lodge on Skull Mountain.' Nevertheless, he took off his shirt and pants and mounted her.

Susan moaned, and a shudder wracked her body as he entered her. She reached her orgasm quickly; but Kevin was not fulfilled. For some inexplicable reason, he was overwhelmed by remembrance of that nightmare so long ago in the seedy whorehouse in Honolulu, and the same phrase that had leaped into Nancy's mind when she'd written her confession now leaped into his:

'Though the mills of God grind slowly, yet they grind exceeding small.'

12

At exactly 10:00 A.M. on September 16, 1980, Susan Brandon walked into the grand-jury room in the Hartford Federal Court Building, escorted by two plainclothesmen who had been watching over her since she and Kevin arrived from California two days earlier. She was questioned first by a county prosecutor about the events of the two days the survivors had spent on Skull Mountain, from the time the Cessna 431 crashed until they were airlifted off the mesa by helicopter:

'You say that Mrs Nancy Ames made an oral confession to you and Miss Jan Danzig before she did so in writing in this letter?' He brandished the letter in the direction of the jurors.

Susan had anticipated this line of questioning. In fact, she had stayed up until four o'clock that morning making a list of queries she might expect from the prosecutor. 'No, Nancy had already written the letter. She told us what was in it so that we would understand her motives for writing it.'

'Didn't you and Miss Danzig think it was peculiar that she should confide in you two?'

'Yes, we did. I told Nancy that a written confession was uncalled for, that she should go straight to the authorities as soon as we were rescued. Her explanation, however, was quite logical. She said that we were in grave danger on the mountain, and that if she didn't make it through the ordeal, she wanted us to carry out her final wishes. Of course, we had no inkling that she was contemplating suicide.'

'Speaking as a lay person, Mrs Brandon, how would you evaluate Nancy Ames's state of mind when she made her confession? Was she overwrought emotionally? hysterical? angry?'

'No. As a matter of fact, she was astonishingly calm and dispassionate when she told us how she and Walter Ames had murdered his first wife. One thing I did feel – that she was seized by an irresistible compulsion to cleanse her mind and soul of the insufferable secret she had been living with for so many years.'

'Did you and Miss Danzig have any cause to doubt her story?'

'None whatsoever. As I say, she was extremely rational and convincing.'

'All right, Mrs Brandon, that will be all for now.'

The next witness to testify was a handwriting expert.

'Have you studied samples of Mrs Ames's handwriting made prior to her suicide?' the prosecutor asked.

'Innumerable samples.'

The prosecutor held up the letter in evidence. 'And you compared those samples with this confession she wrote just before her death?'

'Yes, sir. Beyond the shadow of a doubt, the confession was written by Mrs Ames.'

'Thank you.'

Dr Lewis Lanz was called to the witness stand.

'Dr Lanz, I am going to read a transcript of the testimony you gave before the coroner's jury on September eleventh, nineteen seventy-five, in the investigation of the death of Mrs Kate Ames, to refresh your memory and to acquaint this jury with the events leading up to her death, which that jury subsequently judged to be accidental.'

Dr Lanz listened intently, head bowed, one hand absently stroking his tie clasp as the prosecutor read the transcript of his testimony.

'Dr Lanz, is that substantially how you recall the circumstances of Mrs Kate Ames's death?'

'It is. I remember everything quite vividly.'

'Let me assure you, Doctor, that in this interrogation, I have no intention of challenging your veracity with regard to your previous testimony before that coroner's jury. What I want to determine is whether or not, in retrospect, you entertain any reasonable doubts about what happened on the morning of Kate Ames's death, about what you saw or *thought* you saw.

'Now, you heard Nancy Ames's letter of confession read here in court when these proceedings commenced. In light of what that letter contains, are there any emendations you would care to make in that previous testimony?'

Lanz's brow furrowed. 'I don't quite understand what you mean, sir. To the best of my recollection, what I told the coroner's jury was the truth. Yes . . . yes, I'm sure it was Kate Ames I saw that morning by the fountain in the garden.'

'How far away from the patio would you estimate she was?'

Lanz hunched his shoulders. 'Let's see . . . Oh, I'd say roughly one hundred and fifty yards, give or take a few.'

'Dr Lanz, how is your eyesight?'

'I have a slight astigmatism and myopia, correctable to twenty-thirty in my left eye and twenty-forty in my right.'

'I see . . . In view of that, can you be absolutely certain that it was Mrs Kate Ames you saw sitting in her wheelchair on the morning of September sixth?'

Dr Lanz was plainly befuddled. 'Well . . . reasonably certain.'

'You could positively identify the details of her face?'

'Well, no; but, after all, Kate Ames was the only blonde woman on the premises that morning – the only crippled woman.'

'Precisely!' the prosecutor said with a note of triumph. 'You saw a blonde woman in a wheelchair and naturally you assumed it was Mrs Ames. Anyone would make the same assumption . . . Dr Lanz, if you could, in hindsight, give testimony once more at that same inquest, would you be so emphatic in identifying the woman in the wheelchair that morning as Kate Ames?'

Without hesitation, Dr Lanz replied, 'No, I would not.'

'That will be all, Dr Lanz. You may step down.'

Walter Ames was the last to testify. A rueful smile played across his lips when he took the oath, and he glanced down at his shoe tops.

'Mr Ames,' the prosecutor began, 'you are familiar with the contents of this letter your wife, Nancy Ames, now deceased, wrote just before she committed suicide, in which she alleges that on the day of September fifth, nineteen seventy-five, you and she did conspire to kill your then wife Kate Ames?'

'Indeed I am, and it is a blatant lie.'

'That will be for the grand jury to decide . . . Mr Ames, do you have any idea what motive Mrs Ames could have had in accusing you and herself of murder, assuming the allegation is false?'

'She had a very strong motive, sir,' he said without hesitation.

The prosecutor looked surprised. 'Then, would you be so kind as to enlighten me and the jury as to that motive?'

'One of the oldest motives for damning a man since the world began: She was insanely jealous. If I so much as looked at another woman, she'd rave and rant and threaten to kill herself, or to kill me. One of the reasons she liked it so much up on Skull Mountain was the total seclusion.' He smiled at the jurors. 'No other females to distract my attention from her.'

'Then you never gave her just cause to mistrust you?'

'Not in more than five years of marriage.' He paused and sighed. 'Not until I met Susan Brandon.'

The prosecutor's eyebrows lifted, and the jurors bent forward in their seats attentively.

'Susan Brandon? Do you mean to say that you and Susan Brandon were lovers?'

'Yes, we *are* lovers.'

'Now, wait a minute, Mr Ames. Had you ever met Susan Brandon before the day of the plane crash on Skull Mountain?'

'No, we met for the first time that day.'

'Hold on, Mr Ames. You were all rescued from the mountain on the following day. Do you mean to say that, in that space of two days, you and Mrs Susan Brandon became lovers?'

'It's the truth. The instant we looked at each other, we both sensed it, that we shared a simpatico chemistry. I don't know what else to call it. We made love in my study that same night.'

'Does her husband know?'

'I can't say. But someone must have known about it and told my wife.'

'Your wife confronted you with this charge?'

'She did. I denied it at first, but she had the facts, and this time there was no appeasing her. She threatened to kill herself. She threatened to kill me. She threatened to kill Susan Brandon. It was the old story of the boy who cried wolf. She had been through the routine so often, I dismissed it as just another tantrum.' He leaned over and cupped a hand across his forehead, the picture of dejection and regret. 'This time I should have listened to her.'

'Mr Ames, have you been seeing Mrs Brandon since your wife's death?'

'No. This awful, senseless, bizarre tragedy has left its mark on both Susan and myself. Nancy would always stand between us, the spectre of her slumped over the desk with her brains splattered all over the blotter and wall. That very day we both came to the conclusion that ours was a star-crossed relationship. I haven't seen or spoken to her since.'

'This "chemistry" that attracted you and Mrs Brandon to each other, it must still be there even if you both exercise restraint in demonstrating it? And, if so, why would Susan Brandon level such vicious accusations at you?'

'Because I honestly believe that *she* believed the preposterous lies Nancy told her and Jan Danzig. My wife was a dyed-in-the-wool psychoneurotic. They can be very convincing when they lie; ask any psychiatrist.'

Walter Ames was watching the jury surreptitiously. His antenna for human responses was highly sensitive, and he could literally feel their collective sentiment predisposing in his favour. *I think we've got 'em, Walt, old man!*

'Mrs Brandon told you she believed that you and your wife Nancy killed your first wife?'

'She did, and nothing I could say or do could convince her that Nancy's fabrications were devised to wreak vengeance on me from the grave. That is the truth, so help me God!'

'Mr Ames, I'd like to digress for a moment. Did you know Lawrence and Jennie Bostwick?'

'Yes. They were among the survivors of the plane crash on Skull Mountain. A handsome couple, and he was a brilliant writer. I read about their tragic accident. Terrible . . . terrible.'

'There has been some speculation that it was not an accident, that the brakes had been tampered with.'

Walter Ames's face registered shock. 'Someone wanted to kill the Bostwicks? Who? Who would be so savage?'

'There is further speculation that the perpetrator killed the wrong people, sabotaged the wrong car, that his intended victims were Mr and Mrs Brandon.'

Walter shook his head, expressing absolute bewilderment. 'Speculation, is it? I don't know. It all sounds too far-fetched to capture my imagination, sir. Frankly, it boggles my mind, it's so outlandish.'

The interrogator and Walter Ames locked eyes, and it was the prosecutor who wavered. He did an about-face and walked right back to his seat:

'You're right, Mr Ames, it *is* mind-boggling. I just thought I'd introduce it as – Never mind. That will be all.'

Walter had all he could do to restrain himself from leaping over the rail and doing a buck-and-wing. He had pulled it off! The only thing the prosecutor had accomplished by bringing up the Bostwicks' accident was to confuse the jury even more, thereby reinforcing the doctrine of 'reasonable doubt.' Walter was confident of the verdict even before it was announced two hours later:

No true bill.

13

GRAND JURY REFUSES TO
INDICT WALTER AMES:
CITES INSUFFICIENT EVIDENCE

Kevin Brandon put down the newspaper. 'I don't understand it, Susan. You said it was a *fait accompli*, that there was no way in the world he could get off.'

'I underestimated Walter Ames,' she said, some of her prior smug self-confidence gone. 'He's a survivor; but so am I,' she said with determination. 'This affair is not over yet.'

Kevin's face darkened as he continued reading the account of the grand-jury hearing. 'Speaking of affairs, what the hell is this guy talking about?'

She had anticipated this. Although the press was barred from the proceedings, there was no way to keep a bombshell, such as the one Walter Ames had dropped, under wraps for long: The accused had been having an affair with his accuser!

He screwed me up on Skull Mountain, and yesterday he screwed me again in court. 'Put down the paper, Kevin. I'd rather tell you about it myself.'

He was staring at her strangely.

'Tell me what?'

'The reason that Walt got off scot-free. He persuaded the court that Nancy committed suicide because she found out he and I had slept together. I told you, he's diabolical.'

'And they believed him?'

'He was extremely convincing, apparently. He claimed Nancy wrote that damning letter to gain some sick kind of vengeance. It raised doubts in their minds – reasonable doubts – and that proved insufficient grounds for killing the indictment.'

'You mean the grand jury accepted his word above yours? That's outrageous! Didn't you tell them what a fucking liar he is?'

Her eyes were the hue of polished gun metal. She placed a hand on his arm. In a quiet voice she said, 'Kevin . . . I was recalled to the stand and questioned about his testimony that he had sex with me that first night on Skull Mountain.'

Kevin's countenance mirrored the sort of shock displayed by the humans in *Invasion of the Body Snatchers* when confronted by the hideous truth that their friends and loved ones had been taken over body, mind, and soul by an alien species. 'You're lying,' he said in a hoarse whisper. 'Why do you want to torture me this way?'

'I'm grief-stricken, darling, believe me, but it has to come out. If I hadn't tried to protect you and save myself from humiliation by hiding the truth, he never could have gotten away with what he did. I should have accused him in front of everyone right after it happened.'

'Protect me? Save yourself from humiliation? Accused

him of what?' Kevin was totally bewildered.

'The thing is, Kevin, that night when I couldn't sleep and went downstairs for a drink, Walter was there in the den. He made me a drink; we talked for a while. Then I said good night and started to leave, but he wouldn't let me. He was drunk and sexually aroused. He said he wanted me. I screamed and tried to get away, but he was too strong for me. And nobody could hear my screams over that thunderous storm. Yes, Kevin, Walter Ames raped me on the couch.'

'Jesus Christ!' All of the blood drained out of his face. He tried to stand up but fell back into the chair. 'That rotten sonovabitch! If I could get my hands on him, I'd kill him here and now.'

'That's why I didn't tell you,' she lied glibly. 'I was afraid that, with all the tension and strain we were under, you *would* kill him. It wasn't worth the high risk. And can you imagine how I felt – how I still feel – after I learned that Nancy found out and it drove her to kill herself? Oh, admittedly she was an unstable woman, but I still feel partly responsible. You see, she went to her grave believing that her husband and I were having a torrid affair. If only I had told her what really happened; at least she wouldn't have blamed me.'

He clasped his hands on each side of his head, fingers splayed as if to keep it from shattering. 'This . . . this . . . I can't get my head together. I keep hoping I'll wake up and find out this has all been a horrible nightmare. I mean, it can't be real – seven of them dead, and now this with you.'

'The medicine man was right after all,' she said once again. She was constantly seeking to undermine his impatience and contempt for the supernatural. 'All of them dead but for you and me . . . and Walter Ames.'

He sprang up, his strength revitalized as murderous rage pumped adrenaline through his body. 'No! Not Walter Ames! Walter Ames is just as dead as the others. At least, he soon will be!'

She went to him and put her arms around his waist, pressing her cheek against his heaving chest. She could feel the trip-hammer beat of his heart. 'Kevin, that wouldn't solve anything. You'd go to jail, and I'd be all alone.

Darling, let's put it out of our minds. You were right when you called it a nightmare. But it's over now.'

'Is it?' His voice was empty, dead.

'The chapter is closed. Tomorrow we start anew. Tell you what: Let's take that cruise around the world we've been planning so long. You could take a sabbatical to complete your paper.'

'We can't afford it yet; you know that.'

She laughed. 'Can't afford it? Kevin, you know perfectly well that when my mother died, she left me a rich woman.'

'I won't live off my wife; you know *that* damned well, too!'

'We'll talk about it when we get back to California.'

Abruptly he turned away from her and walked to the door of their hotel room. 'I'm going out for a while. Have to think. I'll see you later.'

'Don't be too long. I'm famished.'

While she was undressing for her shower, a furtive, secretive smile flirted over Susan's face. She was utterly confident that no matter how much things appeared to be working *against* her and *for* Walter Ames, it was pre-ordained that she would be victorious in the end. Her destiny was in the hands of the gods. Generation after generation of Norton women had dedicated themselves, with religious fervour, to revenging Ike Norton against the infamous clan, and had succeeded.

She was on her way to the bathroom when the phone rang. She picked it up. A man's voice, a familiar voice:

'Hello Susan.'

For a moment she was speechless.

'Hello, Susan? Are you there?'

She recovered. 'Yes, Walt, I'm here. Once again you caught me off guard. Congratulations.'

'Congratulations?'

'Yes, it was very neat the way you pulled it off yesterday. That's twice you've beat the same rap. It takes a bit of doing.'

His laughter was congenial, the magnanimous victor consoling the defeated foe. 'You have class, Susan – grace under pressure, as Hemingway once described it.'

'What in the hell do you want, Walt? To rub my nose in it?'

'To the contrary. In spite of what you tried to do to me, I'm still attracted to you. You exude the fascination of a cobra. Being close to you is dangerous – it was near fatal to me – yet . . . well, here I am phoning you.'

'You're right: I *am* a threat to you, just as all the Nortons are a threat to all the Ameses *ad infinitum.*'

'Jesus! You *are* obsessed – crazy, maybe – like a dog chewing on a bare bone. That's what your case is, Susan, a bare, dry bone. Give up on it.'

She remained silent.

'Susan, is Kevin with you?'

'No, he's out.'

'Good, then I can speak frankly. After that one marvellous night we had together, I made up my mind to steer clear of you; but now that Nancy's gone . . . well, I keep thinking about you, your sensual body. You're the most desirable female I've ever made love to; the most passionate, too. Don't deny it, Susan; you enjoyed our sex as much as I did.'

'You son of a bitch! The gall of you! Two weeks ago you sent a goon to our home with orders to kill us – kill *me* – and now you're making love to me over the phone!'

'That's ridiculous. I had nothing to do with the Bostwicks' unfortunate accident.'

'You're a damned liar! Never mind, let's terminate this conversation. If you called to gloat, all right. You won, and it's water over the dam. Is there anything else?'

'Yes, I want to see you.'

'You must be insane.'

She held the phone poised over the cradle, about to slam it down, but an inner voice stopped her: *Don't do it, Susan! He's vulnerable, still within your reach.* It was true. She had lost at the grand-jury hearing, and had resigned herself to it, but now here was Walter Ames tempting Fate, offering her another go at him. Her heart accelerated. She was hot, feverish.

'Why do you want to see me, Walt?'

'Isn't it obvious? You're in my blood. I want to screw your ass off.'

'You're crude; but then again, you're an Ames.'

He laughed. 'There's more to it than that. I want to make a proposition to you.'

Susan laughed. 'Isn't that redundant?'

'Not that kind of proposition. Look, I'm down in the hotel lobby. Leave a note for Kevin and come right down. I'll be outside the back entrance, the dark-green Caddy.'

She was besieged by conflicting emotions: *I'd be a fool to meet him; he may have a plan to kill me. Only a bigger fool would even consider such a thing; he'd be the obvious suspect. I can't pass up such a golden opportunity. So long as Walter Ames is accessible, the game's not over.* 'All right,' she said, 'I'll be down shortly. I have to dress.'

She dressed quickly: a white jersey blouse with blue binding around the neckline and short sleeves, and a light-blue wrap skirt overlaid with a green shell-print. She ran a comb through her hair and applied lipstick and eye shadow, then scrawled a brief note to Kevin on the pad on the bedside table: 'Got restless. Went shopping. Be back soon.'

Though it was mid-September, it felt more like a sultry summer afternoon, and the glare caused her to squint as she exited the hotel onto the sidewalk. A horn beeped twice, and then she saw the green Cadillac with Walt behind the wheel. She took a deep breath and walked purposefully to the car. '*Yea, though I walk through the valley of the shadow of death . . .*'

He leaned over and opened the door for her. 'Thank you for seeing me.'

She got in and pulled the door shut. 'I must be out of my mind.'

'You did the right thing.' He offered her his hand. 'What do you say, no hard feelings?'

Arrogant bastard! She managed a brittle smile. 'I suppose so.' She held his hand briefly.

'Good.' He pulled the Caddy away from the curb into the main flow of traffic, very heavy as the rush hour approached. 'There's a quaint little joint not far from here – Anselmo's. They've got some tables in a garden out in back.'

'I could use a drink, a tall, cold one.'

'Yeah, today's a bitch: Indian summer.'

Throughout the drive they made small talk, studiously avoiding the subject of the grand-jury hearing and the events that led up to it, behaving like casual friends rather than mortal enemies.

At Anselmo's, the head waiter gave Walt the VIP treatment: 'Mr Ames, what an honour! We haven't seen you all summer.'

'I was out in New Mexico.'

'Yes, we read all about it in the papers and – ' He broke off awkwardly and averted his eyes from Walt's impassive face. 'Now for your table.'

'In the garden, Enrico.'

'To be sure. You and Mrs Ames always – '

Walt patted his shoulder. 'It's all right, Enrico, these things are difficult. Nancy is dead, and I've been through hell, but it's all over now, so let's forget it.'

Susan looked at him. *It's not over – not quite.*

They were seated at a table for two underneath a small palm tree. The garden was ablaze with lush, colourful tropical plants and trees.

'In the winter they put a top over it, and it becomes a solarium,' he said.

The waiter served them two tall gin and tonics. Walt offered her a cigarette and took one himself. Inhaling deeply, he leaned back in his chair, studying her quizzically through a veil of smoke.

'Well?' she asked.

'I was wondering why you agreed to come with me. You could have a pistol in your bag.'

'Don't be an ass. Your hide isn't worth my freedom.'

'Yeah, I suppose not. You're a realistic, hard-nosed broad. So why *did* you come?'

'Curiosity. What's the proposition?'

'There's a big package of land out in Lincoln County up for grabs, an amalgamation of Ames and Norton land. I've got first crack at it. Yesterday, after the hearing, it came to me like a bolt out of the blue: you and me in partnership on the deal. We'd put up a million apiece.'

'You're mad.'

He reached across the table and grabbed her hand. 'Susan, I'm holding out an olive branch to you. Don't you grasp the symbolism? No more battling between the Nortons and the Ameses; partners at long last.'

Susan was silent. *Screw your olive branch, Ames!* As she

thought about it, however, she became intrigued. It was a fanciful notion.

'How does it sound to you, Susan?'

'It's worth considering.'

'Good girl!' He smiled and squeezed her hand. 'There will be fringe benefits, too.'

'Such as?'

'Such as you and me. We'll build a ranch house, buy stock, hire a few hands. It will be like the spread on Skull Mountain.'

It was the first mention of anything relating to those two tragic days.

'You forget, I'm a married woman.'

'So, get unmarried. You're not in love with Kevin.'

'How would you know?'

His eyes were wise. 'Because you are incapable of being truly in love with anyone. Human relationships are secondary to your life drive. I'm not talking about sex – you're as ravenous for sex as I am – but that's another thing: Your husband is a bust in bed, right?'

'He's not a bust at all.'

'But not as satisfying as I am?'

She shrugged. 'So, not every man is a stud. I make do. Kevin and I get along fine.'

'Bring him along, then, if it pleases you to play mama to him.'

'You're obscene.'

'I'll leave that arrangement up to you. Well, do we have a deal?'

'I told you I'll consider it.'

'How long will it take for you to make up your mind?'

'One week. We're going back to California tomorrow morning. You phone me a week from today at Palo Alto. I'll give you the number.'

He noted it in his address book.

'I've got to get back to the hotel before Kevin calls Missing Persons. He's been jumpy ever since this business began.'

'Poor Kevin,' he said with sarcasm. 'Come on, I'll drive you back.'

Enrico stared after them as they left. *That Mr Ames sure don't waste time. His wives die off like flies, but he always comes up with another broad even sexier than the last.*

14

Kevin Brandon stood at the end of the patio, gazing across the lush green valley below. It was cool on top of the mountain, and a refreshing breeze against his cheek smelled and tasted of the Pacific Ocean.

'It's going to be an early fall.' Susan came up behind him and rested a hand lightly on his shoulder.

Since their return from the East, their days and nights followed a singular pattern. Breakfast at nine; then Kevin would retire to the study to work on his thesis, and Susan would drive into town to do her marketing. When she returned, Kevin would, invariably, have forsaken his efforts – his mind distracted by lurid fantasies of Walter Ames and his wife on the couch that night on Skull Mountain – and retreated to the chaise on the patio, baking his already bronzed body in the midday sun. After a light lunch, during which conversation was spare, Kevin would walk in the woods, and Susan would take a nap, after which, heavy-lidded, puffy-lipped, and cranky as a cat, she would drag her feet into the shower. Then she would join Kevin on the patio, where he was intent on his electronic chess game. Some days she put on a bikini; others, she would be nude. The Brandon house was thoroughly secluded.

The nights were the worst, for Kevin, at least – so many sleepless nights, turning, twisting, or lying immobile on his back, staring at Susan and Walt on the ceiling. Ever since Susan had related her creative version of the sexual encounter between her and Walter Ames on Skull Mountain, Kevin had been impotent. No amount of coaxing by Susan would stir his inert member. Neither her teasing fingers nor her lips nor her own eager and ready parts could arouse him sufficiently to consummate a sexual union.

'It's like Sleeping Beauty,' he would joke bitterly about his impotent organ. 'Not even the beautiful princess's kisses can awaken it.'

'I said, it's going to be an early fall,' Susan repeated, jarring him out of his painful reveries.

'Yes, I think so,' he said with detachment.

'Kevin, do you know what I think? I think you should get away by yourself for a few days – go back to New Mexico and Arizona and finish the research you should have done at the beginning of summer.' She felt his body tense.

'Leave you alone?'

'What's the difference? I might as well have been alone for the past three weeks.'

'Christ! Don't rub it in. I know what a poor joke of a husband I've been lately.'

'I don't mean to rub it in, Kevin. It's just that I feel a period of separation would do both of us a world of good – clear the air, give us both breathing room. A couple of weeks and you'll see things in their true perspective, and when you come home, the dark cloud that's been hovering over us will have dissipated. You will have regained your manhood.'

'Regained my manhood?' His laughter was self-mocking. 'How mid-Victorian. What you mean is, I'll be able to "get it up" again.'

'I'm sure of it. You know, it might have been different if you *had* sought out Walter and belted a couple of his teeth out.'

'Why?'

'Because Walter Ames, in raping your wife, castrated you at the same time. You still feel a strong need to wreak some kind of vengeance on him. It's like a cancer eating away at your manhood.'

'You're right about that, but belting him in the mouth wouldn't accomplish anything. What I should have done was cut off his nuts.'

'I don't think the law would approve of that.'

'Damn the law! Remember what you told me about your frontier ancestors in New Mexico? the code they lived by? What do you think old Ike Norton or his sons would have done if somebody raped one of their women?'

'They'd have cut out his heart,' Susan said forcibly. 'But

the world has gone soft. Instead of an eye for an eye, the way it used to be, today it's turn the other cheek, let the other guy kick the shit out of you and kiss his boot in the bargain.'

'Yeah, well, if I ever get another shot at Walter Ames, I won't be kissing his boot; I'll be cutting his throat!' He stamped out his cigarette savagely on the stone and turned to face her. 'I think you've got a point. I *will* go away for a few weeks. I'll leave tomorrow. In fact, I'm going to make reservations right now.' He strode into the house with great determination.

Susan looked after him thoughtfully. A faint, self-satisfied smile played across her face. After a while she followed him into the house. He was in the study, on the phone. She went up to their bedroom, opened the top drawer of the night table, and withdrew the small piece of paper she had secreted at the back. On it was inscribed the date she and Walter Ames had discussed his business proposition over drinks at the Italian restaurant in Hartford. He had promised to phone her one week from that day. If he kept his word, he would be phoning her tomorrow. She smiled again. Perfect timing.

The next morning Susan drove Kevin to San Fransisco International Airport. They were late, and the last of the passengers were boarding the 727 bound for Albuquerque, New Mexico. She gave him a farewell kiss and patted his cheek:

'Everything is going to work out fine; don't worry about a thing.'

'You take care of yourself, you hear?' He gave her a final bear hug. 'Jesus Christ! I love you, Sue. God, but I'm going to miss you. I'll phone every night.'

She laughed. 'Such extravagance, and from the practical pig of this family.'

He recanted. 'Well, every other night.'

Susan pushed him towards the gate. 'Go on, now, before you miss your flight.'

After he left the boarding area, she went up to the bar and sat down at a table by the window overlooking the runways. She ordered a gin and tonic and sipped it slowly, her attention on the 727 as it taxied to the head of the runway and awaited permission from the tower to take off.

Feeling someone's eyes on her, she turned around, and saw that a tall, good-looking man – his hair, greying at the temples, and craggy features reminded her of the actor Michael Rennie – was staring at her. Susan was delighted. She was wearing a light, frothy sundress – lemon-yellow voile, with a short flared skirt and strapless bodice – under which she was totally naked, and she had a wanton feeling that this man, with his penetrating gaze, sensed her nudity. Kevin's jet was already airborne when he sauntered over to her table.

'Good morning. I'm glad you came in when you did. I feel self-conscious drinking alone, particularly at this hour of the morning.'

She looked at her watch. 'It isn't all that early: eleven thirty-five.'

'So it is.' He smiled. 'Do you mind if I join you?'

'Please do. I don't care to drink alone, either.'

'I'm Sam Bradshaw,' he said, extending a hand.

'Susan Brandon.' Her watch was swallowed up in his huge paw. Static ran up and down her spine. One of the first things she looked for in a man was his hands. She admired large, broad hands with long, tapering fingers, hands like Sam's.

His gaze rested on the fourth finger of her left hand, on her wedding band. '*Mrs* Susan Brandon.'

'That's right. I just drove my husband to the airport. He's on his way to Albuquerque.'

'How long will he be gone?'

'I can't really say.'

'Well, he's a very foolish fellow to abandon an attractive woman like you to the wolves. Fortunately for him, I am hereby appointing myself your guardian in his absence.'

She smiled. 'I am perfectly capable of protecting myself from wolves or any other species of predator.' Her grey eyes sparkled like flints.

'I do believe you are. In any case, I would like it very much if you'd have lunch with me.'

'I'd be delighted,' she said without hesitation.

Susan found Sam Bradshaw sexually stimulating. It had been a week since she had enjoyed sex, what with Kevin's impotence, and her libido was easily aroused. Raw animal heat inflamed her loins as she cast a furtive glance at his well-endowed crotch, boldly apparent in his form-fitting trousers.

Her mother and her grandmother had instilled in her at an early age the belief that guilt was a futile and wasteful emotion. If you yearned for something very dearly, then you did your damnedest to acquire it, and the end always justified the means. She had been unfaithful to Kevin twice before her fling with Walter Ames. In each case she had been deprived of carnal pleasure for lengthy periods of time when he was away on business, and not once did she think that merely because she had slaked her burning desire with a man other than he, she was any less of a wife to him.

Sam reached into the inside pocket of his jacket and took out his wallet. 'Let me get the cheque and let's get out of here. I'm the new kid on the block, so I'll leave the choice of the restaurant to you.'

'First time in San Fransisco?'

'Yeah – business trip. Be here for just a couple of days.'

'Good. I'll give you the Cook's tour. We'll take a cable car down to Fisherman's Wharf and have a drink at the Buena Vista. Then we can eat at the Kuo Wah Café in Chinatown. They have the best pressed duck in the world.'

'Whatever you say.'

'Where's your luggage?'

'Checked it in a locker here. Thought I'd have a drink before seeing about renting a car and — '

'No need. I'll take you to your hotel. Where are you booked?'

'The Mark Hopkins.'

'OK, we'll go there first, you can check in, and then we'll do the town.'

That afternoon, over drinks at the Buena Vista, Susan told him, 'This is the first place in the United States where Irish coffee was served. It's traditional, almost sacred. Every night, I think at five o'clock, it's Irish coffee hour, and during it, that's the only drink the customers can order; all others are taboo.'

'Quaint custom.'

'Sam, you never did tell me what line of business you're in.'

'I'm an insurance investigator, but I can't say more than that; you understand.'

'Of course.' She lifted her glass. 'Here's to happy hunting.'

He lifted an eyebrow. 'So far my luck has been smashing. I no sooner step off the plane than, literally, I fall into the arms of a gorgeous woman.'

'Not all that literally, Sam. Remember what I told you before about my ability to handle predators.'

He placed a hand over his heart. 'Scout's honour, my intentions are strictly honourable and pure.'

Susan laughed. 'What a dull fellow you must be, then.'

He finished his drink and let his hand fall casually on her knee. 'Let's be off to Chinatown. I'm famished.'

Long after they left the Buena Vista, she could still feel the heat of his fingers where he had touched her leg. She closed her eyes and pictured his hand sliding up the inside of her thigh under her skirt. An ecstatic sensation commenced in the very core of her womanhood, and goosebumps covered her arms.

'Are you cold?' he inquired. 'I'm roasting, myself.'

She smiled. 'No, this is the other kind.' She rubbed her arms, and the condition subsided.

'What other kind?'

'The kind that comes from undue heat.'

'Is that so?'

He gazed intently at her, and received a cryptic smile that gave her the aspect of a more-lovely Mona Lisa.

Luncheon at the Kuo Wah Café was a huge success.

'You're right about the duck,' Sam said as he washed down the second plateful of the succulent bird with a swallow of green tea.

They spent the rest of the afternoon sight-seeing, and arrived back at the Mark Hopkins just before eight o'clock that evening.

'Supper?' Sam asked Susan.

'I'm still stuffed from lunch. I couldn't swallow another morsel.'

'I feel the same way. Shall we go up to the top of the Mark for a drink?'

'Marvellous.'

They took the elevator up to the famous cocktail lounge,

situated on the roof of the hotel. No tourist passing through San Fransisco would pass up a chance to have a libation at the top of the Mark. Couples sitting at the bar or at the tables had a panoramic view of the sprawling, 'cliff-hanging' city that had been glamourized in countless novels, movies, and in songs. 'Glass, brass, and glitter' was an apt description of the landmark watering hole.

'Trysting spot for thousands of soldiers in both World War Two and the Korean War, bound for the Pacific,' Susan explained. 'Usually the last place lovers came before they separated – in many cases, forever.'

'It's intriguing, all right,' he said. 'But I don't believe we're going to get a table or a spot at the bar for a long, long time. Must be a convention here.'

'I've never seen it so crowded at this hour,' she replied. 'Well, the drinks will taste as good downstairs.'

'I've got a better idea. Why don't we go down to my room, kick off our shoes, and relax? Room service will take care of all our needs.'

'Will it, now?'

The innuendo was clear, and Sam put his arm about her waist.

'That remains to be seen. Are you game?'

'By all means. I can't wait to take off my shoes and let my aching feet breathe.'

Sam was booked into a modest suite on the twelfth floor, consisting of a foyer, a large, well-furnished sitting room, and a small bedroom.

'Make yourself comfortable,' he told her. 'I want to hang up this jacket.' He went into the bedroom, calling back to her, 'Why don't you phone room service and order us some ice and tonic. I've got a bottle of gin in my suitcase.'

Susan promptly removed her shoes, sprawled on the couch, and dialled room service.

When Sam came out of the bedroom, wearing only trousers and a T-shirt, she was lying back with her eyes closed, her legs propped up on the coffee table. Barefoot, he padded quietly across the carpet, staring raptly at her long, slender, shapely legs. Her dress was hiked up to mid-thigh, and she was truly a feast for the eyes.

She sensed his presence, and her eyes opened slowly. 'Didn't your mother ever tell you it's impolite to stare?' She tugged the skirt down to her knees.

'Don't blame me. You invite such discourtesies because you are an unusually lovely female.' He sat down beside her and took a cigarette from the pack on the table. He handed it to Susan and lit another one for himself.

'Thanks,' she said. 'The drinks will be here presently.'

A heavy silence ensued as they smoked and gazed out the window beside the couch. The towers of the Golden Gate Bridge were shrouded in golden and purple mist, a refraction of the sun, which was setting behind the horizon across the gentle curve of the Pacific Ocean.

It occurred to Susan that two strangers, meeting for the first time, can quickly exhaust the superficial topics of conversation available. The common ground of a loquacious and three-dimensional relationship had yet to be established between her and Sam Bradshaw. And so, by the time the waiter brought their drinks, and Sam had signed the cheque, Susan had made up her mind. Anything further they could impart to each other was superfluous. It was time to get to the business that had drawn the two of them together in the first place.

'Sam, I feel I must smell like a mountain goat. Do you mind if I take a shower?'

His smile was radiant, that of a child on Christmas morning ogling all the goodies under the yule tree. 'Be my guest. I can use a shower myself.'

She leaned over and patted his cheek. 'Then, what are we waiting for?'

His eyes widened. 'You mean – '

'Yes – together. Haven't you heard? There's a water shortage. Our city motto: Conserve water; take a shower with a friend.'

With a single supple motion, she stood up, grasped the hem of her dress, and slipped it over her head. Sam was stupefied. He hadn't expected her to be stark naked under the dress.

Susan walked towards the bedroom door, tossing back over her shoulder, 'Last one in the water is a rotten egg.'

He unfastened his trousers as he went after her.

All her life, Susan had savoured the intimacy of bathing naked with a male. Her initial experience had taken place when she was fourteen years old. She and another girl had been walking in the woods while on a summer vacation when, unexpectedly, they came upon three older boys skinny-dipping in a secluded cove. Susan had readily accepted their joking invitation to join them, while her chum had fled like a scared doe.

Even at her tender age, her body was well developed and nubile. The sight of her undressing on the beach and walking nude into the water had been sufficient to trigger instant erections with all three lads, and Susan had been vastly amused to see three youthful right arms and hands moving in furious piston rhythm beneath the surface of the waist-deep water.

Cliché had it that women wore their hearts on their sleeves. Not true; men did. Male sexuality was right out in the open, exposed, vulnerable, whereas female sexual emotions could be easily concealed. It was an enormous advantage, an invaluable trump card, that women enjoyed over men in the battle of the sexes.

The shower was ample, and they were not cramped. Susan boldly admired his lean, tight body, his broad shoulders and narrow hips – maybe a little too narrow; she was turned on by some plumpness and contour to the male backside. Nevertheless, he would serve admirably.

They soaped each other's bodies, hands moving in circular fashion, fingers teasing erogenous zones: nipples, navels, buttocks, groins. Sam slipped down to his knees and put his arms around her, his hands kneading the soft, plump cheeks of her behind. He lavished kisses on her trembling belly.

Susan moaned and gripped the back of his head, pushing his mouth down lower. His tongue found the tender cleft, and she arched her back, grinding her pelvis against his face as she commenced the orgastic rhythm.

'Fuck me, Sam – now!'

He stood up, placing her so that her back was against the tile wall, his large hands braced firmly against her buttocks, cradling the cheeks. 'Put your legs around my waist and hold on for dear life. You're going for a ride, baby.'

She did as he said, and their organs meshed, both slippery with soap and body lubricants. He entered her with the ease of a hand sliding into a silk glove.

'That feels so good,' she said, and bit him on the shoulder.

It was a bite that broke the skin, but the pain was overshadowed by his exquisite pleasure. Their strokes were as coordinated as the graceful steps of a dance team. All the time the fine spray of the shower laved them with hot, steamy water, which intensified the sexual sensation.

She climaxed before he did and immediately strove to achieve a new high. Even after he had his orgasm, he remained turgid until Susan reached a second climax. They clung to each other a long time, leaning against the wall. Finally, with a groan, he let her down gently, and they emerged from the shower and towelled themselves dry.

Wrapped in terry cloth, they went back into the living room and had cigarettes and another drink.

'Want to spend the night?' he inquired.

'I'd like to, but I have a dog and cat to take care of,' she lied.

'Oh?'

She sensed that he didn't believe her. No matter. 'I feel terrible about that hickey I put on your shoulder. I go crazy when I come.'

'I'll always cherish the scar.'

'You really should put some peroxide or alcohol on it; it's badly inflamed.'

He frowned down at the afflicted area. 'You're right. There's alcohol in the medicine chest. Will you excuse me while I tend to it?' He stood up and went into the bedroom.

As soon as he had absented himself, Susan reached for her large handbag on the end table, opened it, and removed a small, round, metallic button. She slid across the couch to the far side and picked up the telephone from the other end table. Working swiftly and efficiently, she unscrewed the mouthpiece from the instrument, placed the bug against the magnet, and screwed the mouthpiece on again. She placed it back in its cradle and moved to the other side of the couch. When he returned, she was smoking another cigarette and sipping her drink.

'Feel better?' she asked.

'Much.'

She looked at her watch. 'I really have to be off. Call me tomorrow,' she said, slipping her sun dress over her head and quickly running a comb through her hair.

'You can count on it.'

She turned to him, smiling, put her arms around his neck, and kissed him on the mouth. 'It's been a wonderful day, Sam.'

'My best day,' he affirmed. He squeezed her buttocks.

'Naughty boy. If you keep that up, I'll never get out of here.'

He walked with her to the door. 'Good night, Susan.'

'Good night, Sam. I'll expect to hear from you tomorrow.'

Once out in the hall, Susan headed for the small reclining area between the two elevator banks, where there were two armchairs, a couch, and a glass-topped table with ashtrays and a stack of magazines. Though no one was seated there, still she was cautious. She chose a chair and picked up a magazine. Then, from her purse, she took an oblong of black plastic that looked like a pocket transistor radio. She extended the steel antenna and jacked in an earphone with a long cord. When she'd placed the receiver at the side of her chair in deep shadow, and fixed the earpiece into one ear, she settled back and pretended to read the magazine.

She did not have long to wait. Soon after she left the room, Sam Bradshaw made a phone call:

'Hello, Mr Ames. This is Sam Bradshaw.'

'What's up, Sam?'

'I moved in on the Brandon woman today. All this time I've been tailing her, she only went to the supermarket. But today she drove her hubby to the airport, and I followed her up to the bar after he took off. I just walked over to her table and asked if I could join her. I could tell right off she was hot to trot.'

'Are you sure she wasn't suspicious?'

'Why should she be? She's a good-looking broad and must get plenty of passes tossed her way. Anyway, I told her I had just arrived on an incoming flight, that it was my first time in San Fransisco. She offered to show me the sights.' A note of lewdness crept into his voice. 'Man, did she ever show me the sights!'

'Not so fast, Sam. How could she buy that line that you had just arrived? I mean, what about your luggage?'

'A good detective always comes prepared. I'm staying in a motel on the outskirts of town, but I always have a couple of suitcases in the car trunk for emergencies such as this. I phoned the Mark and booked a room for one night, and I took Susan Brandon there.'

'Very clever, Sam . . . What did you learn?'

'She's on the level about your business deal. Oh, she didn't mention you by name, but, during the course of conversation, she said she was waiting to hear from her "business partner" and was anxious to get the deal finalized.'

'Oh, it'll be finalized next week, and I don't mean *just* the deal. That cunt came within a whisker of sending me to the electric chair, or don't they have capital punishment in Connecticut anymore? Well, life imprisonment is even worse. Yes, sir, I am going to finalize Susan Brandon once and for all! By the way, did you lay her?'

'Did I ever, man! That one is hot as a pistol. Let me tell you how – '

Susan pulled out the earpiece and stuffed it back into her bag, along with the receiver. Her expression was grim and brooding. One thing was undeniable: The century-old Ames-Norton feud was not over yet. Walter Ames was out to get her as certainly as she was out to get him. But she had the drop on the bastard! She knew what his game was, whereas he had no reason to suspect her motives, not after the reassuring information Sam Bradshaw had given him. The two of them believed that she was conned by their game. All to the good. Yes, Sam Bradshaw had done her a great service, the patsy.

Susan smiled as she pushed the elevator button. In fact, Sam, good stud that he was, had done her *double* service!

15

At noon the next day, Susan received a phone call:

'Hello, Susan, this is Walter Ames.'

'I see you're a man of your word.'

'An Ames trait. Well . . . have you made a decision?'

'I have. The deal is on.'

'Fabulous! I must confess I've jumped the gun a bit. I had my attorney draw up the agreements, and all we need now is your signature. How soon can you get out here?'

'That's a problem. Kevin is away. In fact, he's in New Mexico completing his research for his doctorate.'

'So, what's the problem? You're a free woman.'

'You're right. Tell you what: I'll catch a flight to Lincoln City tomorrow . . . What else is happening?'

'I've started work on the ranch house. It will be done sometime next summer. Meanwhile, I've moved into an ancient Mexican villa. Must be one hundred years old, adobe walls a foot thick . . . You'll like it.'

'Walt, you take a lot for granted. Remember, I'm still married.'

'So? As I said, get unmarried. No, don't tell me: You'll "*consider*" it.'

'I will . . . I'll call you back after I make the reservation, let you know what flight to meet.'

'I'll be straining at the leash until you get here. Would you believe I've been celibate since last I saw you?'

'No. Would you believe that I have?'

He hesitated. 'I'll believe whatever you tell me.'

'I think I'll leave you in suspense. All right, stay near the phone. As soon as I hang up, I'll phone the airport. Goodbye, Walt.'

She phoned Southwestern Airlines and booked a flight to Albuquerque, New Mexico, with a changeover flight on a local airline to Lincoln City. In bold print, she noted the information given to her by the reservations clerk on a pad on Kevin's desk – 'Flight 51 to Albuquerque. Change there for shuttle to Lincoln City. Notify Walter Ames' – and placed the pad beside the phone, under Kevin's favourite talisman, a plastic-block paperweight with a shamrock sealed inside. Smiling smugly, Susan stood up.

The die was cast.

That afternoon she was sunbathing naked on the patio when Sam Bradshaw phoned. She took it in the den.

'How are you today, gorgeous?' he said.

'Naked.'

'Naked?'

'Yes, I'm adding to my tan.'

'By God, I knew there was something different about you, only I couldn't put my finger on it. You don't have white bikini stripes across your boobs and pussy, like most gals.'

'I think you put your finger on it very nicely,' she said archly.

'When can we get together?'

'I'm afraid we can't. Something's come up. I'm going to New Mexico tomorrow. Business – you know, what I told you about yesterday.'

'That's great. I'm glad things worked out for you.'

'You sound relieved to get rid of me.'

'Sugar, not so! Hell, I'm wild about you.'

But not as wild as you are about scoring points with big bwana Ames. 'I may not be back for some time. You'll probably be gone by then.'

'Yeah . . . Well, maybe we'll catch up some other place, some other time. I've got your number.'

And I've got yours! 'Even if it was only one day, it was worth it, Sam. Good luck and goodbye.'

Susan hung up, went into the kitchen, made herself a lemonade, and toasted herself in the mirror over the table: 'Happy hunting!' While she sipped the cold, tart beverage, she ran her hand up her waist and onto her left breast, toying idly with the nipple until it was taut and crimson. She wished like hell that Sam was with her. *What you need, my girl, is a cold shower, otherwise you'll end up diddling yourself.*

That night she retired early and lay propped up in bed reading a historical novel titled *So Wicked My Desire*. At midnight Kevin phoned her.

'Where are you, darling?' she asked.

'El Paso. I got a lead on a retired director of the US Bureau of Indian Affairs. He's a gold mine of information. I'll be here at least another two weeks.'

'I'm glad you called tonight instead of tomorrow. Sue Lyons and her husband invited me to go on a camping trip with them to Mount Saint Helens.'

'No kidding. Has it blown its top again?'

'Not since you left. You don't mind if I go, do you? It's

boring as hell without you here.'

'By all means go, hon. And give my best to Sue and Jerry. Listen, don't get too close to the crater. It could go off again at any time.'

'Not on your life. I'm allergic to molten lava. Thanks for calling, darling. Don't run up your phone bill. I'll send you a postcard, if you'll give an address.'

'I'm mobile, Susan. Bring it home with you. Good night, sweetheart. I love you.'

'And I love you.'

When Susan heard a buzz at the other end of the wire, she hung up, put away her book, fluffed up her pillow, and lay down. Tomorrow was going to be a long, arduous day. She fell asleep instantly and dreamed that she was being chased by a man with a monstrous penis. And she wasn't a bit afraid.

Early the next morning, Susan marched to the boarding gate at San Fransisco International Airport with the determined stride of a soldier going into battle.

The flight from San Fransisco to Albuquerque was uneventful, but the air was bumpy all the way from Albuquerque to Lincoln City. The rumble of distant thunder and flaring sheet lightning made Susan mildly apprehensive. It reminded her of the fateful flight on the Cessna *Golden Eagle* in the early summer. The tension drained out of her as soon as the wheels touched down on the runway.

Walter Ames was waiting for her outside the boarding gate. He was wearing a black cowboy outfit, with a matching wide-brimmed Stetson and patent-leather boots. He looked tanned and rakishly handsome.

'Hi there, beautiful,' he greeted her. He removed his hat and bent to kiss her cheek. 'Good trip?'

'There'll never be another good air trip again for me after the crash.'

'You'll grow out of it. How about a drink?'

'I'll wait until we get back to your place. I'm grimy and sweaty. I can't wait to get into a tub.'

They picked up her luggage and went out to Walt's black Cadillac.

'What is it with the black motif?' Susan asked.

'The Indian hands call me the "black angel." '

Susan sighed with relief as the air conditioning whirred to life. 'God, that feels good.'

'Yeah, it's a hundred and seven degrees outside, hottest summer of the century. Maybe it's a backlash from Mount Saint Helens.' He pulled out of the airport parking lot onto the highway and headed north. 'About a half-hour ride,' he informed her.

'How is the new house coming along?'

'Fine, although the extreme heat wilts the workers in the afternoon. Anyway, there's no hurry. The old house we'll be staying in is more than adequate. It was built by the foreman of the spread your great-great grandmother, Molly Norton, sold out to after the Norton Massacre. In fact, it's directly on the site of the old Norton place that burned down.'

'That your great-great grandfather burned down,' she said bitterly.

'Come on; I thought we'd agreed that it's ancient history.'

She said nothing, but was sullen and silent for the remainder of the trip.

The instant they drove through the ranch gate, Susan was overcome by an eerie feeling of *déjà vu*. 'Somehow it's all so familiar,' she said, 'yet I've never been here.'

'You feel the ghosts. I know I do. Sometimes I wake up at night scared to death. I hear voices calling to me. Just last night I got up and went to the window. There was a full moon, and the landscape was luminous. I mean it glowed so, it hurt my eyes. And I saw them – shadowy figures standing beneath the window, inviting me to come outside. Christ! I pulled the blinds and locked my bedroom door.'

'The vengeful shades of the murdered Nortons come back to haunt you for the guilt of your ancestors.'

'We'll bury them once and for all when our partnership is finalized. No longer enemies but partners, friends . . . lovers.' He placed a hand on her thigh.

Though she hated his guts, the sensual female within her responded to his touch. He was a healthy stud, and he knew how to please a woman. No personal feeling involved; no more than the satisfying of a natural physical function, like urinating. She took his hand and moved it to her inner thigh, pushed it all the way up to her crotch. She felt his fingers groping her through the flimsy panties. Susan reached out and put her hand on the erection ballooning out of his trousers.

'Whoa, little filly; let's save it for the bedroom. Here we are.'

From a distance, the sprawling, low ranch house was nearly visible, blending into the rugged, desolate landscape like a chameleon. The adobe mud walls were the same pale lemon as the sand and rock.

'It's ugly and beautiful at the same time,' she observed.

'Like the desert,' he replied.

As they mounted the steps to the broad front porch, the front door was opened by a small, dark man wearing a white jacket. He so resembled Pedro, who had been cut down by lightning on Skull Mountain, that Susan shivered.

'This is Garcia, Pedro's brother. I had him come up from Mexico for sentimental reasons. He's almost as proficient as Pedro, too. It's remarkable.'

He spoke to the man in Spanish. Garcia nodded and responded in kind. Then he picked up Susan's bags and carried them upstairs.

'He'll draw your bath. Meanwhile, let's have a drink.'

As he led her through the house and out to a side porch, Susan commented, 'I adore it. It's so primitive, the absolutely perfect mood.'

Broad archways divided the rooms and gave the airy effect of total continuity. All of the ceilings had natural-wood beams sealed with a light coat of shellac. The appointments were rustic, too, and gave the impression that the craftsman who had made the furniture had stopped work a fraction before his handiwork was completed.

When they had their frosty gin and tonics, Walt outlined their business transaction:

'Daniel Collins is bringing out the agreements for us to sign tomorrow morning.'

'Collins? The name sounds familiar.'

'Four generations of Collinses have practised law in Lincoln City. Going way back, a Bob Collins handled legal work for both the Ameses and the Nortons before the Cattle War and after it.'

Garcia appeared and spoke to Walt.

'He says your bath is ready. You go ahead and wash up.' His eyes narrowed. 'I'll be up in a little while.'

She groped him as she passed. 'Bring your little friend along.'

'We're inseparable.'

Her bedroom was large and airy and had a Spanish flavour about it; also, a distinctly feminine atmosphere. The four-poster bed was fitted with a lacy canopy, and the furniture was honey-coloured and adorned with delicate hand carvings.

Susan stripped off her clothing and went into the bathroom. It was dominated by a sunken tub large enough to hold four people comfortably. *What time does the orgy begin?* she mused.

She was stretched out languidly in the tepid water, drowsing, when Walt appeared in the doorway:

'That looks very pleasant. May I join you?'

'By all means.' She was wide awake and alert now. She began to sing the golden oldie *'Strip Poker'*; ' "Take it off, take it off, yelled the girls from the rear . . . " ' With building desire, she watched him undress, licking her lips in anticipation when his immense hard-on popped free from his Jockey shorts. 'Come to mama.'

Walt stepped into the tub and lowered himself into the water. She floated into his embrace.

'What nice water wings you have,' he quipped.

Her breasts were buoyant, and her red nipples thrust up at him temptingly. He bent and mouthed them, first one and then the other, teasing them with his tongue. Susan put her legs around his waist and locked her ankles together. Her hands caressed his member and rubbed it up and down against her labia.

His tongue probed the inside of her mouth as she manoeuvred him into position and, with a deft lunge of her pelvis, impaled herself on his swollen lance. She cried out in blissful delight as her contractions began. He came an instant after, and they rocked back and forth in the water, splashing it out of the tub and across the floor.

When they had recovered, he picked her up, carried her back into the bedroom, and placed her on the bed:

'How about a little variety?'

He straddled her body in the 69 position and lavished kisses all over her heaving belly and her thighs. He nuzzled the fur of her *mons veneris* and sought her clitoris with his skilled tongue. Her mouth could accommodate only a small section of his erection, but she ministered to it with consummate artistry. Kevin always said she gave the best head he had ever had.

Kevin, my love, if only you could see me now!

16

Kevin Brandon arrived back in Palo Alto one week earlier than he had anticipated. He phoned home from the airport, but there was no answer. Unperturbed, he booked a limousine to the house. The car was not in the driveway, so he assumed that Susan had gone shopping.

He let himself into the house and immediately filled a brandy snifter with ice, then poured it to the brim with gin. While it was cooling, he carried his bags into the bedroom and undressed. Wearing only his Jockey shorts, he went back into the kitchen to retrieve his drink and took it into the den. He did not glance at the pad under the paperweight.

For a long time, he sat smoking and sipping his outsized gin in the comfortable swivel chair at his desk, oblivious of the pad under the paperweight. On a quixotic impulse, he picked up the phone and dialled the Lyons' number. Sue Lyons answered.

'Sue? This is Kevin Brandon.'

Her voice rose an octave. 'Kevin! Long time no see. We were just talking about you the other night.'

'I can imagine who was doing the talking – my prodigal wife. Is Susan with you now?'

'Susan?' There was a heavy pause. 'Why, no. Did she say she was paying us a visit?'

It was Kevin's turn to be silent. Then: 'Well, no,

but . . . I mean, your trip to Mount Saint Helens. When did you get back?'

Her mystification was absolute. 'Mount Saint Helens? Kevin, are you all right?'

'Of course I'm all right,' he snapped. 'What the hell is this all about? Susan and I spoke last week – I've been in El Paso – and she said that you and Jerry had kindly invited her to go on a camping trip with you to Mount Saint Helens.'

Silence.

'Sue! Are you there?'

Still no response.

'*Sue!*' Kevin was at the raw edge of his patience. 'Will you please *answer* me?' He could hear the sharp intake of breath:

'Kevin . . . there's been some kind of crazy mistake. We haven't seen Susan since you guys came back from Connecticut. That party at the Leones . . . Wait! That's it! You misunderstood the name. She must have gone away with the Leones! I know Carl is on vacation. Kevin, do you have their number handy?' She heard the phone smash down on its cradle.

Kevin sat there staring at his drink. He picked up the glass and downed the raw gin in a single gulp. His eyes cut to the shamrock paperweight, and a name, magnified by the plastic, assaulted his optic nerve:

Walter Ames.

'Sonovabitch!' He swept the paperweight off the desk onto the floor, picked up the pad, and read his wife's message. Numb with shock, he got up and went back into the kitchen, where he drank straight from the gin bottle until his throat muscles contracted smotheringly and he almost retched. It wrenched him back to reality.

'Fucking cunt! Fucking prick!' he brayed hysterically, like a jackass. The metaphors so apt – Walter's prick in Susan's cunt; Kevin the cuckolded jackass . . .

He hurled the empty gin bottle to the floor, shattering it into infinite shards, and stormed around the kitchen, a bull in a china shop, flailing his arms wildly, devastating every article on the table, sink, and breakfast bar. After he had spent his fury, he sat down, Indian fashion, in the midst of the rubble and covered his face with his hands, mind, flesh, emotions all turning inexorably to ice.

Moments later he stood up and walked like a zombie into the bedroom – his and Susan's bedroom, for so many years a temple of love and desire where, time and time again, they had paid homage to the god of sex. He walked to the closet, reached up to the top shelf, and grabbed the cowhide case. He carried it to the bed and unzipped the cover, flipping back the lid.

Nestled in a case lined with purple satin was a pearl-handled Colt .45 US Army automatic pistol, a souvenir of his hitch in the navy, purchased from a black-market entrepreneur the day his ship had sailed from Honolulu. The clip lay in a niche beside it. He inserted the clip into the weapon and laid it down on Susan's pillow. Then he went back into the den and made his airline reservation.

At four o'clock the following afternoon, Kevin Brandon walked into the law offices of Collins, Collins, and Worth, located in Lincoln City, New Mexico – a prestigious legal establishment with oak-panelled walls and two-inch-pile carpeting in the reception room. After a wait of a half-hour, he was informed by the plain, sedate receptionist:

'Mr Collins will see you now, Mr Brandon.'

An equally plain secretary came out to escort him into Collins's office. It was obvious that the firm selected its female employees with an eye towards their blending in with the austere woodwork.

Daniel Collins was something of a surprise, in that he wore a checkered sport jacket, contrasting slacks, and a flamboyant tie. He was about Kevin's age, perhaps a few years older: attractive, slender, debonair, with a beguiling smile. He stood up when Kevin entered the room, and offered his hand. 'So sorry to keep you waiting, Mr Brandon. I didn't expect you, and was tied up in an important consultation.'

Kevin shook his hand warmly. 'I'm the one to apologize. I cleaned up some business down in El Paso earlier than I expected, and flew up here on impulse to surprise my wife.'

Collins smiled. 'Yes, your charming wife, Susan . . . You know, then, that she and Mr Ames concluded a business arrangement earlier in the week?'

'Yes, I do,' Kevin said without hesitation. 'We've been in

touch every day by phone. To be truthful, though, Mr Collins, the world of commerce and finance is way, way over the head of his absentminded pedagogue.'

Collins laughed politely. 'That's what attorneys and accountants are for, to guide the uninitiated through the wilderness. Now, how can I be of service to you, Mr Brandon?'

'Well, I thought you might give me directions on how to get to Mr Ames's place.'

'Why, all you had to do was phone Walt from the airport, and he would have sent one of the hands into town to pick you up.'

Kevin smiled and lit a cigarette. 'The point is, I want to surprise Susan. Besides, I don't like to impose.'

'Oh, I see. Well, you won't have any trouble finding the Ames spread. Are you in a rush?'

'Not at all.'

'Then, can I offer you a drink?'

'Love one.'

Collins got up from behind the mammoth desk and walked to one side of the spacious room. He pushed a button, and the panelled walls parted, revealing a well-stocked bar. 'What's your poison?'

'Gin on the rocks.'

'Rugged customer, for a college professor.' He filled Kevin's order and poured bourbon and branch water for himself. 'Sit down and make yourself comfortable.' He indicated a leather easy chair, one of a pair, and sat down in the other. 'What shall we drink to, Mr Brandon?'

'Please call me "Kevin." '

'Swell, and you call me "Dan." '

'Do you know what I'd really like to drink to, Dan? I'm so damned grateful that this asinine feud between the Ameses and the Nortons has finally come to an end.'

'You don't know how relieved I am to hear you say it. There hasn't been a day since Susan's arrival that I don't get up in the morning and say, "Danny boy, this is the day when somebody is going to rock the boat, when the shit is going to hit the fan." I never put much stock in these so-called armed truces.'

'Oh, but it's more than an armed truce, Dan. Sincerely, Susan is determined to bury the hatchet. Hell, I should know; I'm her husband.'

'I guess you should, of all people. All right, then: To harmonious relations between the Ameses and the Nortons for all time to come.'

'*Harmonious relations*' – *quite a euphemism!* Kevin swallowed his gall and drank the toast. 'Tell me something; How long has your law firm been representing the Ameses and the Nortons?'

'Ever since the Lincoln City Cattle War. My great-great grandpappy, Robert Collins, started the firm. Jim Ames and Ike Norton were his first important clients.'

'That's one hell of a spot to be in, representing two powerful conflicting interests like the Ameses and the Nortons. That's one fence I'd hate to straddle.'

'Not as bad as you might think. Ike and Jim were not the top dogs, as most uninformed people believe. The big wheels were the Chisums and the Murphys. The Ameses and the Nortons were caught in between the two sides in the big struggle to muscle each other out of the big US-government beef contracts. You could say they were both victims of circumstance.'

'Yet, when you get to the nub of it, Dan, it was Jim Ames who ordered the Norton Massacre.'

'Yeah, and all the Ameses ever since have been wearing it like an albatross around their necks, generation after generation. There are superstitious folks in these parts believe to this day that Molly Norton put a curse on the Ameses that has dogged the family for more than a century.'

'I've heard something like that from Susan. What sort of curse?'

'Not long after the massacre, Jim Ames was gunned down by an anonymous assassin, motive unknown. Generation later, his grandson Stan fell off a cliff to his death during a Fourth of July picnic. Then Walter's father, Glenn, he came home to the big house in Connecticut, Manorhaven, to find that his wife had blown her brains out. He hanged himself the following week. It's struck Walt twice. Both of his wives have perished from violent deaths.'

'That *does* give one pause for wonder, I must admit.' Kevin shook his head. 'However, I don't believe in spells and curses. Just rotten luck.'

'I'd have to agree. Still . . . ' He did not complete the thought. 'Well, whatever it was that plagued the Ameses, let's hope that, with the reconciliation of Walt and Susan, there's nothing but good times from now on.'

'I'll drink to that. In fact, I'm looking forward to one very good, high time tonight.' He winked at Collins. 'It's been a long time since my wife and I have been together.'

Collins's blue eyes twinkled. 'I sympathize with you, Kevin. A wonderful-looking woman like that has got to inspire a heap of missing.'

Kevin stood up and extended his hand. 'It's been a pleasure to meet you, Dan. No doubt we'll get together soon out at Walt's spread or here in town.'

'I'm looking forward to it.'

'Well, thanks again for your hospitality.'

'I'll have my girl type out directions for you on how to get to the Ames ranch. You take care, now.'

Fifteen minutes later, Kevin was on a four-lane highway heading north.

17

Susan sat on the porch glider with her legs drawn up underneath her haunches. Walt was leaning against a column on one side of the front steps, smoking a cigar. It was an unusually warm night for October, as the Midwest was in the throes of the most torrid Indian summer of the century. The sun was just setting, and the horizon was a ring of crimson fire.

'Looks like red rain falling through the dusk mists,' Walt said absently.

'Blood on the sun,' the Indians called it, remember? It happened the night before the Norton Massacre.'

'Why the devil must you turn every conversation, no matter how remotely connected, back to the Norton Massacre? It's an obsession.'

'Yes, it is,' she readily conceded.

Night came, and a half-moon ascended in the sky in the

northwest; even thus diminished, it bathed the desert in brilliant, silver light. The sky was a soft black velvet, the stars a multitude of sparkling diamonds. A gust of hot wind brushed Susan's cheek like human breath, followed by the rumble of thunder to the north. Over the distant mountains, forked lightning rent the tapestry of the heavens.

'The devil's pitchfork,' Walt commented. 'More ancient Indian folklore.'

'They could be right. Remember, Gall said that all of us who were there that night at the ceremonial lodge would be punished for our sins.'

His laughter was dry and tinged with annoyance. 'He said no such thing. He said just enough vague and menacing things to whet the imagination and stimulate the conscience. You know the old saying: If the shoe fits, then wear it.'

She wasn't listening to him. 'Of the nine of us – ten, including Pedro – who were on the mountain, only three of us are alive.'

'Poppycock, as the English say.'

'Walt, are you going to rebuild the house on Skull Mountain?'

'No. I've received several offers from local people. I told Collins to go ahead and sell it if he gets a fair price. There's one outfit that wants to open a summer resort up there, but I wouldn't sell to them for any price – too dangerous with the lightning storms.'

'Your concern for human life and welfare is really touching.'

'Skip the sarcasm. Coming from one of your impeccable moral fibre, it's too ludicrous for words.'

She got up from the couch, walked over to him, and put an arm around his waist. 'We're good for each other, don't you think, dear?'

'I think we have a lot in common,' he returned, equally sarcastic.

'The human condition is both absurd and frightening,' she observed. 'Here I am, waiting to go to bed with a man who murdered one wife, was responsible for another's suicide, and had two of my friends killed because his hit men got our cars confused.'

He pulled away from her impatiently. 'I refuse to listen

to your claptrap another instant! You're a raging paranoid. I'm going up and grab a quick shower. Won't be more than five minutes. Have Garcia bring out a tray of ice and booze. I smell a storm brewing, and we'll have front-row seats.'

'I have a hunch that Garcia is in the sack with the cook. I'll fetch it myself.'

'Very considerate of you.' He went inside and up the stairs.

The tempo of thunder and lightning was building, approaching from the mountain range miles off, which was now obliterated by the sheet of heavy rain on the leading edge of the storm. In their immediate vicinity, however, nature was serene and harmonious but for an intermittent flow of wind that kicked up dust in the front yard and sent tumbleweed bouncing across the plain; it reminded her of the lightning balls on Skull Mountain pursuing their eerie, slow-motion course over the mesa.

Susan went to the kitchen and filled a bucket with ice cubes, then carried it into the den. She was just placing it on a silver tray that held an array of bottles and glassware when the phone rang. She picked it up on the first ring:

'Hello, this is Susan Brandon.'

'Susan, this is Dan Collins. I should have phoned sooner, but I was indecisive about what to do. Your husband was in my office earlier.'

'Kevin?' Her adrenaline began to flow, kicking up her heartbeat and respiration. 'I don't understand.'

'He said he had finished his business in El Paso earlier than he'd expected and flew up here to surprise you.'

'And now you've gone and ruined his surprise, Dan,' she baited him.

He laughed uneasily. The woman had a way of confounding him every time he met her. He could never be sure what she was thinking and feeling. Everything about her was a pose, he suspected.

'No problems you can foresee, then?' he said.

'Why, of course not, Dan. Walt will be delighted. He and Kevin have become good friends, now that all of that past mess is behind us. Let's drink to new beginnings; that's what I always say.'

'Yes, to be sure . . . Uh, is Walt available?'

'Not this minute. He's in the shower. Can I have him

phone you back?'

'No, that won't be necessary. I'm meeting my wife for dinner in fifteen minutes . . . Look, Susan, I'd appreciate it if you wouldn't mention to your husband that I phoned. He *did* ask me not to.'

'Mum's the word, Dan. It'll be our little secret,' she said sweetly. 'By the way, Dan, why *did* you break your word?'

Momentarily tongue-tied, he found his voice at last. 'I . . . I don't really know. Call it a premonition.'

'Don't be such a nervous Nellie, Dan. Kevin, Walt, and I get along so famously, we may even start a *ménage à trois*.'

She was in high spirits when she hung up the phone, and whistled as she carried the tray out onto the porch. She mixed herself a drink and sprawled out on the glider, watching the approach of the storm.

Walt appeared a few minutes later. 'Did I hear the phone?'

'Yes; it was Dan Collins. It seems we're going to have company.'

'Dan's coming out here tonight?'

'No, darling – Kevin.'

'Kevin? What the hell!' He sat down in a chair and stared at her.

Susan told him about Kevin's visit to Collins's office in Lincoln City.

His face looked gaunt and deeply lined as he demanded, 'How in hell did he find out where you were?'

'I haven't the foggiest. Does it trouble you that he's coming here?'

'That depends on *why* he's coming.'

'After all, Walt, it was you who told me I could bring Kevin along with me.'

'I was kidding, and you know it.' He stood up and started back inside.

'Where are you going?'

'What's the cliché: Forewarned is forearmed? Well, now that you have forewarned me, I am about to forearm me. I'll be back presently.'

Susan lit a hurricane lamp, and as she bent over it, her eyes and teeth gleamed in the pale light. She lit a cigarette and walked to the far end of the wide porch, then back to pour herself another drink. Carrying it with her, she began to pace back and forth. Filled with excitement and anticipation, she would not rest until Kevin arrived.

Walt came out of the house, carrying a sawed-off shotgun. He patted the double-barrelled lethal weapon fondly. 'This little baby has been my life insurance on more than one occasion.'

'You mean to kill Kevin? Be careful, Walt. It would be the one rap you couldn't beat.'

'I don't want to kill the little prick. But he sure as hell wants to kill me.'

'You don't know that. Maybe he's coming out here to talk. I mean, he doesn't have an inkling what's going on. He has a right to know why I walked out on him without any explanation.' She laughed. 'Maybe it's *me* he wants to kill.'

'He's not going to kill anyone.' Hs laid the shotgun across his knees and lit a cigarette.

The two of them sat on the front steps smoking in silence, watching the storm move slowly across the prairie like a dark curtain, heralded by an overture of thunder and lightning that played ticktacktoe all over the brooding sky. A light rain had just begun to fall when they saw the headlights far, far down the road that ran in front of the Ames property.

'Here he is!' Walt stood up and moved back into the shadows of the porch. He flicked off the shotgun's safety.

Susan remained seated. Her excitement was near uncontrollable, excitement akin to sexual arousal. She would eagerly have made love right then and there on the porch. As the vehicle approached, the headlights grew larger. About a quarter of a mile off, they were switched off, and the car reduced its speed and finally stopped short of the gate. A figure got out and vaulted the fence, heading for the house.

'It's Kevin,' she said. 'I know his walk.'

'And he's carrying a gun,' Walt said tersely. 'Listen, you'd better go inside. This could be a real shoot-out.'

'But you said we'd have front-row seats – *we.*'

He kneeled down beside her and put a hand alongside her chin, tilting her head so that he could look into her eyes. They were aglow with the reflection of the myriad stars, swirling like golden atoms in a miniature atomic field. Her smile was that of a death's-head in the pale moonlight.

'You unholy evil bitch!' he snarled. He slapped her as hard as he could, knocking her off the side of the steps onto the sand. Then, cradling the shotgun in the ready position, he walked down the steps and across the yard. Susan's jeering laughter carried to him on the rising wind, a banshee wailing.

Susan got to her feet and wiped the blood off her mouth with the back of her hand. She tore open her blouse and cupped her breasts with her hands, savouring the thrust of the nipples against her soft palms.

And then it happened, suffusing her with awe. Materializing out of the mist preceding the storm, resurrected like Lazarus after a century in the grave, came Ike Norton, and behind him a long, straggling line of ghosts, hands raised all, walking across the yard towards the barricades where the infamous Ames clan lay in wait, marching into the valley of death. Atop the barricade stood Jim Ames, surrounded by his hired killers, their teeth bared in ghoulish leers. A clap of thunder that shook the earth signalled that the carnage should begin. From the barricade, the first fusillade erupted. The Norton men spun and whirled and twisted in a wild dervish dance of death. Susan saw their contorted faces in vivid detail in the stark strob-light glare of the lightning. The storm was upon them.

The rain whipped Susan's skirt about her waist and she ran across the yard towards the fray, crying, 'No! No! *No*!'

Just before Nature unleashed the full force of her fury, Walt yelled to Kevin, 'Put down that gun, you crazy man, and let's talk!'

The reply was a muzzle flash from the Colt .45 in Kevin's hand. The slug went far wide; the distance was too great for accuracy. But the two men were closing on each other fast.

Walt held the shotgun at waist level, muzzle tilted down. He did not want to kill the other man – too many legal complications compounding his suspect past. At thirty feet, he tried for a low blast and succeeded. The Double-O slammed into Kevin's leg, and he was flung back and to the side, rolling over in the sand; but he held on grimly to the automatic. Lying prone, he braced the Colt on his left forearm and squinted along the barrel.

'Gotcha!' he muttered, and fired.

Walt grabbed his groin and screamed in agony as the

bullet shattered his pelvis. He went down backwards, pinwheeling from the force of the shot, and flopped around like a beached fish. Miraculously, he remained conscious and alert. He swung the muzzle of the shotgun in Kevin's direction. The second blast of double-O shot shredded Kevin's head and chest and shoulders. He died instantly.

The majestic symphony of rain, thunder, and lightning was Walt's swan song. As his strong heart pumped the life's blood out of the wounds in his lower torso, in his fast-dimming vision he saw Susan race to Kevin, kneel down, and cradle the gory head and shoulders in her arms.

'My knight in shining armour! I knew you wouldn't fail me, darling.'

She turned her face up to the angry heavens and laughed wildly. The rain pounded on her head and bared breasts, stinging her eyelids and her nipples.

'Oh, Holy Spirit,' she recited in the singsong rhythm of the Indians chanting in the ceremonial lodge, 'the sky is holy, the earth is holy, the rain is holy, the thunder is holy, the lightning is holy, everything that is is holy . . . '

The earth was wracked by lightning bolts striking all around her. Still she sat there, clutching her dead husband to her bosom, a wide and pacific smile on her upturned face.

And the ghosts of Ike Norton and his sons, and Jim Ames and all the other Ameses who had felt Norton vengeance, were joined by those of Molly, Amy, Candice, and Peggy . . . and Nancy and Dick and Laura and Jan and Larry and Jennie. Impervious to the storm, they formed a circle around Susan. Solemnly they converged on her, the circle growing ever tighter.